"Miss Paul writes with an icicle, in a fine and distinguished way that is quite her own . . . the effect is sombre, impressive, moving."

—*Times Literary Supplement*

"Phyllis Paul was that rare creature, a puritan with a passionate and colourful imagination . . . [Her] quintessential novel, and arguably her finest, is *Twice Lost* (1960). Here she is writing at the height of her powers, combining even more successfully than elsewhere a mystery story with a metaphysical fable . . . *Twice Lost* is an unforgettable portrayal of the human capacity for self-deception, and of the vulnerability of the innocent to the inroads of scrupulosity. It is a novel of a uniquely unsettling kind, the definitive achievement of the possessor of such a fascinating . . . and disturbing gift."

—Glen Cavaliero, *Wormwood*

"An almost medieval sense of good and ill. One enters a different world—compelling, fearful, mysterious. The characters live, the place has frightening reality . . . a kind of violent beauty."

—Elizabeth Jane Howard

TWICE LOST

TWICE LOST

PHYLLIS PAUL

WITH A FOREWORD
BY JEREMY M. DAVIES

McNally Editions

New York

McNally Editions
52 Prince St., New York 10012

ISBN: 978-1-946022-48-6
Ebook: 978-1-946022-49-3

Design by Jonathan Lippincott

1   3   5   7   9   10   8   6   4   2

FOREWORD

Everyone gets forgotten. Writers more than most. They send their names into the world, names they by and large didn't choose, and then with those names try to sell us a few thousand or hundred thousand words, words that are already public property. Their faces, voices, behaviors, transgressions . . . these might survive them a while, as they would any nonentity who's cast a shadow, cooked a meal, bred a few kids. But, for writers, these are meant to be secondary matters. Marketing material at best. At worst, indictments. What a writer worth her salt cares most about is what's most perishable. It's what goes away first. For a writer to be remembered, and so briefly, as nothing more than another human being who had the misfortune to live and breathe is the most abject of all literary failures. Also the most common.

The majority of writers are forgotten before they have the sense to die. The rest melt away within a few years of their final byline. The radiant constellations of a mere twenty years past are full of dark patches today, where we can see—or, rather, not see—the entropy of fashion at work.

That said, even in a firmament this gloomy, there are singularities so dense that nary a sigh of resignation can escape them. There's obscure and then there's obscure.

For a novelist who published eleven novels over three decades, whose books were widely reviewed and reprinted within living memory, the novelist Phyllis Paul has become the blackest of black holes. She's vanished about as completely as anybody can. She is, and is likely to remain, an enigma that no search engine, no university's special collection, no clandestine archive will ever illuminate.

How much those eleven books of hers, published between 1933 and 1967, might have borrowed from her life story is impossible to know. In the words of British publisher R. B. Russell, these "dark and unhappy books often feature murder, disappearance, suicide and insanity . . . It makes it all the more tempting for critics to look for autobiographical material in [Paul's] writing, but all that can be said with any certainty was that she was preoccupied in her imaginative life with dysfunctional and morbid relationships."[1]

We do happen to know how Paul died: in a traffic accident, struck by a motorcycle as she was crossing the road. According to the late Glen Cavaliero of Cambridge University, the world's first and (to date) final Pauline scholar[2]:

Phyllis Paul died on 30 Aug. 1973, in Hastings [England] . . . The account at the inquests suggests that she was not known locally as a writer, being only identified by the . . . nametag on her handkerchief. A neighbour commented that 'Miss Paul kept herself to herself. When she walked she had a habit of looking quickly to one side

---

1 R. B. Russell, *Past Lives of Old Books*, Tartarus Press, 2020, 93–94.

2 Cavaliero (1927–2019) was President of the Powys Society for thirty-four years, an organization that was founded to celebrate and study the writing of the Powys family, "particularly John Cowper, Theodore, and Llewelyn." It was John Cowper Powys's enthusiasm for Paul that first intrigued Cavaliero and sent him looking for Paul's work, which even then was by no means easy to acquire. Cavaliero's continual drumbeating for Paul's books—his insistence that she was "a writer who deserves to be taken with total seriousness"—carried the conversation about Paul's work into the digital age when by all rights it ought to have disappeared.

and then the other, and then she would look down again.'
A witness to the accident was more graphic still, remarking that what he saw was 'an old lady going across the
road like a sheet of newspaper.' The phrase might have
been coined by Paul herself (see *Hastings Observer*, 8 and
15 Sept. 1973).[3]

The phrase might have been coined by Paul herself, as
might the detail of the handkerchief. By the time of her
death, she seems to have scrubbed the record of her existence,
leaving only the barest facts. To wit: She was born in Kent
to Alfred Ernest Paul and Edith Jane Hartley. She was the
youngest of three; an older brother died in childhood the
year she was born. Paul's father worked as a commercial and
mercantile clerk. In her twenties, Paul may have done work
as an illustrator of children's books. She published her first
novel, *We Are Spoiled*, in 1933, when she was thirty years
old. This and its follow-up, *The Children Triumphant* (1934),
were published by the London house of Martin Secker, in
the company of such celebrities as D. H. Lawrence, Thomas
Mann, and George Orwell. Then there was silence for fifteen years—a rehearsal? an interruption? a crisis of faith?—
after which Paul published nine more novels, now with
William Heinemann, home to Henry James, Joseph Conrad,
Graham Greene, and, in time, the justly lauded African and
Caribbean Writers Series, respectively. Paul's oeuvre con-
tinued, and ended, with *Camilla* (1949), *The Lion of Cooling
Bay* (1953), *Rox Hall Illuminated* (1956), *A Cage for the
Nightingale* (1957), *Constancy* (1959), *Twice Lost* (1960), *A
Little Treachery* (1962), *Pulled Down* (1964), and *An Invisible
Darkness* (1967). According to Cavaliero, who interviewed
Paul's solicitor, she left behind a substantial donation to the
League Against Cruel Sports, as well the manuscript of an
unpublished novel, "Hedera," rejected by both Heinemann

---

3 Glen Cavaliero, *The Supernatural and English Fiction*, Oxford University Press,
1995, 259.

and Chatto and Windus. These pages were sent by the solicitor to the friend who was Paul's primary legatee, but has since been lost.[4]

Paul never married, lived quietly, and—according, as always, to Cavaliero—she "resolutely maintained her privacy, believing strongly that a writer should be known only by [her] work."[5] She avoided literary circles; indeed, her novels won her famous fans whom Paul did her best to spurn. Among these admirers was John Cooper Powys, who proselytized about Paul to his friends, including the American novelist James Purdy: "Do try and get from some library this Book—*Rox Hall Illuminated* by Phyllis Paul and published by Heinemann. Like your own writing it shows some subtle demonic-angelic influence emanating from Edgar Allan Poe."[6]

Paul "is a puzzle to me," Powys went on, some weeks later,

> I wrote to her once and she answered to my letter politely but by some psychometric spirit emanating from her letter (if that is the right word) I got the feeling she doesn't want to be praised by anyone. She writes to write and she must until we are all turned to dust. I'd give a lot to know whether she is Roman Catholic . . . Phyllis Paul might I feel (like the angels and devils) easily take the form of either St. Augustine or, or someone else! She is deadly subtle."[7]

Subtle to the point of total occultation. Paul's great subject, on the page and off, was darkness—darkness both mundane and metaphysical. To survive, her characters cling to the dark,

4 Mark Valentine, "The Last, Lost Novel of Phyllis Paul," *Wormwoodiana* (blog), January 15, 2019, http://wormwoodiana.blogspot.com/2019/01/the-last-lost-novel-of-phyllis-paul.html

5 Glen Cavaliero, "The Novels of Phyllis Paul," *The Powys Review* 14, 6–10, https://www.powys-society.org/1PDF/PR_14.pdf

6 Michael Ballin and Charles Lock, "The Correspondence of James Purdy and John Cowper Powys, 1956–63," *The Powys Journal*, Vol. 23 (2013): 23.

7 Ballin and Lock, 24.

as much to hide their sins as to keep the truth at a safe distance. What is or isn't "happening" in a typically plotty, mystery-driven Paul novel—*whodunnit, whydunnit, wuz it even ever dun*?—tends to be as difficult to distinguish as your fumbled housekeys on a moonless autumn night. Not because of any overt postmodernist trickery, but because her characters flee, en masse, from the very secrets they yearn to penetrate, chiding themselves all the while for their weakness. To quote Cavaliero once again: Paul "has a chilling gift for showing how careless laziness, or willful blindness to the truth, provide the soil in which more purposeful malevolence can flourish."[8]

Four of Paul's novels were picked up for hardcover editions in the United States. Two of these, *Twice Lost* and *Pulled Down*—the latter retitled *Echo of Guilt*—were then reprinted in 1966 as the inaugural novels in the "Lancer Gilt-Edged Gothic" paperback series. These were emphatically pulp editions. Nowadays, even the less pedigreed Lancers—*Don't Look Behind You!, The Devil's Church, Evil Became Them*, et al.—are treasured for their lurid, painted covers of women in flowing dresses, or else torn shifts, fleeing across cliffs or marshes in the shadows of rambling, Gormenghast-like estates. Might this be the key to Paul's peculiarities, her relentless secrecy, her novels about secrets never quite coming to light? Was Phyllis Paul a "gothic writer"? Gothic like a twelfth-century basilica, gothic like *The Monk* or *Dracula* or *Melmoth the Wanderer,* gothic like the skinny fellow with stringy hair throwing shapes at a Legendary Pink Dots concert in '99?

Of course, anything and everything can be termed gothic if it aspires to horrify in a less-than-blatant manner. But Daphne du Maurier, as a preeminent latter-day popularizer of the mode, makes for an instructive comparison with Paul. The gothic has never really been out of style, but it seems likely that whatever measure of success Paul's novels enjoyed on the American

---

8 Glen Cavaliero, "Mysteries of the Thirteenth Hour: The Enigmatic World of Phyllis Paul," *Wormwood* no. 9 (Autumn 2007): 1–15.

market, in their pulp incarnations, owed something to the enduring popularity of *Rebecca* and its many daughters. But a *Rebecca* flirts with the abyss only to return its narrator, and the reader, to the drab everyday of consequences and regrets. If Paul is gothic, she is not gothic like *that* du Maurier, but like the du Maurier of "Don't Look Now," which ends, famously, with a moment of terror, insolubly absurd.

Which is not to say that you'll find any homicidal dwarves in these pages, nor that Paul was "against the world, against life," as Michel Houellebecq has characterized H. P. Lovecraft's fiction. But there is a misanthropy here that runs deep, which must have undermined contemporaneous readers' desire to take *Twice Lost* for a simple romp over the moors.

Paul's books aren't just gothic. They aren't just pulp. In her sentences you will find the filigree of a Henry James at war with the heaving bodices and adverbs of the drugstore spin-rack. But it takes as much squinting to fit Paul into the context of literary fiction as it does to exile her as a writer of potboilers. Paul's work shrinks from labels as it does from the light. Part of the fascination it exerts is precisely in leaving us wondering which of Paul's effects were intended and which dictated by commerce, a very bleak sense of humor, or a streak of irrepressible neurosis. Until the last lines of *Twice Lost* you may find yourself doubting that Paul was in control of her materials—wondering whether this book is above or beneath you. The question is settled with a final cruel fillip. It's difficult to think of many other final sentences in "serious" fiction that hit with such an authoritative, undermining effect. It is subversive. Even malicious. And, for that, delicious.

Paul was rather more successful in erasing herself than fellow recusants like Kafka or Rosemary Tonks. Were it not for the spell she's still able to cast, it might be the polite thing to let her spend eternity in the oblivion she chose, without the hiccup of a revival.

But cast a spell she does, and no author so able to beguile should be allowed to rest easy. Besides which, this is a different world—bleaker, weirder, ruder—than the one Paul left behind. Where once she came across as eccentric, a bit troubling, she now reads as alien. In its unique amalgamation of guilty pleasure and inscrutable modernist paradox, *Twice Lost* is utterly out of place in the fiction of our moment, where obviousness is king. To me, that makes it a tonic.

Surely we've had too much of authors who must telegraph their every valorous opinion. Let us read *Twice Lost*, and be led back out of the light.

Jeremy M. Davies
New York, 2023

TWICE LOST

ONE

They had separated and were creeping about the grass, bowed over, with their eyes on the ground. But it was too near night-fall. Through the gateway with the flanking piers topped by urns, whose pale, classic shapes were enveloped in savage tufts of ivy, the rest of the tennis-party had already drifted, and out in the lane voices rose boldly above the din of bicycle bells and hooters, and the stuttering of a motor-cycle on the point of moving off. Only the three of them remained in the big, wild garden. Christine Gray and a friend of her own age, Penelope, had good-naturedly stayed behind to help the little girl in her search for a lost treasure.

'A charm of some sort?' Christine questioned her. 'A shiny thing? Goldy? Silvery?' But the child was upset, did not seem able to describe the object she had lost, and could only say it was 'a thing to hang on a necklace'. 'Well, a sort of pendant,' Christine decided.

But having come to the verge of the cleared ground surrounding the courts, she paused, straightened her back and remained gazing dubiously over the great spread of knee-high, feather-headed grass which stretched away to a con-fused region of thickets where the flower-garden had once been, or was swallowed up under the pyramids of the horse-chestnuts whose shadow was so dense. This outlying domain was extensive enough to be called a park and had long been out of any sort of cultivation. Forest trees had room there; they spread at ease and freely brandished their great limbs in windy weather. But neglect preyed on them. Ivy embraced them in its deadly clasp. An innumerable progeny of saplings had struck root at their feet and were thrusting up lankly to the light. Even the garden itself, in which the courts were situated, was a wilderness. Paths had long ago been obliterated by weeds which had forced their way through every crack in stone-work, and trails of climbing roses, unpruned for years, sprawled on the ground and mingled with the long grass, forming entanglements as effective as barbed wire. In short, the only quarter open enough to allow of any sort of search at this gloaming hour was that of the two rather rough and indifferently levelled courts which the young tennis players themselves had cut and patched and rolled so enthusiastically in the spring. They had hired the ground for the season from the agents of the empty house.

Vivian Lambert, the little girl, bored by the tennis, had been running all over the garden the whole afternoon. Somewhere, at some unguessable point in her solitary play, the string on which she had threaded the pendant and had knotted inexpertly herself, had slipped unnoticed from her neck. So that her helpers should not be discouraged, she had at first pretended to know in what part it had fallen; but Christine and Penelope now realised how entirely fanciful the pretension was. While they did their best to comfort her, therefore, the search was becoming more and more perfunctory. Christine, at least, saw that it was hopeless.

The voices were dying off down the lane, the courts themselves were engulfed in shades, the air pinged with insects. The last of the sun, still on the upper parts of the house, produced a somewhat sensational display of gleaming windows. She looked round and saw Penelope across the courts, still groping energetically over the shadowy ground, with the child trailing behind her at a slack, uncompanionable distance of many yards. Penelope's optimism reproached her.

So she went on a little way into the wild part, moving irre-solutely; pushing aside the large weeds on which the flecks of cuckoo-spit, beginning to show like cotton-wool, touched her exploring hands with sudden, cold dabs. Moths, clouds of moths, minute or big and whirring, were shaken out of the disturbed grasses. They sometimes blundered into her face, star-tlingly, before reeling off into the dusk. Some night-breathing weed exhaled a harsh scent. She began to find it all discom-forting. And she was about to call out, 'Look, Pen, how odd those little bushes look in this light,' when, through the thin shrieking of the cruising swifts, she fancied she heard a wail or screech of another kind, distant, seeming to her to come from a particular far corner of the garden. At that, she stopped dead.

Then, moving abruptly out of the wild part and drawing near to Penelope, she began saying in a nervous tone, with a sort of annoyance, 'There's that old gate again———' But her friend, calling out at the same moment, did not hear her. 'Shall we look in the well-house corner?' cried Penelope. 'I saw her playing around there—at least, I saw her hanging over the fence under the chestnuts.'

'Oh, *no*!' Christine exclaimed, the words bursting from her spontaneously. Then she added, feeling that so flat and decisive a refusal required explanation, 'It's much too dark now.'

'Well, I suppose it is.'

'Besides . . . someone has just gone through there.'

'What—the iron gate? Go on. Now you *are* imagining! *I* didn't hear anything. Perhaps it was cats. Hi, Vivian!'

'Where is she?'

'Behind you.' No, she had not known that the child was anywhere near her, and she looked round sharply; to see the small figure hovering at a little distance with a kind of cra-ven, dodging air which somehow expressed itself in spite of the darkness. As the two girls faced round on her, Vivian spoke in a hoarse half-whisper. 'I don't ever go near the well-house,' she said quickly, in a denying tone, in the manner of one who expects to be accused of something, or to be disbelieved. And she stood there, keeping a wary distance.

And now Christine felt that all her growing discomfort came from that; from the strangeness of the child.

Indeed, perhaps both girls now became conscious of the agitated, tense and unchild-like quality of the silence in which the little girl had been trailing at their heels throughout the search. They began to concentrate upon getting her away peaceably. But Vivian at first silently circled from them, like a dog who does not want to be put on a lead; trying with a sort of dumb tenacity to detain them. Penelope lost patience. She caught the child by the arm and began to pull her out of the garden.

Christine resolved to come back the next day in her lunch-hour and continue the search. But she did not say so, for fear of raising false hopes. She had just left school and had a post in the new public library, and it seemed to her very important that she should not over-run her lunch-hour; still, she would risk it. She felt sorry for the little girl.

Vivian walked between them with a drooping head. A light curtain of straight, shoulder-length hair fell forward, her face was hidden, and one did not need to be peculiarly sensitive to feel anxious about its expression. She was not crying, but her cold hand clutched Christine's very tightly.

A child should not be included in a tennis-party, Christine thought. And Penelope openly said it was a nuisance—a child was in the way, listened to gossip too old for her and was bored and lonely. But Vivian was tolerated because her young stepmother had nowhere to park her and she was 'too much of a little coward', as Rosalie Lambert put it, to be left by herself.

Thinking of this, Christine leaned over and said to the child kindly, 'No one else will find your treasure—it's quite safe. Because no one but ourselves knows it's there, you see. When we come up here next time, we'll look for it again.' And then she added what she had not meant to say, impulsively wishing to give comfort, 'If it's fine, I'll come up in my lunch-hour tomorrow.'

Outside the gates, a little knot of people still lingered and were in quiet discussion. But the attention of the two girls was first caught by a noisier group higher up the lane, where a young woman surrounded by several boys had just got into a car with one of them and was about to be driven off. The boys' affected drawl and the girl's bubbling, empty-headed laughter, which broke out every few moments, sufficiently indicated the nature of this little gathering; and Penelope, a sturdy, intolerant young person, at once raised a ruthless shout. 'Here, Rosalie—here's your child!' She was too late; the car had just started amidst cheers and cries. Rosalie Lambert had not heard her—could not have heard her. And Penelope flounced with temper.

'Oh, never mind,' said Christine quickly, sorry that the little girl had perhaps noticed their reluctance to have her on their hands. 'I'll see her home. It's not far out of my way.'

'No, but it's disgusting!' bawled Penelope. Christine was not of Penelope's war-like make, but still she was a good deal annoyed. It was like Rosalie's cheek.

But the next moment their indignation found another outlet. Having joined the confabulating group, the young girls learned that the club might soon be called upon to give up its use of the garden. There was a rumour that the agents were in treaty for the sale of the house. So little had this event ever been anticipated by the young people that they had put all their work into the making of the courts with minds quite at ease. A clatter of protest and argument had arisen. The house had been empty for years. And what of all their back-breaking labours? Christine was also much disappointed for a secret reason; she took great delight in their right of entry to the romantic garden, with which her imagination was so familiar. It had been the scene of many visioned adventures of childhood, of not a few enchanted trespassings. But of course the tennis club had accepted the proviso that it should give up the courts immediately if ever the house should be let or sold, and the others were already laughing and joking as they discussed new plans. Penelope thrust forward and joined in ardently.

But Christine, on the outskirts of the group, with face turned back upon her shoulder, was asking herself who on earth could have bought such a place. Reckless and lavish they must be, indeed! She hoped with all her heart that they would not fell the trees, and her spirit stole back and glided anxiously from one great bole to another, swamped in darkness under their rustling canopies.

Suddenly she became aware of a pull on her arm which made her look down sharply at the child. She saw a little blanched face with staring eyes. Engrossed in private dreams, she had almost forgotten their business in the garden, and now she cried, startled, 'Why, darling, was it a very great treasure?' And then tried to coax her, 'Can't you tell me just what it was?' The child seemed almost speechless with some emotion—could it really be fright? Christine was shocked. She began to make out that it was something borrowed, and to suspect that it was something borrowed without permission. She hoped it was nothing valuable, and felt uneasy when she remembered that the child's father was supposed to own a collection of rare and costly bibelots; she wondered if jewelry made part of it.

There was nothing to be done but to say comfortingly, 'Now, don't worry, we shall be coming up here again once or twice more at least. And I'll come up in my lunch-hour, unless it's wet. We shall have plenty of time to find it.' She imagined the child to have jumped to the conclusion that they were already ejected, that the domain, having swallowed up her treasure, was closed to them, once and for all, now that they had shut the gate. And she excused herself for raising false hopes by thinking, 'This time tomorrow, she'll have forgotten it.'

A little worried, however, in a rather plaintive tone, she called to her friend, 'Come, Pen—if you're coming with us. I've got to go a bit out of my way, you know.'

Christine, though sympathetic, was only a big child herself; she was only seventeen, and had never taken much to the little girl, whom she privately judged 'sly'. In spite of that, the child was apt to attach herself to her, no doubt because she was one of the younger ones and spoke to her kindly. Christine was not old enough to recognise and compassionate properly that shifty, abject, propitiatory manner—to understand it as the sorrowful characteristic of the unloved, neglected child. She felt awkward with Vivian.

This intangible uneasiness was too slight a thing to weigh on her spirits at the moment. With the child between them, she and Penelope went along in cheerful, voluble talk about the house and about the afternoon's play. But Penelope's road did not lie with the others' and they soon parted company.

TWO

Unwillingly, Christine's whole attention was now turned upon Vivian again. Having gently extracted the fact that the ornament had been worn tucked inside her dress, she was struck by a new thought. 'Shake yourself, lovey,' she adjured her, stopping. 'It may have fallen down inside you. Stretch the elastic.' It was here that she noticed how little Vivian had to shake. Why, she surely had nothing on under the top part of that frock—and for the first time Christine's eye was properly caught by the extraordinarily grubby little rag of a dress the child was wearing. It was of a peculiarly unpleasant, cheap, crude pink and was, besides, very much outgrown, too short, and only not too tight because its wearer was so skinny. Perhaps she had been adequately clothed for the warm afternoon; but no one had thought to make her bring a coat, and now she was shivering. She was quaking. Christine stood and surveyed the child with a shock of compunction. She looked at her with new eyes. What a miserable little object! And the young girl's judgment of those who were responsible (herself included) befitted one of her age—it was sweeping and merciless. She started to pull off her own coat—the beautiful, long, white, fleecy coat, so extravagantly expensive, which she had had for her birthday; but then, realising that it would swamp Vivian, and also that she herself would be chilly, she drew it on again, opened it and took Vivian inside, making the child put an arm round her waist to keep them close together, and herself holding the coat snugly about her shoulder. Then, laughing at the odd arrangement, she hurried the child along, looking down on the little head peeping out under her arm. After a moment's awkwardness, Vivian had clasped her tightly.

An intense consciousness of the little bird-like frame pressed to her side suddenly took possession of the young girl, rousing in her an anxious, pitying feeling which was by no means agreeable. For it was a gloomy feeling. She was conscious of a kind of dismay. She had an impression of great timidity and weakness, and it affected her deeply but very oddly. She felt it as more dismaying than pathetic. It was a dragging, clinging thing from which something in her shrank. She had sensed the chilliness, the initial hostility, in the little body she held against her. Vivian was perhaps one of those delicate children who dislike contacts. However that was, now she had attached herself; now she clung. Christine was not much used to children, being greatly the youngest of her family. But she had always been petted and tenderly loved, and with this poor little one she used instinctively the winning manners, the tone of rather emotional affection, which had been used to herself; until at last the child's dull unresponsiveness seemed to yield slightly.

Then there followed a brief conversation which Christine was never to forget.

'I've torn my dress. Did you see my old dress, Christine? Now I've torn it.'

'Well, it isn't a very new one, is it? I think really you need another one—you've grown out of that.'

'Yes—did you look at it properly? Isn't it an old thing! But I don't have new dresses. I wish I could mend it so she doesn't notice.'

'Rosalie won't blame you, I'm sure.'

'Rosalie hates me.' The child's voice was curiously hoarse, perhaps from nervousness; she whispered. And this hoarse, privy little voice, so close that it was as if it proceeded from herself speaking in sleep, too close, yes, too intimately in contact with her own body, affected Christine with a half-physical uneasiness. 'Speak out,' she felt, almost in irritation. 'What is there to be afraid of?' A voice which wormed itself in. She did not, of course, quite formulate such thoughts.

'Nonsense!' she cried out briskly. 'That *is* nonsense!'

There was no answer. 'Why do you think she hates you?' she asked, drawn on reluctantly. As the child still said nothing, making a guess, Christine added, 'No doubt just because she tells you to wear an old frock when you come up here, thinking you'll tear something, all in that wild part. And you see you have.'

Then she had the unexpected answer. 'I put it on myself.'

'Because you were afraid you'd tear anything nicer?'

'Yes,' the child said, primly and quickly. Then, once more in a whisper, so that Christine had to stoop to catch it, 'She'd pour boiling water over me again.'

Christine's first reaction of horror was abruptly tinged with doubt. Hadn't the child magnified and misinterpreted some small accident? Little as she liked Rosalie, she felt through all her instincts that she was not a cruel woman. And the strain of distaste mingled with her pity deepened.

She said severely, 'You mustn't say things like that, Vivian. If Rosalie ever did such a thing to you, it must have been the purest accident. I'm sure she looked after it. Didn't she?'

The child was silent and went on with her head lowered.

They had a good way to go. They had walked some distance through unspoiled country, down a winding, steep, tree-arcaded lane, before parting with Penelope; but all the while they were approaching a new and spreading district, and their glimpses of the valley and the surrounding hillsides through the leafy gaps of the hedgerow had shown a boundless area of roofs. This scene was already spangled with lights which the misty shades of the lower ground seemed to put forth as the sky puts forth stars. Down they came into this cosy cup of domesticity. Farms, ancient cottages and country houses together with their lovely settings, century-old trees, hundreds and hundreds of them—all had been swallowed up in a flood of new building which had engulfed a whole countryside. Christine and Vivian were lucky to inhabit such a spot. It was orderly and salubrious.

Indeed, those who made their homes there thought it remarkably pleasant and prided themselves upon living almost in the country. It was a region of pretty suburban roads, of avenues in fact as well as in name, half woody still in the better parts; a region of long passages between well-kept back gardens—sad travesties of the sweet meadow footpaths they had superseded, and yet, as everyone said, countrified. A place of prideful gardeners; where lawn-mowers snored away on all sides throughout the summer evenings, up to the very verge of nightfall, and garden shears chipped and chattered among the darkening herbage, busy and destructive, up to the last minute. In the autumn there was sawing, clipping and the long, sad squeak of the tree-pruners; for everything, everything without exception, had to be felled, lopped or trimmed.

It was a prosperous and expensive district. Christine's family liked it extremely. They were sensitive people, highly civilised, and, as they said, quite truly, such a district does not give scope to the cruel diversions of the country. Then, everything is settled—or, as some might put it, nothing worse can be done to the place. It is safe from speculative builder and local council. It is built-up. Even the few large trees that remain are likely to be spared, being privately owned by eccentrics who admire these untidy and shady vegetables, so out of scale with modern life.

But here and there some humble cottage property remained obstinately embedded, and made certain hands itch to be at it. There were even some remnants of wild wood which had not been absorbed owing to some exceptional difficulty about the ground—it was too steep, or it was marshy; or a stream, un-regenerately natural, took an open way through a small meadow. But such picturesque corners and relics were considered untidy and poor, and were held to lower the general tone. Almost every piece of remaining 'country' was a 'site' and carried an agent's board, and the ground was highly priced.

It was a place which had never had a village nucleus. So it had been called Hilbery Village. The churches were new, the public house was new, there was no cinema, the shops were ranged in 'parades'. There were, as yet, no low corners, no dubious dens. Not a single building had any roots or history. There were those who were known to jeer at Hilbery, but to jeer was foolish. It was a pretty place and a well-conducted one, and hundreds of people lived there in reasonable comfort and contentment. It was of no interest to the police. Nothing had ever happened there. Crime was unknown.

Into the outskirts of this ingenuous version of a town, the two young people entered a little after the lights went on. One minute more, and Christine would be free.

At the corner of her own road, the child suddenly spoke up sharply. 'And you don't think it'll rain?'

For an instant, Christine did not grasp the allusion. Then, saying to herself, 'Well, now I *am* committed,' she replied cheerfully, 'Goodness, no. Look at that sky.' But she was a little concerned on finding that Vivian seemed to be building so much on her rash promise.

Here she could have left her little charge, with a clear conscience, for they were within sight of the Lamberts' house and some window at the back was throwing a light, cautiously dimmed by curtains, out into the garden. The same light was weakly reflected in the panes of the front door. She was much relieved to find that someone was in. But she did not content herself with leaving the child at this point. She went the whole way with her.

Arrived before the gate, she pulled gently at her coat, waiting for the child to let go of it. The coat was held against her, feebly but quite distinctly. 'Hurry up, darling, now, or you'll feel the cold,' Christine was obliged to say. The child for a moment more clung to her, bat-like, and even turned her face against her body, so that all of Christine's sensations seemed gathered in the weighty pressure under her heart of the warm, hard skull. So consciousness centres upon a sudden hurt. Curiously affected in the nerves, affected to the point of having to restrain an impulse to tear herself away, she brought herself to add gently a few more words of encouragement. Then, at last, only then, Vivian lifted her head and relaxed her clutch—nor could the young girl help noticing the spiteful thrust with which she suddenly disengaged herself. Christine opened the gate. Vivian dawdled a little way up the path, walking sideways, with her head hanging. Instead of turning into a beam of welcome, the bleared and niggardly glimmer in the glass was suddenly all but extinguished, as if by the partial closing of a door within. Christine's nervousness burst out in impatience. She waved, calling urgently, 'Hurry, hurry!' and then, thinking, 'She'll go quicker if I don't watch her,' turned from the gate and sprang off beside the hedge with a running step. She drew a deep breath; she was intensely relieved to be rid of her charge, and she bounded off, swinging her racquet blithely, and was once more thrillingly conscious of the evening, of the air and sky.

Turning her head at the corner of the garden with the idea of getting a view of the Lamberts' front door, which by now should be opening to Vivian and casting out a cheerful beam, she was halted by the discovery that the level of the road had dropped so that the hedge was now much too high for her to see over. It was also too close to yield peep-holes. But she barely paused; the matter seemed to her so unimportant that she walked on without giving it another thought.

She did, however, tell herself that it would have been better if she had gone up to the door with the child, for she might have made an explanation which would have broken the ice for her, supposing the thing she had borrowed was of any value. She did not realise that she had thought of this even while standing at the gate, but had pushed it out of sight. A mild, instinctive aversion from the Lamberts as a whole had actuated her, unconsciously. She had felt shy about facing the child's father.

THREE

Walking on with the soft, light step of freedom, Christine had soon dismissed any troubling thoughts and felt glad that she had come this way. For when she raised her eyes, she saw a moving sight. She had taken a short cut through one of the garden passages, and at the far end of this, raised on a slight incline, a group of great elms fountained up splendidly against that pellucid sky filled with the afterglow. A few rooks still sailed about their summits and the darkening air was full of their pleached notes, but thinned and muted now to a dreamy conversation between individual voices, pitched variously. Morning and evening, this noise like the noise of a pebble beach when the sea drags at it could be heard all over Hilbery. The rookery was bad enough. But crouched at the foot of these majestic trees, on an uncultivated piece of ground as spacious as a meadow, was one small, ancient cottage; a little garden patch before it, and all the rest wild. Here, in fact, was an out-standing example of that obstructive cottage property which many a good, dull, tidy mind in Hilbery lusted to sweep away. It was felt to be the nearest approach to a slum that the district possessed.

This lonely relic of wild beauty caused much unease in Hilbery Village. For the elms were 'wild'! Efforts were there-fore continually being made to prove that they were dangerous. Everyone knew that this cry of danger was a bare-faced pretext; the elms, if dangerous at all, were not remotely as dangerous as the near-by road since that had been straightened and turned into a speed-track, and there was no proposal to scrap that. And in fact, as always in such cases, all sorts of humane and public-spirited reasons had been put forward to mask a simple lust for destruction.

There was, of course, the opposite camp. The elms had their partisans. Even in Hilbery there were those whom wanton destruction enrages—and those who are perhaps even more enraged by the tidy mind. And among the first of these was the owner of the ground, a Mr Parmore, who lived opposite in one of the rejuvenated farmhouses, and he was a man as determined as wealthy, and doted on his view. In the second class was the tenant of the cottage.

Enraptured by the sight of the trees, Christine heedlessly drifted across the road and stood at gaze in the dusk before the gate of the cottage, motionless and lost in conjured visions; a white-clad figure with a lifted face on which the light from the west fell. It gave the skin a delicate glow, made the eyes look unusually large and liquid, shining as they moved, and showed the lips curved into an unconscious smile of bliss. She took a deep breath, put both elbows on the gate and leaned her chin on her wrist, turning her head a little to one side; a gentle, pensive and faintly sentimental habit which she had from her mother.

But suddenly she was aware of a voice calling to her out of the field.

'So you've come to say good-bye to me? How very nice of you!' it cried, somewhat satirically.

Christine jumped, and was conscience-stricken.

A woman in slacks and a pullover had come to the door of the cottage, a mat in one hand and a brush in the other, like a good housewife at the start of her day's work.

'Tomorrow! Why, yes, so it is! It's tomorrow you move. Well, there, Miss Freemantle, I shall just have to admit I'd clean forgotten!' Actually Christine was not much to blame, for Miss Freemantle was no real friend of hers; she was only an acquaintance, though a valued one. The value was dubious. It was one of those wayward tastes for the highly-coloured to which young girls are sometimes prone, betraying an attempt to extract a little excitement out of conditions too insipid.

For Miss Freemantle, like her cottage, or rather the cottage she rented, was one of the oddities of Hilbery—some would have added, one of its doubtful spots. A woman of about forty, she seemed to possess no ties or family and had no visible profession. She was a bohemian of some sort, perhaps, though she was not known to write or paint. Christine had always felt her rather basely fascinating. Her pleasure in the woman's company was almost entirely due to Miss Freemantle's talent for being funny, excruciatingly funny on occasion; Christine was still child enough to enjoy that. A woman who was, presumably, very fond of children, since she drew so many round her, she could be wonderful at children's parties; and yet she was not so much in demand at these functions as would have seemed natural. It was not merely the unsophisticated whom she had the power to amuse. She could suit her performance to her audience. And perhaps, with careful mothers, the rumour of certain exhibitions in the bars of the district and other such free-and-easy places, weighed against her. In short, there was a good deal of the buffoon about Miss Freemantle. She had a small rubber-face which she pulled about for the general amusement without any considerations of vanity. Some of her effects had the fine craziness of a good clown's.

But what kind of a woman is it who deliberately adopts the role of comedienne—not for the sake of a livelihood, but from choice, in private life? She was an educated woman, too, or so her speech and manners (when she was not playing the buffoon) led one to suppose. Perhaps it was only that she had an unruly sense of humour, that she was simply one of those people who have an ungovernable itch to cock a snook at society.

Christine had never asked herself these questions.

Leaning over the gate, she called out earnestly, 'I'm really very sorry you're going—it doesn't mean anything that I'd forgotten the exact day!' Still carrying mat and brush, Miss Freemantle began advancing down the path at a decrepit hobble. It made Christine laugh. But at the same time she said with compunction, 'Are you so very tired? You must be, of course!'

A thin, black-haired, spider-limbed woman, slightly simian in appearance, Miss Freemantle was an impudent-looking creature.

Christine could not quite make out her friend's expression in the dusk, the light quarter of the sky being behind her, but fancied she was being looked over teasingly; and no doubt she was. With her mild, sincere eyes, to which the level brows gave a character of gravity, with her fair hair tossed up carelessly from her round, ingenuous forehead, Christine looked so simple and sound, so lambent with that quality which might justly be called innocence at her age (because she was not a child and it was not ignorance), that it might well tempt a certain kind of person. Miss Freemantle said, whining a little, 'I thought it was an angel leaning over my gate—all in spotless white, with a halo, and gazing heavenward. I thought, "*Now* what does one do? What's the correct thing?"'

Christine, though laughing, retorted indignantly, 'Don't be silly! Can't I look at your trees? Oh, those trees!' she cried, enthusing again, now half in fun. 'Oh, the beauties! How I do hope nothing will be done to them when you're gone.'

'Don't worry. Ted Parmore will hold the fort.'

Christine was a little struck by this saucy way of referring to one of the foremost denizens of Hilbery, a dignified, formidable person, in her estimation.

'Daddy says it would destroy the whole character of the neighbourhood if we began cutting the trees down.'

'Began cutting the trees down!'

'Well—*right* down.'

'I get you.'

'Oh, now you're teasing . . . Well, I'm ever so glad I happened to come by. I came this way,' Christine went on to explain scrupulously, 'only because I had to see little Vivian Lambert home.'

'Poor little wretch,' said Miss Freemantle, and suddenly shook out her mat and began beating it with the back of her brush with a terrific, suggestive gusto.

'Why do you say that, really?' Christine asked, rather uncomfortably. And she waited anxiously for Miss Freemantle's explanation. But Miss Freemantle said nothing.

Christine lowered her voice. 'Well, yes, they do neglect her rather, I'm afraid. Still, after all, we oughtn't to talk as if they ill-treated her—ought we? No one says *that.*' But she could not help adding (because it secretly weighed on her), 'She hadn't even got a coat tonight. She was so cold, poor little thing, that I had to wrap my coat round her—like this—walking home. No. Rosalie should have seen that she brought a coat! She had one herself.'

'Trying to get rid of her. Funny, too—because she's not a bad-looking little thing, apart from those teeth. And they could be corrected, if anyone liked to bother. Well, they deserve to lose her,' Miss Freemantle pronounced. 'Or, rather, no, they don't deserve it, for they'd *be glad* to lose her.'

'Oh, I don't think we ought——! Oh, I wouldn't say that!' And Christine, scrupulously familiarised with the principle of being silent if one could not say anything pleasant, thought she had better turn the conversation, and so offered to come back after supper and give Miss Freemantle a hand with her preparations for the move, if she could be of help in any way.

This offer, however, was rejected. 'No, you can't do anything, child. I shan't get off till about one tomorrow—I've only a few bits and pieces, so Hope is moving me, and he can't start early.' Then they discussed her plans a little. She was going a good way, to Southampton, in fact, as Christine already knew. 'Leaving my stuff with friends there.' But, Miss Freemantle added, in due course she would be going to South America. 'God, the business! Still, I've got us all settled at last, thanks to nobody.'

'Oh, so you're going with a friend? I *am* glad. I didn't like to think of your going quite alone. It's rather a wild country, it seems!'

'Didn't like to think of me——? Well, yes, dry your eyes—I'm taking someone with me.' They were going to Peru eventually, or Ecuador.

Christine had already heard of this, and the fact had coloured her dreams. It was Miss Freemantle's coming venture which had recently fired her to borrow from the library a few books on these exotic lands, and then every book she could lay hands on at all related to the subject, which had ended in fascinating her out of measure. So now she began to talk eagerly and to put various questions; to all of which Miss Freemantle returned her nothing but nonsense.

'What a place to take and live in! Well you may say it! Why carp, though? It has its compensations. 'Tis no great matter there. 'Twill not be seen in me there. Everyone there has sticky fingers——'

Christine blushed and was silenced; she blushed so deeply that she could be seen to blush even in that light.

'You *are* a tease,' she said in a low voice at last, but without conviction. Her voice carried a tone of reproach, unknown to herself. 'Well, then, I must say good-bye to you. I *am* sorry you're going and I do hope you'll be happy in your new home, wherever it is.'

'Happy and honest! Good-bye, Christine—I shan't forget you. Or your name, either. I shall remember those eyes of yours to my dying day—grey as the summer skies! Good-bye, my lass—God bless you.'

Christine walked on and instinctively quickened her pace, conscious that she was late. But her thoughts remained with Miss Freemantle. She had blushed so when the woman had spoken of 'sticky fingers' because she was ashamed. Yes, perhaps it was as well that Miss Freemantle was going, for there were one or two things about her one could not care for, and they were worrying things. Christine would never forget that day when she had met the woman near the shops and they had walked a little way together. A greengrocer's bore the usual display on an open stall before the window; and from this, as they passed, Miss Freemantle had slyly whipped off a handful of nuts and popped them into her bag. Christine, expecting her to turn in at the door of the shop a few paces further on to pay for the goods, had naturally made to stop there—and then, what was her confusion on realising that her companion had no such intention! They had simply walked on: and for the moment Christine was more dumbfounded than shocked. 'But that's stealing,' she had thought stupidly. But Miss Freemantle, who had made no attempt to hide her action from her young friend, had made so light of it, had treated it in such an amiable, comical, matter-of-fact manner, had so merrily rolled her eyes at her, that Christine had felt in confusion about it, and had felt so ever since. She had been too much ashamed and shocked to mention it to anyone, feeling that she had as good as stolen herself, because she had connived at it. Yes, certainly she was an accomplice, she was an accessory after the fact!

Yet now here she was, still taking unscrupulous pleasure in Miss Freemantle's company. She saw this was not right.

Going thoughtfully on her way, she suddenly decided that she was *not* sorry to have said good-bye to so disturbing a creature; and this meant that she had lied in professing herself sorry. She continued at a slower pace, with her eyes on the ground. It was quite true, it was just as they said; once you had taken a wrong step, another presented itself as a necessity.

Thus searching her conscience, she returned to thinking of the little girl; she was thrown back upon a line of thought which had already made her feel painfully that she was to blame. This sense of guilt seemed to be connected with a critical attitude in herself.

In spite of what Miss Freemantle had said, Vivian was not a nice-looking child, and Christine recalled this distinctly (with a shamed sense that she recalled it with an unkind alacrity); for her eyes were peculiarly small and deepest and her two top teeth protruded a little, so that they usually showed slightly, resting on her lower lip. It was not really ugly, but the tips of the teeth were visible most of the time. (But they were her first teeth, no doubt, Christine thought, and the others might grow better.) Her chin, then, receded. With her light hair, she was sallow. Anyway, she was darkly sunburned, which made her hair seem the lighter. A large nose with a prominent bridge always makes a face look unchild-like. Yes, she was an odd-looking little person. But it was her expression, abject, shifty——

As Christine dwelt upon the little girl's appearance, the impression became less and less pleasant—it became distasteful. Suddenly realising this, she was well-nigh horrified, protesting to herself that it was an abominable way to think of a forlorn little creature whom she knew to be unloved. Think kindly of people, think the best of them! She could hear her mother saying it. But the fact was that that touch of spite which the child had displayed at the last moment, so unexpected, so uncalled for, had shocked and hurt the gentle, affectionate young girl, herself accustomed to a world of kindness, and now that she could no longer suppress the memory, it became almost frightening. It seemed charged with sinister meaning. She did not like to think of it. She reminded herself severely that it was her own fault. One could not blame the child. So she walked on and was overwhelmed by an unhappy sense of failure, a deeply uneasy sense of being in some way very much in the wrong.

But these feelings gradually succumbed to the natural bravery of her youth. When she raised her eyes, she was at once happily distracted by all they rested on. All the small, common beauties of the way delighted her. The avenue trees bending over with the lights raying through them imparted a touch of drama, a scenic character, to the simple suburban road; it seemed vaguely portentous. Sometimes the rays escaped in large whorls through the leaves, as if some heavenly apparition might be stationed behind the tree. The touch of fantasy thrilled her. Thoughts of adventure in regions alien and disturbing were still lending their rainbow colouring to this tame world when she arrived at her own gate. The wind was freshening. All the little trees within the fence were agitated and sibilant, it was dark beneath them, and suddenly, with reminiscences of the low, black aisles under the forest monsters of Carlotta House garden, she felt as if something might be hiding there, having run on before her; and so, in a spasm of childish panic, not quite serious, she sprang up the path and, with a sensation of comfort out of all proportion with the trifling convenience, felt her key slip familiarly into the lock and the lock respond friendlily. She was home.

FOUR

No sooner had she stepped into the warm, bright hall than her mother opened the kitchen door and her father came out of the sitting-room; and both looked at her solicitously. On both faces was the same faint smile of relief—though her father's bearing was a little jocular as if to indicate a sensible carelessness. Christine was so much the baby of the family that her two brothers had already left home and made their own lives while she was still at school. Her father was almost an old man, but her mother, who had married very young, was not much above fifty. Still, her hair was white above that delicate, short little face with the dancing bright blue eyes which Christine's pensive ones (the straight, long eyebrows giving them a shade of melancholy) so little resembled.

Turning to see that the door was properly shut, the young girl made this an excuse to look away, to bend her head and so avoid their fond scrutiny. Her comfort was gone. There was a sudden breach in it. She had been struck and was petrified inwardly by a glaring, heart-rending contrast. Here she was, a full-grown woman (as she considered herself), and here were both her parents hastening to meet her with anxious faces because she had come in a little over half an hour later than usual from those quiet, innocent roads where nothing ever happened. *Yet a trembling little girl of seven*——And, far-off, she descried the sombre, churlish light in the glass of the Lamberts' front door.

Christine's greeting was rather severe—not unkind, but grave. She was old enough to perceive the quality of the emotion which made the poor dears fidget so, but not old enough to accept it quite patiently. It originated, she knew, with her father. Of herself, her mother would never have worried. Sensitive, delicately made in mind and body, he was inclined to melancholy views. Christine loved both her parents dearly, but her mother most, because that light-hearted nature reassured her. A weakly sensitive strain in herself shrank from the same in him. She did not, of course, know it.

But she could not at this moment respond to either of them. Something had happened to her that evening, something which had disturbed her whole nature in a dark, premonitory way.

As she went upstairs, it seemed as if a fresh eye had been given her and she saw the familiar details of the little well-kept house as if she had been long away from it. Biblical texts, simply lettered and without offensive ornament, hung in many places upon the walls, but were not there in any vestigial fashion, or merely because they had not been swept away; they were there because Mrs Gray loved and drew comfort from them. They were to her what authentic works of art would have been to the aesthetically-minded. She changed them frequently. She delighted in them. She would pause thoughtfully by them in the course of her duties, and then bear them in mind as she went about her business, alone in the house. The habit had grown on her; she was sometimes teased about it. They were not church- or chapel-going people. Christine was so well used to the texts that she thought nothing of this old-fashioned peculiarity about her home.

But pausing on the landing outside her own door, now she read, in straight, dark lettering, 'Take heed how ye offend one of these little ones.' For the first time she felt a stirring of discomfort. It amounted almost to dread—she had seen suddenly that these words could sound in another tone than that comfortable one she had heard in them as a child, as she well remembered, when they had seemed to promise kindly protection against night-fears. (Yes, for all the tender care lavished upon her, she had been a frightened child—no one about her would ever have understood how frightened—for she had an excess of sympathetic imagination.) Now she was on the other side of childhood, the threatened, the unprotected side. And she saw this for the first time.

'Drowned in the depth of the sea!' she thought, and seemed to catch, from far, far down, a reverberation of the icy, massive waves.

Almost at once, this passed and she forgot, and began thinking of the rumour that Carlotta House was sold and the probable loss of the courts.

When she came down again, having hurried so that she could help her mother with the supper, her reserve and her gravity were quite gone and she chattered at length about the prospects of the tennis club—the rumour, she thought, must be false, for who on earth would be rich and reckless enough to buy Carlotta House? But her father, joining them at this point, had to dispel her hopes.

'Yes, dear, I'm afraid it's true. I had it from Moulton himself today—at the agent's, you know. But, fancy, we're to have a celebrity in Hilbery! And our own famous man, too—a home product! I confess I didn't even know that he had once lived here, in the days before he had become famous, but Moulton tells me he did. Yes, the place has been bought by Thomas Antequin, the celebrated playwright—or novelist, isn't he? And the son, Keith Antequin, is almost as well known. In fact, I get them muddled. I stick to the old writers. Still, a distinguished man. He must be very well off. I suppose he's fond of the place and has come back to it for that reason.'

From working in the library, Christine knew the name of Antequin—a name of renown in the literary world of that time; that she had read scarcely a word written by either father or son was explained by the fact that her tastes had not yet aspired to genuine literature. But she had heard of them; and now, after wrinkling her forehead, was able to supply the titles of some of Thomas Antequin's works, to her parents' admiration. She herself felt disappointed, all curiosity flattened by the name of a public person too far out of her orbit to be of any great interest to herself. Also, Thomas Antequin must be old. 'What a shame! To come and take our courts,' she said reproachfully.

But her mother was crying, 'Oh, dear me, yes. And wasn't there a Mrs Antequin—who used sometimes to come to the women's meetings? I really don't remember anything of her but her very odd name. How nice it will be to meet the dear woman again! There's no one like an old friend.'

'Oh, I think you'll find they're quite out of our class nowadays,' her husband warned her. 'Besides, I believe Mr Antequin is a widower.' Mrs Gray, deprived at a stroke of an old friend, gave a sad cry. He went on, 'It'll be good for the neighbourhood. We must think of it like that. We're very lucky that the buyer is a private person. It might very well have been turned into a convent or an approved school. Part of the estate is to be sold off and the hill will be developed——'

'Oh, I should so grieve to see the hill road spoiled!' exclaimed Mrs Gray; and Christine joined in with protests and lamentations. Mr Gray, too, was disturbed at the prospect; but he said, sighing, 'Well, we mustn't be selfish—houses are wanted. I shouldn't imagine that they will be council houses—but, even so, we must think of other people. We have a good home ourselves.' Then they all agreed, sadly, that they must not be selfish. But at length Mr Gray allowed himself to express a cautious hope. 'I should say it will be good-class property. And Mr Antequin himself is probably a man of taste and feeling, and, if so, the trees may well be spared'; and he quoted, with emotion, '"Old trees in their living state are the only things that money cannot command."'

This made Christine think of Mr Parmore's splendid championship of the elms and she expatiated upon it; and so was led to refer to Miss Freemantle and the fact that she was leaving the district on the morrow.

Finally, she just mentioned, while out in the kitchen with her mother, the cause of her lateness. Little Vivian Lambert had lost some trinket in the garden and she had stayed to help look for it and had afterwards seen the child home. And really that was all there was to the matter. Or so it seemed now.

FIVE

'But, Father, I've arranged for you to go to Granada! The little inn is really comfortable and clean. I've been at the greatest pains to make certain of that. The hotels would not do—that shocking bogus-Moorish would surely amount to a most disturbing element among the impressions? It will be beautiful in the south in the early spring, the heat will not be excessive up on those hills.' The young man spoke winningly.

Thomas Antequin gave a soft sigh, which he smothered with a cough. The noise of the London traffic went on droning and vibrating comfortably through the room. Thomas, a countryman by birth, loved the noise of traffic and loved London, yet had sometimes considered going to live at the antipodes or retiring into a monastery, and was even now considering settling in the outer suburbs. Something was driving him to this extremity.

The young man was pacing up and down between the window and the gloomy depths of the room. Turning at the end of the long apartment each time, he was seen advancing from quite a distance, and, looming nearer, seemed to have suffered, unknown to himself, a kind of transmogrification which had turned his flesh transparent, so that his emotions were all made visible; now was faintly green about the countenance, now fiery, now leaden; and finally, emerging into clean daylight, he was just pale. The window had a number of coloured lights which stained and falsified the daylight of this gleaming spring afternoon. Yes, he was a little pale, but that was all. And that was admirable; in the circumstances, really admirable.

Pale, tall, slim, with high, unequal shoulders, he had brown, wavy hair, longish, rather untidily disposed, and there was a softness about his face, perhaps because of its plumpness and its delicate, small features. There was a kind of vague 'niceness'. There was a conscious sort of sensitiveness in his glance, an almost appealing air, faintly sweet, like the glance of a nice woman who has always relied, quite innocently, upon her looks. (But a man can always pride himself on a feminine strain—it is an attribute of many great artists.) The face was youthful; it matched the graceful awkwardness in that high-shouldered gait of an over-grown boy. At the same time, it looked a shade dissipated; one saw that the nice boy had gone a trifle to seed—though it was certainly a dissipation of the emotions, not physical. And if his looks were a little the worse for wear, well, the young man was past thirty.

But the brow, the large, noble brow, was a wholly praiseworthy feature. Partly due to the fact that, young as he was, his hair had receded over the forehead, it was not due to that alone. The brow was good. However, if one happened to glance at the other occupant of the room, who was seated meekly in a corner by one of the windows, the carefully dressed, brushed, trimmed and yet insignificant little elderly man with the thin, lined face and small beard, one made the discovery that the brow was Thomas Antequin's. The brow was borrowed.

It was so much borrowed that it did not fit very well. The face beneath the brow, with its trifling features, seemed as if built on a different scale.

Arrived before his father, the young man smiled; a crooked smile which twisted up the right corner of the mouth; a smile of humour—or perhaps one might say a *cultivated* smile of humour.

'I've gone to some trouble about the arrangements, which are all made,' he said pleasantly. 'You yourself admit that you require a Spanish-Moorish colouring—you'll remember that you yourself first spoke of Granada——'

'Pooh. I don't need to *go* there,' muttered Thomas, with a sort of artless surprise—with a disconcerting crudeness of feeling, as it seemed to Keith; who laughed and said, 'You know, when you talk like that, I'm reminded of a hack-journalist vamping up an article—or an artist who paints from photographs!' Such moments with Thomas always sent a shiver of angry shock and apprehension down Keith's spine. Had he, after all, backed the wrong horse? The eyes of father and son met for an instant in profound incomprehension.

'I'm particularly thrilled at the prospect of seeing what you'll make of this new departure. Spain is still very much to the fore—it's the Catholic influence. But, well, a faithful portrayal surely depends on first-hand knowledge——'

Thomas looked at his son dumbly, wondering how he could be such a fool.

'Has the boy *no* imagination?' he asked himself; and then thought grimly, 'Imagination? Oh, yes.' Keith had imagination, too, and the quality of his imagination had sometimes struck Thomas rather awfully. It was of the emotional kind which inclines the happy sufferer to see only what he wants to see. An inherently untruthful mind, a mind trained in ways of untruthfulness, is the ground in which it flourishes.

'Pooh, stick to your last, my boy,' he said, with unusual irritability. He was emboldened by Keith's final piece of impertinence.

But the young man appeared not to have heard; still smiling, he approached the desk behind which his father sat penned. Thomas averted his eyes, and his firm manner covered panic. 'I'm already negotiating for Carlotta House. I don't intend to leave England just now. I'm already, I say, negotiating for Carlotta House.'

Keith then turned a little aside and glanced round the room. His gesture was subtly dramatic. The room belonged to a tall redbrick and terra-cotta mansion in the neighbourhood of Sloane Square. It was darkly paneled, had insufficient windows for its great depth and much dark furniture; so it was already dusky at the end on this weakly lighted spring afternoon. A fire on the huge hearth seemed merely to intensify the shades and to hint at the presence of an untimely night.

It was a room in which every effect had been carefully arranged by Keith *to express Thomas Antequin*. Rage seethed in the young man.

Much research, much reference to authorities, much frequenting of artistic circles and pumping of painter friends had gone to the creation of Thomas's present setting. There had been trials and errors. Obviously some semi-barbaric Jacobean mansion, some modified form of a pile like Hatfield or Audley End would have formed the most sympathetic frame for Thomas's strange, naive, massive and extravagant genius, in which the element of the macabre was strongly discernible, and the lineaments of the gargoyle—that rich, strong mixture which baffled orthodox criticism, and, with every canon of art against it, achieved its triumph. What was really needed was something with the flavour of old Holland House. Arcades of lacy stonework, oriel windows, Dutch gables, little towers capped by pointed roofs—the whole like the scenery of a grim, powerful fairy-tale. West End London (where Keith liked to live, or thought it necessary to live) provided nothing in this genre nowadays. Still, London abounds in Ruskinish fantasies. Victorian Gothic, some product of the romantic revival of the 'seventies, had at first seemed the nearest equivalent. With this might go a semi-Jacobean décor, a little of the neo-primitive judiciously mingled with it, to sharpen it up, or to provide a line of retreat should the Victorian revival collapse upon them. Thus Keith had discreetly edged his effects towards the neo-Gothic; and this, he thought, really suited Thomas's genius with delightful subtlety.

Red brick and terra-cotta! Frightful, indeed, to weak modern eyes resigned to childish simplicity. But Keith had known what he was doing. The very fact that it was frightful would endow it with a vicious fascination for that type of mentality he had wished to attract—for the people who made the noise. Refined perversity of taste had boosted the baroque of late.

But all this had required the nicest handling. The Victorian revival was already a little stale, and there was constant danger of being suspected of over-seriousness. One must never appear beyond being amused. On the other hand, there must be no suspicion that the matter was not serious. The least suggestion of cynicism must be avoided at all costs. Thomas's genius was devoid of cynicism. A delicate situation.

In short, the carrying out of his conception had called for the most exquisite judgment and had taxed Keith's ingenuity to the full. Moreover, it had been difficult to arrange, and costly.

And now, at a mere whim, one thoughtless fancy on the part of the great man, in the twinkling of an eye, all his work was to be undone. Hey presto!——Regency and the outer suburbs! Hilbery Village!

For a moment, the young man seemed about to weep with rage. His face crinkled distressfully. (Thomas, after one peep, kept his eyes lowered.) 'But, Regency!' Keith protested, laughing slightly and his voice was a little shrill. 'Now, one of those Victorian family mansions—the kind of place from which Papa drove up to the city in his gig every day—turrets, gargoyles—a soupçon of the fairly-tale—*that* would have been more in keeping. Something truly *out of touch* with the contemporary spirit——' Although curiously sugared with playfulness, the angry irony in these words was very perceptible, and the almost fooling gestures which accompanied them, as the young man sketched a curlicue in the air, smiling crookedly the while, were in some way unpleasantly impressive; and the worst part of it was that the light eyes with the dark markings, rather small, yet handsome, stared too fixedly and did not smile in the least. In fact, there was an air of hysteria about the whole performance.

Thomas, peeping again, experienced the sinking sensation.

But it was all over in a minute. The young man was not only angry, he was also at a loss, he was deeply astonished; and this restored him to caution. 'Why? What a choice! Extraordinary! Hilbery! (*Where I picked him out of the gutter!*) One really cannot understand the attraction,' he thought, and glanced sideways in suspicion. And almost at once he was calm. His hard common sense was already at work; his natural opportunism was already on the hunt for spoils and advantages in the new situation. He was a man who could adapt himself infinitely in his own interest.

So now he calculated. Supposing the worst came to the worst and Carlotta House was their fate, and was as he could only suppose it to be, then there was but one type of ménage possible and he and Thomas would need a capable woman to run it, one conversant with social usages and one who could not give notice. Just such a woman he had in reserve. Whatever happened, sheer comfort became very important to the elderly, and he had recognised of late that it would not be amiss to provide his father with a more easy-going, a less exacting, home-life. He had been thinking of marriage for some while, but any wife of his must fit into his life with Thomas. Helena would do so without a murmur.

'Well, if you really have made up your mind——' he resumed, but in a very different tone, blandly accommodating. 'An earlier or a later style would have lightened the difficulties. It will have to be an entirely new décor,' he added, in a careless and slightly teasing manner. 'Time and money, and a great deal of fuss and botheration for *me*. *You* need not trouble about that, however, *you* need not suffer. Just put it all in my hands as usual, won't you? Why you ever took it into your head to deal personally with the business, I can't quite fathom. What am I here for but to relieve you of all the unpleasant practical problems? Your department is the imaginative one, the sphere of art——' The young man now spoke with a warm vivacity, a seeming eagerness to be of service, which was very attractive. 'But, now, two months—two months or so—could very well be spent in Spain, while I make all the preparations at Hilbery Village.' He uttered the name with a slight emphasis, a little humorous lilt. (Absurd as he knew it to be, Thomas always shriveled before that note of restrained amusement at his own simplicity.) 'Well, don't trouble yourself any further about it, I'll arrange the whole thing for you. We'll look into it all some time when you are less occupied. And you can just go and gather honey in the sun, and when you come home again I shall have everything in train. Of course, always provided that no insuperable difficulties arise.'

And insuperable difficulties would arise, Thomas instantly perceived.

But the young man's tone was now so pleasant, so sunny, that it cost him a visible effort to say, 'This time, Keith, I wish to have the arranging of it all myself. I've got my own ideas on this occasion and have a whim—a tiresome, old man's whim, if you like,' he added cravenly, 'to carry it through personally.'

Keith was silent and looked thoughtful. But Keith, as Thomas well knew, had acquired the art of looking thoughtful as he listened, as if considering one's words carefully. It was a graceful touch in his social repertoire. It meant nothing. Or, rather, it meant that he was simply pursuing his own line of thought and his already determined course.

'Oh, you will change your mind when you thoroughly realise what the purchasing of such a place entails. It's a pestiferous business—nothing but delays and aggravations, and jiggery-pokery by the legal personalities—which has to be dealt with pretty firmly, or they'll maunder on for months. An old house, too—there are sure to be snags—trouble with the deeds, lost documents—and no damp-courses, you know, and dry-rot, and the like. These Regency houses were sadly jerry-built, actually, and are usually in a hopeless state. I do trust you realise what it will cost you . . . But, first of all, I'll run down there and see if it's at all worth while.'

The great writer sat sadly through all this, like a captive bird without a song in him.

Left alone, he began pushing his palms up his forehead in a gesture of despair which was, at first, consciously comic. But he continued for some minutes to make these instinctive soothing gestures again and again.

SIX

Thomas Antequin was afraid of his son.

To begin with, the boy was illegitimate; and how that had happened Thomas himself scarcely knew. It was not his fault— no, it was not. He had not married the boy's mother for the sufficient reason that he had not been allowed to; and indeed the circumstances were of a kind to make such an outcome unthinkable. A simple, penniless boy with a faun-like charm and a pleasant animal gaiety, he had been put into service in a large and famous country house; and there a young girl of good blood, a very little older than himself, had fallen in love with him and he had later been accused of seducing her. Unfortunately, nothing of their childish liaison had been found out until it was 'too late'. But still the girl was of a social standing which, in those days, had made any acknowledged connection between them out of the question. An iron hand had parted them. And Thomas, at least, had never had a moment's thought of appealing against his sentence; for nothing had ever more surprised, shocked and shamed the well-brought-up young man, a son of chapel-going country people, than this wicked adventure which had befallen him.

It had been a very shallow and almost wholly animal experience on Thomas's part, and he was hardly to be blamed if he dismissed it readily, fruits and all. He wrote no poems to his young love. Inspirations he may have had at that time, but they were never given artistic form. Any thought of putting pen to paper of his own free will had not yet visited Thomas Antequin. This passionate interlude, which, for want of any other evidence of sexual passion in the whole course of Thomas's life, would certainly be cherished and hailed solemnly by future biographers as the 'fructifying experience', had obviously left Thomas much as it had found him. It did, however, throw him out of a job and rather unfairly deprive him of a reference from his employers, and so most fruitfully force him into another and wider way of life, one more favourable to a developing artist.

But instead of taking advantage of this situation, he had almost at once made a humdrum marriage with an unattractive woman much older than himself; and this had continued, to his contentment, for a little over fifteen years, with his wife earning enough to keep them both and himself making laborious efforts to prostitute his abnormally slowly awakening genius. Then she had died. They had had no children. She was a serious woman, above him in station but not very cultivated; did not think a great deal of her husband's talent, yet saw that she must encourage him in what she took to be his one earthly chance of ever making a livelihood. She criticised his work very severely, from the moral angle, and frowned upon the least tendency to freedom of thought and expression; and many a lovely phrase and situation had Thomas abandoned for the sake of peace and quiet. Something of this sentimentalism and slight falsification was to cling to his work for the rest of his life and to become a major matter of reproach with his critics. Still, it was possible that Thomas would never have found himself as an artist at all without this woman's aid. She took upon herself the duty of seeing that his gifts, such as they were, should at least be employed to the full (and of this came Thomas's habits of obedient industry); and she protected him against interruption (by which his original practical weakness was much augmented). When she died, therefore, he was like an abandoned child. However, he continued for some years struggling to support himself by his pen in his obscure corner; and during this time, free at last from moral censorship, his gifts expanded, thus late and unexpectedly, to their giant stature.

Still, his material success declined; it was far more limited than it had been in the days of his wife's management, for his changed style, expanded and uninhibited, lost him the artistically infamous market she had discovered for him. Socially, he sank, his circumstances became so desperate that he at last scrambled into a minor clerkship in the council offices of the Hilbery district; and it was under these lamentable conditions that his best work was done. But possibly it was a strain. And Keith's sudden entry at this juncture must have had the appearance of a heavenly intervention. Poor Thomas had suspected nothing. The tempter was of such pleasant exterior that the bargain had seemed all advantages.

Thomas had never seen his son in childhood; as a parent, he had been swept imperiously out of the picture. He had not met him until this moment when Keith had reached manhood and introduced himself.

Keith's lot had been hard in its own way; he had not much to thank Thomas for.

As if left an orphan, the child had been made the ward of a solicitor friend of the family. He had been given a good education and had had modest provision made for him; but he had never known any family life, there had never been any human contact with his mother's people. The boy had existed in a social void, one indifferent stranger after another had tended him; he had gone through childhood as a little homeless, placeless, unloved creature who had had no background to set against other boys' talk of home and family, and no hospitality to offer to school friends. He had had nothing but himself and his own individuality; and as for a background, he had had to create one. So it was not surprising that he had come to overrate these things.

In the circumstances, it was especially unfortunate that Keith's native qualities were not equal to doing much for him. Added to his natural failings, he had the defects of his upbringing. He had no affections. He was calculating. He was suspicious. Self-esteem was his strongest passion. He had much too great a regard, a really morbid one, for appearances. His own talents were trifling. His brains were by no means first-class, as is apt to be the case with the children of very young parents—a shallow, spontaneous nature which had soon been modified by events and had achieved a sensitiveness and also a shrewdness and agility it would not normally have possessed. He was a natural climber. There was an aura of mystery about his person, which he had the wit to turn to account, and he had the knack of laying out such money as he possessed to advantage; which is to say that he had a fine gift for self-advertisement and a hard business-head.

In short, he was well-equipped to make good as a modern writer; it was but a minor drawback that he could not produce a single original idea, since he had other talents more important. Having fallen in with a smart, fashionable, semi-aristocratic literary set, he had made shift to keep himself afloat by light journalism. A flair for ingratiating himself with influential people was already pronounced, and even in his early twenties he had made many useful contacts.

Then, one day, pondering a notice in a literary paper, he had had the idea of exploiting the talent of his father, who was at this time one of the obscurest of writers.

But although cultivated and possessing enough literary feeling to suspect that here was something good blossoming in almost total obscurity, to suspect neglected talent, Keith had taken some while to become aware of the oddity, the absolutely original and individual quality of his father's work. A certain critic had been inclined to smile and had dismissed Thomas as a curious throwback—had spoken of an archaic style which fell fatally between prose and poetry. Here was one, he had said, who wrote with an artifice, who employed a strong, unblushingly ornamental language and a wildness of plot reminiscent of Elizabethan drama. Here was one born out of his time.

That had set Keith thinking. And as he pondered, he became deeply excited. (His excitement was not, however, the selfless enthusiasm of the art-lover.) His eyes were opened.

Now he saw those strange and roughly formed works for what they were—atmospheric effects, spiritual adventures in the trappings of a dark, wild and powerful imagery. Through all Thomas's pages ran a breeze of terror, arising in the metaphysical world; the air was sinister. The leaves shivered in the dark forest. Something flew behind the million leaves, always out of sight—mystery. Thomas was afraid neither of the romantic nor the wondrous, the hellish or the sublime. (And was not aware of being unafraid.) So they had said that all this was not to modern taste? But already the clever young man knew better. It was like nothing else in print at the moment—and that was enough, that was its real beauty, in Keith's judgment. The critic, the young man concluded, had done very foolishly to laugh.

But such works needed to be presented, and presented cleverly, the modern literary world being what it was they would sink without it.

Hungry and subtle, Keith had suddenly glimpsed vast possibilities.

The son of a famous man is well known to be in an unenviable position. This is so even when he has talent in his own right. But when his gifts are trifling?

In boyhood, ignorantly overrating the few lines of laudatory criticism he occasionally saw of his father's achievements, he had felt somewhat overwhelmed and frustrated, as if by a connection with an overshadowing fame; and for some years his interest had been deep and uncritical. Nevertheless, it was by no means a hero-worship. It contained an element of jealousy. The lonely, placeless, unyouthfully cynical boy, perhaps scraping to himself every morsel of consideration in a wolfish world, had taken a secret interest in a father whose name might one day be famous enough to reflect fame upon his son. He had collected his father's press-cuttings, and in time had found himself in a position whence he could add to them himself with little flattering, anonymous articles and notices. Till at last, observing the effect of one of these clever little eulogies of his own, observing it in dry astonishment, he had stumbled upon the inspired thought, 'Why not *make* this man famous?'

Thus had come his awakening, his conversion. It was at this time that he changed the modest utility name with which he had been ticketed at birth for the distinctive one of Antequin.

Then, tactful and modest, and immensely delicate in his approach, he had introduced himself to Thomas; with the suggestion, made with a charming hesitancy, that he might perform certain practical services. (And he would never forget the shocked astonishment caused him by the first sight of his father, the author of those powerful, half-barbaric works; a little, quiet, diffident man living in a single rented room on a housing estate in the outer suburbs. Nor would he cease to admire his own perspicacity, which had led him to put his money on Thomas in the face of that.) Half alarmed, half bewitched, Thomas had fallen easily into the trap. Indeed, it was a temptation, to a man whose practical inefficiency amounted to imbecility, thus to sell his freedom. Not that he had realised what he was about. Though at first greatly upset by this sudden resurgence of his past, the simple man was also touched, moved by fatherly affection, and, perhaps more than anything else, flattered by the impressive young man's acknowledgment of himself. He had also, in his innocence, rediscovered some remorseful feeling of having wronged the boy and a feeling that he owed him some fatherly attention. In any case, he had not liked to repulse him.

Keith had begun by taking the whole of Thomas's business affairs upon his shoulders, by re-adjusting matters with his publishers, and shielding the poor man with relentless efficiency from all those who would have preyed on him.

Soon, with his experienced charm and his gift for ingratiating himself with useful people, he had found it possible to assemble the *claque* he had dreamed of—the set of literary fashionables whom he had worked upon, through this or that channel, to see Thomas as the newest thing. But Thomas was not merely the newest thing. No sooner had the applause broken out than it was drowned by the noise of wings, the powerful wing-sweeps of ascending genius—an awe-inspiring and uncustomary sound to follow upon such an introduction. Other voices, of better repute, began to acclaim him.

But Keith's view of the triumph lacked proportion. He was undeniably the *deus ex machina*, but he saw himself as something more than that. Regarding himself as the architect of Thomas's fame, he was inclined to regard himself as Thomas's equal. And he meant to be seen as such. As soon as the results of his exertions were felt, as soon as the money began to come in, he had set up his father in a proper establishment and had joined it himself; and thus had started skillfully to impress their relationship and their double personality, the picture they presented, upon the public. His tastes were expensive, perhaps deriving from the aristocratic strain in him. But if people ever said he was living on Thomas, they were very wrong. He worked extremely hard. He took an immense and conscientious amount of thought and care and devoted himself entirely to his father's welfare, for it had become his business. His devotion was unsleeping. And Thomas had very soon begun to find it so.

But it was undeniable that from the day when Keith had taken him in hand, Thomas's stock had soared. In ten years, Keith had made his father's fortune.

Through it all, he had never owned to himself that he had intended to exploit his father. A well-loved public figure, with himself smiling winningly behind the chair, had been the ideal in view. But it had not turned out like that. Anyway, it would not have been easy, perhaps it would have been impossible, to make such a figure of Thomas.

SEVEN

Thomas was a man of middle height, skinny build and undistinguished features, excepting the good, massive forehead— and the forehead merely made his head look too large for his body. He was not physically strong. His dark, kindly eyes were full of humour and sadness, and the delicacy of his mouth was half concealed by hair. He had not worn a beard, or ever dreamed of doing anything so bold and youthful, until Keith had got at him. But his chin was not his strong point, as Keith had at once perceived. The beard was Jacobean. Dressed and arranged by Keith, he could muster a touch of distinction, but on the whole he was not an ornament to public occasions and was best kept immured from them. Thomas had made no difficulty about that. It was not that he was too shy for human intercourse, or that he was of an unsocial spirit, or that his manners were too uncouth for exhibition. On the contrary, his manners were engaging. But sophistication frightened him. He did not take himself seriously. He could not be brought to conduct himself like a man who recognised his worth. Left to entertain people, he would be found bridging the top of a glass with matches. In short, he shone in simple company. He *was* simple.

But the really insurmountable embarrassment was his almost infantile goodness.

Keith was at heart amazed on first discovering the purity and simplicity of his father's life. There was nothing to hide, there were no private indulgences, no irregular connections, not a touch of vice. Tactful researches had soon laid out the whole field of his father's experience before him, every corner exposed. It was insipid as a child's tale. But that was incredible! And Keith had never quite believed in it, dark suspicions had continued to gnaw at him. For was it possible, when one considered the roots of the creative power? Can a great artist be devoid of passion? Can he live like a curate? One knows it cannot be. To all appearances, Thomas was of blameless life. A sinister innocence! There was always, of course, the one youthful slip, which Keith could hardly overlook, but that was a mere bagatelle, psychologically speaking. Or was it actually the cause of so much virtue? As for his marriage, one had all but extracted the confession that Thomas had married a mother. No wonder that Keith was tormented by a restless and disbelieving curiosity, a perpetually irritated sense that Thomas was contriving to deceive him—that he was having his leg pulled by a man far simpler than himself.

From the first, Keith had been startled and dismayed by Thomas's inadequacy as a person to bear the load of his genius. He perceived that Thomas's character was pitifully commonplace. He was a normal, or even a slightly sub-normal person—with genius added, genius extraneous, as it were, to his own personality. An ordinary, perhaps even a sub-ordinary person, who was at times inspired. That was all. Whose mind, with triumphant spontaneity, sometimes threw out great branches lit with magical flowers out of that quiet field in which he lived in isolation; out of that very quietness.

It was really no mystery. The whole of Thomas, all his badness and all his goodness, all his heart, soul, strength and mind, had gone into his work, and there was nothing left but a little animal, sometimes well and gamesome, sometimes ill and sad. His books were his life.

Keith could only conclude that he was best kept out of sight of a public which revels in personalities.

So a curious thing had happened. Keith had become the public face of Thomas Antequin, the ideal portrait of him turned to the world; and so skillful was this illusion that many among the ignorant were misled and identified his features with those of the famous man himself. That really did not matter; Thomas's looks were of no importance. But in a photograph the noble forehead, properly treated, gave Keith a likeness to his father. He was 'one of the Antequins'. He gave curiously possessive talks about the Antequin works, he appeared on television. Thus many people, even among the cultivated, began to get the impression that it was a dual genius. And the question, which was the author of which book, was sometimes asked. Or was it a collaboration? Indeed, a few of the lesser works apparently came into this category; or, at any rate, Thomas had consented to his son's name appearing on the title-page; whether under pressure, as the malicious asserted, or simply out of kindness, to please the boy, or because there was some truth in Keith's pretensions, none would ever be able to say.

Thus Keith enjoyed fame.

He did not bear it well. Confused with Thomas by an ignorant section of the public, recognised by the cultivated as a power with the great man, he was flattered and placated, and he became very spoiled. From displaying manners all attention and eagerness, all pliancy and sympathy, he became arrogant. He had a very sharp tongue and he indulged it now. His criticism of 'enemies' took a tone of waspish ridicule (which was to recoil upon him later, when he was in need of support). He was highly-strung, and this little harmless indulgence afforded great relief to his nerves; the nerves so often privately exacerbated by the strain of the situation, by contact with the personality of Thomas—it could not be hidden!—an antipathetic personality.

It was inevitable. Keith, in daily contact with his father, could no longer look at him with any vestige of tolerance. His attitude towards the great man had changed and developed as might have been expected. There were secret irritation, contemptuous surprise at the shortcomings and infirmities of genius, a clash of character, of tastes; and then a very large admixture of jealousy, and even of hatred. 'Who would ever have heard of him, but for myself?' Keith was apt to exclaim in private. And he had a right to ask the question. And always in fear that his father did not fully realise what he had done for him, and might even imagine that he had attained fame and fortune through his own powers, he could not resist attempting to make the true facts clear. A life-time's allegiance! Well, half a life-time's.

Oh, how often had Thomas heard this. At intervals, these emotional scenes took place, for Keith was a highly-strung person and lived on his nerves. Thomas could not abide emotional scenes—not in real life.

Not for nothing was he in awe of his son. A young man who had the manners and social equipment of a class worlds apart from Thomas's own; who had a far greater empirical knowledge of the world, if not of human nature, than Thomas would ever acquire, and of course knew it. A young man who was so easily upset!

Now the great writer, finding himself alone at last, first rubbed his forehead soothingly for several minutes, and then began to attempt concentration upon a certain paper which Keith had just laid on his desk. One of those flattering, perceptive articles, he discovered. But, dear, dear, was *that* what he had meant? In truth, he had never dreamed of any of those subtle points which his critic had perceived, with the masterly plotting of which he had been credited. It had all been instinctive. The things had come to him.

He suddenly felt ill, hot in the head and angry as he seldom was.

And was he now to be at the trouble of going to Granada— to see with his fleshly eyes what he could see already, transfigured, and what crude facts would only confuse? The more you see with the bodily eyes, the less you see with the spirit. Of what use was the imagination, did they suppose? He would have been afraid to admit, to these knowledgeable persons, what small seeds had yielded his forest trees.

For ten years and more he had borne this handling and this business of living in settings.

'And what settings,' he paused to think, looking round on the heavily Jacobean interior with the beamed ceiling, the monstrous ingle nook, the black wainscots, the insufficient light seeping in through leaded windows under projecting gables. And then that loathsome modern stuff! He had always been surprised at Keith's taste, though he had never presumed to say anything. He had failed to see why his rooms should offer such a strange mixture of churchiness and the South Seas. Besides, it was knobby. It was true that his own taste was for the magnificent. He liked size and could hardly have found anything too massive, but he had a weakness for the classical column. A district like Bayswater, grandiose and slummy, was what he had always fancied.

For ten years he had his shoe-laces tied for him. For ten years he had borne it, that breathless, incessant care which anticipated every move, obviated every exertion, which never allowed him to take a holiday in the normal rough and tumble of daily affairs, but drove him on to unrelieved brain-work, conserved him for that alone, forced him to live, without respite, in a rarefied atmosphere in communion with his muse, when perhaps a little practical exertion would have been by way of relaxation. It seemed strange that he could remember a time when he had raged and groaned against the miserable commitments of daily life which interfered so disastrously with the creative mood! For ten years or more, he, a man of no ambition, had been frog-marched to fame.

And all his disorderly scrapbooks and notes (God knew, no need to go to Spain!) which he had understood perfectly, filed away into neat cabinets under some system he could never bother to master.

'A pact with the devil!' he suddenly cried aloud. But here, of course, he was speaking with shocking ingratitude and with some exaggeration.

The truth was that he was getting ominously tired, self-control was slipping. Often his heart fluttered in panic.

The explanation of his sudden move, the mystery of his fancy for Hilbery (for a key to which Keith was even now solemnly seeking high and low), was pitifully simple. It was bleak, crude, selfish and innocent as a child's reason. Carlotta House had been remembered by Thomas as a quiet, secluded old dwelling, with good large windows and of the classical style which he preferred—and, above all, he believed that Hilbery, now developed into a nasty, dormitory, bourgeois 'setting' at which all Keith's friends would scream, was *a place where Keith could never bring himself to live.* Yes, that was Thomas's secret, unnatural, graceless thought. He wished to throw Keith off. To unseat him and throw him off as Sindbad threw off the Old Man of the Sea.

Thomas now took a resolution. He would not go to Spain; (his weak stomach turned between the triple horrors of air-travel, Spanish cooking and smells); he would manipulate the purchase and supervise the rehabilitation of Carlotta House in person. He had not dared to tell his son how far on in the business he already was.

Then *perhaps* he would marry. Yes, he had even thought of marriage as a way out. A desperate remedy; but he was at such a pass that he had thought of it. Some sensible, elderly woman who could protect him, and perhaps one who could whack out his things on a typewriter—for that, he thought, was all he needed of a wife. Someone who would be a match for Keith, and could oust him. He knew just such a woman, had known her for years, and thought it possible that she would marry him out of kindness if he explained things to her; or if not that, for the sake of his riches.

Had Thomas, then, forgotten what he had heard so often? That all the best years of his son's life had been given up to a loyal, self-effacing, tireless service to himself? That it was not many young men who would have abandoned a brilliant career, in their finest years of promise, to promote the career of another? No, he had not forgotten. Thomas was selfish. He was growing more selfish every day.

Keith could go to Spain and could collect the Spanish-Moorish colouring. He deserved a holiday.

A hidden struggle began. It turned out to be fierce, exhausting; a contest which never came out into the open, never developed into a brawl, but was conducted with appearances intact. Keith stalled and obstructed in masterly style. And in that velvet-handed grip, under that suave pressure, Thomas had almost succumbed.

But the struggle exhausted the ageing man whose brain had been working at high pressure, with scarcely a break, for so many years; and although he finally won, it was a tired victory, and he felt old and desperately impatient at the end of it. Moreover, it was the violent, stubborn, half-childish impatience of old age, when the judgment is already disturbed. And Carlotta House had become something of a senseless passion.

For all this impatience, however, it was three months before the beautiful June morning when he got out his car, the shabby, antiquated Wolseley he kept in the face of Keith's disapproval because he liked driving it, and ran himself down to Hilbery to have another look at his property and to meet the builder on the spot.

A shattering experience awaited him.

EIGHT

The noonday was warm. On the long hill, one always had to alight and walk. For this reason, she did not usually take her bicycle when she went up to the garden. But today it was a question of time and she was counting on a rapid run home.

It was, if you liked, a matter of looking for a needle in a haystack. But it was also like a difficult game at which one had at least a sporting chance; a thing which was undoubtedly there, must be findable. A still, bright noon, the searching eye of day, was now her ally. Her doubts of the evening before were forgotten. Success did not seem so improbable.

She was vividly happy at the prospect of having the great, wild garden all to herself. She felt adventurous, in a half disturbed fashion. As soon as she entered the enchanted place, the thick greenery, the exuberance of all the growths and the vertical rays of the sun pouring into these enclosed, leafy chambers with a concentration of heat not felt in the open places began to work strongly and excitingly upon her imagination. These things translated the scene for her to another world than that from which she had come—the world where nature was tamed and every green thing was shaped to neatness by the shears— and an inexpressible hunger for strangeness, for the marvels, the colours and natural riches of wild tropical lands, seemed to her almost to be satisfied. The chestnuts were in fullest leaf, their candles spent. In the deep green twilight of their own canopies, under the mountainous piles of shade formed by layer upon layer of their own large green hands, their boles looked as black and massive as if they belonged to the giants of an exotic forest. Amazonian exploration was a passion with her at the moment. Beyond, fringed by the dark, splayed leaves, the sun blazed down and silvered the heads of the tall grasses. And all this lush growth and the fierceness of light and shade, the subtle touch of riot, encouraging the dream, she began pretending to herself that she was an explorer in a deep jungle country.

She did not, however, let these visionary adventures interfere with her serious business in the garden. She had planned to work systematically, to quarter the ground and search one small area thoroughly each day—for she intended to repeat the lunch-hour expedition, if it should be necessary; and remembering, rather reluctantly, Penelope's words about the well-house corner, she first went in that direction, entered the kitchen garden and, standing at the iron gate, gazed doubtfully for some minutes into the field beyond. She did not go in.

The piece of ground known among them by this name lay at an acute-angled corner of the garden, from the rest of which it seemed of a different character, possibly because it had been even longer out of cultivation and was also lower-lying. It was a small, irregularly-shaped field, bounded on two sides by the outer wall and on the third by a lofty hedge of elders, growing quite wild, which, in their season, made the whole field smell rankly. This hedge shut the place off from the kitchen garden and had the iron gate in it. And a row of chestnuts on the long fourth and garden side cast over the whole of it a heavy, dark green shade. It was a sombre spot, overgrown with coarse grasses, among which docks lifted their broad, dull leaves and the shadowy clocks of a host of dandelions were now mingled. The very grass was of a different type from the sweet, fine meadow-grass out in the sun of the garden. It had broad, ribbon-like blades which were looped over and gleamed in the pallid light. This gave a scribbled, restive character to the surface of the field. In the midst stood a little building of crumbling terra-cotta brickwork with a door shredded by dry-rot. It had no window, but a small barred vent under the eaves on the further side. The little ruin was topped and seemingly almost borne down by a huge bush of ivy larger than itself. It was supposed to be a well-house, or perhaps at one time it had been a privy of the most primitive type, and was so old that from inside one could see the wooden pegs with which the timbers were joined. There was a hole in the floor covered with heavy planks. The ivy had peculiarly vast leaves which, in the shade, were touched by moony gleams. All the high lights in the little field were reflected lights and so had the whiteness of a blind eye, an opacity, a muted pallor, dull and unwholesome.

Christine had a distaste for the well-house corner, which might be no more than natural. The spot was dank and gloomy, and the idea that the building had once been a privy was repellent. It brought with it vaguely a sense of soilure. Looking over the gate into the field she could hardly believe that a nervous little girl would have chosen to play in such a spot. Moreover, although she could see a thread of path leading to the well-house, no doubt made from time to time by a few curious explorers of the tennis party, the corner as a whole looked undisturbed. So she felt justified ill concluding, 'Oh, she can't have played there. I shan't bother.'

At any rate, she would leave it for another day.

Then suddenly and gladly she remembered that Penelope had merely described the child as hanging over the fence, or playing near it, the fence between the chestnuts on the garden side; and so she resolved to begin under the chestnuts and to work back towards the courts to the place where there were some old fruit-trees with low-spreading boughs, which she knew Vivian was fond of climbing.

She went to work very methodically, going in a straight line and returning upon a parallel track, like a person mowing a lawn.

At first, under the trees where it grew almost in twilight, the growth was sparse and coarse and gave her little trouble; but the terrain rapidly became more difficult, a mingling of over-grown beds, their very shapes swamped by weeds, bristling with a thicket of suckers and saplings from the old fruit-trees. However, she went on, resolute and earnest, not deflected by any obstacle, nor giving way to daydreams inordinately; hardly raising her eyes, and even shining a torch down to the roots of the grass in shadowy patches, in the hope that the ray would draw a responsive glint from metal, stone or crystal. There were a good many vague beaten trails and she gave these her particular attention. They had no discoverable objectives. She set them down to cats.

At intervals she darkly and uncomfortably remembered the well-house corner, but pushed it out of her mind. Nevertheless, the sense of failure or discouragement which began to grow upon her perhaps emanated from that quarter, for she was pursued by a feeling that it was there her search should have begun. After all, to follow any paths or trails would have been comparatively easy in that place which was all but untrodden. No, *she had not wished to.*

However, she at last shook off the thought of the well-house, absorbed in her quest.

She had brought a package of sandwiches and had intended to eat while searching. But finding it unpleasantly hot, moving slowly, bent over with the sun pouring on her back—combined circumstances which seemed not to favour digestion—she decided to break off halfway and give herself ten minutes in the shade for lunch.

Settling herself on one of the low-growing branches of an apple-tree, she undid her sandwiches and bit into them with zest. At once she felt better. She had chosen, too, a delightful position. The rather sparse-leaved tree allowed the sun to stream through in a cascade of soft, gliding light-spots, and yet subdued its fierceness. Small golden flies hung in the air with wings vibrating at such speed that they were invisible. Little apple-green insects with stilted legs walked delicately upon her arms, and she studied them benevolently. About her was a sea of grass, so pierced and riddled with sun that one could peer into its reedy depths as into new-washed hair.

She now tried to recall any casual, far-off glimpse she had had of the child during the previous afternoon. She had seen her climbing in these low-hanging boughs, these old twisted apple-branches which wound into the undergrowth like snakes—like the huge serpents of the Amazonian forests! 'Look, there one glides and raises its blue-black coils out of that riot of vegetation loaded with incredible blossoms, and one of us seizes his machete——' And surely she had seen the child in this very place? She remembered feeling mildly concerned at the height the little girl had reached and her rather dangerous-looking perches. An attempt to revive in her mind's eye the view she had had of her then, yielded a curious impression, an impression of fierce, wild movement and the agility of a monkey; and this seemed out of character.

Or did it not? Certain overtones from the conversation of the walk in the dusk had perhaps crept in here to mislead her, to falsify the memory picture. Her mind flicked down a shutter.

The child was fond of climbing. Her hopes rising, she thought that this, then, was the most likely place of all. In no other circumstances could it have happened more easily that a string caught on a projecting twig or an insecure knot came untwisted. She must give special attention to the ground under these trees.

With that, she raised her eyes, turned her head, and found she had a view of the house, at which she continued to gaze dreamily without really seeing it.

A small, rather plump, fair girl with a gentle, meditative expression, her face short and round, flushed and sunburned, she sat there munching unselfconsciously, with visible enjoyment, sometimes licking her fingers; and at that moment any adult touches about her person seemed to be quite incidental, with no significance. She looked a happy, quiet, slightly greedy and good-hearted child.

Her mind abruptly acknowledged what her eyes had been resting on for some minutes, the only token of humanity in her surroundings, Carlotta House.

It had always pleased her, but chiefly because of its romantic setting—*that* had delighted her. For the building itself, she had hitherto had no eyes. Its comparative antiquity, its melancholy disrepair, and her totally untrained taste, had made her think of it simply as old-fashioned. She had thought of it as hopelessly decayed. She did not realise that its air of dilapidation was mainly a matter of cracked and fallen stucco; a paintless shutter at a top floor window, hanging by one hinge, seemed to her proof of ruin. Its day was over.

But the house at which she was looking was actually a building of great distinction; and something of this came through to her now and pierced her ignorance because she looked at it in a new light, with the wondering knowledge that a man of taste had made choice of it. It was pure Regency; not a mansion, merely a large villa; with a wide, gently swelling central bow rising the whole height of the house to a flat cornice; the bow gave a graceful roof-line. But the house, in Christine's opinion, had no roof, which she reckoned ugly. That iron verandah on the first floor, with the crinolined hood, looked of course very old-fashioned to youthful eyes; but, carried right across the façade, the hood under the top windows, the balcony railings overhanging the ground floor, twice repeated, a little more heavily in descending order, the elegant line of the cornice. The iron-work, rich and light, supplied beautiful and effective ornament to the plain walls. A small pavilion or lower storey attached to the side of the house contained the front door. This stood in a round-headed recess, and had flanking pilasters, with roundels between them, and three blind lights above it. The cornice of the pavilion carried a small pedimental ornament.

No, she could not quite admire Carlotta House.

Still, she felt it to be romantic; it seemed to her to have a foreign air which, together with its name, brought vague dreams of distant countries where white walls cast back the rays of a fiercer sun.

Now, what sort of man could he be who had bought such a place? she asked herself, marveling mildly. No answer suggested itself. The unfurnished chambers of her ignorance contained nothing for fancy to build on.

Turning her mind to business again, she wondered, rather uncomfortably, whether the child had gone into the house itself on the previous afternoon; for the young people of the tennis club did sometimes break in and poke around out of idle curiosity, and everyone knew that an entry could be made through that low window at the back. At least once, she knew, Vivian had gone inside, for she herself had been of the party. With that, her spirits sank a little. She could not tackle the house as well! Indeed, the bare thought of a solitary tour of the old echoing building affected her with a slight chill; the whole place suddenly looked to her heavy and secretive in the broad sunlight. It was surely not at all likely that the timid little girl had really entered the house alone?

And so she had said to herself in the case of the well-house.

But a child would not know bad and nerve-racking things such as Christine knew.

She gave a final lick to her fingers and then, glancing down at her person, was sorry to see that she would have to leave at least ten minutes earlier than she had intended, for she would require something beyond the sketchy wash and brush-up she had planned for herself. This duty of getting oneself up was still a trial to her; she had no elder sister to rouse her to emulation, and the standards of the girls in the library still seemed to her formidably high. Left to follow her own taste, she would have preferred to remain grubby and playing in the sunshine of the vast, wild, secret garden for the rest of the afternoon. She looked frowningly at her hands; and then found herself observing them very closely and seeing them very distinctly, every soil and blemish. She had suddenly become extremely, peculiarly conscious of herself sitting there.

She was aware of her solitude, tinglingly aware of the lack of anything human in this garden, which was silent in the noon-day heat but for the murmur set up by a million infinitesimal stirrings of leaves and wings, or an occasional rich, warm phrase uttered by a blackbird. She was cut off, quite out of reach or call! No one even knew where she was—and as soon as she had thought of her position like this, her sense of it increased and she paused and sat quite still to savour more fully this exciting and yet faintly uneasy experience.

She could only have compared her recognition of these facts to a return of consciousness, a feeling such as one has on finding oneself observed where one had thought oneself alone. A little shock had resulted.

She had half wondered whether the child, who seemed to have fastened so on the idea of a lunch-hour search, would perhaps take it into her head to come running up here to join her after her morning school.

Well, yes, it was true. She felt jumpy, unnaturally alert. Not exactly nervous—for why should she be? But a little anxious.

She dropped off the bough and rolled into the nest of grass which her own trampling, despoiling feet had made; extending herself deliriously, blissfully, among the sweet, warm stalks. For two minutes, for three minutes, perhaps, she would relax completely.

And she turned her head sideways, as on a pillow.

Instantly, she sat up.

Out of the corner of her eye, imperfectly, she had seen a patch of pink lying at a little distance, a scatter of light hair and a stick-like arm thrown backwards. When she sat up, the leafage of the low boughs intervened.

Her eyes grew huge with shock, her whole face lengthened and sharpened, and all the secret sicknesses of her nature started forth as if extravasated by torture.

'Oh, no, I am never going to find the body of a poor little murdered girl!' she thought in anguish, her breath nearly stopping and the scene going dark before her. And she rose to her knees, with bowed head, joining her hands and wringing them across her breast. After a time, she forced herself to her feet and thrust through the grass towards the place. Her heart-beats nearly choked her now and she heard herself whimpering.

She had perhaps started in the wrong direction. No, look where she would, nothing of what she had seen, nothing suggesting it, was to be found. She stumbled at last back to her first position, stooped, squatted, and then, in fear and trembling, lay down again and looked sideways as before. No, nothing.

She continued to be there. She had had such a terrible shock that she felt quite ill, and although relief went on pouring through her, it was not perfect relief. What secretly continued so to frighten her was that she had found nothing to account for the illusion—no garment left behind by trespassing picnickers, no pinkish fungus, no patch of flowers or remnant of coloured paper.

Suddenly, however, it occurred to her that, in a slight daze from heat and sleepiness, one might have had an instantaneous glimpse of some small object quite close and transferred it to the distance with a momentary loss of the sense of scale. She had not seen directly, but out of the top of her eyes, as it were—she had glanced sideways and upward. She rolled over and looked eagerly, and there, sure enough, caught in the grass a few inches from her head was a bright pink rose-petal. At this she lay staring for a full minute in a kind of blank, fatuous ecstasy. She disentangled it from among the grass, she caressed it and almost wept over it, pressing its velvet surface to her lips, as if in a passion of gratitude.

Then, very quickly and quietly, with not another thought of searching the garden, she got up and scrambled in panic haste through the wilderness to the tennis-courts where she had left her bicycle. The sun shone out brightly here, and now there was a lark risen from the fields. Relief was uppermost. Yet the shock had left her with a tremulous, oppressed, sickish feeling, and she hurriedly pulled out her bicycle from among the bushes and wheeled it into the lane. It was fortunate that she had plenty of time and could spin gently home without effort; fortunate, too, that she had no traffic to cope with, for at a little distance down the lane she came upon a large, dark car standing half on the grass verge, empty, and all but ran into it; so nerveless was her progress.

But what ominous, buried chain of thought had so translated a rose-petal? The young girl did not ask herself this. Some illusion of light and distance had combined with a hidden fear she had felt for the child. That was strange, too, because although it was common knowledge that, between the father's unamiable character and the step-mother's indifference, Vivian was an unfortunate child, yet there had never been any suggestion that she was ill-treated. Or none that Christine had ever heard. The truth was that there had been just such a horrible case blazoned in the papers recently, the case, staged in some remote country spot, of a child murdered in a privy, which the young girl had absorbed with secret, silent horror, dreading to hear anyone mention it.

She bowled effortlessly down the hill and, on turning into the high street, was in time to catch sight of a shabby little van with the name of Hope upon it. In the back of the van lolled Miss Freemantle, raffish as ever, in the same dirty slacks and pullover, tilting a bottle to her mouth—though the bottle appeared to be labelled 'Jeyes' Fluid', and it was obviously but a parting gesture made in the face of Hilbery Village. She waved to Christine and pulled one of her faces, indicative of intense grief at departure. It was so very funny that Christine could not keep her own face straight but burst out laughing where she stood at the side entrance of the library. She laughed certainly a little too much and was still shaking with laughter when she went inside. And it was some moments before she observed the odd and solemn looks of her two companions at the counter. Then they told her that she was to go to the police station without delay; Vivian Lambert was missing.

NINE

'What can have happened, Mother? What can have happened? *Missing*!'

Did they answer her? She did not know. She went on thinking, 'She was close to the door of her own home—only a few steps from the door!—she looked back at me, and then she vanished. She vanished, vanished. She is missing. She is lost. Lost, lost, lost. A little girl in my charge.

'Listen to the voices! The neighbours, the papers, the talking in my own head.

'To think of such a home! "The facts throw a remarkable light on the Lambert ménage." "A household which has its peculiarities." "When Rosalie has an evening out, which is more often than not, the child is left to her own devices. Her father ignores her. He does not even put out food for her, as one puts out food for a cat. She is left to get her own meals, to take anything she fancies out of the larder, or to go without, if she prefers it. She puts herself to bed. She is a child who requires no attention."

'Miserable, miserable little being! That I did not see it! A little creature who clung to me in desperation, and then flung away in bitter resentment because I did not respond. And I thought her spiteful. "Our last sight of her shows her standing a few yards from her own front-door, throwing a farewell look at Christine Gray—and thereafter she vanishes." She vanishes, vanishes, vanishes. She is missing. "She vanishes and yet she is heard. She is heard by her father to come in by the back-door and move about in the kitchen. Such is his tale. The back-door is usually kept locked, but it is not locked this night, apparently. And yet Lambert, said to be abnormally concerned about burglars, does not investigate the sounds."

'Oh, it's plain, plain! "He never heard her come in. Simply forgot about her, but felt he could hardly admit that when the police questioned him. So he made up his tale; committed himself to it before realising that he might come under suspicion, feeling that he could not take the risk of being thought an unnatural father, hideously callous and neglectful. It might have been, for a man in his position, wiser to admit that he had not heard her—wiser to deny that she came home at all. And George Lambert, *because he did not think of this, must be innocent.*"'

'Then she is alive somewhere, safe and sound?' Her mother's voice answered her, 'I am sure of it, darling.'

But the talking went on, everything heard and read, buzzing like a hive. '"Still—come in she did. She is said to have taken some food from the larder, some scraps, a remaining sardine or two, leaving an empty tin, some milk drunk from a bottle—something of the sort." "You mean we have Rosalie's word for it."

'"The tale of the Lambert pair is that she wasn't missed till next day. Of course they have an explanation. Mrs Lambert got in very late after an evening of pleasure, both of them assumed that the child had put herself to bed, and neither even looked in on her. The father, who is in business in one of the fruit and vegetable markets, is in the habit of leaving the house well before dawn and driving himself to town. He did so, as usual, on that day. Mrs Lambert didn't get up till halfway through the morning, and going at last into the child's room, noticed nothing to show whether she had slept there or not; for the child makes her own bed—another good custom of the house—smooths it down and draws up the sheet and blanket again, and hides up all imperfections with the bedspread. So it wasn't till she should have returned from school at midday that she was missed. Then Mrs Lambert learned that she had not been to school."

'What can have happened?

'"Yes, true enough, she might creep round to the back of the house in the hope of getting in without facing her father—for the poor little wretch has a guilty conscience, she is possessed by a terrible fear that her theft has been discovered in her absence. And she is returning empty-handed. But almost certainly the back-door will be locked.

'"The odd fact is that no one knows what this trinket was which she is supposed to have borrowed. Lambert has a collection of bibelots which are said to be of some value. But he denies having lost anything. He denies it—and whatever the truth may be, no wonder he denies it! It cannot be long, they say, before the body is found, and everyone believes that if the police come upon some trinket in the garden, can prove it to belong to Lambert and to be of value, they will arrest him."

'Why, why? Oh, I can see it. The door opens. I know the hall, for I once called there. It is narrow, dark, a mere passage, with dark green paper and a bulb with no shade to it. "He opens the door and she falters in, she cringes along by the wall and makes to creep past him. A blow from an angry man who has extracted a confession from the miserable little creature that she has lost something of his which is of great value. A blind blow in that little cramped hall, out of sight and hearing, with no fear of a witness—no one else in the house, the neighbours out—with ample time and opportunity to 'clear away'—a blow of unguarded fury so violent as to kill her. Or at least to injure her in such a manner that he was terrified into silencing her. The body put out of the way for the night, probably stowed in the garage. And it is all too easy to prevent a neglectful, tipsy woman from bothering about the child that night. Then, in the morning, precisely at his usual hour, the man eats his breakfast, gets out his car and drives to London, unloading the body somewhere on the way. Have the police some reason to think that he unloaded it at Carlotta House? We locals hold that he did. Not, of course, on his direct route, Carlotta House, yet only a slight detour was necessary. Still, it cannot be found that he diverged by a hair's breadth from his daily routine—he arrived at his business at his usual hour. Coming home in the early afternoon, as he sometimes did after starting his working day in the market at dawn, he walks calmly into the house pretending ignorance that anything is wrong——"

"'Or as an innocent man who has not even heard that his daughter is missing?" "Well, perhaps such he really is.'"

Now a real voice, her mother's. 'Christine, love, drink this.'

It was her father who lifted so gently her burning, talking head from the pillow so that she could drink the cool stuff. 'Of course, of course. Poor old Lambert—a man who would not harm a fly. We must be charitable. Musn't be prejudiced because we don't care for what little we know of him. Poor, poor man! Terrible enough to have lost his little girl. A man deeply to be pitied. Just a heavy, self-centred fellow, you know, a man who isn't able to live up to the tragedy, who has no adequate poses for it, so to speak, and can only take refuge in a lumpish silence, which appears like callousness. Look how he continues to plod crassly about Hilbery, for which everyone blames him, going about his business just as usual, with that blank face and his eyes cast down—suspicious looks from all sides and everyone shrinking from him in abhorrence—but I would wager that the poor beggar simply does not know what else to do. A simple chap.

'And if perhaps he does look rather like a haunted man at the moment, which of us wouldn't if we knew that the police were only waiting to arrest us? It is, of course, generally meaningless to say of a person that he does not look a criminal type—still, we will say it of poor George Lambert.'

'Of course that's the truth. Of course it is. God will take care of His lamb.'

'Then she is alive somewhere, safe and sound?'

'I'm sure of it. Just trust in God, my darling, you've done nothing wrong. God will never forsake you.'

'Only, you see, if I hadn't left her alone, none of this would have happened.—Listen! Oh, do you think that could be her crying, now that it's dark?'

TEN

Keith had been to Paris for a few days and when he returned was told that his father was unwell in bed, 'because of the Hilbery business'. Having missed the London newspapers, he took the servant to be referring to some new worry connected with Carlotta House. 'Better and better!' he thought with grim triumph; and he hastened, in no very charitable spirit, to take a look at the sufferer.

Thomas welcomed him brightly. He was lively and talkative, like a person exalted by excitement, with nerves a little out of control. In fact, Thomas had had a shock.

'Well, my boy, I've got myself mixed up in a horrible disaster down there. A crime appears to have been committed and is suspected to have taken place somewhere in the house or garden. At least, so some think. A little girl lost and probably made away with.'

'Good God, you don't say so? What a business!' Keith cried, his private satisfaction warmed by natural, simple enjoyment of so sensational an event. 'Do give me the details . . . So the deal is off?' he could not resist adding in a voice of indulgent sympathy.

'Off? The deal? What, the buying of the house? Off? Oh, no. No, no. Why should it be?' Thomas asked rather airily.

'Well——' Keith began, taken aback.

'The place has been thoroughly searched and nothing found. Pooh, they're entirely on the wrong scent, that's obvious. Still, it *is* annoying to be involved, even in such a completely fortuitous way. I hope the police won't find it necessary to pull the place to pieces. Actually it's not a body they're after—or, rather, a hypothetical body—but a lost toy—trinket—which is supposed to be connected with the disappearance.' And he began an account of the affair as seen from the local angle— for he had remained in Hilbery and spoken to almost every-one in the place, it seemed—breaking off somewhat abruptly, however, and tossing a daily paper across the bed to his son, saying, 'There, read it yourself,' as if the effort of explanation had suddenly become too much for him. Thomas sank back on the pillows and turned his face from the light; but after listening to Keith reading and commenting for some minutes, he added, 'There's this young girl, you know—the poor girl involved—the chief witness—the one who was the last to see her. Decent local people—used to know them by sight—see them about the neighbourhood. Remember them well. A nice woman, the mother. Used to admire her. My wife used to speak to her. I should like to be of some help to the family. A shocking experience for a young creature. She forms an interesting con-trast with such a murky, squalid, yes, probably blood-stained drama—as it seems likely to be. A creature of light . . .'

Keith did not quite care for this tone, which seemed a little excessive. But he was not warned. The thing was too far from his experience of Thomas.

'I hope the upset won't put you off your work upon *The Inquisitors*,' he said sincerely. 'Coming in the midst of a great creative effort—how very unfortunate! A disrupting influence. A veritable "person from Porlock"! But, then, the whole thing——'

'Oh, dear, no,' returned Thomas, lightly. 'I find it stimulating.'

'What odd things Father does say,' Keith thought as he closed the door. And suddenly it struck him that of late Thomas's odd sayings had become frequent and marked. There was often a kind of tactlessness, an insensitiveness, as if Thomas did not stop to think what he was saying.

Then for some minutes Keith stood in the passage considering this rather uncomfortably. He remembered several instances—and they were particularly unhappy ones. He remembered with a sudden flood of distaste the nature of the material he had been amassing for Thomas's latest work . . . Morbid stuff. Records of the Spanish Inquisition at its vilest. And a play, too. Thomas, although he had had one or two stage successes, was not primarily a playwright. Keith went into his own room and there pondered what he had gathered of this work. What was the theme? he asked himself, point-blank, having so far fought shy of the question. In essence (as far as he could judge), the play was to be nothing more nor less than a justification of cruelty. But surely Thomas himself hardly realised that? Cruelty sometimes performs a catharsis. It is an antiseptic in society and as such to be employed and admired. Yes, that was the argument of *The Inquisitors*. A calm, detached plea for the use of cruelty and force in modern society—the brazen, impudent, scientific type of cruelty which has performed the damnable feat of self-justification. Thomas's Inquisitors were to possess modern minds, they were to go as far as our own scientists and medicals into the base depths of insensibility and indurated conscience; but they were to surpass them in honesty, for while making no pretence that they inflicted tortures to save souls and admitting that they acted merely for their Church's worldly salvation and aggrandisement, they brazenly, unashamedly, were to confess to their sensual pleasure in what they did.

That the spirit of cruelty cleanses society, that it is cathartic in action, is a theme sadly familiar to the modern world, after all. Too familiar. Schoolboys strut in it. Yet what banality could not genius exalt and transfigure?

Yes, it would be a freak among his father's productions, Keith decided, a freak and a *tour de force*; one of those brilliant freaks which genius sometimes throws off. One of those triumphs of pure inspiration, one of those works in which the artist seems to rise above his normal powers, to be discoursing, with marvelous insight, in a tongue he never learned by normal means, of things clean out of his experience, as if by a black miracle.

So Keith sought to dismiss his doubts. His objections were of course not moral, not at base. Success sanctifies the most evil theme. One could but hope that the present adventure, coming at a time of creative tension, would not endanger the work, which at least promised to be of sensational quality and to make no little noise.

But Carlotta House with this new stigma upon it had surely become impossible in anyone's estimation! Struck by this happy fact, he returned to question his father more closely, pressed his inquiries with gentle diligence and found that Thomas had not even now advanced too far with the negotiations to withdraw, if he really wished to. A small money loss that was negligible was the only bar to such an act of commonsense. So with tactful and friendly insistence, Keith urged this course upon him, sitting on the foot of the bed and talking long and earnestly—until he perceived that Thomas was looking rather flushed. Then, with his usual delicate feeling, he withdrew; believing, from Thomas's amenable manner, that at last his words would be heeded.

Keith was vividly interested in the drama at Hilbery. Greedy for details, he ran about gossiping and gleaning news of the case, and even pushed his inquiries as far as Hilbery itself. It seemed to him that the whole trouble was about to roll away; he hoped that the police and sightseers would work such havoc between them that all further thought of the house would have to be abandoned (whatever Thomas might feel about it at the moment), and this made him very cheerful.

On joining a party at a friend's house at Campden Hill that evening, he found the case under discussion—for it had figured sensationally in the evening papers.

'So, Keith, we hear that Thomas is in trouble with the police?'

Keith responded with an amusing account of Thomas's adventures, giving these a slightly ludicrous turn (an odd little fact, noted with surprise and interest by that intelligent gathering); and he was also able to supply vivid eye-witness portraits of certain of the chief actors. He had been down to Hilbery. Talking to excited locals, he had had a plentiful choice of theories. He had run about like a good newspaper man and had stuck his nose into everything. He was a bold and assured talker, and the attention of a critical company, which was already amused and agog because the Antequins were involved, inspired him to give of his best.

Someone remarked that the young witness was very pretty and produced an evening paper in support of his words.

'Ah, let me see her,' said Keith, and he looked with professional interest at Christine Gray for the first time; for in her case his reporter's tactics had been of no avail, he had caught no glimpse of her. The snapshot, slightly out of focus, gave a curiously impressionistic view of the young girl's head, which was both flattering and misleading. Juvenile delinquency was very much in the air at the time, and someone now suggested that Christine Gray might be the criminal; whereat Keith smiled and declared, 'She's an innocent little schoolgirl, as normal and healthy as daylight, greatly distressed by her position. A little suburban nobody. But pretty, yes. Everyone is falling in love with her.' These words were remembered and he was laughed at later.

'A highly unattractive child,' was said of a similarly falsified portrait of Vivian. 'But her home-life explains her.'

'Those teeth should make identification easy,' Keith said, his odd humour seeming to relish this little detail. 'Not many people are really buck-toothed. It will lighten the task of the police.' And, pleased with himself and in high spirits, he had one of those lapses into bad taste and coarse feeling to which the egoistical are prone, however cautiously they conduct themselves. He allowed himself to be facetious about this unfortunate trait in the little victim's features; and he repeated the bad joke more than once, as if the detail intrigued him.

At the end of the evening, he found himself leaving the house at the same time as a middle-aged woman with a dark, plump face made piquant by its big, shallow dimples. He knew her and could not avoid walking a little way with her.

She was a Mrs Harrel, a friend, or, rather, a gossip of his father; one of those people who by dint of taking upon themselves all the active and initiating side of friendship, or being abnormally thick-skinned and persevering, are able to force their friendships upon the very shy. Thomas had been helpless to repulse her, Keith supposed, and then had found her a soothing habit. But it was regrettable.

He had seen her at the beginning of the evening, made a mental note to avoid her and then had forgotten her presence. She was there in such circumstances, probably, that she had had the discretion to keep in the background; and this although her attractions were of a kind not easily subdued. That she had contrived to introduce herself at all into that somewhat exclusive company did not in the least surprise him. Such catlike insinuations were her forte. She herself was a literary personality. There was hardly a famous man, so it seemed, with whom she had not been intimate. Book after book of light, gossiping reminiscences had borne her name, all full of scandals, old and new, lies and libels of the comical sort which the victims dare not rebut. She was patently a dangerous person to know or to be known by, and had little trouble in pushing her wares. Her style was execrable and amusing, Much too lazy and impatient to do the writing of her books herself, she was known to employ other hands; little but the inspiration was her own. Most of them were supposed to have been written by her schoolboy son, which accounted well enough for their peculiar flavour. She was rather better than her books, and made this perverted use of a considerable intelligence; was good-natured, if in a selfish, eupeptic way, and was not incapable of gratitude and loyalty. So her charms were not entirely base, and few people resisted her long when she determined upon their capture. Keith had resisted her. He was cold by temperament and was armed with jealousy. At the same time, he was wary. If she had ever fancied his job, she could perhaps have relieved him of it; and he was not without some inkling of this.

'How oddly your father seems to be taking it,' she said, in the familiar manner of an old friend.

'Oddly?' Keith was, of course, all the more struck and annoyed because the same thought had occurred so uncomfortably to himself.

She laughed. 'But he *is* taking it oddly, you know. Lightly.'

'*Lightly*?' Keith repeated. He was most unpleasantly surprised.

'Yes, I happened to drop in yesterday morning when he had just got back from Hilbery, and so heard the whole story. You had a few points wrong.'

Keith had regained his self-possession. 'Oh, one needs to know him as well as I do. Lightly?—no, far from it. One cannot expect a man of his sensitivity not to be upset.'

'I shouldn't have been surprised if he *had* been upset, my dear man! No, not a thing to take lightly.'

'Lightly!' Keith cried again; unable, through shock and annoyance, to avoid the echoing trick, the word had irritated him so. At which Mrs Harrel laughed again. 'Why, what's the matter with you? You're like a cuckoo this evening.' And then she went on to speak with the impudent frankness of which she made a specialty.

'Do you notice that he's rather changed of late? Not ill—I don't mean that. Not precisely. But altered.'

Keith rebuffed her. 'Oh, a passing mood—which might be taken by anyone who did not know him very well——'

But Mrs Harrel interrupted, turning her head after some passerby and speaking casually, 'For instance, he's forgetful, abnormally so. You must have noticed that, at least.'

Exasperated, Keith replied, 'He works too hard—and sometimes gets very tired. He's not a young man.'

'So you *have* noticed, then! I thought you must. But, my dear, who encourages him to work too hard? Why, *you*.'

'I? I make him over-work?' Keith cried, sincerely amazed and then deeply hurt. He was devoted to his father, who could doubt it? She saw with amused surprise his worried air and was agog to find out the real reason. He had grown slowly pallid with indignation under the street lights.

'My father works when and if he wishes to. Like all artists, he's inclined to over-drive himself when he's in the vein.'

'He's by no means so thoughtful as he used to be for other people,' Mrs Harrel resumed, quite as if he had not spoken. 'In fact, there's a peculiar insensitiveness, which really one can't help noticing—it's so marked, so odd.'

Keith was silent, determined to give the intrusive, dangerous creature no more handle.

But she hung on, in the face of these snubs, in her usual brazen manner, because she had an exciting feeling that Thomas had returned from Hilbery in some sort of trouble, and she would have given the world to find out what it was.

'You don't mind my speaking like this to you, of course,' she said cheerfully. 'Now, this play he's working on at the moment—it's surely something quite out of his usual line of country?'

Keith was incredulous. Was it possible that his father had opened his intimate thoughts to this woman, so slight and so shifty an acquaintance—a woman who was known to be passionately inquisitive and an unscrupulous gossip? Concerned as he was with the documentation, he himself always had a good idea of his father's works at their inception, but it was not that Thomas ever discussed them with him; and, noting this sorely, Keith had always made it his pride to ask no questions. But it was a tender point, a secret grievance. And had he now to learn that Thomas had indulged in such incontinent babbling to a mere casual acquaintance—and a female at that?

'A Spanish story!' she went on. 'The Inquisition! Why, golly, how crude.'

He was silent from excess of feeling.

'Oh, I know, of course—medieval Granada's only the setting—the spirit of the play is anachronistic and entirely modern. And that's intentional, naturally. Just one more transcription of the modern nightmare—but I should have said we've had too many . . . Do you know, I have the impression that he has suddenly felt his age, has become conscious of murmurs of disaffection among his admirers—for such I'm afraid there are, my dear!—and has suddenly decided he must attempt something more in the contemporary spirit. Fatal, don't you think?'

'Well—fatal to anything short of genius,' he admitted dryly.

A furious barking of dogs, an obscene yapping and squealing, almost drowned their exchanges at this point. Mrs Harrel's lips twitched. 'What Thomas has always wanted is a girl-friend,' she remarked, taking leave of him. She went off with her soft, lazy, heavy yet enticing walk, the walk of a woman whose body was still provocative and beautiful in spite of increasing fat. He had not offered to put her into a taxi. He was reckless in his displeasure. At the corner she waved to him.

He went home with his head full of this woman. It was Mrs Harrel, no doubt, who served to distract his attention at this time from events at Hilbery and the quarter of real danger.

In an hour he had recovered his exceptional spirits. And although a little surprised, he was not much alarmed to find, on the morrow, that Thomas had suddenly risen from his bed of sickness and gone down to Hilbery. And he was totally unprepared for the sequel.

There had not appeared to Thomas any reason why he should not be friendly with the people of the neighbourhood in which he had once lived and proposed to live again. He had begun by calling upon the Grays. He called with an offer of such support as a man of standing in the district might give. His harmlessness and sincerity had met with equal harmlessness and sincerity, and he had made friends with Christine's parents. It would be useless to say that, unworldly though they were, they were not a little flattered and dazzled by the attentions of so famous a man; that they did not automatically attribute to him motives quite superior to those of others who had breached their privacy. Besides, of course he was not quite a stranger. Many queer proposals, or offers of help, had been received by the Grays, and of these the majority had appeared to them inexpressibly offensive. Thomas, in short, was not the only one to be sentimentally affected by the pathetic distress of a pretty young girl.

But it was a long while since this ageing man, with his inflammable, artist's nature so long harnessed to an ascetic discipline, had come so dangerously close to a young female creature of this sound, pure pattern as to feel her very heart-beats. He was deeply charmed. He lost his head. In sad fact, there was truth in Keith's savage conclusion that his father had acted on a senile impulse and had fallen a victim to his own psychological history. Thomas had certainly succumbed to a temptation which would never have been felt as such in his days of vigour. Then he would not have thought twice of a young girl. The grey-haired man had suddenly acted with the suscep-tibility and precipitancy, and perhaps even the innocence, of a youth. All prudent ideas of an elderly partner had been entirely banished—but not the thought of marriage, not the pressing need of enlisting help against Keith.

Yet Thomas had had the guile to make a cautious approach during Mr Gray's lifetime. He had given sympathetic sup-port, both moral and practical, throughout Christine's ordeal. Then, when only a few months after the Lambert affair Mr Gray had died with great suddenness, there was Thomas, a rich, trusted, knowledgeable friend at the service of the two helpless ones. Undoubtedly Mr Gray's death had smoothed Thomas's path.

The young girl was scarcely eighteen. She was far too young to withstand flattery. She could not even have been expected to distinguish between her natural pleasure in being chosen and any genuine feeling she might have for an elderly man. Thomas Antequin was perfectly presentable. His simplicity, a charm-ing natural gaiety, an ability to enjoy himself in simple ways, were quite to the taste of his new friends. Mrs Gray herself had married at eighteen, and had married very happily. But, as is often the way in such cases, an emotional development out of all proportion with the intellectual had taken place. She had never developed intellectually, and had remained, for all her experience, a little childlike. Besides, simply because he was of her own age and generation, Thomas had seemed to her to have right ideas and right notions of behaviour, and when she had compared him with the shoddy, irresponsible, amoral boys who were Christine's contemporaries, she had forgotten his years and seen only the shining virtues of maturity. Yes, he had seemed to her a good human creature whom they could trust whole-heartedly. With Thomas, her darling would be safe. Moreover, she was a sorrowing widow and a woman greatly at a loss without a man's guidance.

In place of advice, Christine had had only her mother's romantic, ingenuous approval.

ELEVEN

It would not be in Keith's power to oust a wife, Thomas had fondly supposed. Yet that was what the young man had achieved. Thomas had underrated him. From the first moment of outraged shock, he had been determined to recover his position with his father. He had only just married Helena when the incredible news that Thomas was committed to do the same by a young girl in Hilbery had burst upon him. His first furious conclusion was that Helena was redundant. After viewing the little suburban wife, however, he had seen that the running of his father's household would not, anyway, be left in the hands of this poor child. Helena would be useful. And for the wretched little stepmother his plans were soon prepared.

But, obliged to give way at the outset, to act gracefully, concealing rage, he had known better than to force himself in while the two innocents were still in the flush of their small triumph. For a judicious space, he had left Thomas to flounder.

What, then, had happened? Christine herself had never known, and never even suspected, the part Keith had played in it.

The marriage had gone wrong; or, rather, it had simply become least painful for two people of hopelessly discrepant age to lead sundered lives. And Keith had gently, subtly assisted the process. It was he who had first made them unhappy about it, filled them with doubts. By hinting, and finally warning Thomas with affectionate candour that his talent was suffering, by working upon an ageing man's fears of a mental decline, by suggesting that so young a girl had not known what she was doing, that she was unhappy and only put on a happy face in her husband's presence, perhaps even by insinuating that her heart was elsewhere and that it would be a kindness to release her, he had soon worn away Thomas's resistance. In fact, it had been all too easy to introduce into that weakening mind suitable ideas.

But the ugly truth was that Thomas was a not unwilling dupe, that his behaviour was weak, selfish and cowardly. He had soon tired of playing the husband; he had wanted to get back to his work—wanted it with increasing impatience—to his whole days and nights of silent productivity. The tension, the nervous and emotional havoc, which checked inspiration induced in his mind had been too much for him. It had become like an illness. A suspicion that his creative powers had in truth declined since his marriage had terrified him and roused up in him, rampant, the selfishness of the dedicated artist, to whose work everything else in life always has been, always will be, pitilessly sacrificed. Then he had desperately missed Keith's efficiency; he had floundered despairingly in the midst of the terribly laborious business of documentation, for which Keith had such a flair. So when Keith and his newly married wife at length joined the helpless pair at Carlotta House, it was by invitation. Thomas had simply given up—he had had enough of difficulties and confusion; a spoiled and wearied old man who had lost the knack of managing his practical affairs at all.

After that, everything had been easy. With Christine, with that gentle, inexperienced creature, so uncertain of herself, so easily shamed and startled into humility, it had been enough to insinuate that she was hampering a great man.

Yes, it was Keith who had broken the marriage, and he was far from blinking the fact. For he saw nothing wrong in what he had done. He had merely done what was best for her as for Thomas. He had performed a painful little operation for them both, neatly and delicately, with a virtuosity which few could have equalled. The marriage ought never to have been made, and so he had unmade it.

In such wise had every stone been removed from Thomas's path by his devoted son, his exemplary son—whom, in the end, some twelve years later, Thomas saw fit to reward through an iniquitous will leaving to that son Carlotta House, which that son had always hated, and everything else he possessed to his young widow, carefully tied up so that she should have no power to rectify matters from generosity. Cruel requital for so many years of pure devotion, monstrous ingratitude such as no trusting, honest mind could have foreseen!

Pure devotion? Perhaps Keith had a right to call it so. To steer upon a reputable course a mind subtly swung off its balance, given to sudden gross follies, unseemly impetuosities, and, before the end, to shifts, lies, reprehensible quirks of every description, had been a labour which would have defeated love itself, through love's very tenderness. But self-love had achieved it. By an exertion of main force, with a desperate determination, he had held the old man upright with the pen still in his hand. For the intellect had remained almost untouched to the end, that department of the mind which had learned its trade so thoroughly, so magnificently, seeming to proceed for a long while under its own power, unaffected by the creeping ruin all about it. This disintegrating personality had been a truly fearful charge. But Keith could not be taxed with heroism, since all he had done for his father he had really done for his own benefit.

He did not see it like that. He would declare with modest conviction that no son could have been more devoted.

That long strain, crowned by the shock of Thomas's vengeful blow and all the resulting trouble, threw Keith into a condition verging on illness. His complexion yellowed. He was inclined to shamble slightly. His attacks of ironical fooling became more frequent.

To the world, he kept up appearances; indeed, at first had put up a brave show in the face of that terrible will, that mocking, humiliating situation; going about in the rather unwholesomely elevated spirits which the death of a dear one who has lingered too long often gives rise to. He had carried himself jauntily.

'All my friends think it very original of me to choose to live in Hilbery.' It could be passed off like that. In any case, he did not feel about living at Carlotta House as he had done earlier in life, in the days of his pride, when he had had to overcome a disgust, a chagrin and genuine mortification at being obliged to own to such an address. Carlotta House had its distinction, if Hilbery Village still took some explaining. Walking round his little estate, he was sometimes quite proud of it and indulged in grandiose schemes.

But no scheming, planning or expenditure of charm could cause literary society to flow into such a backwater. Keith Antequin was not, in himself, a magnet of sufficient power to draw such congenial company about him. Stranded here, he was cut off from his proper milieu, from the West End bars and clubs where the artistic, journalistic and stage worlds met, where his own kind congregated, where the useful, entertaining and necessary intelligence circulated; cut off from the pleasant, informal little lunches where the real business was done, where things were managed, the vital contacts made. Among the weeping trees, in the grey, dripping weather, when no one came near the house for days on end, he was a prey to his nerves and the melancholy which so easily afflicted him.

He had only the society of the neighbourhood, the retired professional classes to which the local gentry was reduced.

With this, however, he might have had a certain position, oddly enough, both because of Helena's aristocratic blood and because of his own status as the son of a famous man whose name, to these literary innocents, was still respectably eminent. Only it soon became clear that even such an amelioration was beyond his means. He could not offer these people a good table or a good cellar. Indeed, it was glaringly obvious that a household run by Helena herself with nothing but a little fitful assistance did not permit of entertaining at all. Old friends, visitors who would not mind giving a hand, were all they could manage.

It was Carlotta House itself which he could not afford.

But it was a place abominably difficult to let, as he had experienced; while the sale of such a property was scarcely worth considering as an emergency measure. Unnerved, over-strained, he had acted, perhaps for the first time in his life, with financial folly. Things went from bad to worse, and, a few months later, came to a crisis, when he was thankful to accept Christine's veiled charity. She had rented the house from him and invited him and his family to stay on there as her guests. It was understood that she herself just at present did not wish to leave London.

It should not have irked him so bitterly. It was a free and willing gift, made in the simple belief that she was acting only fairly, a gift offered with anxious kindness. Moreover, she had already been very generous in doing what she could to counteract the effect of the will.

TWELVE

Mrs Gray, having stopped before the door in the wall, was wondering whether she would take a short cut through the garden. It was a long walk up to Carlotta House, and the twelve or thirteen years since her husband's death had made her an old woman. And the hill-road was not nowadays the old, rough, country lane to which her memories were attached. It was one of the groomed and carefully tended kind to be found in all such districts of the home counties, with a surface made for expensive cars and verges mown like lawns, not seriously a country lane at all. Yet it was still very pleasant, very lovely, with its large, silent domains at intervals, mysterious behind trees and well-clipped hedges, and now it was filled with the pure, strong, exclamatory cries of a darkling thrush. The bird seemed to be giving voice to an astonished joy—perhaps at that sky. A cloudless, shining, rosy-golden sky which might have overarched paradise.

But suddenly she had felt that a lonely saunter through the garden at this soft, dusky hour would give her intense pleasure. Pleasure? Well, something better than that. A moment of communion.

She stepped back into the road and looked up. Laden with their tiers of candles in fullest flower, the massive, rounded heads of the horse-chestnuts towered above the wall, with a few great conifers in the background, black, loftier still, prick-summitted—vast trees, forest trees, they banished petty thoughts and expanded the human scale, they instructed the sense of the majestic; they exalted and solemnised. Their blossoms were shadowy against the sunset, their beauty seemed veiled, mysteriously, as if at the light of a superior glory. The paradisial air of the whole scene brought the Garden of Eden to her mind.

She would go through the garden, she had chosen.

But it was a moment to be cherished, so, suddenly fearing that the door might be locked, she lingered to enjoy the fancy that in another moment she would be walking so close under the massive, drooping boughs that she could touch the flowers. The beauty of the evening filled her with a serene, prayerful happiness—she was a woman with a mind so steeped in the Bible that half her thoughts clothed themselves naturally in biblical phrases. With all this she was so intent that she was not aware of someone coming up behind her, walking soundlessly on the grass verge. In the lane, under the overhanging boughs, it was now so dusky that this person had drawn in upon her like a shadow, with the slinking, all but invisible progress of a black cat over a lawn at night.

Only when quite close did he speak and wish her good-evening. But his greeting had an uncertain note and sounded abrupt, as if he had intended to add a name and had only at the last moment realised that he did not know it; or else had suddenly perceived that she was someone other than he had thought. It did not matter. Mrs Gray, a little hard of hearing, remained unaware of his presence.

With her face still raised, 'They heard the voice of the Lord God walking in the garden in the cool of the day,' she said in distinct, low tones.

'Eh? What's that?——Oh, good-evening! (Rather an anti-climax, I fear),' the stranger sang out with a touch of imper-tinence; and he came forward, strolling on the grass verge towards her. 'Sorry I forget what was said on that occasion, or I'd have played up to you in the role of the Lord God.'

Mrs Gray was of course startled, but did not start noticeably. Her nerves were good. 'Ah, I thought I was alone,' she said with serene good-humour. 'I have this habit of speaking to myself.'

'A bad habit, of course.'

'I suppose it is—but I don't know why.'

'Well—as you see—someone may be there unknown to you and may be encouraged to answer.'

'And thereby some have entertained angels unawares,' she murmured, being still alone in spirit.

The young man, now standing more in the open, could be seen to smile; a deep, sneering fold from the nostril to the corner of the mouth indicated this. Mrs Gray perhaps took in his presence properly for the first time.

'Were you thinking of cutting through here?' he asked briskly.

'Yes—yes, really I was wondering——But perhaps it *is* locked. Perhaps I had better go by the road.'

'Well, let's see.' A cautious twist of the handle disposed of this question; and having pushed open the door and thrown a glance inside, he stood back with an inviting gesture which had a little impudence in it.

Mrs Gray, however, made no move and was silent. Now that her exaltation had faded, more wide-awake now, she was attacked by a deep reluctance, a disappointment so keen, so impassioned, as to proclaim an evil origin—so she assured herself—at having to share her little coveted, precious, almost mystical experience with a companion—with *such* a companion, one so uncongenial, as the young stranger seemed likely to prove. So she remained silent, praying against this infirmity of spirit.

Had she been a more worldly person, more concerned with purely reasonable affairs, she might have felt at this juncture a little uneasy wonder as to whether this young man really had the right of entry to her relatives' household. But any judgment she might bring to bear would be moral. And her mild, 'You're a friend of the family, I suppose? I think we haven't met before——' was innocent of any catechising note.

'Oh I know old K. very well,' was the answer, uttered carelessly.

She had almost at once recovered from her disappointment—or, rather, she had thrust it behind her as something less than worthy and believed that she had purged her mind of human antipathy. In two minutes, she stood there prepared to love the sinner and hate the sin. As this is, of course, not really possible, Mrs Gray deceived herself. She had taken a keen dislike to the young man in the depths of her soul; she experienced a sense of repulsion. She therefore resolutely turned on him a courteous attention and submitted herself to contact with him. At the same time, she studied him as well as she could for the growing dusk. That profile, with its loose lips and receding chin, with its small, deep eye set too close in to the base of the nose, a nose large and Punch-like, was not an endearing one. It made a poor claim on sympathy.

'My name's Shelley,' the profile added. A most unlikely name, anyone else would have thought it. Mrs Gray merely wondered incuriously whether he was a descendant. She thought of all extra-biblical poets as small fry.

But now, behind her as they entered, the young man was saying in a tone of artless disgust, 'Lord, do we plough through all this stuff? Must be chock-a-block with midges.' Beams of light escaping through the trees streamed away across the long grass and searched it like shining water in which the green blades stood upright, translucent and glowing, and in this lovely dazzlement thousands of little common flowers were netted, and the fallen florets, all transfigured. 'There is a path,' she said, and they came upon it, threading a way under the trees.

'Let me take that bag. Have you walked up from Hilbery? Or did you come by bus? Quite a stretch, either way.'

'It's not at all too heavy for me—but as you please.' She yielded up the bag without further protest. Another little trial, welcomed if sent. And so, with the door quietly closed behind them—for the young man's movements tended to be cautious, she noticed, he insinuated himself, there was something of a prowler's air about him—they began walking through a green darkness under the sweeping boughs. Doves murmured aloft in a world of leaves; up where the rosy light lingered, birds continued to cry out; the small flowers, the pale discs, the lacy cow-parsley, seemed to swim off their stems above the grass in the dark places. But all the value of the scene was lost to her. It had not lain in mere sensuous images, and communion was destroyed for the moment.

They came in five minutes to the holly-hedges and followed a winding path within these, very close and dark, and arrived presently at a big expanse of mown lawn where stood an immense black obelisk of a conifer to mark the point where the avenue from the gates ended and the drive branched. Flanking trees half obscured their sidelong view of the building with the flat cornice and central bow. Here they both stopped and seemed like people who had the purpose of saying something further before venturing out of cover. With Mrs Gray, however, this was not so; she had stopped, with a little secret impatience, and was merely waiting for her companion.

The sun had withdrawn completely from the deep green garden, and the house had a pallid, bluish shade, the eastern sky being still suffused with a little brightness behind it. Then a light went on, and the delicate trellis piers of the verandah on the first floor showed like black lace. Other gleams escaped through the leaves. Opening straight on to the lawn, the ground floor windows were dark, peering under the shadowy limbs of the trees with the enigmatic gaze of eyes in the gloaming. They two, on their side, lost in the dusk, merged with a leafy background, were probably invisible. Mrs Gray had a strange feeling that their approach was secretive. She felt bodiless as a shade.

'Well,' the young man said in an easy, jocular tone, though softly (and she realised that he had not spoken for some moments and was like a person taking his bearings), 'Keith has a nice little property here. Phew, that must take some keeping up. It's quite a little mansion. He must be filthily rich.'

She was surprised and felt she must correct him. 'But of course Thomas left Keith nothing but the house. (Thomas died, you know, about a year ago.) And we all thought that rather odd, rather naughty of him, for he must have known that Keith never liked the place. And, anyway, how was he to afford its upkeep? It seemed almost like an unkind joke. My daughter, however, has rented the house from him. It was a way she saw of helping him—for of course she doesn't really need such a place and rarely stays here long. But then, so far—or perhaps just temporarily—Keith and his wife and family are staying here. Yes, it's really a little topsy-turvy! Or so it seems to me. But I dare say Keith is hard up . . . We knew the Antequins many, many years ago when they lived in Hilbery, before Thomas became famous, and I was so fond of his dear wife,' she said with emotion (for she had come to think that this was true). 'Christine prefers to live in London nowadays, but she often visits Hilbery. Keith and Helena are so fond of her. We are all great friends——'

Here the young man exclaimed, somewhat sharply, 'Christine? Ah, that would be Christine Gray.'

'Why, yes,' she answered, laughing a little. 'Of course I'm Mrs Gray. We seem to have been talking at cross purposes.' She felt she had better explain. 'My daughter, you know, married Thomas Antequin (let me see—about twelve years ago, isn't it?).

But Thomas didn't leave her the house—he thought it would be a burden to her. Very wise, I think.'

Then, as he had expressed no surprise and made no comment upon his various mistakes, she had a queer fancy that he might simply have been fishing for information. For surely he must really be aware of Keith's circumstances? How, indeed, if he was at all intimate with Keith, could he not know them? Or perhaps he had merely been trying to find out who she was. She said vaguely, 'Yes, it is a fine house. We always admired it and in later years thought it was a shame to see it so neglected. But it was occupied when we first came here, and well kept-up. We came here when our boys were small—our house was all new, and Hilbery, too—all new—and we loved it, of course, only I used to feel it was very restful to see something old. And to see these great trees, which were never felled or lopped, except by way of tendance. And so this was a favourite walk with us. I used to come up here very often with the children, pushing the chair—a climb, but well worth it. Then, when the boys were at school, I would come with Christine alone. And I'm sure I little dreamed, then——But how strangely things do fall out!' Reflecting at this point, however, 'Here I am, an old woman with her reminiscences,' she drifted off easily into her own thoughts.

But much to her surprise, he drew closer and said in a low, pleasant tone which seemed to her extraordinarily sympathetic, betraying genuine eagerness to hear, 'She must have been very attractive as a young—a young girl. Seventeen or so. Has she altered much?'

'Oh, she was a darling!' Mrs Gray cried out, the tears starting to her eyes. She was carried away at once from any thoughts of discretion, she could not withstand this voice of sympathy. And why did her tears spring up like this? She did not herself know, or at least would not have admitted that it was because the past tense was the one that came naturally; that she wept because of a secret consciousness that the happy, transparent child had been lost to her all those years ago and replaced by an enigma, a sad riddle. She went on, in this moment of emotion, to give the little homely details on which the bereaved heart dwells and for which it can so seldom find a listener; speaking of the young girl's looks and ways; saying the fond and foolish things one can sometimes say to a stranger. 'And at that time she used to wear her hair rather long, brushed back like wings—such bright, fair hair, but so silky that it would never stay put, you know—and I remember she made herself some little filigree butterflies—and had them in her hair on that very night, the last night—I mean the night she came in after seeing the poor child home. She didn't wear them again . . . And only the next spring she was married.'

But Mrs Gray's voice had not the proper note of triumph. Too young? Yes, of course, she made confession to herself at last.

Yet it was not that she had over-persuaded her girl. Christine had needed no urging to accept Thomas for a lover—and that was the first sinister note. She had seemed to her mother suddenly to wake from that apathy and nervousness into which the Lambert case had thrown her and to come to a rather febrile life, even to be a little wild and difficult, a thing she had never shown herself before or since; and certainly to be inclined to throw herself into the first-comer's arms. And that had frightened Mrs Gray; the girl had seemed to her in need of protection, and even to know it herself.

But why had it been? She had always been a bright, normal, happy-tempered child. It was true that she was a little younger, as well as a little older, than her age, as the only child is apt to be (for that was really her status in the family), and that she had just lost her father. But why that need of protection in a girl of sensible independence? Obviously because of some overwhelming shock which had shattered all confidence in herself.

As deep as that, Mrs Gray had been compelled to look. It was as deep as was given her to look, perhaps.

This only she knew clearly: that the night on which Christine had taken Vivian Lambert home was the last night on which they had seen her in her full brightness, the shining bud unblemished, in all its lovely promise; and she had a vivid, anguished remembrance of the curve of the child's neck under the bright hair as the young head was turned to the door, making that self-conscious movement, that simple, subtle, defensive gesture against scrutiny. Always romantic, Mrs Gray had only wondered at the moment whether someone had given the child a goodnight kiss which had made her feel shy. Never, never had she suspected a kiss of death, of poison, disease, destruction.

It was the last night, she thought, that all was well with her.

She was recalled to herself by a light touch on her arm. Her companion had actually touched her—perhaps he had spoken before without making her hear—and was leaning over her and murmuring, 'What about going in?' in as stealthy a manner as if he had been proposing something nefarious to her.

She replied quickly, hoping he had not noticed her instinctive recoil from his touch. Suddenly all belief in his sympathy fled like a foolish dream.

THIRTEEN

But instead of acting upon his own suggestion, the young man began skirting the shrubbery at the edge of the fine-turfed lawn with rather the air of one who hesitates to break cover. And after a few paces of this, he stopped again. Mrs Gray, following his lead with absent docility, stopped also and turned her eyes on the house. Now it seemed quite dark because of the lights in the windows.

The young man suddenly reverted to his first manner—that impudent jauntiness with which he had first accosted her.

'K. pretty hard hit by the old boy's death, I dare say? And a lot of unkind talk, too, isn't there?'

'Yes, it was a great blow, I believe. Unkind talk? I don't know.'

'Why—you must have heard? The old man's work went badly to seed before the end. And one or two really business-like debunking articles can do a great deal of damage. It's always a ticklish moment, an author's death is. Just when they're scraping together all the fragments and sweepings. Isn't Keith botching up some sort of biography?'

'I believe he is,' Mrs Gray answered in some bewilderment, 'writing *something*.' Then she gathered herself together to reply intelligently, as befitted one related to genius. 'But not the official biography, as I understand. Some well-known author—I forget his name—is to do that. Keith's, I think, is just an introduction to some of the last writings. A diary, I think? Yes, I think Helena mentioned something about a diary.'

'Ah! Of course you know there's a rumour that something rather spicy in that line has been dug up? You don't think K. would be willing to have a chat about it—supposing, for instance, that you were to put in a word for me? Ah, you wouldn't know.'

'I've no influence at all with him—none of that sort,' Mrs Gray hastened to assert, mildly astonished that anyone could think otherwise.

'There's a rumour going round that old Thomas was a bit of a sly-boots. Now, what was *your* impression? A good husband, should you say, and all that?'

'I think you must have forgotten that Thomas Antequin was my—yes, my son-in-law,' Mrs Gray said, not exactly rebukingly, but with a sort of gentle, distasteful wonder at the young man's gross unmannerliness.

Her companion slapped his thigh. 'The devil he was! Why, of course. So he would be. But such an ancient, you know! Doesn't seem natural.'

Mrs Gray fell into pensive silence.

'Ah, but what about the rift in the lute, though? Thomas and your daughter. You wouldn't say there's anything in the story that K. was a bit of a mischief-maker?'

As this was exactly what she did think, Mrs Gray was brought to a stand, taken aback twice over, and also much distracted between the young man's unsnubbable spirit and her own inability to give a firm denial.

She spoke with feeling and dignity. 'Thomas was a good, kind man. I was very fond of him. It was all a sad mistake—but there was no ill-feeling. They had a great affection for each other to the end, and merely agreed to live apart for reasons to do with age and taste. There was no bitterness . . .'

No bitterness. But suddenly her distress returned. Indeed, it was seldom that she allowed herself to think on these lines, for they showed Providence in a bad light. Had she not prayed for guidance at the time? Yes, she had always felt that things should not have gone so very wrong—that inherently there had been nothing impious about the marriage, or wrong with her own sponsoring of it. After all, they had had so much in common— poor dears, they were both so fond of Thomas's little conjuring tricks! And such love as there had been was obviously the love of a good man; many times she had thanked heaven for that. She had always liked Thomas and had continued to like him in spite of the human blemishes which had all too soon been exposed; and she had never understood the sad break which had come later. There had been weakness on Thomas's part, undoubtedly. Yet she had never blamed him. For she had always suspected Keith.

Now impulsively she cried, 'I'm afraid any trouble existed only in Keith's imagination.'

'Ah, you think that?' And a long, low, chuckling laugh came from the darkness. This laugh, so full of impertinence and with such a note of conspiracy or of collaboration about it, really startled Mrs Gray. For it opened her eyes. She was suddenly conscious of having too easily taken for granted that this stranger was what he claimed to be, a friend of Keith, and moreover that she had been misled almost entirely by that abbreviation of his name—an affectation, as she had always thought it, peculiar to an inner circle of his literary friends. And she had been silly enough to take it for proof of intimacy. However, to be abased by one's own silliness is to make it a matter of importance. Mrs Gray was slightly amused.

'Well, I see I've been talking to you too freely,' she said with quiet candour. Words and tone, it was a statement which might have reduced some people. But not this young man.

'Yes, friends, so that's the way of it. Old Tom Antequin has fallen like Lucifer. Oh, that's only to be expected, you know.

One might say it's bound to happen to a writer who in his lifetime receives his good things. I can quote Scripture, too, you see.'

Mrs Gray, arrested by these words, stood there dreamily, these phrases with their biblical provenance having a natural attraction for her and sending her into a bemused state. But the allusions were not happy ones, as she suddenly realised. The sneering voice saying, 'I can quote Scripture, too,' revived her strong antipathy; and of her own accord she began to walk over the lawn, feeling unable to respond. In a moment more, she could see into one of the ground-floor rooms where there was a light, and could see Keith and Helena; she standing with her arms folded on her bosom in one of her fishwife's attitudes, and he gesticulating. But they would not be able to distinguish anyone in the garden, she fancied, it was too dark. Keith seemed upset. But Mrs Gray observed all this with half her mind, because of the troubling presence of her companion. He came up with her silently; and then she thought she heard him mutter, 'By the way, did you mean anything just now by talking about the Garden of Eden? No, I take it, not.' Distrusting her own ears, she did not attempt to answer. They walked on without speaking again; she still trying to conceal from herself her extreme dislike, which was so very wrong—and appeared to be upsetting to the nerves also. Passing soundlessly over the turf (she was very conscious of the young man's noiseless, springy stride), they crossed the drive and approached the main door, the fanlight of which, a shell-like design of iron fronds, they now saw boldly and gracefully inscribed upon a bright interior; she feeling an extraordinary relief at the thought of parting from her companion. So she did not wait to ring, but, knowing that the door was rarely locked, turned the big knob as she had a right to do; and then suddenly, with jumping nerves, she noticed how closely he was craning over her shoulder, like one eager to see into the hall before entering. The next moment, he had pushed forward, fairly thrusting her out of the way, and she was watching him bolting up the staircase at the side of the hall, two steps at a time, and seizing the rail with such a pouncing grip that she heard the ironwork creak.

'Well, he must certainly be very intimate with them—it's odd I've never met him before,' she thought, looking up the empty staircase doubtfully. Now indeed she began to feel like someone who, on opening a friend's door, inadvertently lets a cat slip into the house without knowing whether it belongs there, and rather dubiously trusts that the animal will do no harm.

FOURTEEN

'The cult of Thomas Antequin was a strange phenomenon. Although retaining, until quite recently, his popularity with a wide public, he had long been ignored by the discerning. Today, even with the public of the lending library, Thomas Antequin is a sinking sun. It is a sad comment upon the vagaries of fashion, and a still sadder comment upon what can be done by a determined publicist, that only a decade ago he was acclaimed, by so influential a critic as Willoughby Bacon, as one of the greatest of living writers.'

Here, the article (a serious one, as can be judged), went on to explain that Thomas's work was without social significance, his language was non-contemporary, his scope was gravely restricted; that he was basically an uneducated man, that his experience was unusually narrow and limited, his knowledge of the world laughably circumscribed; while, in an age of science of unparalleled brilliance, he showed no more scientific awareness than a bird on a bough; and that of all this came a *naïveté* intolerable to modern sophisticates. He had a vicious taste for a story—even for a 'plot'. He had a propensity to write prose like poetry, his subjects, his themes evoked the emotions proper to poetry, his matter was unrealistic, his imagination was 'gothic'. In short, one had had enough of this Antequin fustian. Modern life was too grim for fairy-tales.

Thomas had outlived his time, that was all. The usual slight revival of interest had been excited by his death, the death of a famous writer, but the usual reaction had been swift and dire beyond what one's worst fears had foreseen. In short, Thomas had been in his grave less than a year, and his position was exactly what this article indicated.

Yes, Thomas was dead and the ghouls were upon him. Their ravages might cause considerable pain to anyone who had valued him and his works, but they were not actionable. The ghouls were in no danger.

Other judgments, less measured and less serious, had followed.

'It is time that someone asked a straight question—whence came this immense prestige? A careful examination of Antequin's career will throw some light on the matter. Up to middle-age, his reputation was very modest; if he was not entirely unknown, still, who had heard of him? He was in the forties before his name was noticed; and then, almost over-night, he became the darling of a small but powerful literary clique which professed to see in his works far more than he ever saw himself, we will hazard a guess, for poor old Tom was a simple-minded, modest man, as all who met him will testify. It is all something of a mystery.

'But we do observe that he is a man with one rare advantage; he has a son. We are all familiar with the Antequin antiphonies . . .'

Here the writer was getting towards perilous ground but was not yet in danger. If, sinking to personalities, he now glanced at Thomas's private life and late marriage—from which date, he implied, the great man had gone entirely to pieces—if he now allowed himself to poke sly fun at Thomas and show him up in the light of a silly old geezer, and even to hint that he was an old dodderer who could not fulfil his marriage obligations, still all was well with him. For Thomas was dead.

But at this point, carried away by his own eloquence, per-haps, intoxicated by the pleasures of malice indulged with impunity, fatally carried away, the writer had extended his personalities to include Keith Antequin, 'the lesser half of the Antequin turn, *the backside of the Antequin animal*'. (What a brutal insult! Worse and worse, the more one pondered it.) And Keith was alive. And he could be shown by any clever counsel to have been actionably defamed. Doubts had been cast upon his honesty, he had been presented as the true begetter of the 'Antequin ballyhoo', vain, greedy for money and publicity, and a liar. Moreover, it had even been hinted that he had interfered disastrously between his father and his father's wife.

Such is literary spite. For there was not a vestige of truth in all this—or so the wretched defendants, if tackled and beaten to the last ditch, would be eager to acknowledge, in the hope of saving themselves.

A libel case at this juncture of flagging interest? For a space, Keith's imagination had played joyfully round this theme. But in fact he knew better.

No, there was no redress; such an attack, derisive, belittling, with its tone of malicious caricature, more deadly than serious calumny, was of a kind to render the victim helpless, for if he chose to draw the attention of a wider public to charges such as these, what better would the enemy ask? Such ill-judged defences can only make a laughing-stock of the victim. The Antequins would have a free show—but what sort of a show? In a court of law, those grotesque libels, those poisonous innuendoes, would be treated with an unpleasant flippancy; more damaging things would be boldly broadcast to the public than ever the libel had ventured upon; the papers would all carry the story, and from end to end of the literary world a merry laugh would run. Keith Antequin would be finished.

It was true that Thomas himself would be none the worse for it all. The obloquy and neglect would probably last for several generations, but he would be revalued later; at some far-off date his fame would revive, beyond a doubt. Only, that would be too late for Keith. *His* end would be now.

He was on the verge of editing Thomas's 'fragments', he was at work upon a biographical sketch of a great and serious artist, which would precede the definitive Life (for Keith knew his own limitations and the writing of the official biography which had been in contemplation for some years before his father's death would be entrusted to some celebrated author); and such a sketch from the pen of one uniquely close to the great subject would, of course, always hold an unrivalled place as a work to which every other biographer coming after him must apply. His most urgent need of the moment, therefore, was to appear in the role of a serious person, a person of integrity, a critic of weight; one of whom it might even be said, 'Keith Antequin is by no means without a share of his father's genius.'

Clearly it was not advisable to call attention to spiteful chatter about, 'poor old Tom' and 'the backside of the Antequin animal.'

The study had grown quite dusky; but he had not turned on the light. He was waiting for Helena to come in and find him brooding sensitively in the gathering darkness.

A comparatively easy and rewarding task, one would have thought, the writing of the biographical sketch, for he had but to skim the cream off the whole vast mass of material to which only he himself had so far had access. Yet, taking into account his own inaptitude for such sustained efforts—but that was nothing. No, it was the extraordinary vacuity, eventlessness and insignificance of Thomas's life before which one sat down in despair.

Stuck was not the word for it! Bogged. Sunk in the quicksand up to the chin.

What a temptation was that shabby journal which Helena had discovered hidden away among Thomas's great, secret collection of bargain underwear.

He sprang up, and, forgetting the little pathetic effect he had prepared, switched on the light, flung open the door and bawled for Helena.

FIFTEEN

She came in with obliging alacrity; a tall, big-boned, very plain woman with a florid face and red hair, and a huge, good-humoured mouth. To her he spoke with a mixture of frankness and guile, of hard sense and reckless fancy, which might have had an ill effect upon the nerves of any less seasoned woman.

'Helena, I believe I must be on the verge of a breakdown.'

'Oh, cheer up, old boy. No, on the whole I wouldn't say so. I haven't noticed anything more than usual—unless it was your going and filling a scuttle for yourself the other day—that *was* a bit out of character, I thought at the time.'

'Well, never mind—who cares? It's only an unpleasant fullness in the head—a touch of dizziness. A matter of nervous exhaustion, no doubt. Months of grinding, gruelling work, and to tell you the truth, a more thankless job I've never had in my life. I wouldn't have thought it possible to meet with such difficulties. The fragments alone—the most exasperating, intractable material imaginable! As for the sketch—I don't mind admitting that the miserable paucity of incident has almost defeated me—there's really no making anything of such a life! Yet I'm loth to put it into anyone else's hands——'

Here he dropped the dramatic tone as readily as he had assumed it and spoke with unaffected eagerness. 'Helena, you'll remember that little old notebook you found? The diary you turned out of the old portmanteau along with all that indescribable junk? I suppose you didn't tear a page or so out of it—before realising what it was, perhaps?'

'Tear anything out of it? What chance did you give me? You were there, weren't you? And fell on it like a dog on a bone.'

Keith sighed heavily.

'But I thought you told me there was nothing to it? Just a record of what he'd had for dinner, and so forth.'

'Well, that was my first impression, I'll admit. Yes, my first impression was that it was a thing so abysmally dull that nothing whatever could be made of it—just a collection of private jottings of the most commonplace kind, totally useless for publication. That, I say, was my first impression. And of course I was bitterly disappointed. Bitterly. But I've studied it very carefully since . . . very, very carefully indeed. There's one particular section which interests me extremely. What first drew my attention to this section was that there are a few pages missing—three pages have been torn clean out, as if Father had had second thoughts. And when one studies the few pages immediately preceding the gap and those following, one receives the strangest impression. In short, I've decided to publish it, after all—or at least extracts—with a slight biographical sketch as a foreword. Of course, the loss of those pages is a disaster. Yet I do feel that perhaps enough remains to arouse *very wide interest.*'

'But, I say, old man, hold hard. Oughtn't you to consult Christine—if it's anything of *that* kind?'

'Well, it's hardly a case of "ought". Father left everything to my judgment, as you know. And you must remember that Christine has, very naturally, put everything literary into my hands. The task of preparing all the remaining works for publication falls naturally to me. If anything is to be held back, the decision rests with myself. Christine was in full agreement about that. She trusts me absolutely. There is no need for further discussion . . . Besides, none of this will keep . . . However, if it relieves your mind,' he added with weighty irony, 'I *did* hand the journal to Christine, and she kept it about half an hour and then returned it to me with the remark that she didn't think anyone would ever be able to wade through it. But I could do what I thought fit.'

'Oh, good. "Wide interest", though? What sort of interest? Spicy?' said Helena matter-of-factly.

'Tending towards the self-revelatory, you mean? You have visions of a little book which could be reviewed under some such headline as *Antequin's Secret*, and live up to it?' And he laughed excitedly. 'No, Helena, I'm laughing at you! How is it you can never distinguish when I'm merely laughing at you?'

Helena did not know how this was.

Keith continued to laugh, somewhat excessively, for several moments. But then his tone changed again; a strained look came into his eyes. 'I will say this for myself—no son could have been more devoted. As you know very well, I've suffered enough during the past ten years to drive anyone mad. It was no easy matter to keep it up before his public—it was an appalling labour, it took constant vigilance, to keep him together at all before the end. You women have never appreciated that sufficiently, Helena. As for Christine, of course she never even saw it——'

'Well! I say, whose fault was that?'

'A mental deterioration which began in the higher reaches of the brain—which left his intellect practically unimpaired for so long, but not his moral nature—a malady so insidious that he was probably profoundly ill long before we even suspected it. In fact, I have proof——But leave that now . . . *You,* of course, had to deal with his condition privately, to some small extent—but I, added to that, had to hold up the screen before the eyes of the world . . . The section of this diary which so interests me deals with the time when he was negotiating for Carlotta House, and there are references to the Lambert affair—and it is very strange, Helena—I've received a very strange and startling impression—a flood of light seems to be thrown upon that business—a murky, lurid ray it is, but still——It is so suggestive that those few pages should have been destroyed! You remember what play it was he wrote at that time? Its theme was cruelty—the pleasures of cruelty . . . Then there was his marriage—a senile impulse . . .

'Well, I've had a considerable shock, I will not deny—— Oh, don't ask me to explain. I'm a bit unnerved at present and might say more than I intended to. Forget it, Helena, forget it . . . Father's was a strange, divided personality,' he resumed feverishly. 'It was a case of still waters, I'm afraid. He was a very, very secretive person. An introvert, of course—a mass of inhibitions—and the implications are obvious.'

He had uttered the greater part of this speech in a *distrait,* disconnected fashion, throwing out each inspired statement just as it came to him, reckless of the effect of his words—and in any case there was always this advantage in speaking to Helena—that she did not take in half one said. But the mere formulating of suspicions often results in strengthening them. They acquire substance.

'There were times when he was not responsible—one has only to think of that iniquitous will! It should have been opposed, there were grounds enough for it, God knows—only there was his reputation to be considered. And our dear Christine, also.'

His voice tensed. 'Living here, as I am, in my own house, on sufferance, as a guest of Christine——'

'Yes, it is a bit thick, isn't it?' Helena agreed earnestly.

'My God, what a situation! Father cannot have foreseen it. I put that past him——'

But actually Thomas had made the will at the time of his marriage, well before there was any question about his competence, and it could not have been upset, as his son well knew. Had it been possible, Keith would have leapt to action. As it was, it was nice to think of the consideration he had shown Christine.

Helena cast round vainly for a happier subject. But with an effective gesture which seemed as if it should have been accompanied by some such histrionic outcry as 'My father, oh, my father!' he turned to the hearth. (This was the gesture seen by Mrs Gray from the garden.) 'Leave me,' he said deeply. Helena grinned and went off. She closed the door with the minimum of noise. Clumping though she was, Helena never slammed a door.

'Swept and garnished!' she thought, influenced by Mrs Gray in advance of her appearance; and she went humming back to the kitchen sink. They could not afford resident servants, but had two helpers, and so Helena did all the drudgery herself. She was infinitely glad that Christine was coming; it would create a diversion. Besides, she was extremely fond of her.

Keith, in the workroom, continued in his tragic pose, but now all unconsciously. It was genuine.

In the final event, it was not a question of money, or of prestige, or of the collapse of that profitable world of his own creating, but of spiritual loss. For years, in his prosperity, he had been living in a dream world; he had been apt to talk and even to think as if the contributions made by himself and his father to their partnership had been equal. How bleakly did it now appear which of the Antequins was of moment! The loss of Thomas had revealed his own hollowness. But to say that it had revealed it was hardly the case with this habitual self-deceiver. Only somewhere, in the depths of his heart, the fact was there.

If only he might ride upon Thomas's shoulders a little further!

Faced by the carroty visage of Helena, by her earthy presence, he had for an instant seen recent dreams of his, based on the diary, as unrealistic. But now that he was alone again, their charm had returned, he was once more in their power. And he stood by the hearth lost in fascinating speculations; his pale face, lacking its conscious, social expression, looking doughy and dogged, oddly fixed and set.

He came to at last in the light, elegant room—which had been redecorated so beautifully of late at Christine's expense—which his father had so cruelly or mockingly bequeathed to him in a condition of sorry disrepair. (For Thomas had long and stubbornly refused to keep the place up properly. With that very bequest in his mind? Heart-rending!) He found his hands clenched, his entrails quaking. The shutting of the hall door had made him jump like a cat. He had not heard it open.

Christine, after all? No, it could not be Christine, for only an hour ago she had spoken on the 'phone to Helena, saying she could not come that night. But, with the very thought of Christine, a conscious air at once settled upon him; his features resumed their normal mobility.

His manners had always been at their best with Christine. From their first meeting, he had treated her with tact and kindness, and made a pleasant, easy thing of their odd relationship; and she who, at eighteen, had been much frightened at the prospect of such a stepson, had been very grateful.

Yes, he had always been very attentive to Christine; suave, brotherly, serviceable. After the rift with Thomas, in particular, there had been nothing he would not do for her. He had been sympathy itself. His sympathy, too, had taken a practical shape. He was for ever performing thoughtful little acts for her comfort and convenience. It was thus that Keith had kept in abeyance, during his father's life-time, an inexplicable uneasiness in her presence.

One could not all of a sudden cease to be suave, brotherly, obliging!

But decidedly his feeling for his little stepmother had acquired a morbid tinge. He was abnormally conscious of her; he watched her, thought of her, took a sort of strained interest in her movements. Moreover, the keen eye he kept turned on her was strangely like the eye one is apt to turn on a sick person, on the look-out for symptoms. (But this proneness to seeing ill-health in other people, is it not sometimes a symptom of illness in oneself?) A sick person from whom one expects to inherit, perhaps it should be added. He was, in fact, her heir; though of course the possibility that he would ever benefit by this was too remote to be considered. He did not consciously consider it at all—he was too decent.

Sometimes, curiously, he would deliberately call to mind that pale, pretty face, which looked gentle and good, touchingly so; as one nurses the thought of some bitter, unendurable injury.

Could it be that he did not love their 'dear Christine'? His was a jealous nature. But to hate an attractive and lovable creature, merely for getting innocently in one's way, shows an ominous fault in the sense of proportion, only excusable in the very young.

Now he felt unusually conscious, nervous, at the thought of a meeting. Christine, he felt sure, would not normally make much of a study of the literary columns of a newspaper, if she glanced at them at all. But Keith well knew how readily kind friends draw one's attention to any published utterance which will cause pain or breed trouble. That article had contained statements about himself, in relation to Thomas and his young wife, which he could only hope would never reach her. He did not want to offend Christine. He did not want to figure badly in her eyes. He did not wish her to know, he did not wish to know himself, that he hated her.

SIXTEEN

He crossed the room and opened the door a little way, quietly.

The hall was large, it was furnished in pale shades and was lightly classical, and the staircase rose in a lobby to one side, behind an arch with columns. Mrs Gray was standing at its foot. He could not see her averted face; but her stillness, her intent air, as she looked up at the bend of the staircase, which was out of his sight, gave him the impression that something up there had surprised or even alarmed her. The house seemed quite silent. That in itself was unusual. Perhaps because his mood was nervous, he felt sharply that something was wrong. She had not heard him. So he called out, 'Mother?' She turned; smiled quite naturally, with her warm cheerfulness, and came towards him. And then he said quickly in a tone of affectionate reproach, 'But you told us you wouldn't come tonight—you know how willingly I'd have fetched you! Why, dear, didn't you give us a ring if you felt inclined to come? And what were you looking at, up there?'

'Just a sudden, silly change of mind—and I fancied the walk—such a lovely evening!' She had failed to answer his last question; not because she had not heard it.

Keith did not for the moment notice this, her cheerful aspect having dispelled his nervous fears.

There were not many people he would have been glad to see at present, although he was a man who drooped in solitude. He could not just now have stood inspection by any of his clever friends, or by anyone really capable of understanding his plight. But he was pleased to see Mrs Gray. She would keep the talk to the surface, her presence would deliver him from any further temptation to open his heart to Helena. He had moments of ultra-sensitiveness when he felt Mrs Gray's imperturbable simplicity curiously chilling; when that perpetual floating lightness of spirit seemed to him suspect, like an attitude tinged with irony of the most devastating kind. But there, he knew, he was only attributing to her his own subtlety. At his better times, he imagined himself to be a favourite of hers—a soothing persuasion. Then he saw her as a pleasant, innocent old woman who diffused a gay kindliness. It was what he needed now. He needed gentle treatment, after the manhandling he had had. He relied nowadays far more than he would have admitted on Helena's ugly bulk to sustain him—but one did not look to Helena for gentle treatment.

So, as Mrs Gray came towards him with those peculiarly young, clear, blue eyes out of which, at this moment, all her soul looked as she put her silent question, he was appreciative, he approved of her. Smiling, at his conscious nicest, he said, 'No, dear, no—poor you!—she won't get here tonight. She rang us up this afternoon. No, she didn't give any reason. Something had cropped up and she wouldn't be able to make it, that was all.'

'Oh, Christine—my darling! Never mind—tomorrow, then! I have you two.' And she spoke with an unclouded face, so as not to let her disappointment trouble him; such was her delicate kindness.

How she disliked him to call her 'Mother'! (Yet she liked it when Helena did the same.) The truth was that she had never been able to reconcile herself to Keith. It was Keith's incipient baldness when she had first met him which had brought her nearer than anything else had ever done to facing the false and lamentable nature of Christine's marriage. That this elderly young man should actually have the right to call her poor child 'Mother', had seemed to her the height of indecency, a horrible absurdity, grotesque.

Besides, of course he had been a little shock in another sense. Although Keith had later acquired a right to his father's name, still, Thomas Antequin had not married his mother.

However, she had got round this by being vague—Thomas, after all, *had* had a wife, whom one could quite well think of as the mother of Keith.

But she had soon had other and legitimate cause for dislike; and latterly there had at last penetrated into her serene miracle-world hints of an even darker perfidy than she had ever suspected. Still she smiled upon him, as she had smiled upon him throughout. It was not pretence. For she conceived it to be both right and possible to forgive injuries and to love enemies.

So she had taken him in all these years, without once striking a false note, this subtle man with all his psychological knowledge—so deadly is the guile of the simple. And it gave her a little secret amusement, there was a touch of childish slyness in her charitable duplicity.

She smiled, she began laughing a little as she came to meet him. Her manner was, as always, delightfully natural, and like this, easily, she said. 'But, Keith, I hope I've done nothing wrong. A young man, a stranger to me, overtook me in the lane and came in with me. Evidently an old friend of yours, by his account, and he has now run straight upstairs. It took me rather by surprise—his running into the house like that. I've no idea who he is—I've never heard you speak of him. A Mr Shelley . . . Oh, well, yes, I suddenly felt I'd like to be here when she arrived. So I've brought some night things—I know Helena won't mind.'

'Certainly, Mother, stay—we love it,' he answered, mechanically gracious. 'Shelley?' he then added, having had time to consider what she had said. His voice rose a little. 'But I know nobody whatever of that name.'

She stood there with her air of tranquility, and repeated, 'He told me he knew you well.'

'Shelley? Shelley? Faugh—ridiculous! Good God, how annoying——' However, he curbed himself. 'Well, Helena's upstairs——'

'I'm so sorry,' she said cheerfully. There was a remoteness in her apology, as if the matter did not strike her as being of much consequence. She was not, of course, indifferent to any annoyance she had caused. But, looking dreamily about her with those ecstatic eyes of hers she was thinking of God in the garden, beside which other sensations paled.

Still, she could not but notice his face. 'Oh, I do hope I haven't let a burglar into the house,' she exclaimed, with a more proper concern.

'If that were all——!' Keith cried. And then he burst out in excitement, 'A fellow from some paper, of course. Wanting me to express an opinion—or find out whether I'm hitting back——'

But here Helena came out of a door down the passage. At this, his voice rose a shade hysterically. 'Why, worse and worse, I thought you were up with the children. Helena, one of those damned reporters has got into the house, sneaked in with Mother, on some pretext—actually run upstairs—must be snooping about up there. Well, this is enterprise, with a vengeance!'

Helena swept forward and drew the old woman into a bear's hug. She was very fond of her.

'Oh, rubbish, Keith—that would be a bit much,' she said over her shoulder, between one smacking kiss and another.

'A thin, dark young man with a large nose,' interposed Mrs Gray, persuasively, as if still in hopes that he could be identified as an old friend, if they really tried. 'I think you *must* know him. For he spoke of wanting a chat with you.'

'Pshaw!'

Helena said she would soon winkle him out. She plunged up the stairs and then could be heard tramping overhead and opening and closing doors and occasionally speaking to someone. But only a child's voice answered her, and then a young boy's. Keith stood as if prepared to dive back into his study and lock himself in. But his look was one of excited expectation, Mrs Gray noted.

Helena's clumping feet slowed down. Joining them again after a few minutes, with a perplexed face, she said, 'It's very odd—not a sign of anyone. And nothing to be got from the children.' This last statement was a little ambiguous, and

Helena's expression matched it. The others looked at her in astonished silence; Keith's face falling. Mrs Gray, somewhat disturbed now, asked in wonder, 'Then—what can he be? Really a burglar? Dear me, what have I done?'

'Of course he could have run down the back staircase. Unless he's hiding in a cupboard somewhere? I didn't look in the cupboards!' Helena cried cheerfully.

Keith suddenly fell into an odd mood of clowning. He seized a stick from the umbrella-stand and, brandishing it extravagantly, capered about the hall for a moment, crying in a falsetto voice meant to mimic womanish alarm, 'Oh, whatever have you let into the house, Mother?' Then he ran off down the passage to the kitchen quarters, with Helena following. There they could both be heard inquiring of Mrs Jebb, who cooked for them, whether she had seen the burglar. Much chatter followed, Keith's voice still high, and a noisy exodus of the three of them to see if the back staircase yielded any clues.

There is something disturbing, and even sinister, in the clowning of an unhumorous man. Mrs Gray made this reflection while glancing into one or two of the rooms; then came back and stood thoughtfully in the hall to await the return of the others. She turned her mind back to the walk in the garden, and saw it now in a changed light. Suddenly the dusky setting seemed to her almost unreal, its invisible flowers, its unearthly beauty. A slight *frisson* took her. She remembered the young man leaning over her in the darkness of the close bushes.

When she looked up at a slight sound, she saw a little girl in pyjamas gazing at her over the handsome iron banisters with her chin resting on the rail. This little head, with face pale and round as a dandelion clock and upstanding red curls, might have been decapitated and balanced there, so unresponsive was it to Mrs Gray's fond greeting. It did not smile. The unusually large, round eyes had the offended, the curiously solemn, bored and affronted expression of a spoiled and precocious child.

'Mirry—think. Are you sure you didn't hear anyone go along the passage up there just before Mummy came up?'

Miranda shook her head, making her eyes larger and blanker than ever; then, hearing the voices of her parents returning, no doubt, she soundlessly withdrew, scampering upwards.

Keith and Helena came back into the hall, talking argumentatively and no longer laughing.

'And you're quite certain, Mother, that he actually went up the staircase? Did you turn away, for instance, or look elsewhere, if only for a second?'

Mrs Gray answered without hesitation. 'I particularly noticed the way he sprang upstairs—two steps at a time.' Suddenly, even in her own ears, this had an unpleasant sound, and that it had struck the others, too, in the same way, she could see; they were silent. Mirry's little offended face again appeared, peeping through the iron-work.

'Are you sure he was flesh and blood, Mother?' Helena then asked ghoulishly. She loved ghosts, burglars, anything dramatic.

Mrs Gray looked about her and answered at length in a tranquil manner, 'How strange you should say that, dear! Do you know, at that moment when he came up behind me—which he did so quietly and suddenly—I was just thinking. It was the garden, you know, the garden looking so lovely "in the cool of the day". And these words had just come into my mind: "The serpent beguiled me".'

The two younger people glanced at each other in astonishment, and then, without any attempt at hiding their feelings, went into laughter. Mrs Gray did not mind. She smiled at them with indulgence.

Keith threw a filial arm round her shoulders. 'I hope he didn't beguile you into telling him anything unsuitable, Mother,' he said pleasantly, but not without a questioning note. Mrs Gray was spared answering, for he went on, 'Helena, I do wonder you haven't thought to put on a fire. *We*, of course, are hardened to the perpetual chill of the place, but Mother must feel it. This infernal dampness!—just what I always predicted—exactly what I warned Father it would be.'

'Not for me, Helena!' Mrs Gray hastened to cry.

But Keith liked an open fire. 'And you might put one in my room also, while you are about it. Just a very small wood-fire will do—you needn't trouble to make a big one—it'll be just nothing in the morning! I have an immense quantity of work to get through and shall be working very late.'

Helena plunged obligingly towards the drawing-room to start a fire.

'Go back to bed, Mirry,' she shouted over her shoulder, catching sight of her daughter. But Mirry did not stir. Helena was a lazy mother, or perhaps a disheartened one, and did not often bother to make the children obey her. So Keith, more conscientious, was left to be worsted in the usual arguments which always ensued with Mirry:

'I can't go back, Daddy. It isn't possible.' 'Why not?' 'Because you can't go back to where you've never been.'

Keith came into the drawing-room after the women, rubbing his large brow distractedly. 'Where is Leslie? What do we pay her for? Her beauty?' This was the young woman with the exotic training in child psychology who was supposed to understand and control Mirry.

Mrs Gray had followed Helena and spoke in a low tone. 'I only hope the child didn't hear what I said. I didn't realise she'd come back. It might well have frightened her.' Helena did not treat this as a matter for concern; in which she was right.

No, Miranda was not frightened. She went along a passage on the second floor and opened a door cautiously. A boy was sitting at the table in the large, comfortable playroom with the child's furniture painted in various bright colours, the cuckoo clock and the instructive frieze round the walls; he was tilting his chair on its back legs and reading with an air of connoisseurship. The shelves were full of children's books, toys both fanciful and mechanical lay neglected about the floor. And surrounded by this almost unlimited choice of juvenile pastimes, he was reading *Nana* in French. He glanced sideways and winked at Mirry.

He was a very stout young boy; a fat, yellow-faced boy with heavy, dark eyes, and he was one of the banes of Keith's life. He was not a child of the Antequins, but a vague and distant connection, and his presence in Carlotta House was the result of a sensational act of charity on Thomas's part, long since deplored. His father had been some obscure Antequin, but he had had a Syrian mother and had spent his early childhood somewhere in the Levant. Taken out of that milieu and sent to a good prep school in England, he had been expected to lose some of the worst characteristics. But he had not done so. He was fat, yellow, shifty, irretrievable. He was twelve, but so large and stout that he looked years older, and his face was oddly inexpressive. When he winked he did not smile. Nor did Mirry. Perfectly solemn, she essayed a wink in return, but it seemed doubtful that she had seen any joke.

'Well, my word, they are all in a flap down there,' she said in a tone of quiet superiority. 'What did he give you?' she added bluntly.

'Nothing.'

'Liar. Well, where did he go when Mummy came up? Has he gone now? Perhaps he has got into a cupboard somewhere.'

'No, he's gone. Garden way.'

'What did he want?'

'Wanted to look round. Asked whether the house had been changed much since when Grandpa took it.'

Mirry could not make anything of this.

'I could have had a lot of money out of him,' Jo pronounced slowly, rolling the words on his tongue; and his blank face suddenly shone with ardour and intelligence.

Mirry looked scornful. 'And you didn't get any.'

Jo had no answer.

'They won't like your reading that book,' she said shrewishly, having peeped at the title.

'They won't have the chance.'

'That's a bad book.'

'Now say you can read French.'

'I know it is—the women all so fat—I looked at the pictures. Besides, it comes from Daddy's own book-shelves.'

So the two lambs conferred together; while less informed speculations upon the strange event engaged their elders downstairs.

SEVENTEEN

'What did you talk about, I wonder?' Keith began again, on finding himself alone for a few minutes with Mrs Gray. His manner was pleasant but persistent.

She answered with caution. 'Well, Keith, I thought it was Christine he was interested in——' For so it seemed to her partial view.

Keith smiled dryly. 'Why, it's true, of course, that she's Thomas Antequin's widow! Oh, no doubt he would have been very happy to contact Christine. But what did he say to you? Or, rather, what did *you* say to *him*, Mother?—for that's the point.'

'Very little, dear,' replied Mrs Gray with her most other-worldly air. (Very little, but a great deal too much, she now realised.)

But here again she was saved. Helena, who had run upstairs to settle the children, now burst into the room, announcing cheerfully, 'I thought as much. Mirry did see him. She was lying. And Jo of course lies from pure habit.' Mrs Gray, if not shocked, was at least grieved. But Keith revived. He made an exaggerated gesture of despair; not because of the children's moral condition, however, but because he knew what was coming; his worst fears, or his highest hopes, were realised. And when Helena added, 'He told them he was from some newspaper and gave them each a bob to be quiet,' Keith shrugged, laughed, and appeared in a state of irritable amusement, which his wife could only view doubtfully. 'Good,' he said ironically. 'Now we shall have a revelation about Mr Keith Antequin's home life—the kind of toilet paper he uses and the pattern of his dressing-gown. Some women's feature page, most likely.'

Mrs Gray saw that the subject could be changed with advantage. 'The *Advertiser* this week has something in it about George Lambert's collection, Keith, which I thought might interest you, if you hadn't seen it. So I've brought it with me. Helena, I've just brought a little bag with a few night-things, for I thought that tomorrow——' But here she stopped short and cried, 'My bag! Yes, he has gone off with my bag! He insisted on carrying it for me——'

'This at least proves his fleshly existence.'

'Why—but how ridiculous!—it has nothing in it but my night-clothes,' Mrs Gray protested, laughing happily.

Springing up in a new burst of animation, Keith went to look in the hall, in case the bag had been deposited in some corner. However, within the next few minutes, the young woman Leslie came in and was able to tell them that it was standing by the glass door which opened on the garden near the foot of the back staircase; putting away her bicycle, she had seen it there and wondered whose it was. Also, she had found the door ajar. So he had run right through the house, they concluded; but by no amount of puzzling and speculation could they arrive at the intruder's motive in doing this. The contents of the bag had not been disturbed, the newspaper was still at the bottom; and was, anyway, merely the current edition of the local paper which could have been bought anywhere in the district. So their excitement and their ingenuity petered out together. But the production of the newspaper set them talking again of George Lambert and the strange posthumous blaze of publicity in which his story had lately closed.

Helena brought in the tray of drinks, Mrs Jebb and Leslie came into the drawing-room to take their nightcaps, and Keith continued to sit with the women as he did not usually when the company was merely domestic. Mrs Jebb, a little person with a huge head and a deep voice, was a local woman and could contribute a host of local rumours; and suddenly Keith began questioning her with a particularity which seemed a little odd at this time of day. He had the manner of one whom the subject had struck from a new angle.

George Lambert's death—or, rather, the sequel to his death—had recently fluttered the whole neighbourhood. In fact, he had died and no one had given that event any special attention. But, shortly afterwards, Hilbery had had a vast surprise. All those foolish, useless little bibelots of which this unobtrusive neighbour of theirs had made a life-time's collection, but had kept so jealously in the dark (yet who knew if that had not been merely for the want of a fellow-enthusiast?) when handed over by the widow for disposal in a London salesroom had all of them fetched incredible prices. Iniquitous prices, Hilbery considered. That heavy, lumpish, taciturn man in their midst, whom nobody had ever known properly, who had lived in one of the shabbiest houses in Hilbery and had gone about for the past twelve years suspected and shunned because of the Lambert mystery, had accumulated possessions which realised for his widow a fortune of some thirty thousand pounds.

No one had been more amazed than Rosalie. She was at first so much affected that she could hardly rejoice for thinking and talking of the number of years she had been forced to pinch and scrape and put up with every sort of insult while 'sitting on a goldmine'. She could find nothing strong enough to say of her deceased husband who had treated her so scurvily. A mean hound. If only she had had an inkling—the barest inkling—she would have taken a hatchet to those cabinets of his! He had not even had the decency to take her away from the neighbourhood after the tragedy, he had not used even the minutest portion of his wealth to save her feelings, and Rosalie had been forced to brave it out all those years, suffering untold miseries. She had been ostracised. Very few people had been charitable. (Mrs Gray had been one of the few.) The revelations at the inquiry had turned everyone against her. And what did Lambert care? Apparently he himself had cared for none of these things. He had cared only for certain shabby cabinets in a little dull back room.

Now, speaking of the collection, Keith said thoughtfully, 'No, I never saw it, Mother. I don't know anybody who did. One had always thought it must be phoney . . . An odd point is that he died intestate. So that if ever that miserable little girl of his should turn up again——Well, *that's* unlikely! *That*, I think we can say, is impossible,' he added, and smiled to himself and relapsed into thought; but did not quit their company.

Helena referred regretfully to their unknown visitor. 'What a pity,' she said. 'It would have made a nice ghost-story.' She delighted in the occult, it made her laugh, for she took the sheet and turnip point of view, being unburdened by up-to-date psychic lore of any description. So, loth to let the subject drop, she continued, 'But after all, if this house is haunted by anyone, it should be by little Vivian Lambert.'

'I should much like to see an apparition,' said Leslie indulgently. 'I should find it a most intriguing experience.' Decima Leslie was a small, hard-favoured girl, whose face behind glasses with bizarre, jewelled frames was touchingly chubby. She spoke in the casual, loud, rather husky voice she cultivated, coughing a little over her cigarette, as she had noticed inveterate smokers sometimes do.

Keith shot a malicious look at her. He disliked the girl extremely; or perhaps he liked her as a stooge, and it was an interesting symptom that he thought it worth his while to dislike seriously so harmless and insignificant a creature. He was apt to take these extreme, violent, irrational dislikes; and then, if there was no need to control himself, he sometimes became prankish even to cruelty with their objects. So, with a side-glance at Mrs Gray, he said solemnly, '"A spirit passed before my face and the hair of my head stood up." It can be no light matter to see a ghost. Not all of us have Leslie's singular strength of mind.'

'I should be frightened to death,' Helena cried, her gargoyleish features appearing in the light of the lamp all sanguine and enjoying.

Leslie looked tolerant. 'There's nothing whatever to be frightened of, as we now know,' she explained patiently. 'Anyone may have a hallucination—and that's what they are, in nine cases out of ten. Just an interesting phenomenon which might be experienced by you or by me. It doesn't happen only to people of mental *instability*. That's an exploded notion. It's not at all discreditable. The chief thing to remember, with these psychic experiences, is the importance of writing it all down at once, you know—it should be written down immediately, without a moment's delay, and the account sent off to some responsible person—preferably an expert——'

'Thank you, Leslie, thank you,' said Keith.

'An *expert*!' Helena cried, delighted. 'No, really——!'

Then they listened to a long, old-fashioned, well-spiced account by Mrs Jebb of a neighbour's experiences on passing by the wall of Carlotta House on a suitably sombre evening. She had seen a light over in the well-house corner, a bluish light.

'How I should enjoy such an experience!' said Leslie. 'Now, *my* reaction would be one of purely scientific interest. I believe I could observe any sort of supernatural appearance quite objectively. And I can quite credit your story, Mrs Jebb—at least in part—for of course if the child actually died here, it may well be a haunt.'

'That's a very nice idea, Leslie,' Helena declared approvingly.

To all this Keith had listened while openly mimicking the expression of Leslie's solemn, chubby face. But now he suddenly dropped his nonsense and asked with an interest such as he rarely accorded to his wife's remarks, 'Helena, why did you say just now, "It should be Vivian Lambert"? Do you really suggest that the child came to an end *here*?'

This started them upon the Lambert story again. Mrs Jebb said, yes, it was well known; local opinion had always had it so. And that the murderer was Lambert.

'George Lambert,' said Keith categorically, 'was of course as innocent as a babe.' Then he left them to argue and leaned back, sitting quite still with his eyes fixed upon one or another of the speakers in a brilliant stare, as if his thoughts were strongly concentrated on some inner point.

Mrs Gray never listened to these allusions to the Lambert case, which even to this day sometimes cropped up in local conversation, without a painful interest. But not too painful. For she had sublimated the tragedy, to a large extent; it was no longer quite real to her. The poor lost lamb was long since safe in the arms of God. Yet she did begin to feel that she might not sleep very well if they went on like this. It was long past her usual bed-time; and her thoughts had suddenly reached out to Christine and were saddened.

EIGHTEEN

But she did sleep, and almost at once; and some incalculable time later, woke from a confusion of dream and lay there uneasily for a good while, attempting to recall what it had all been about. Her bed faced, a little from the left, one of the high, narrow windows whose lower sash came almost to the floor, and its slender bars were visible on a background of faint light. She listened to a sighing wind. A melancholy dream with strange features, a sense of contacts, very unusual in dreams, of physical sounds, weeping, broken words, a pursuing sense of lamentation. She felt troubled. Turning over, she looked down the bed towards the window—to see the little girl standing near the foot, leaning against it, supporting herself on her hand, while her head hung down somewhat. Facing her, the child's figure was dark.

'Mirry, love, what *are* you doing? What's the time? Why are you out of bed? You frightened Granny!'

The child did not answer. But she moved, turned her head sideways and, passing before the window, was suddenly gone.

Then she said to herself, '*That was not Mirry*! . . . I have had a very vivid dream, that's all. A terribly vivid dream!' She began to pray. And, calmer after a few minutes, she concluded, 'All that nonsensical talk downstairs—serve me right.'

But she felt sad and frightened in a way she rarely did, and her solitude, the narrow bed, the unresponding darkness, made her think of her husband. 'How I miss him!—my loneliness!' she thought grievously.

And Christine, whose husband also was dead? But it was not possible to think that she had grieved at all; what had she to grieve for, poor child? No one could help seeing that Christine's widowhood had been nothing but a release. Suddenly, at this cold, grey hour of low vitality, Mrs Gray was overwhelmed with pity for her daughter, who had had nothing to weep for. But this heartrending pity was poisoned by a rare sensation, by remorse. Remorse was a feeling unfamiliar to Mrs Gray, whose way was to shed sincere, refreshing tears and then feel herself forgiven.

It had all to do with a peculiar glimpse she had had of Christine recently, which she had not been able to forget. Of all unlikely things, a chance view, and the view of an onlooker or stranger.

A friend with a car had unexpectedly taken her to London. She was to do a little shopping in the West End while her companion attended to that business for which she had come to town; and afterwards, sitting by herself in the restaurant of one of the big Oxford Street shops, waiting for the friend to fetch her, Mrs Gray had had her little experience.

Suddenly she saw her daughter moving among the tables only a few yards distant in the company of two other women. But Christine had not seen her. She came on, with her friends, and finally settled at a table nearby, so close that much of their talk was audible, and even intelligible, and still it so happened that she did not glance in her mother's direction; and so unexpected was this circumstance, so sure was she that the next instant would bring the recognising look, that Mrs Gray allowed the natural moment for standing up, for signalling her presence, to slip past her. Christine sat down, not quite facing her mother and yet not in profile, and thenceforth it seemed, with every second, that their eyes must meet. Yet still by an odd chance they did not.

Perhaps now Mrs Gray felt a little shy; Christine's companions were smart women and not known to her. She had let the right moment go by and already felt that she had behaved oddly. Not that she minded that. In fact, it was more than half deliberate; she had suddenly had the queer notion, the rather reprehensible notion, 'I'll wait till she sees me.' It was partly childish, a sort of impulse of mischief. But from that ultimate core of hardness, that base of ruthlessness, which unusually soft, kind and benevolent exteriors often conceal, particularly when they are child-like, she set herself to watch. Drinking her tea slowly, with enjoyment, she watched this young woman who had secrets from her.

It was a picture of which any mother would have been proud; a vision too wonderful, too polished and stylish, ever to have entered the tousled head of the sunburned child who had sat licking her fingers in Carlotta House garden, while earnestly wishing she had not to tidy herself. But something was gone, something in that artless figure was missing from this later and polished version—a hardiness, a healthiness, which was not merely physical.

Christine was considerably taller than she had seemed to promise at that time. A frame built sturdily had grown rather thinner than was natural. But she moved well; she sat, and was at once still. Yes, she was very still—she did not even look about her. She was still as a person is when listening to his own thoughts.

It was a charming face that Christine nowadays showed, mild and gracious. The beautifully set grey eyes had lost their wideness and limpidity, the rounded forehead had lost its smoothness; two upright lines, faint but immovable, stood between the eyebrows; but Christine was nearly thirty and these marks of experience were only to be expected. The mouth was soft and youthful. She was beautifully dressed; she obviously cared a good deal for her person, but showed no consciousness of her appearance. She wore little or no make-up. She was pale. The frosty fires of her small diamond earrings emphasised the pallor, and this gave her a look of delicacy which she had not in the usual way, as did also the subtle shadows under the cheekbones, which the lighting cast. She was tired, perhaps. Placing one elbow on the table, she some-times rested her cheek on her hand sideways. Then she looked languid. The mouth was perhaps too youthful. A nervous mouth, indeterminate in expression.

The charming exterior of a nice, natural, simple woman, whose every slight contact with her neighbours revealed courtesy and kindness and a modest opinion of herself.

But the party seemed to be a serious one. The tea-rooms were quiet, it was early, there was no orchestra. The young women were talking soberly, with some leaflets before them, and were not laden with parcels. Their meeting had perhaps some social or charitable object which required grave discussion. Thus it was that there was little vivacity among them, and a smile or laugh were infrequent. It was a severe test. The other faces, though pleasant enough, were seen to be not beautiful; and Mrs Gray looked at her daughter and glowed with loving admiration. But this mood gradually chilled.

For there was one strong impression which intermittently made the whole infinitely disquieting. It was an air of deep anxiety. In serious mood, the tender mouth became pained and pitiful, the line of the brows tragic. The stillness seemed tense. Oh, what an overcast look it was—a late spring landscape under the silent, dark presage of a storm. The enigma was before her.

A secret love affair, pitched tragically? How thankful Mrs Gray would have been to think so. But she well knew it was not that—nothing natural, nothing comprehensible.

The young women were finished before herself, after all, and standing up, took smiling, friendly leave of each other, as if going different ways.

Then at last Christine's eyes fell upon her mother. An astonished smile, a sudden kindling, was succeeded by a look almost of shock. 'Mother, how long have you been here? Didn't you see me?'

'Yes, dear, I saw you. I've been here quite half an hour,' Mrs Gray replied peacefully.

'Sitting here—and looking at me—and not speaking!' And Mrs Gray could see that she was so greatly surprised as to be a little distressed. 'What a funny thing to do, Mother!'

Then Mrs Gray laughed and said mischievously, 'Yes, I was spying on you!'

She was ashamed of herself now for having behaved so, and, above all, for having made such an answer. What had led her to do it? She could hardly say. She feared it was simply one of her bad impulses.

But in the moments which had followed, while Christine, having thrown off her surprise, talking and laughing, delighted at the unlooked-for meeting and the opportunity for a gossip, had become almost her youthful self again, the cheerful, prosperous, healthy young woman Mrs Gray loved to think her, that unhappy, shocking glimpse had been lost.

Only it had recurred since—it had recurred many times—revelation and mystery in one. Now, in the cold, low hours of the morning, she wept because of it.

She rarely repined in this fashion, but (beginning with the remorse-provoking sight of Keith's bald brow) it had been an upsetting, over-exciting evening. She felt shaken by her eerie dream, she wished the light in the window would strengthen—that barred, crepuscular background which, for one flicker of time, had seemed to show her a little profile that was not Mirry's. Whence had her dreaming brain dredged up that slightly rat-like profile? Ah—the young man in the garden! But what a muddle. All the events and the hints of the evening jumbled together, she perceived, after the manner of dreams.

So there she was, back under the trees, in the growing darkness, with the young man—and now all too aware of the feeling on which her repulsion had been based—fear, superstitious fear. Not of course at the young fellow's person, weedy and unimpressive as that was. No, spiritual fear.

If Mrs Gray had come to the conclusion that she had walked with Satan in the garden, she would not have considered it an hallucination. The evil spirit was a reality; whenever he so willed, he clothed himself in flesh, going to and fro in the earth, walking up and down in it. Such as he wished to appear, he appeared to all. He might well (and, indeed, quite suitably) have clothed himself in the envelope of a minor journalist.

In short, the idea crossed her mind and was not rejected by her imagination. But, believing that such a thing *could* happen, she did not perhaps quite believe that it *had* happened.

NINETEEN

'Come and sit by me, Jo,' said Mrs Gray with tender kindness. She thought of him as an orphan and a foreigner, and was the one person to have hopes of him.

Not that Jo required much attention, or desired any. He did not ask for sympathy, and to be understood was probably his last wish. Quiet and docile, and a dullard at school, this strange boy was capable of very ingenious arrangements for his own well-being. He had lately written a letter to his headmaster containing detailed instructions for the comfort of J. Antequin during the opening term, and had signed it K. Antequin. He had typed it on Keith's own typewriter, and had typed the signature also; Jo had looked ahead and had thought to avoid a charge of forgery. The letter was quite well composed—it was, in fact, an uncannily good imitation of Keith's style; but the matter was very strange and the spelling was rather below Keith's standards. Still, it was a good try.

The incident had shaken Keith; not so much because it had revealed that Jo had the makings of an excellent crook as because of the strange facility with which his own somewhat mannered literary style had been attained to. Of course, imitation is not creation. Still, it had left him uneasy, pensive.

Jo was at home at present because his school had tired of him.

Not put off by any of this, 'Come and bear me company, Jo, come and talk to me,' Mrs Gray said, wanting to make much of him, the poor little fellow. She was sitting in a shady corner of the kitchen garden, topping and tailing gooseberries for lunch. Refreshed by the good sleep she had finally enjoyed, she was feeling remarkably well this morning, so that she had not even been much cast down by the news that Christine had again rung up to put off her visit yet another day; a little trial of patience, she had called it cheerfully. The morning was breezy, the boughs tossed livelily, the sun-flecks poured over the satin foliage of the beech-tree. Snowy, round-headed clouds drove rapidly across the blue. Many birds were singing. Mirry was laughing in the garden as she played with her new puppy. Someone was whistling. It was a different world from that of the night and Mrs Gray had quite dismissed her nonsensical dreams and morbid woes. And Jo's fat, knock-kneed legs coming into the range of her vision as she dealt with the gooseberries had filled her with compassion.

'Do you like gooseberries, Jo? What—sick of them? But the gooseberry season is barely started and these are very young. Oh, a gooseberry pie is extremely nice when made of really young fruit. The bushes are weighed down again, I see. Yes, those great old bushes are simply laden every year, and have been so as long as I can remember . . . Dear me, I never do this but I think of poor George Lambert. Why, he used to pop the Carlotta House gooseberries among the stuff he brought from the market and charge a good price for them, too, as if they came from London. So it was well known, in those days, that if you were thinking of making jam, you had to forestall old George. Of course, Jo, we mustn't lose sight of the fact that the gooseberries didn't belong to Mr Lambert, strictly speaking— or to anyone else, either. I myself always had doubts as to its being quite honest. Still—just enough for a pie!

'Poor George! Or perhaps I ought to say "poor Thomas".' And here Mrs Gray stopped and seemed to fall into a reverie, and one which was not unamusing.

'Why ought you to say "poor Thomas," Grandma?' Jo inquired with unnatural vivacity.

'Well, let me see, I don't know why I shouldn't tell you that story, either. Dear man, he *was* in a way, that day he spoke to me. You know, Grandpa and I were such good friends. Of course I promised him at the time not to let it go any further, but it can't possibly matter now. Actually, it was rather funny. Seeing that he was not at all himself for a little after the Lambert trouble, I one day said to him, "Thomas, I feel you have something on your mind," and after a bit of hesitation he took me into his confidence. He was in such distress because of a foolish thing he had done. He had seen George Lambert in the garden here, during that lunch-hour—or a man he afterwards recognised as George Lambert—a man with a sack, and afterwards was filled with all sorts of misgivings—about the child—and about the well-house, near which he first saw him—and in fact had actually convinced himself that he had seen the murderer. And yet he had kept quiet about it! Well, you would not know, perhaps, but your grandpa was a very sensitive man. He shrank from a fuss or a scene, or the least unpleasantness. And so, between a sort of shyness and that hatred of publicity which he had, and a horror of being dragged into the case—and then, on the other hand, the dreadful possibility of getting an innocent man into trouble—he foolishly said nothing to the police, until it was too late to say anything—which of course was very wrong. Or would have been, if things had been as he thought.

'But luckily I was able to reassure him, I was able to laugh at him and tell him that poor old George was only after the gooseberries. You see, going off so early in the morning on that dreadful day, Mr Lambert wouldn't have known that his little girl was missing, he would have known nothing about it. He didn't know, and couldn't know, that there was anything at all wrong at home. So there was poor George, come to pick his gooseberries, just as usual. As for sacks, his car was always full of them.

'The sad part of it was that Grandpa, I think, was never entirely convinced—and later I had a feeling that the dear man had not told me everything—everything quite as it was——' But here Mrs Gray stopped short. In fact, to a large extent, she had been talking to herself. 'So I never liked to tell Christine,' she finished, rather sorrowfully, 'lest she, too, should feel George *might* have been there—for some other reason.'

Jo's mouth had fallen open and his flat face betrayed, as much as it could betray any feeling, interest. It was puckered with thought.

'I say, does Uncle Keith know about that?'

'Oh, no—and perhaps I ought to tell him. What do *you* think, Jo?' But Jo was against it. 'It would upset him,' he said considerately. And Mrs Gray couldn't help smiling to herself at the dear little fellow's acumen; for she, also, was under that impression. This was Keith's own fault. For the fact that the diary had been found and something of a startling nature elicited, and something to do with the Lambert case, was an open secret in the household, owing to Keith's inability to refrain from giving dramatic hints.

'Then what do you think happened to that girl, Granny?' Jo lingered to ask.

'Oh, just some nasty accident, I should judge. Perhaps she fell into a river,' said Mrs Gray soothingly, having her mind elsewhere.

'What river, Granny?'

'Why, any river, Jo. Any river would do.'

Jo mooched off; he went round the corner of the house and stopped to think. He was full of ideas. He remembered that he had been asked for information, offered money for it. Only he did not know whether this was the type of information required. Should he get in touch with the tempter and tell him this story? Jo did not know how to go about it, but was capable of finding out.

But as he turned over in his mind what he had just heard, his faith in his windfall began to be shaken. In the first place, the information was not exclusive; and, secondly, if George Lambert, when seen by Grandpa in the garden, had merely been after the gooseberries—well, Jo felt keenly that it was not a front-page story.

The idea that Uncle Keith himself might be inclined to a deal had at the first blush seemed not impossible—but Jo foresaw unreason in that quarter. Yet a dim, sensational idea that Uncle Keith might be glad to 'buy his silence' was still feebly afloat. Care puckered Jo's low and narrow forehead.

Mrs Gray compassionately watched the poor little man out of sight.

But it had been her happy creed all through that the child had been kidnapped by someone—and of course it would have been someone who was fond of children. 'A river?' she thought, suddenly surprised at her own morbid inventiveness. Then she recognised from what source the idea had come to her. Thomas had more than once mentioned his belief that the child's body had been disposed of in a river; had been inclined to dwell on the thought, she remembered. She went on snipping absently while thinking of Thomas. But the slightly pessimistic frame of mind continued. Already ill, could he perhaps even have feared people would suspect himself? And could he really have contemplated turning suspicion from himself by throwing it upon George Lambert—who had denied having been in the garden? Helena presently came out with a cup of coffee.

'How you do spoil me, Helena! Well, dear—Keith, I see, is in one of his nervous states. He misses Thomas, I suppose.'

Helena looked gloomy. 'Yes, we all do. I only hope he isn't about to take to himself seven other devils, like the chap in the Bible. That's all I hope.'

'Oh, Helena, think what you are saying.'

Then they went on talking for a good half-hour, Helena laying up trouble for herself in the shape of a late lunch.

She seldom entered into accounts of her feelings or discussed her husband and children, but such reticence was not due to delicacy or loyalty, it was to be feared, but merely to inarticulateness; and now she stood diffidently before Mrs Gray—a big gawk bursting out of a dirty overall very much too small for her—and was moved to declare, in a modest and unpretentious fashion, her inmost thoughts. Why, she wouldn't mind being shot of the lot of them. There were their two great boys, away at school, already ugly and hulking, like herself; while the little moon-faced Miranda, apart from her red hair, had her father's looks. 'Heaven send they don't take after either of us,' Helena said, simply and earnestly. But she feared they did; and, to be honest, she was sorrier for Mirry than for the others.

'So you're not very happy with Keith?' Mrs Gray mused pityingly. She was of course well aware of this; but spoke from the heart. Helena rubbed her forehead and was obliged to admit that it did look like it. 'I myself was always so happy in my married life,' Mrs Gray murmured in sad wonder.

And then Helena, in her artless language, supplied certain details of a startling character. Her husband, she said, was an odd fish. She had sometimes doubted his sanity. Mrs Gray was shocked. Well, he was tiresome. In what way? Well, it had always seemed to her not so much that he took up with an idea, as that an idea took up with him. He would 'keep on' about it, to a weird extent—and, as Helena described it, this tendency seemed of an obsessive nature. He was what she called, with palpable moderation, obstinate. There was plainly something quite abnormal about this 'obstinacy' that it had struck Helena so. However, she had no other word for the phenomenon.

Then she branched off into telling the story of her wooing, which she did with a bleak candour. She had known perfectly well, even at the time, that it was her social position which had attracted Keith—yes, even more than her prospects of fortune—but she had been mad on him, believe it or not, and mad also to get married. Although the daughter of an aristocratic house (but one much decayed), she had had a wretched home life, hardly any education, and had also been wretchedly treated by nature in the matter of looks. Her people, nevertheless, had objected to Keith, they had regarded him as a detrimental, and he had been grossly insulted by them, time and again, and once had even been treated to physical violence and thrown out of the house—out of the tomb-like family mansion near Regent's Park with the great sooty windows, the ceilings which kept falling down, and the Irish family in the basement. Yes, time and again she had thought it was all over, she had thought such treatment would never be tolerated by any man in his senses. But Keith had hung on like a limpet. He had simply swallowed it all and kept a pleasant face, 'fairly making a doormat of himself sometimes'; and at last had actually succeeded in ingratiating himself with the most hostile of the pack. She believed she had been hypnotised. For she had not been able to deceive herself, even then, and had never been so far gone as to imagine he was thus conquering his feelings out of love for herself.

The aristocratic connection had perhaps done him some good, if largely in his own eyes; but the prospects, by an awful fate, by an unforeseeable and ironical turn of fortune, had all come to nothing. Yet Keith had never reproached Helena with that; for he had never recognised her prospects as among his motives. 'I tell you, he is decent. A decent fellow in his own eyes. You know what I mean? Conscientious.'

'Oh, Helena, what a good thing!' cried Mrs Gray, with her head sideways inclined.

Helena made a face. However, she admitted that it was a good thing. She had never had any trouble with him because of other women. He did not drink. He was steady. It was ideas which seduced him. He became 'set on them'. They took hold of him. Once started, he kept on, she thought, as if he really could not help himself, like a man under a spell, bending everything round to fit in. But she obviously found her real meaning too difficult to explain; perhaps had not the vocabulary for it.

Clearly such 'obstinacy' was quite neurotic, and Mrs Gray, although having only the haziest knowledge of fashionable psychology, saw it as such.

'And what the devil is it he's running his head up against now?' cried Helena. 'That blessed diary!'

'Oh, if he merely thinks he has found proof of George's innocence, as he seems to——'

'Well, but if George was innocent, somebody else wasn't,' Helena reasoned. 'Not that I care.'

Then she remarked, apparently going off at a tangent, that they had all been through too much with Thomas; adding mildly that Thomas in his last years ought to have been shot.

Mrs Gray had never heard Helena speak more unkindly.

TWENTY

There stood Carlotta House in a wide blaze of sunshine, with its dead windows and its fallen shutter.

This vision at the end of sleep was so sharp that when Christine opened her eyes the darkness of the room bewildered her. It took her several moments to get her bearings. Then she remembered. She had just begun packing her case for Hilbery, meaning to make her preparations overnight, although she would not be going till the afternoon, because she wished to spend her morning leisurely; she had a little shopping to do of a kind which required time and care. A recent secret distress had thrown her into a worried, nervous state and made her reluctant, as she had rarely been, to go down to Hilbery at all; and so she had rung up Carlotta House to put off her visit to the next day. She had felt ashamed of this weakness at the time; now, however, she was thankful. Tired after her work at the clinic where she did voluntary duty, she had found this final small but exacting job of filling a case intelligently almost too much for her. Leaving it half done, she had thrown herself down in an easy chair and had allowed this dusk to gather round her—while she had stepped out into the sunshine of a past day.

The thought of the coming visit had aroused the usual mingled emotions. That was the cause of this sharp dream.

She had leased the house from Keith only half in charity; she did not want to live there, but she had so feared he would sell it. The selling of such a place was, of course, a most unlikely eventuality; yet it had not seemed so to her. She had been filled with a great fear. She had panicked, and had rushed in with her offer without seeking advice from anyone. That her motive had been taken for pure generosity had caused her some shame. For it was not that. Intense, irrational feeling against being cut off from the house had actuated her, not precisely superstition, but a faint, far-off, secret thought that the key to the mystery lay there, and her last hope of rescue.

Yet it was also true that she had a healthy fondness for the place and had sometimes wished she could make up her mind to live there. In childhood, she had stood entranced at the gates, lost in dreamy bliss at that glimpse of wild nature, of a house set in a forest, the solitude, the luxuriance—an excited bliss wherein her heart beat strangely—and if anyone had then prophesied that one day she might live there she would have been transported with delight. The house was also connected with such small happiness as her marriage had held, for Thomas had treated her very kindly in those days, indulging her like a child.

Again and again, during her later solitude, the young woman had sadly and blindly attempted to fathom Thomas's motives, but she had never been in a position to see the matter clearly. She had never been in possession of the simple facts.

The whole episode of her marriage had been to her a humiliating, mystifying one. She had not even been able to help Thomas with his work, of which she had no critical understanding. It was true that for about a year she had innocently thought and attempted to take Keith's place on the secretarial side; and, thanked, loved and indulged, had had no inkling of her own shortcomings—for which she had a sad smile now. She had laboured with great earnestness and good-will, under the impression that she was of real use to Thomas; and those were the days she had enjoyed at Carlotta House, in the sunny spring, under the flowering towers, the romantic, giant candelabra, of the horse-chestnuts, with the larks singing over the fields which were then all around them. Indeed, she marvelled and was filled with something like horror of herself in looking back at this insensate happiness—for surely it was insensate, when so much evil, even down to the death of her dearly loved father, was then so recent? Her insensibility had extended even to that quarter of her heart, too, it seemed. But, in fact, transplanted and out of sight of the daily reminders of this natural loss which her own home would have pressed on her, perhaps she had merely displayed the normal resilience of youth. It seemed to her now that she had been entirely happy—though not in an adult way, for her role had almost at once settled into that of an affectionate daughter; and this had satisfied her at the time, so childish was she, so delicately, so kindly and so cruelly had her inexperience been cheated by Thomas. She had run about like a child, romped in the hay of the still wild garden, entertained her young friends royally, played tennis to her heart's content. Then the work, the striving with intellectual problems, had had a great savour for her at that awakening stage of her development. Above all, the immediate details of living, new and complex, had occupied her whole attention, so that she had thought far less of the desperate, unnatural wound she bore inwardly, though it was so recent, than at any other time. A point of sinister peculiarity, as it seemed to her now.

In short, her marriage had been a distraction which had perhaps saved her reason. That had been the happiest year of her life since the tragedy.

Dawning doubts of her own aptitude to help Thomas had at first only fired her to greater effort. She would probably have done well enough in the end, for she had native intelligence and a perfect will to learn; and although she could not bring an instinctive understanding to his art, she might well have attained to a cultivated one.

But Keith had not given her the chance.

At first she had been glad of the arrival of Keith and his wife, she had welcomed Helena with pleasure. That gawky, modest woman, so friendly and easy-going and ready with her admiration, had been a great comfort to her in her growing uncertainty.

But Keith had not intended this. It was not his design that a pair of contented couples should settle down at Carlotta House. He had had no intention of sharing Thomas with anyone. He had had no intention of allowing Thomas to be distracted and softened by a young wife. It was he who had disrupted the household.

She and Thomas had found themselves wintering abroad, enjoying a forlorn, homesick spring spent on the outskirts of Keith's circle of friends in Rome, paying a nightmare visit to New York. And this was where things had gone so badly wrong, for Thomas was a helpless man, and Christine was still more helpless, and with a better right. They had been equally unhappy and lost in an equally childish way. Thomas had shown up badly and Christine had shed many tears. Then had come a few months' holiday apart, which was to do them both good. Of course there had been no legal separation. Keith had seen to that. A wife in the background did very well to keep his father from any similar prank in the future. It was just that she and Thomas had lived together less and less, and finally had lived apart. At last (and she, at any rate, had never known how), the final sundering of their lives had come about. She had gone on living in London for no better reason than because she had been abandoned there, and because Keith had been clever enough to find an unexceptionable tenant for Carlotta House.

So she had made her own life in London, as well as she could, and her time had not been unoccupied, for she was a girl of too much sense and conscience to exist in idleness. At first, she had patiently tried to continue her studies, but all the motive power for doing so was gone, and she had plodded joylessly through a solemn curriculum of her own devising. After a while she had given it up for want of encouragement. Then she had done a good deal of thankless drudgery among the poor; yet nothing had claimed her attention properly, nothing had satisfied her with herself. Her zest was gone. And perhaps those whom she attempted to serve felt the distraction in her, the divided spirit.

It was not that she was such a commonplace young woman that she could not satisfy herself apart from a domestic life; her intelligence was good.

But she had been neither one thing nor the other; she had been nobody's wife; and that Thomas had so soon tired of all she had to give had humbled her pitifully. Religion had been offered her, but could not appease the guilty, anxious heart. She observed with tender envy her mother's happy friendship with God, but had no such assurance herself. Her charities were nothing but a heavy duty to her. And how deeply she sometimes longed to be like her mother who went about impulsively doing good in her own oddly light-hearted way. A little feather-headed, perhaps it was; still, she did it and was loved.

The young woman read much, but her natural taste was not exacting. It had remained quite artless. It was not only that her education had not taken her far. She was like a person waiting at a station, anxious and distracted, able to give only half her mind to some light, adventurous story. Her chief diversion was the reading of travel books of the picturesque, sensational kind, the absorbed following of adventure in strange lands; and it did not matter to her if sometimes these books were of a kind which would have been found unreadable by people of any taste because of their illiterate style. This did not offend her, even when she was aware of it. It was the adventure to which she gave such bemused attention, the exotic scenes in which she wandered almost in hypnotic state, and she coloured the poverty of these narratives with her own imagery. But it was no longer with delighted zest that she dreamed. The exercise merely gave her the relief of stupefaction; even her sleeping mind was affected. For this imagination which worked so vividly also worked unconsciously, uncontrolled like a child's. She had been driven into this unreal world—she was no genuine inhabitant of it.

Such reading was not food, only a drug or a stimulant. She had become addicted to it as another to drink.

Yet it was true that she could never have been happy with Thomas with an adult happiness, for she had never loved him as a husband; and true that the separation had spared her much human trouble and suffering. She had not been forced to witness and endure the old man's deterioration; nor could she blame herself for her exemption from that trial.

In fact, all those years as a neglected wife, without children, without even the management of her own household, would probably have done her little harm—but for one thing. This married yet deserted state, this sense of belonging nowhere, had left her peculiarly alone—and alone with a destructive thought. She walked apart from the common stream of life, absorbed and staring at one inner point, at a black vortex within herself, at the increasing ravages of a moral sickness.

Whatever she had done or failed to do on that fatal evening, it had never been the offence the young girl's delicate conscience had made of it. She knew that well enough with her reason. Yet the knowledge was useless—the iron weight remained.

Because of a secret, selfish desire to evade a few embarrassing moments, she had omitted to deliver the little girl safely into her father's hands—a child who was so much afraid, so palpably afraid. And the child had been lost.

TWENTY-ONE

Some weeks ago, apparently on a pure impulse, Christine had gone to see Rosalie Lambert.

Mrs Gray had been kind to the woman at the time of the tragedy, when Rosalie had been censured and avoided by all Hilbery, and with a simple deftness of touch, all her own, had quite comfortably sustained an awkward and highly incongruous acquaintanceship ever since. She had happened to speak of Rosalie to her daughter and say of her that she was a pitiably lonely person, and so Christine, on a visit to her mother, had screwed herself up to the act of charity. On the face of it, she had been fired by her mother's example, was conscious of nothing but a natural shrinking from the encounter and had a conscientious belief that she should therefore face it. An act of kindness which she should have performed years earlier suddenly seemed to her obligatory.

It was true that she had once wished for courage to speak to Rosalie and to ask her certain questions. But that was a desire long ago shelved.

So there was the gate—the gate, now almost paint-less, which she had fastened after the child. And there was the front door, deep in the porch, deep in a dusty mass of half-dead creeper, with a step never washed, a mean, skulking door, just as she remembered it. And in face of these memorable things, she felt nothing but a dull, fretful surprise at having come. A hidden impulse perhaps existed. It was buried deeply.

The same mean little villa, many degrees shabbier than in those days, the paint split and peeling, the garden a spread of tussocky grass, a disgrace to the neat road, still housed Rosalie. Nothing whatever had been done to it, although the turn in Mrs Lambert's fortunes was now several months old. Christine had not seen her except in distant glimpses for many years. Rosalie had always been considered very common—but not of course by the charitable Grays; and if Christine had hardly known her even in the days of the tennis club, it was not for that reason, it was because Rosalie had never had any interest to spare for girls, and certainly had had none for one so much her junior. Now something of the diffidence of those days descended upon Christine.

The door opened—but fortunately the business of greeting and recognition could be gone through by rote, whatever one's feelings. Christine had heard a good deal about Rosalie from her mother, but one never obtained an exact portrait of anybody from Mrs Gray, so benevolently were all hues softened, so romanticised were the features. The moment of mutual appraisement was one of simple astonishment on Christine's part. She was looking at an old picture unearthed and found to have lost its colour, to be faded, to be reduced—Rosalie was even a smaller woman than she had thought her. And her first impression, 'Why, she's really a perfectly simple creature,' made her smile inwardly; so eloquently did it speak of the simplicity of one who had once regarded young Mrs Lambert as stylish and sophisticated.

But Rosalie had plainly been through much; she had suffered, and she looked the worse for it. She had rather the sick and sorry air of an ageing dog which has become so ugly that people no longer caress it, which does not expect caresses any more. Far from rebuffing her visitor, she welcomed her with pathetic pleasure. And this made Christine suddenly, sharply conscious of the impure element in her act of kindness. She had not come there merely to comfort Rosalie. She had come to try to satisfy a furtive and painful query which had risen in her mind of late—she did not know how. She was troubled by a doubt about her own memory at a certain point, and by a strange dwelling upon that point, over which it was as if a slight film had drifted.

But shelving these personal problems, she began by gently opening the way to confidences, and then gave her attention unstintingly—she had had much practice at this in her daily work among the ancient poor. Her experience warned her that here was a tale which would take some while in the telling; she could at least listen and give Rosalie so much comfort.

They went into a little sitting-room with grimy windows and here Mrs Lambert poured out to her the story of the twelve years' troubles, which consisted mostly of neighbourly cold-shouldering. How so social a person, so wholly extroverted a creature must have suffered by that ostracism, Christine now vividly realised. Most of the feeling against her had, of course, faded years ago, she had lived it down; and if she was nowadays as lonely as ever it was only because, when young, she had never had any interest but in men. Now she was past forty and had not worn well. In fact, she had worn very badly. The frizzy hair was dyed, the snub nose, which had looked *gamin* and amusing on a young face, was now merely coarse, and the wide frog's mouth was almost comically lugubrious. She was not thin and yet she was flaccid, and this seemed to match something in her spirit. Body and spirit seemed deflated. And she had neither wit nor kindliness to replace her lost animal charms. So here she was, stranded high and dry, and no woman would ever really like her, for she was shoddy, she drank more than was good for her and looked it, and her greatest virtue was perhaps a blunt honesty. This, however, she had, as Christine quickly recognised while they talked, and it was not at all a bad thing; even though it probably came of nothing more exalted than a dully realistic mentality. With another woman, at least, she would bluntly tell the truth.

'Why have I never come to her before?' Christine suddenly thought—though with vagueness.

Rosalie passed on to a pathetic tale of a fortune which appeared to have come too late. For years she had passionately longed to get away from Hilbery, and now that she had the means she did not know where to go. 'I don't seem to fancy anywhere—not by myself.' Then she looked at Christine plaintively, as if hoping she might offer to introduce her into circles where wealth was enjoyed. On her own, she was so reduced and disheartened a creature that she had begun to wonder whether it might not be better to stay in Hilbery, where, after all, she had a niche of sorts and a few boon companions—to stay in Hilbery and throw her riches in its face. One of those swish bungalows on the hill, for instance, that was what she was thinking of. A car—yes, and a chauffeur, and a young one, too, and let the neighbours say what they liked. She had plainly not enough imagination to see what she might do with her money, other than buy herself such Hollywood luxuries; she could not entertain an idea of doing anything unusual with it, anything of a kind she had never done before. In place of sham jewels and furs, she would now have real ones, that was all. No one could have called her an ambitious woman even when she was young and in full bloom. Had she not married George Lambert and contented herself with a little simple fun in the hayloft with an Allan Ruby? 'Why don't you travel?' Christine asked with a dreamy gaze upon her. But, no, she did not like her habits upset.

Christine found these confidences unexpectedly moving, in spite of the touch of farce, or perhaps because of it. Her emotions were worked upon.

Still, she could not deceive herself as to her feeling for the woman; it was little but an attraction towards one who, it was felt, had something she needed, one who might settle something for her. Good sense warned her that to indulge morbid queryings could only be harmful—it did not restrain her stealthy, timid attempts to push the talk into the desired channel.

And Rosalie, perhaps influenced by some feeling of the same nature, met her more than halfway. To Rosalie, words came easily enough. She began to talk freely of the tragedy, and it was obvious that she had never felt any inner shrinking from the subject, although probably in the habit of avoiding it out of an instinct to let sleeping dogs lie. An original dread that people might think she knew too much if she wagged her tongue too much, that her tongue might get her deeper into trouble, had in fact silenced her most unnaturally. With Christine she had no such fear, and the flood-gates were opened.

'Well, yes, I often wonder how the kid would have grown up. She'd never have been much to look at, of course. But she'd have been tall. She had those long hands and feet. She was that build.'

Christine felt curiously in disagreement with this judgment. 'Still,' she objected, 'sometimes, for one reason or another, people don't grow as much as Nature seems to have intended. I suppose there may be hardships—food may not be suitable—bad conditions. And then sometimes in foreign countries girls develop too early and stop growing too soon——But, no, of course it's not a question of foreign countries. Only, don't you think it's easy unconsciously to exaggerate such physical traits in remembering people? *I* do.' Why she troubled to argue against Rosalie's impression, however idly, she did not know. Sometimes one takes such contrary stands out of nervousness.

'No, no,' Rosalie declared. 'I tell you, she'd have been lanky, like her father.'

Christine could not rid herself of a curious desire to continue to contradict her, of a feeling that she was mistaken on this point.

But Rosalie went on, 'Oh, no, she'd never have been much to look at. Remember how her front teeth stuck out? Yes, they did—just a bit. No, she'd never have been a beauty. Not in *that* sense!'

Then Christine asked in a voice which came out breathlessly, 'Rosalie! What do you really think? I've always wanted to ask you, You've always felt quite certain, I suppose—quite, quite certain that she—died somehow?' She was aghast at her own words and faltered over them.

Rosalie took them as a matter of course. 'To tell you the truth, I'd a deal rather think it!' she declared with energy. 'And I don't say that because of the money, either. Not at all. Believe it or not. The money bothers me. Such a pesky lot of it, and I've no business head—and I get that suspicious! Feel they're all doing me. It's a worry. Mind if I ask how *you* feel about it? *You*'re pretty well feathered, too, I suppose?——Mind you, though! *I wouldn't like that kid to walk in on me one day—I wouldn't like it*! That's what I think of her . . . No, let's hope she's safe in her grave, say I, and that she'll stay there.'

But here, perhaps remarking Christine's look and misreading it, she became a little shame-faced.

'I know, I know—I didn't treat her very well. But I'm a selfish sort and I do like plenty of fun. Mad on it, in my young days. Oh, I did neglect her a bit, I'll own it.' She sighed gustily. 'I was a selfish flighty young fool who wanted a good time. And I didn't get a good time at home. All the same, if she'd been a nice, pretty child, I'd have taken trouble with her and liked it, but I got disheartened . . . I had a grand time with the child's father, too. I married George Lambert straight out of the hospital, where I'd nursed him. You know how illness sometimes softens people? I got the impression he was an ordinary chap. There you are—such is life. Well, I stuck to him. And I don't see why I shouldn't benefit from having been a good wife. Get the full compensation, like. *You* know how it is—you're a widow yourself. Enjoy my retirement . . . That kid! What I suffered from her!'

So heartfelt did this last cry sound, that Christine turned her eyes on her and then saw in astonishment that Rosalie's features worked for a moment as if she was about to weep. She could only protest hesitantly, 'Oh, surely the poor child was not much trouble? Such a quiet, timid little thing! Surely she was?'

Rosalie's face twisted into a wry smile. 'Oh, *was* she? *My* guess is that she wasn't really at all a nervous child, though she was shy—what I mean is, she wasn't the sort to be frightened of the dark, or of storms, or burglars—that sort of thing. Yet, if I'd left her at home, for instance, or sent her to play with the other children, when I came up to tennis, she'd have turned it against me in some way—gone whining to the neighbours and telling them I'd left her alone and she was frightened. I don't know whether you'd call it timid. She was cowardly—just that. A little sneak.'

But Christine had a memory of a small, terrified face white in the dusk of the garden. She said faintly, 'Perhaps she was really frightened? Timid people become very resentful——'

Rosalie patted her arm and, looking at her with a wide smile, said, 'No, no. Now, you listen. If ever that kid got a good-looking bruise or scratch, she'd go round hinting that I'd done it. You'd hardly believe some of the tricks that child played on me. You know our garden's pretty long and there's a shed right at the top? Well, she shut herself up in that one day, and she locked the door and pushed the key underneath and outside. She waited till she knew I'd gone out, and then she began shrieking and hammering on the door till the woman in the next house went up the garden to the rescue. Then that little treacherous so-and-so said I'd locked her up there as a punishment—and a nasty cold winter day, too. And when they looked, oh, yes, to be sure, there was the key on the ground outside, fallen out of the door, of course, as the poor kid shook it! Good show, eh? What do they call it—original sin? Yes, I *do* believe in that. I should say so! Of course, everyone believed her, they were only too delighted to think bad of me. But that's the truth of it, so help me God. And I haven't a doubt that by the time they got to her she'd succeeded in frightening herself so much that she was having fits. And—who knows?—she may even have brought herself to think it was true, what she said, to imagine I'd done it. Kids are so odd—sometimes seem to swallow their own make-believes, don't they? Not that some of us older ones are above cheating ourselves, either, when it suits us.'

Christine listened silently, with a startled look.

'Yes, that went off very well, that was a great success, like a good many other of her little tricks. And I've often thought that perhaps—well, who knows?—she may have over-reached herself in some way at last.'

'You mean some accident? The cause of her disappearance?' Christine spoke slowly, with a horrified thrill of the nerves. The idea was perfectly new to her; it seemed to burst up in a dark, static landscape, where she had been straining her eyes for years, as a confused flare which cast wild shadows. She fingered her lips, hesitating. 'Did you ever tell the police she played such tricks?'

'Not me!' cried Rosalie, and laughed, but not at all gaily. 'Oh, no, my dear. I never dared say a word against the kid, *after that*. No, I never said a word of what she was like or what I'd suffered from her. I didn't dare. You can just guess how people would have taken it—I should have been lynched. I can tell you, it struck me pretty forcibly that it would be as well not to show unkindness against the poor little victim. And I only say this to you now because I take it you're not one of those motherly creatures with pink blancmanges in their heads who think you're capable of murdering a child because you dislike children.

'Well, I could go on about her little ways, but I'll spare you. There was a time, though, when she went about telling people I'd poured boiling water over her. What happened was this. I turned round quickly with the kettle in my hand, not knowing she was right behind me, and it splashed a bit over her leg. It was nothing—just a bit of a scalding through her clothes, and I didn't send for a doctor because it wasn't necessary. I was a nurse, you know, before I married, and I'm quite capable of dealing with something a lot worse than that. And I did, I treated it properly. Granted, it might have seemed a lot worse than it was to a kid of that age. And for all I know the little wretch may have been so morbid as to take it into her head I'd done it purposely.'

'Yes, Rosalie, as it happens, she spoke to me of that incident. Morbid! Yes, that is a little my own impression of her. And yet what do we mean by that? Do you know anything of her own mother—what she was like?'

'Why, George hadn't much luck, really, that I'll admit. She was a dead loss—went off with another. Not that I blame her. And George never noticed the child, unless to tell her to hold her noise. He wasn't unkind to her, you know. Most of the time, she just mightn't have been there.'

Christine shuddered inwardly. She wanted to ask whether Lambert was a bad-tempered man, but did not know how to put it. He had not looked it exactly, only glum and dull. 'Was Mr Lambert a hasty man?' she said at length.

'Hasty? Lord, no. Hasty! Anything but. An old slow-coach. Just mean, that's all. He was what I'd call pretty level in the temper. Only thing known to rouse him was his treasures. Lay a finger on one of those bits of rubbish—for that's how I used to think of them, naturally, and don't take back my words now——Well, as I say, lay a finger on one of his treasures, and he was like a madman. I know, because I once tried. I waited my chance and sneaked a ridiculous thumping old watch with only one hand, and came down to supper with it pinned to my chest. Just for a lark, of course—to tease him, you know. Those were early days—you know how it is. It was the only time he ever lifted his hand to me, I'll say that for him, and I hit back with the poker and he got the worst of it. I don't stand for being beaten up, it isn't decent . . . Well, you may say it's a wonder that didn't open my eyes a bit to their value, but you see I just thought it was one of those childish crazes men have. P. S.—that watch, my dear, went for seven hundred in the end. A real snip!' And Rosalie clapped her visitor on the shoulder and laughed heartily.

Christine had listened with a surge of startled feeling; distaste and a sensitive dread of violence preventing her from getting Rosalie to elaborate the scene with her husband; and so the dark questions it aroused in her went unformulated. Half distracted by these, she sat listening with somewhat slackened attention to Rosalie upon the theme of her husband's character.

'Dear me, when I think of the way he went on, and those doddery old cars of his—the trouble he had to go to keep them from falling to pieces on the road—and patient as a saint with them—when he had only to sell a few of those bits of rubbish—I can't help feeling it was a sort of disease. Seems like it, doesn't it?'

A memory just below the surface of consciousness stirred in Christine, causing her to repeat vaguely, 'Cars?'

'One at a time was my meaning. He was always changing them. He liked to go in for a big saloon—did for the vegetables, you see. Why, yes, he used often to bring home sacks of stuff from the market and sell it about the neighbourhood. Good cars in their day, but of course just scrap-iron by the time George came by them . . . Well, as I've hinted to you, George was a trial.

'And he didn't make that kid a good father, he took no notice of her at all. And she hadn't a mother, and I wasn't a good substitute. All the same, I wasn't as bad as the stories that got about. That description—all over the place and in all the papers, wasn't it?—of that rotten little worn-out frock she was wearing—well, it was a wicked bit of injustice to me, that one was. When that very day I'd put out a new frock for her and told her to wear it up to tennis—and if a child of seven can't be left to get into a frock by herself——Wicked extravagance, too, to let her wear such a dress up there, for she always got herself in a mess, climbing and so on—more like a boy. But I wasn't going to have the tennis-club people saying things about me. A funny thing, wasn't it!—if only she'd had that new dress on, I should have kept a sharp eye on her that day. As it was, of course it didn't matter.

'Yes, and there it is, upstairs still—I could show it to you this minute. A little green frock with smocking, ever so smart and pretty, like you see in pictures of society children in the women's mags, and cost a mint, and I'd bought it with my own money. George always said I ought to dress the child out of my own old things cut down. I can see myself! I've got all her things up there, but you needn't think I've kept them from sentiment . . . Well, she put on that old one that I'd just rolled up and stuffed away in the back of the drawer, and naturally

I hadn't even washed it. And she put it on and sneaked out before me.'

'She was afraid of tearing the new one, perhaps. Oh, yes, Rosalie, she said something of the kind to me.'

'You might think so, of course. But I know different. I know why she did it. She did it to show how badly I treated her. It was that nice little dress, still spread on the bed in the morning, just as I'd put it out for her before tennis—that's what first scared me. I got a shock when I saw that, I promise you. But I'll tell you what I thought. I thought she'd put it back like that herself in the morning—just to give me a shake-up. She was such a spiteful kid—and in fact I'd got a bit unbalanced about her. Thinking it over at this distance, I shouldn't say she was up to working out anything like that, should you? A child of seven—and not too bright. But, at the time, I did. And I was just going to see what she'd say for herself when she got home at midday.'

'And of course you told the police about it—about the frock on the bed? I don't remember——'

'Not on your life. For, you see, I didn't 'phone the police at once, as I ought to have done—can't be denied.'

'But—she hadn't come in at all that night! The little dress proved it! The green dress——'

'Well, she didn't go to bed,' Rosalie amended doubtfully. 'She came in all right, for George heard her.'

'Ah!' Christine said faintly. 'I'd forgotten that.'

'She must have sneaked out again. Question was—and is—where did she sneak to? Forget it—might as well. Yes, it made a nice tit-bit for the neighbours, the description of that old pink frock. I found I was living in a nest of vipers. The Turnbulls have gone, thank God, but the Riches are still next door to me—we haven't spoken for years. *She's* the woman who found Vivian in the shed up the garden.'

Christine was silent.

TWENTY-TWO

She had taken in with strained attention everything that Rosalie had told her about the case; and with senses so alert that she seemed to be entertaining two trains of thought at the same time, each with unnatural clarity. For as her gaze encountered the various objects in the dull, shabby room, in which the furnishings looked as if they had done duty for decades, sharp and clear messages reached her from these, too. Vivian must have known the pattern of that dusty carpet; and the one light and charming note in view, struck by a small Victorian china house which could be lighted by a candle—that must often have been turned admiringly in Vivian's little fingers, so fascinating a toy! And perhaps it was those same little fingers which had naughtily unwound that tassel, or had broken the knob off the bureau while playing with it. The sleek, fair little head gleamed everywhere before her eyes—no, she could not see it as anything but fair!

'Rosalie, what colour would you say the child's hair was?' But Rosalie, to her surprise, considered before answering. 'Oh. well—fairish—but going darker, you know. She was fair when she was little.'

'And her eyes?'

'Brown—rather small.'

Hazel, Christine would have said; and she tried to recall the long oval little countenance, the recessive underlip, the eyes which, even at that age, were deepest. But the top lip of all small children is apt to protrude, in a way it does not later when the mouth has settled into its adult shape. It was a face which had haunted her long enough—and why did she feel this uncertainty about it now? She was conscious that the values of the picture had altered a little, it had a shade of strangeness; and no doubt that was because Rosalie's portrait of the child, another, a different face, was superimposed upon it. Some strange impression had confused her own. Whose could it be but Rosalie's?

Sitting there, she was faced with the question of what was at the back of her own conduct from the moment of deciding to see Mrs Lambert. She had known there was something other than pure charity, and now she nervously groped for that hidden motive. She had wanted this talk. *She had wanted to discuss Vivian's looks.* Why? She could find no answer. As if she had lost control of herself, she persisted and repeated, 'I find it so easy to exaggerate certain little peculiarities one remembers. I wonder whether you have a photo of Vivian?'

'Not me. I got rid of them. There are only a few snaps, anyway. But of course the police used them and they were in all the papers. Along with everything else about us, all the dirty gossip. Of course, I know *you* had the same to put up with, in a way. But then, you see, no one ever blamed *you*—you never had anything to blame yourself for.'

'You must have had a dreadful time,' Christine said in a low voice, stiffly.

'Well, I did.' Rosalie drew her chair a little nearer and continued, with forlorn emphasis, 'I did, I did, really! And I don't mean only because of the police and all the blame and bullying. It made me sick to take up a knife and fork and begin *eating*. "What's *she* got to eat?" I'd think then, and could hardly push the food down. And him sitting opposite, tucking in as usual, with his book beside him—all just as usual. He always did read at meals, and he had a jolly good appetite, too. So I'd go out and make myself a cup of tea in the kitchen—and then I'd think of tongues swelling and going black. It was enough to choke you! Because, you see, ridiculous as it was, I couldn't ever get past the idea of her wandering about, lost. Lost and starving. People thought I didn't care, but I'm not inhuman—not like *him*. And I'd had that kid almost from a baby. (I see you're looking at that odd bobble on the runner—I couldn't match it. Yes, Vivian pulled that off and threw it into the fire, and I lost my temper and smacked her good and hard, and I often look at it. That little china house I used to let her have by her bed sometimes, with a candle inside. And I often think of that, too. It's those little things you think of when a kid's gone.) Yes,

I've got all her things put away upstairs still—I didn't love the child, Lord knows, and I don't pretend I did, but after all——It wasn't like a death, see? I never cleared them away, because I never could feel it was ended—not for years—and after that I couldn't get up the energy.

'Night was the worst of all. Yes, I know what they all said about that night, but it wasn't like that with me usually, really it wasn't. But the truth of it couldn't be denied—just for once I'd come in buffy. And I never gave a thought to anything. It *would* happen that one night! . . . Well, I didn't have another such night's rest for ages—that I can say. Nights were bad. For quite a long while I used to sneak down after he was asleep and unlock the back door, and that meant going down very early to do it up again, too—*he* was up before four, had to be. Till he caught me and was furious. (And you can understand that, now, with what he'd got in the house. At the time, it didn't seem to me human. His own child!) Then I used to think I heard her calling, and up I'd get again and put my head out of the window.

'She was bad enough alive. But I could never tell you what she got like *after she was dead,* as you might say.'

Christine sat looking on the floor, not trusting herself to speak or to meet Rosalie's eyes. At last she said, with desperate quietness, 'Wouldn't you be thankful, Rosalie, wouldn't you be thankful with all your heart and soul to—find out that she was alive, after all?—alive, and nothing bad ever happened to her?'

'Lord, no—that I wouldn't!' Rosalie cried, in a voice of frank dismay, staring. 'All I ever wanted was that she should be properly dead and buried, and not haunting us all like a ghost . . . My word, I could knock back a drink. I suppose you don't——?' No, Christine didn't.

Christine went away. She was so much shaken that she walked, in agitation, far afield, like one with a dreaded letter in her bosom which she wished to open in solitude, to hide her anguish; and presently came to herself at a wood's edge, where she threw herself down on a bank in the shade from sheer weariness. The April morning shone about her. Great clouds, snowy and shining, towered into the deep blue sky, and for a little while she sat listening with reviving pleasure to a pair of cuckoos at their soft, elusive, beckoning duet within the fastnesses of the woods. Their differing notes were like the magical horns of legend sounded far oft in the depths of the country, in the folds of the hills.

Scarcely audible now was the lamentable cry.

But how many times had she herself, staring up out of her comfortable bed in a sweat of horror, heard that feeble voice out of the night? Or a voice from a lonely dell as she passed? Or how many times, walking alone, had she made herself turn aside to part the matted weeds under a hedge and peer, almost blinded with terror, into the black channel of a ditch, where things rotted, where some rag was caught on a briar? The note of crude pink had flickered like a signal out of the landscape everywhere. The wind or an animal's cry had carried human tones. All these fancies were wildly irrational, yet had the crazed logic of the sights and motives of the dream world.

She had been shattered by this continual pressure of a secret torture, shattered inwardly; she had gone about everywhere, talked and played and joined in all the parties, and, with the other young people, had laughed and sported in the snow of an unusually bitter winter, and in the end had married Thomas. 'In the spring-time—in the spring-time!'

She picked up one of the little honey-coloured posies fallen from the sycamore and tossed it in her palm, smiling at its beauty, thinking, 'What a pity—what did it bloom for?' and then, looking up into the tree, saw the soft, damp young leaves hanging half expanded, bright as silk with the sun burning through them; they, too, torn by the wind.

Presently, calmer for having bathed her senses in the pastoral sights and sounds, her working mind isolated a strange suggestion it had received from Rosalie, but not properly assimilated in the midst of that long talk bristling with shocks and distractions. The words, 'And I've often thought that she may have over-reached herself in some way at last,' ran out like a vividly lettered scroll across the inner skies, always dark—a strip of fire shedding light from an unnatural quarter, beneath which the whole of the interior landscape lay transformed.

For that instant, it was an idea which seemed to possess a perfect verisimilitude. When a problem has been wearily canvassed for years without solution, any new idea, at a stage when all hope of new ideas has been lost, bursts upon the mind with an artificial brilliance, seeming as if it must contain the inevasible truth.

She turned her eyes about, the grey, gentle eyes whose glances were so readily commiserating; but now they saw nothing of the burgeoning earth and the wreckage of its tender creatures, their expression was a little wild; the shade of anxiety had deepened intensely.

Could the child perhaps have gone to bed as usual, waked when her father went out early, lain trembling till she heard his car go off; then, a little later, got up without rousing her stepmother, who was sleeping heavily after her night out, and gone up to Carlotta House to look again? She must have gone early, for no one saw her. But it was summer, fine, warm weather, she might have played quite happily throughout that summer morning, having provided herself from the larder at home in her usual way. She had been known to play truant from school on more than one occasion. Had she intended to lurk in the garden, knowing that Christine was coming, and was she then going to say piteously, making a bid for sympathy, 'Rosalie's told me I mustn't go home till I find it'?

Had she perhaps, while waiting, shut some door which she could not open again?

Played some trick intended to give pathos to her situation, which had turned out fatally?

But the police had searched everywhere, the whole garden, the whole house.

One moment Christine sat there, carried away and trembling, with eyes fixed deliberately on this new, strange scene, horrible enough, and yet having the effect of releasing the pressure of guilt from her own brow. Reprieved?

Then the gleam went out; her interior sight strained after it in growing panic, in an attempt to avert something deadlier far, to blind herself to what was now taking form in her consciousness. 'Lay a finger on one of his treasures and he was like a madman.'

Then, almost fainting, she witnessed a curtain rising, an iron curtain which had been shut down fast years ago, because she had never been able to bear to look upon what was behind it.

A rejected memory—really a blacked-out memory.

She could not be said to have noticed the car she had seen on leaving the garden, except to see that it was there—big, dark, a saloon, standing half on the grass verge near the door in the wall. She had never seen the door in the wall open, and never regarded it as a way in at all; it was locked, jammed or otherwise impassable, with weeds grown up behind it. So she had assumed. It had not occurred to her at the time that the car could have any connection with Carlotta House. Its accidental presence there had not seemed of any importance, a circumstance which had nothing to do with the tragedy. In fact, that she had encountered any car at all had passed clean out of her mind in the catastrophic experiences which had followed. *When she remembered it, she kept silence.*

For she had said to herself it was Thomas's car. And so the matter still had no importance.

Now, suddenly, flashed upon the dark, came a little picture, viciously brilliant and precise, which showed her the front wheel of her bicycle wobbling before a disreputable, battered mud-guard with a large dint in it.

Yes, was it not a huge dint, and the mud-guard very rusty? Or was treacherous memory exaggerating here also?

That was not Thomas's car!—could not have been. Whose, then? Whose but Lambert's?

Another, a more nebulous memory, floated behind this; of a rustling of the grasses, a regular swish as of someone walking, just caught, just brushing the aural sense, while she looked persistently, dotingly, desperately at the pink rose-petal netted in the grass close to her head, and pretended—no, *convinced herself*—that the petal had accounted for a hallucination.

The fair young woman suddenly fell back on the bank at the edge of the wood like one meaning to take her ease—but her eyes were shut, her face dead white, and in her ears was a wave-like roar carrying a great voice. 'Drowned,' was the judgment. 'Drowned in the depth of the sea.'

TWENTY-THREE

The little sprightly clock, so out of keeping with the dull furnished apartment, the little pretty pink china clock, her mother's present, which she had brought from Hilbery, had suddenly uttered its thin, quick chime into her very ear. She had got up, under the agitation of her thoughts, and had laid her head on the mantelshelf, pressing her forehead on the marble. But had she really been cherishing the hope—this vain, irrational hope—that Vivian was alive, all these years? Yes, indeed she had; and was clinging to it so desperately, even now, that the bare hint of a proof that the facts were otherwise had made her faint with horror.

At the striking of the clock, she stood up. The sensation of a fiery bar across her forehead where the cold of the marble had bitten into it seemed to deepen for a few moments, as if she had been branded. She felt curiously dazed.

But then, peering into the face of the clock to confirm her impression of the number of strokes uttered, she abruptly realised that it was not the darkness of night which filled the room. It was not nearly so late as she had supposed. What had happened to the May evening? Startled, she went to the French door on the balcony.

A cold and livid light from the horizon in the north streamed down the road; but, overhead, the sky was hung with a low, bellying roof of cloud so black that it had caused this premature night. Purple darkness covered the west also. Against this, the opposite buildings, a tall stucco terrace, stood up blanched and glistening, for the level light struck the houses sidelong, whitening unnaturally every plane turned to face it, throwing the reverse surfaces into darkness. Shadow and light met at a knife-edge among the classical detail. Recessed features were sunk in black hollows, of a depth not to be plumbed; while the narrow mouldings ran like threads of light; the dentils under the cornice, the triglyphs on the recurring porticos were sharp as piano-keys. Columns had a look of abnormal weight, because of their exaggerated rotundity. All the little balusters on the balconies stood out like nine-pins, and a plaque with a lion's head glowered into life.

This scene at once filled her with foreboding. Anxiety was so close to the surface that it awoke at a touch, for anxiety was here quite baseless, the storm would not hurt her nor was she normally afraid of storms. Yet she began to breathe as if her chest was weighted. Reluctant that the thunder should take her unawares, or so this apprehension translated itself to her, she remained on watch by the open window.

The street was deserted. An occasional car, purring swiftly by, was perceived by her as a straggler in the rear of a flight. There was not a single foot-passenger. But, yes, there was one. Her eyes rested casually on the solitary figure which had turned the corner and, a little higher up the road, was about to cross to their side. Having crossed, the figure was hidden by the projecting porticos. 'She should hurry,' Christine thought fleetingly, turning her eyes again to the sky. There was a smell of rain already. A few large drops glistened on the balustrade in the silver light.

Suddenly a shrill, needle-fine medley of screaming voices reached her ears—so fine, so shrill that it was only just audible over the murmur of the city. She stared upwards, and in a moment made out, high up in the black zenith, so high that they appeared like a swarm of midges, a great concourse of birds. Swifts! Up and up they went, she straining her sight after them, till they were really invisible, till from the ever-blackening sky the rain abruptly plunged in steel rods, drowning out both sight and sound of the mad voyagers. They were escaping—where were they off to? The devil-birds! They were said to sleep in the sky. This glimpse of a wild life, of a fierce, wild physical ecstasy, over the stony gully of the London street, suddenly raised her spirit to a holiday height, she was the young Christine again who had cried out with delight at the 'wild' trees, and, regardless of the torrents, sheltered a little by the projecting cornice, she leaned outside and filled her lungs with the clean-washed air, again and again. A peal of thunder, not loud, but full of menace, a complaining rumble out of the darkness, rolled round the sky vaguely. The light faded perceptibly.

All at once, she discovered that the young woman she had seen crossing the road a few minutes before had got as far as their own portico and had there taken shelter. Christine, looking over the balustrade, looked down almost directly upon her and had an extravagantly foreshortened view of her as she leaned on the low curtain-wall which joined column to house above the area; she had evidently withdrawn as far as she could from the rain beating in on the other side. Seeing this, Christine was about to call down impulsively, 'Oh, don't stand out there—I'll let you in,' but something prevented her. Nevertheless, perhaps she had made some sound, for the girl raised her face and their eyes met. The face seemed abnormally pale, the skin glistened; and this it was, perhaps, which gave the watcher so sharp and gripping an illusion of gazing deep down into water, at a face rising from a river. How drenched the young stranger seemed to have got in those few seconds she had taken to reach the portico! Their joined stare held. There, in that faintly macabre, inverted fashion, in the livid twilight, they silently took stock of each other for what seemed to Christine a long, a curiously prolonged, intense, melancholy moment.

Suddenly the girl vanished, she vanished soundlessly and completely—that is, she moved and was at once hidden by the roof of the portico which formed the large balcony belonging to the floor beneath.

Then Christine withdrew, turned on the light and stood in the middle of the room, like one who hardly knew where she was.

She was recalled to herself by a cold drop trickling from her hair on to her cheek. She was quite wet, and mechanically went to fetch a towel and change her light bolero, soaked on the shoulders, for something warmer.

'No, I am not imagining it,' she whispered. 'It is the same girl!'

TWENTY-FOUR

It had happened on her first day back in London after that visit to Hilbery when she had seen Rosalie. She had returned nervous and thoughtful.

In a bus for Oxford Street, sitting on one of the sidelong seats by the door, she had become painfully conscious of a persistent scrutiny from a pair of strange eyes.

She had first seen this young stranger in her own road. She had first noticed her walking a little distance ahead, and had only become aware of her at all—a commonplace figure, a rather small, stocky girl—because of the way she kept glancing over her shoulder. Christine had not then supposed that the girl was looking back at herself.

Then, on the corner of Sloane Street, by the Underground, someone rather clumsily got in her way; and Christine, just noting that it was the companion of her walk, now loitering like one who had named the station entrance as a meeting-place, half-consciously thus accounted to herself for the backward glances. The girl, she supposed, was waiting for someone. Yet Christine could not help noticing how closely she herself was eyed. This poorly dressed girl had perhaps observed her attractive clothes, her air of fashion, and resented them. But the look was not an envious or an insolent one, and it was to Christine's face that the deep and slightly oblique eyes were lifted at that moment of close quarters. Christine felt a little disconcerted, but thought no more of it. She joined the queue across the road.

But no sooner was she seated in the bus than she found the girl had followed and that they had sat down almost opposite to each other. Attentively as ever, she was being watched—there was now no mistake about it, though the stare was no longer open but shifty, furtive. Christine looked away, sought to ignore it; but their respective positions would hardly allow a convincing display of unconsciousness. 'How unpleasant! No, I don't know her. Is anything wrong with me?' she thought nervously; and she glanced round to see if she had drawn anyone else's attention. The other glances were quite casual.

That rather long oval face with the long nose—it looked, she fancied, sarcastic and reckless; something about the eyebrows made it so. It was quite strange to her.

Then, just for an instant, the thought, 'Well, she no doubt lives somewhere round here—if so, what more natural than that I should have seen her before?' seemed contradictory to the first conclusion.

She was thankful when her short journey came to an end; jumped off the bus without looking behind her and mingled with the crowd with something of a hunted feeling, which lingered with her unpleasantly. But she had seen no more of her pursuer.

This was all she knew of the girl in the portico.

Her shopping of the next morning took her to one of the largest stores in Kensington High Street; she had decided to make a change in her present for Mirry—a difficult child to please, one she always despaired of pleasing. She was nervous with children, frozen inwardly. To be done with the business, she went out early, almost as soon as the shops were opened, and on leaving the toy department on the third floor she chose to walk down the stairs. The staircase was quiet, few people used it in preference to the lifts, and in any case it was too early for the crowd. On each half landing were large windows looking on the high street itself, and at the first of these she intended to stand for a few moments to amuse herself with a view of the diminished traffic—but someone was there already.

Christine realised it was no chance meeting. The girl had probably followed her in from the street, watched her movements through the glass doors of the toy department, seen her approaching and, seeing a chance to meet her in this comparative privacy, retreated down the stairs to the half landing before her. There was nothing of surprise or confusion in her deliberate movement as she turned, leaned against the sill and calmly raised her eyes to watch the approach of her quarry. Yes, there was now no mistake about it, Christine thought in excited alarm—she was being dogged. Self-possession left her. Fully expecting to be accosted, she went down unprepared with any opening move; and then, as nothing happened, found herself passing by helplessly. But this was not to be borne. Moved by indignation as well as by fright, she turned back and said in a tone which was unnaturally severe, though her voice trembled, 'I think you've been following me. Do you mind telling me why?'

Unexpectedly, the girl then gave a smile of a rather timid turn, though looking into her face steadily. There was a certain hesitancy in her manner which did not seem to go with those somewhat bold looks. She sighed audibly, like one in painful indecision. At last, she half whispered, 'Then you don't recognise me, Christine?'

So astonished, so taken aback was Christine by these words, that she gazed silently. Was there perhaps really something familiar about those small, rather narrow brown eyes? For a fleeting moment, Christine thought so.

'Oh, I hoped you would. Well, I suppose,' the girl went on, 'it's too much to expect. You wouldn't, of course, ever have thought so much of me as I of you. You were always sweet to me——'

'Who are you?' Christine asked quietly, but with a thudding heart.

'Vivian Lambert.'

For some seconds, nightmarish with memories, Christine was only capable of thinking, '*What* Vivian Lambert?' and thinking that it was a queer, ugly, cruel coincidence that a stranger crossing her path should be so named.

Then she said with a severity quite mechanical, 'How am I to believe such a thing?'

'Ah, that has you staring. Well, you'll believe it all right once you've listened to me.' And then the girl, coming a little nearer, said in a very natural and feeling and, indeed, rather discouraged manner, 'I really haven't been able to make up my mind what to do! If you'd just listen to my story?' She was very young, still under twenty, Christine concluded. (Yes, of course! So she must be.)

But if her eyes saw, her mind refused to admit anything of the child Vivian Lambert, as she remembered her, in this young woman. Besides, she had thought at once, in the midst of her distraction, 'But Vivian was fair.' And the picture of the child in her mind was still (and in spite of Rosalie) of unmodified fairness.

It had been, according to Rosalie, one of those little heads which are beginning to darken on which she had looked down as it peeped from under the folds of her coat, on which the fair hairs are still so numerous that it shines when the light strikes it and leaves an impression that it is far fairer than it is in fact; and probably it would have been more exact to have said, 'Vivian's hair was light.'

This girl's hair was not truly dark. Neither was it light brown, but a peculiar shade, rather dark yet with a reddish sheen on it. Christine's next thought, 'I am sure Vivian's eyes were hazel,' was amended the next instant. 'But am I sure? For the eyes which watched her were dark, they were dark as sloes, and the eyebrows were pressed down low over them, making them look sunken, driving them inwards; well-marked eyebrows which followed the slant of the eyes. It was this which made the cast of the face a little saturnine. The nose was large and long. The big, sharply-cut mouth she did not remember at all; the teeth did not show; yet the mouth was prominent and the chin receded. But the form of a child's mouth is always provisional; it is only later that its lines are set. Although of a recessive type, it was a strong face, a striking one.

Or so it seemed to Christine's affrighted and bewildered view.

She was hatless and the hair, smoothed down from a middle parting, like a southern woman's, made the long oval of her face look somewhat heavy. 'Oh, no!' Christine cried in herself. 'No, no, no!' Her eyes fell on the hands; they were narrow, long; she could not recall Vivian's.

Yet there was one thing which she could not overlook, which struck faintly a familiar note. She remembered—so clearly!—that manner which had always divided her between distaste and pity—that furtive, slightly whining yet tenacious manner of a timid, neglected child. At the same time, she had a confused feeling that such a manner was strangely out of keeping with these present looks.

But the girl was speaking. 'I thought, if I could get you to recognise me—if you recognised me, and then perhaps could advise me——' She let the sentence drop away as if disheartened by what she saw in Christine's face.

'You had better go to a solicitor, I should think, with your tale,' Christine said, hardening her voice unnaturally. 'It must be a strange one . . .'

She could not help seeing that the girl looked dubious, that she even made a little movement of recoil. However, she merely answered almost impassively, 'Well—perhaps—later. But don't you think I ought first to see what chance there is—whether I can find people to recognise me? You see, when I started thinking of the people who'd be likely to remember me, I couldn't think of anyone who had been nicer to me than you. Of course, I got angry when you didn't kiss me goodnight that evening—but I don't suppose you'd hold that against a kiddie of seven, would you?'

'Oh, hush—please——' Christine cried, sickening with shock.

She turned to the window and leaned on the sill, looking down into the street and feeling a little dizzy, as she remembered afterwards; and, while her mind was thus whirling with disordered surmise, her eyes rested on two strange figures on the opposite pavement, two fantastic-looking foreign figures such as that part of London sometimes had to show—dark-faced people in gaily striped mantles and odd head-dresses. Africans? Indians? She could not give them any intelligent attention; they were but a visual pattern on her brain. 'I'd hardly spoken to you—to Vivian, till that evening when I walked home with her.'

'But you used to smile at me—oh, yes, you were kind.' The girl had turned with her to the window, and after saying this drew closer to her side, silently; and becoming aware, tensely aware, of the almost panting anxiety behind the silence and the too close pressure, feeling it like a hot breath on her neck, Christine was roused to a keen consciousness of danger.

She perceived, with sensations of panic, how any chance word which escaped her might give an impostor material for her deception. 'I'm afraid,' she added quickly, 'that I simply don't recognise you at all!' And she forced herself to turn and scrutinise her companion as she spoke. The girl's face fell. This was so noticeable, and seemed to Christine such a natural, spontaneous reaction to her hard words that her fright was succeeded by a feeling of compassion, almost of shame. Yet she did not really believe she was speaking to Vivian Lambert.

Also, another idea struck her. 'And Rosalie? Haven't you seen Rosalie? Why don't you go to *her*? She would be the one to remember you best! To remember Vivian——'

'Perhaps you've forgotten—I don't know—perhaps you never knew. Rosalie hated me. Besides, Rosalie is now what you might call an interested party—don't you think so?'

'Oh, the money!' Christine cried. She had not thought of the money till this moment, and her tone was one of consternation, eloquent, she felt, too eloquent, of the inevitable reflection, the worldly-wise reflection which must occur to anyone. Still, it was necessary to ask, 'Yes—why did you wait till your father's death to come—to appear—to make yourself known——?'

'I can't very well explain it all here, can I?' the girl said, glancing up nervously. 'People keep going by.'

Christine now noticed that the swing doors at the top of the flight had opened and two assistants from the floor above had started to come down. Abashed because suddenly thinking, 'Am I looking upset? I must control myself,' she turned away sharply, turned round to the window again and stared down into the street. Even then, it seemed to her as if the footsteps lingered unnaturally on the next flight. She kept her face averted.

Then the girl asked, her voice sounding rather loudly, 'Do you remember Lia Freemantle?'

'Oh, of course I do! But, yes, of course!'

'I went with *her*.'

Christine spent some moments trying to assimilate this astonishing statement, but without success. Then she said, with a sense of deeps opening beneath her, 'You must find someone to advise you. I cannot.'

The girl exclaimed sullenly, 'No, I don't want the law brought into it—not yet, anyway.'

'But, Vivian, how can you avoid it?' Christine cried, surprised, favourably impressed, in fact, by this evident artlessness—and using the name unconsciously. 'You can't, surely, suppose that you can avoid it? Your case was a famous one. The police looked for you everywhere—I mean, they looked for *Vivian Lambert* everywhere. There was a hue and cry all over the country—wireless appeals—all of it. Even if you were—even if you are——But Vivian Lambert could never expect to come back quietly, like this, unknown to anybody but a few friends. You must have realised how the police searched for you when you disappeared? Your reappearance—*her* reappearance would cause a sensation. Or so I think. No, I don't see how you can keep hidden—I wonder the police haven't found you already. And then, if you ever intend to claim your father's money——'

The girl listened, looking down, and seemed, she thought, suddenly cowed. She was pale or, rather, sallow, and Christine fancied that she had turned paler. She said with a slight smile, 'Would they give me a rough time, then?' But there was a scared look. And now Christine noticed with a pitiful heart that there was an indescribable air of poverty about her—not altogether in her clothes, but in the pinched, rather sickly face, the stunted growth. However, the girl went on doggedly, 'That wasn't my aim, to have anything made public—it wasn't what I intended! I never visualised any sort of legal business. I just wanted to be acknowledged by Father, and perhaps a few other people who'd seen me about—neighbours. I haven't got anything in the way of relatives who knew me, I think—I never saw any. I just thought of *you*. You see, I came to England with the idea of walking in on Father and telling my tale and just having him recognise me. I thought he couldn't fail to recognise me. I didn't expect him to be overjoyed, but I did hope he'd help me—I mean, with a little money, or by helping me to get a job—well, I thought he might, for the sake of being rid of me. I had a right to ask him to help me, hadn't I? It was none of it my fault I—you'll see when I tell you. I did, of course, think we might come in for a bit of pestering by the local paper, and so forth. But not lawyers!' She added with an attempt at swagger, 'Try to run me out of the house, will they? So what?'

Christine considered, 'Well, she is very young. Whoever she may be, she is very young. In fact, *she is Vivian's age*.'

'When I got to England and found he'd just died, I was quite bowled over, it was a terrible blow! I don't mean I shed any tears over him, for I'm not pretending I had any feeling of that sort for my father, or very little. But it was a facer . . . I came over after a job, but you see I've been short-changed—it hasn't turned out what I expected'; and she muttered a few words, some slang phrase, probably American, which was so obscure that Christine did not understand or even catch it properly, but judged it to mean that she was sick of something, through with it all, had a good mind to pack up and call it a day. An apathetic look, dull and dark, as if her interest had waned, was remarkable for an instant.

'Where did you come from?'

'South America, you know. We lived in Lima.'

'You came over alone?' She thought that the girl seemed to hesitate before she answered, 'Yes.'

'Couldn't you have come before? Why didn't you? At least, why didn't you write to your father—as soon as ever you were old enough—old enough to think? Surely you must sometimes have pictured what he and Rosalie went through when you vanished?'

But the girl looked at her with a smile of astonishment which appeared genuine. 'Why—how could I? I couldn't possibly do anything while Lia was alive. She's dead now, but she died only last year. It was a criminal thing she'd done, wasn't it? And I suppose such an action wouldn't exactly be overlooked, however many years had passed. But, you see, you haven't even given me a chance to tell you how it happened yet!'

Christine cried out again, with a prevision of terrible complications, something quite beyond her management, 'Oh, I'm afraid I can't help you. You should find a solicitor.'

'You won't help me, Christine?' And the girl drew still nearer, unconsciously, no doubt, till her companion, caught in the corner of the embrasure, could retreat no further. 'Surely you will give me a little help?' But again, and overwhelmingly, Christine felt that the tone, humble and appealing, and even timid, did not go with the appearance; the appearance, she suddenly fancied, was desperate. She felt penned into her corner. She touched her forehead and drew her hands down her cheeks, agitated inexpressibly. 'So you are going to pass by on the other side—again, again?' Were these words really uttered, and with a rageful sneer? For the next moment she heard the girl saying, quite nicely, 'I don't want to distress you. I thought you might be glad.'

'Glad! Glad!' Christine cried within herself; but she let the words go by in a flat, cruel silence.

Then the girl said, 'I've a real right to some of my father's money. Why should anyone be suspicious because I want a bit of justice?' But the tone was now abject. Still, she added, 'Will you do this? Make a date with me some place where we can talk and just listen to what I have to say? I'll give you a straight story, sure I will. Only, don't you set the bims on me, will you! Couldn't we fix it for now?'

Christine felt that she must consent to a meeting, though she would require time to consider, and so told the girl to come to her flat on the next afternoon; but felt bound to warn her, speaking perhaps rather coldly, that she would have a friend with her who would know what to do, who had knowledge of legal matters and could no doubt advise her. She could scarcely think of anything but escaping, to be alone with her thoughts. So with a distracted glance, a gentle bend of the head, she left her and went to the staircase and began to run down it. But a sudden realisation halted her, she felt a stab of joy, and she turned back and sprang up the flight again to cry, in a coaxing, affectionate voice which was like her mother's (the voice of a child who wishes to be told only happy things), 'Oh, Vivian, is it really you?'

But the girl was gone. She was too much distracted to feel surprise, she was not in a state to consider the fact properly—the staircase surrounded a lift-shaft and the lift had just passed down. So she turned again and ran fast down the stairs.

She was overwhelmed by a sort of febrile delight; suddenly almost as if drunk, and in the street could hardly walk steadily. Reprieved! 'Oh, God, how good of you! Am I to have a second chance?' Knowing, intensely knowing that she ought not to let her feeling run up to such a height, or to rejoice at all without proof, she still could not prevent this fount of thankfulness. And for a space her thoughts, broken and tumultuous, seemed only to find expression in exclamatory argument. 'It is!——It must be!—"I was angry when you didn't kiss me goodnight that evening." Who else could have known that?' So she reached home and could not have said how. Almost at once, her joy collapsed.

All through this, she had forgotten, she had positively forgotten, that she was going down to Hilbery that afternoon; and she felt shocked at herself, for now there was nothing for it but to ring up Carlotta House again and put them off for yet another day.

Then, thinking things over and remembering a hundred things, and with a mind ringing with questions, she became more and more agitated as she imagined the next day's interview; and she could not bear the thought of trying to explain a story which on her side went to such wounded depths, to any of her London friends.

So she thought of Keith. He at least knew the story of the disappearance in all its details; she remembered his interest in the case at the time.

Impulsively she sent out her appeal to Keith; and then, much agitated and feeling a deep exhaustion, she drew her green sun-blinds—for the day had turned hot and her rooms received many hours of sun—and lay down in the muted, dreamy light to try to recover herself. She had lately been inconvenienced by the full sunshine, which was apt to hurt her eyes. For a long while her heart went on beating quickly and shallowly. Every noise from the street seemed peculiarly loud and jarred her through, as noises do in sickness.

TWENTY-FIVE

'Yes, I remember that evening as well as I shall ever remember anything in my life. You waved to me over the gate and turned and went, leaving me alone. I shall never forget it. I was afraid to go in, I was afraid to go anywhere. I'd stolen that ornament, you see—and thought that what I had taken must have been missed.

'And what *had* I taken? you ask, and impulsively tell me that no one ever discovered what that object was. No, you shouldn't have told me that (and I see you know it). You're right—it gives me a lead. It leaves me free to improvise. Well, that's what has occurred to you, I suppose, with that dubious look. *"An impostor* would feel free to improvise."

'What? Nobody ever missed what I'd taken? Quite likely. It was a thing of no value. I don't remember it clearly.

'Ah, I see you thinking, "That's a false note. Oughtn't she to remember, and that most vividly, an object which she had so intensely admired and which had afterwards caused her such terror?" Well, then I do remember it. But only vaguely. It was a sort of pendant with a big blue stone set in some cheap silvery metal, very gaudy—no, it can never have been a valuable thing, but of course I had no idea of that at the time. Jewellery, I thought, must be precious. I'm not surprised if she never missed it. "Then it was Rosalie's!" you cry. Oh, yes. Why, of course it was Rosalie's. Whose else? *If it had been my father's, he would have killed me.* She had loads of that sort of barbaric, arty stuff. Beads and bangles. She had a whole box-full of such rubbish—I admired it passionately, and I used to creep into their room when she was out and turn it over and try things on, and I'd borrowed things before but never had the ill-luck to lose them.

'Don't ask me what I thought, I can't in the least remember. How does a child think? It feels. I felt misery.

'But I know that at last there came into my head an idea of one person who had always been jolly with me—Lia Freemantle. A person to whom I'd run once or twice before to be comforted. Afraid of overtaking you, I waited a bit, and then I slipped up the road and down the passage—but then there you were, leaning over the gate of the cottage, talking to Lia. That seemed to me final. Hope was crushed. I ran back.

'What a lovely evening, Christine—what a lovely evening! Do you remember our walk? You don't answer.'

Christine did not answer. And the words came again, with insistence, 'Christine, don't you remember our walk? Why, you can't have forgotten our walk!' the girl said, smiling. 'So you ask me what was special about it—and you avoid my eyes. Oh, don't you remember? How you took me under your coat and put your arm round me? We walked on like one person! I felt safe. I thought, "She will kiss me goodnight, as other children are kissed".'

Christine lay back, in melancholy stupefaction. 'How does she know these things?' But after she had been silent a few moments, an explanation occurred to her. 'Wait! Didn't I tell Miss Freemantle that? Didn't I perhaps say that the child hadn't a coat, and that I had to put my own coat round her?' She could not remember. Again, as at the first meeting, she had the sensation of walking among pitfalls, of being drawn in with every word.

'Tell me this, then,' she suggested. 'What did we say—after Penelope had left us?' But, having added these last words, she unconsciously made a helpless little gesture, thinking in alarm, 'Another slip!'

'Don't worry,' the words reached her. 'Truly, I *could* have told you she was with us, and that her name was Penelope. But what did we say?' After considering, the girl replied to this, quite coolly and naturally, 'I can't remember. It would be too good if I could, surely?

'This I can say, though. That evening you had a number of little butterflies in your hair. I loved pretty ornaments——'

'Oh, those butterflies!' Christine recalled; and she lay thinking of the butterflies and smiling her mother's smile, tranquil and indulgent. 'How well I remember those butterflies. I thought them so pretty myself—and still think they must have been—as I was so young! But someone up at tennis twitted me about them, and I began to feel silly, and so I think I never wore them again. Only that day.' But she stopped, shivered in alarm and cried sharply to the figure in the dim room, 'But you ran home? You went in? Quick—on with your story—whoever you may be.' The girl laughed. 'Yes, I ran home—*whoever I am*—ran home again, and this time I went inside because there was nothing else to do. I crept into the kitchen by the back-door and took some food from the larder—and all the while I was weeping bitterly in my hopeless fright. I cried silently, the tears ran into my mouth with the food. I ate, not because I was hungry, but to comfort myself. I could hear Father moving in the back room, where the cabinets were, and he was opening and shutting drawers and cupboards, like a person looking for something. I went and crouched under the shelf in the larder; it smelt nastily of damp wall. I thought he would come out any moment, for he must have heard me. But he did not. I couldn't bear it any longer, and crept out into the garden and clung for a bit to the lighted window. In the end—well, you can see, there didn't seem to be anything for it but Lia Freemantle.'

Then Christine followed an account of her running back to the cottage in the dark, and being taken in and comforted. Miss Freemantle had probably thought that a few hours of anxiety would not hurt the Lamberts; or she might have supposed they would guess where the child had gone. When the incredible thing happened, when the hours went by with no inquiry, and it was past midnight, what had she thought? Perhaps, after tucking Vivian up in bed, she had gone round to the Lamberts' house and found all in darkness. Peacefully retired, with the child's bed empty! What had then gone on in that quirky head? Was she outraged by such evidences of callousness, by conduct so monstrously neglectful? Was she indignant? Did she then and there make up her mind to kidnap Vivian—to give the Lamberts a memorable shake-up—to make a scandal—to publish abroad their treatment of the child? And to give Vivian a bit of fun, though it might not last long?

Christine did not think that anyone could have taken a fancy to the little girl, as she remembered her; yet she recalled how Miss Freemantle had said, 'She's not a bad-looking little thing, apart from those teeth. And they could be corrected.' But pity—pity would do!

A vivid vision of Miss Freemantle slouching quietly through the dark roads of Hilbery, at an hour when everyone else was sleeping, formed before Christine's inner eye. A lawless one, a night-prowler. She was padding softly back to the little rebel cottage under the elms. Smiling to herself, was she? Thinking of the sensation she was going to cause . . . Simple enthrallment held Christine; and now the girl began telling of the morning. When it was time for the van to come, Miss Freemantle had put her into an outhouse in a corner of the garden, giving her some magazines and a pair of scissors and told her to stay there and on no account to show herself. She had already cropped her hair and put her into shorts. Hope and his son filled the van and then went off to lunch, and while they were gone Miss Freemantle put her into the back of the van concealed among the furniture, in a nest of rugs, with a raincoat draped before her hiding-place. Thus she could peep out, without herself being seen. There they had picnicked, in that adventurous fashion, and Miss Freemantle had made such a lark of it all that the whole wonderful affair had seemed to the child delightful beyond belief. She had promised to lie still as a mouse in the recesses of the van, but thought it likely that other measures had been taken, that the food had made her sleepy. She remembered the rest only in the dimmest way. Lying back on her rugs, she seemed to have seen nothing of the journey but the endless stream of the road running away under the tailboard. Nor did she remember anything of the arrival in Southampton.

She remembered a little of the time in Southampton where they had stayed for a while—she believed, only for a few weeks. But it was no good asking her for any details which would serve as proof here—what could Christine herself remember of her life at seven? Shadowy fragments—dates all gone, if ever they were known—times and places jumbled together. Authentic memories? Or things told one afterwards? Above all, disproportion. It is the private moments which the child remembers. She had thought of the place simply as 'the seaside'. But she seemed to have no visual impressions of the town and thought she had been kept indoors, no doubt for a good reason. She couldn't even form the slightest picture of the outside of the house she had stayed in, though she clearly recalled certain portions of its interior—a bead curtain, a great, pink, curly jardinière on the staircase corner, a pudding-dish baked brown—and she thought the people were foreigners.

'And about what Lia did and how she managed with all the travel documents and the rest, I can tell you nothing. At the time, and for years afterwards, such questions never entered my head, and she would never talk of it when I asked her, much later. I can tell you nothing of the way she herself lived in Southampton, either, because I didn't live with her there, oddly enough, and I can't tell you why. I didn't live in the same house. I can't remember her being there at all, and I don't think she was, though she sometimes came to see me, and then brought a boy with her. I do clearly remember that. And I know I had his room in the house I was in, because there were some toy models in it which he forbade me to touch, and also that I wore some of his clothes. But when we sailed, we left him behind. I don't know how she managed, but you're probably aware that she was a woman who could have bluffed her way past Saint Peter.

Later, the boy came over and joined us. It won't do anyone any harm if I tell you that he was in fact her son. Manuel.

'But that time in Southampton I accepted everything, as it seems to me, without question, I never even wondered. It seems as if I kept quiet instinctively, with an instinct for my own safety. If I was ever warned to hold my tongue, I don't remember it. No one ever spoke of my miserable home, so it was "out of sight, out of mind"—as it is with kids of that age. I forgot my home. I dare say I could hardly have told anyone who I was, in the end, or where I'd come from. With Lia, I was happy for about the first time in my life.'

'Did you really leave your home like that—and never think of it again?' Christine said with shocked, pitying incredulity. And the feeling of this was so strong in her that she experienced a kind of vicarious woe. How she herself at that age would have wept, how wild would have been her grief and terror on being torn away from her mother!

'But it was not a home like yours, Christine.'

'*Did* they ill-treat you? Oh, no, they didn't, surely!'

'I dare say not. Not genuine ill-treatment. Oh, well, I'm afraid that's how it was,' the girl repeated, laughing. 'I forgot my home. Lia did give me a good time.'

Then there followed some explanation of Miss Freemantle's circumstances, of which Christine remembered vaguely to have heard. She had English relatives, and by these had been educated in England, but she also had Latin American blood on her mother's side. She had gone over to join these half-Spanish connections, who were in the hotel business, and was to assist with one of their establishments in Quito. And if this seemed a strange choice of occupation for the vagabond Lia, the hotel, as it was briefly described, sounded but an indifferent one; and that the clientele was apparently English-speaking in the main, might have given her services a special value.

However, they had first left their ship and strayed for a while among the Caribbean islands, of which she retained little but an impression of brilliance, heat, and a generalised vision of the negro face, seen then for the first time in the flesh.

The story went on. She spoke of the voyage across the Caribbean, and the high-coloured, fleeting pictures of the Panama region flashed before their eyes, with the spirit of fire everywhere—a sparkling sea, a blinding sea, a sapphire sky.

Then a long, sluggish journey in a river-boat which was like a house of three storeys took them south, down Colombia, between the walls of the jungle, from which Indians sometimes looked out on them; and her nostrils expanded in laughing distaste as she mentioned the reek of that river, the overpowering rottenness of primeval swamp under the sun, which she could recall to this day. The boat glided on, with all its interior surfaces reflecting the shifting, shimmering lights on the brown water; lights which also gilded with varying sheens faces of every shade of complexion possible to the human skin, through pale to ebony black, with features of every race, and these often mingled in one countenance. This rippling and smiling light, which made dark eyes glisten and showed flashing teeth in dark faces, gave the child a sense that everyone was happy and pleased to see her, and to the whole adventure an atmosphere of endless holiday. Red cliffs, trailing vines festooning every branch and surface in wild profusion, pink herons, great parrots of brilliant hue, little black monkeys; small huts thatched with leaves sometimes seen in the forest, like habitations in a children's story in which children go on adventures and live alone: and behind this canvas, daubed by a child with the brightest colours in her paint-box, seemed to crowd all the reputed wonders and horrors of the Amazonian forests; their serpents and alligators, their gorgeous birds, their fearsome insects; their lost trails, their poisoned weapons; and far back in the depths of a low hut, a wizened human head with peaceful eyelids weighted by long lashes.

So they came into Ecuador. The hotel was evidently much like a second-rate hotel anywhere, furnished in North American style, dull and shabby, patronised by Americans. But all round were the monstrous ranges bristling with volcanoes, and you had only to climb out of the town in the ravine to set eyes on the very type and device of the fire-bowelled land in the perfect, dazzling cone of Cotopaxi. She had run about the hilly streets, where the crowds swarmed so negligently among the honking, madcap traffic, and had seen the squat Indian women with ugly baboon faces, billowing skirts and queer bowler hats, flocking in from the country with their produce. The rags and the bare feet, she remembered; and also the innumerable churches, barbarously ornate, with interiors like treasure-caves, every surface encrusted and festooned with ornament, gold, colour and jewels glistening in the light of many candles.

They had stayed in Quito three or four years. Lima next, and the great brown cliffs gloomily fronting the grey, misty sea. The massed flowers glowed in the sorrowful light. Lima, ending on a grey note, as at a tomb, with the floral trappings of a tomb. This time the hotel was a big one in the rich seaside quarter of Miraflores; and here for the first time she had gone to school, amongst English and American children; for the Cazares, Lia's relations, were people of some standing in Lima.

She listened, listened enthralled. It all seemed to her to ring true, and she did not ask herself what knowledge she had to enable her to judge of this South American part of the narrative; but still she did realise that ignorance may account for an easy acceptance of improbable facts. Yet it could not account for this deep, haunting conviction of authenticity. Perturbed, trying to hold on to balanced judgment, she sought to bring the test on to familiar ground. 'What friends had you in Hilbery? Tell me what people you remember. Neighbours, for instance.'

The girl looked at her sidelong, sullenly amused and a bit shrewish. 'But what friends could I have?—a child of seven! And coming from such a home, where we never entertained. Where I never had anyone in to play with me.' She added, with something of a sneer, 'You do oblige me to point out that it would be easy enough, in a place like Hilbery, where everyone's tongue wags both ends, for a perfect stranger to find out a few names of past inhabitants—and a few useful facts about them. Don't you think so?'

'Now you are going too far,' Christine told her gently. They exchanged a long look. Christine's heart sank, a chill of disbelief played on her hopes and renewed the anguish of irresolution. For the girl's manner was bold, far bolder than on the first occasion. Bold, rough, impatient, threatening. It lacked slyness. She could not avoid thinking so. Where was the half-dispirited cajolery, that hint of the abject child Vivian, she had first noticed? She could not prevent the idea that the girl was like one who had started to play a role and had not been able to keep it up—or perhaps had seen that there was no need to keep it up. How unaccountable the change was otherwise! No need to keep it up with such a weakling, such a born gull as Christine Gray? But then suddenly she remembered how Rosalie had said (and how she had then silently disagreed), 'She wasn't really at all a nervous child.' Besides, how easily one could imagine that in those strange, foreign, less inhibited surroundings, under conditions possibly coarse and primitive (for they had clearly had little money at the beginning and had often roughed it), and, above all, under the guidance of a Miss Freemantle, Vivian Lambert had developed into a bolder, hardier, franker character than she had ever promised to be. Of course! What more natural?

As for the looks—the expression of a face can alter completely, no doubt, according to the spirit within, and the expression of a face can change it unrecognisably.

The treacherous nature of memory was already sufficiently clear to her.

Face, manner, voice——She listened with inquiry turned in a fresh direction as the girl resumed, 'Neighbours? Well, Riche was the name of the people next door to us. Turnbull— was it?—on the other side. Or a door or so away, perhaps it was. Allan Ruby was the name of the boy Rosalie was fond of going about with. They used to do a good bit of necking up at Carlotta House. You remember, Christine?'

'Yes, that is right,' Christine agreed in a low voice, somewhat absent. 'He belonged to the club.' Something else had caught her attention.

She had been listening in vain for any trace of an accent, or any mannerism of speech which could be called foreign—and that was surely strange, considering the age of the child when she had left England. That they had lived among English-speaking people in the main had to be taken into account, of course. Nevertheless—a slangy English, mingled only with a few Americanisms such as nowadays are in common use in this country? She had half-consciously worried about this all along, as she now realised. But with the words 'Carlotta House', she had at last actually caught some peculiarity of pronunciation. The barest hint of a foreign accent? Well—of something! But of something ineluctably English—of an English dialect. And suddenly she heard the little girl's voice saying in quick, false denial, 'I don't ever go near the well-house,' giving the 'ou' a flat sound, so that the word was almost 'hay-oose'. The Lamberts had come from the Sussex side. They were country people, they did not speak quite a Londoner's English, like the majority in Hilbery. But could a little trick of speech, such a fragile thing, have survived such experiences, even this shadow of it?

The girl was continuing with rather a manner of humouring a foolish fancy. 'Well, then—so what? I remember Miss Maple's school, and a little boy called Don—and him I remember only because they made a joke about our being sweethearts, or something of the sort, and I didn't like it because I was so shy.'

'Don?' thought Christine; and, yes, she remembered a pretty and rather dull little boy with an almost white mop of curls who used to live in her own road. She could not remember his surname—the people had left long ago.

'Say that again!—"Carlotta House",' she demanded. The girl, a little uneasy, repeated the name. Now the trace seemed fainter. 'Again!' Christine cried anxiously. 'Well, tell me about it, I mean. Say what you remember.'

'Oh, I remember Carlotta House very well indeed. A great, empty, very old-fashioned place which scared me rather. Wasn't there talk of its being haunted? Yes, I know there was.' And she smiled, mockingly, as if at a private joke. 'I used to go inside sometimes, you know, while you were all at tennis, getting in through the little window at the back. Jeez, how scared I was, yet I used to creep in and dare myself to go up the staircase.

I used to lean flat on the handrail—it was of some wood very smooth and slippery—and slide down it, in a funny mixture of fear and enjoyment. Just near the newel, the ironwork "peeps" like a bird, when you pull on it. I remember the little lions' heads at the corners of the door-frames—are they still there? They used to fascinate me. In one of the rooms upstairs there's a curious, high old grate with pilasters each side which have faces on them. Well, I never saw the ghost.'

Sometimes she had ventured into the kitchens, this region evidently having had a fearful, ogreish attraction for the child, with its ancient ranges and stone vaulting, *as it was then*, and the ringing echoes. '. . . And half dark, too, with the green light through the barred windows—the branches pressed right against them.' As they were then! 'There was an old brick oven up in the wall at the side of the fireplace. I didn't realise what it was at the time, of course, and thought it was a secret passage, such as I'd heard of in stories—it seemed so deep. But I only once peeped into it.

'From the kitchen you could look across the garden where the gooseberries were, and those huge bushes of mint—oh, yes, and the well-house corner.' And she laughed and remembered that it had a bad reputation, the well-house corner. For it looked the part—it looked like a place cast for some sinister act. Christine smiled in response.

'That reminds me! Does the iron gate still open of its own accord? When you heard it squeal, you all made jokes about it, saying it was the ghost passing through. The latch was weak. Still, iron gates don't blow open, it was very stiff really. I sometimes opened it and swung it, and then hid—and one or two of you would come running and crying it was open again.

'"So it was you who opened it!" you exclaimed impulsively, and that makes you laugh. But do you see what you've done? *You've acknowledged me.* Yes, *I* opened it. *I*, Vivian Lambert.'

'Yes, I believe in you!' Christine heard her own voice confessing with intense emotion. 'But come again tomorrow, in sign of your good faith. You see, you must come tomorrow, to meet my witness.'

The girl seemed to promise, and Christine put out her hand in friendly salutation to clasp the other's——

But she had retreated, had stepped away from the bed so quickly that she was already at the door—then she was gone. And, listening for footsteps, Christine heard them going off and off, a long way. (Yet the carpet was thick, the stairs carpeted also.) Till they mingled with others, in the house, in the street.

Almost in the dark, Christine sat upright on the bed and remained thus a long while, her first fearful joy gradually darkening into bewilderment, sometimes putting her hands to her head with a sensation of hardly knowing where she was—so far away had she been. More than once, some obscure impulse made her wonder whether it would be as well to ring up Keith and tell him not to come—in case the girl did not keep her promise. So she sat there feeling shaken and uncertain, harassed by indecision.

She was conscious at last of being exceedingly hungry, and perhaps bewildered and faint because of that. Then she remembered with astonishment that she had not eaten since the morning; and now it was evening, almost dark.

TWENTY-SIX

As soon as she had sent for Keith, she had felt dubious about him. But her own brothers were out of reach, and with the legal aspect Helena would be as much at sea as herself. Besides, she had grown used to relying on him. She had had a considerable liking for Keith at the beginning, based on gratitude, but much had happened in the past twelve years to bring about a change in her feeling, and of late there had been revelations and suggestions which even her confiding mind had been unable to discount. If she had examined her feelings honestly, she would have found that she no longer trusted him.

She did not examine her feelings. But she said to herself that he was the right person to consult. He was an intelligent man, would know what steps to take, and she could at least count upon his lively interest. And it was with simple relief that she received him in her green-lighted room on the following morning, returned his friendly handclasp and began telling him her strange tale of one risen from the dead.

Keith at once showed himself entirely skeptical. His customary flattering air of attention was not so perfect as usual. He smiled faintly, was silent, drummed with his fingers, and she felt that he was merely thinking that in another moment he would scotch the whole impudent attempt on her credulity with a few sensible words. But she had the satisfaction of seeing a change in him as the revelations went on. He grew visibly disturbed.

From below, from the road, the dry and resonant air, the gusts of heat and light, were wafted up under the blinds, and all noises from without sounded very clearly; voices spoke clear sentences which floated into the recital with tiresome irrelevancy, putting a strain on the attention; children cried, shrill barking broke out, and all the manoeuvres of a taxi stopping to let down its fare could be followed. It was a wide road and not a noisy one, a good residential district; but, as always happens in London in fine weather, balconies broadcast domestic sound to a distracting extent, neighbours were too close together. All this, to which she was accustomed, now chafed her nerves and increased her sense of speaking under some difficulty to him.

Keith heard her out almost in silence. Then he laughed, shrugged, and asked her how she thought Miss Freemantle could have got out of the country with a little girl who so resembled the missing Vivian Lambert as to be, in fact, exactly like her. He could only point out how fabulous the feat must be accounted. 'But, dear, even in the case of the normal, innocent tripper there is so much to be gone through—so much!—before he can ship to such a country as South America nowadays. There are tiresome enough regulations in the way of the perfectly blameless traveler. And to attempt to smuggle out a kidnapped child, a child the police are looking for——'

But she patiently reminded him that Miss Freemantle was South American by birth. She could also recall clearly that the woman had told her she had 'everything settled', and, moreover, was 'taking someone with her'.

'Are you sure?' said Keith, frowning. He was driven to admit that if Miss Freemantle's nationality was really South American, and if she had also had lawful business in one or another of the republics, her mobility, and her achievements generally, did become a little less of a marvel. They shelved the point. She was perplexed by his attitude. The smile had faded from his face and was replaced by a sort of disconcertion which was almost sulky.

'But the woman was presumably in her right mind?' he said with more than a hint of petulance. 'A crazy, perfectly objectless thing to do! And, besides, criminal.'

Christine was silent. She could not say, 'I once saw Miss Freemantle steal a handful of nuts from a stall. It made me see her as a woman who would do *anything*.'

Instead of answering thus, instead of expounding Miss Freemantle's character, she was overcome by a sense of something hostile and stubborn and, she felt, unreasonable in his opposition, something she did not understand. 'Oh, Keith, I did think you'd at least be interested. But I see you feel just as I did at first. I did feel almost certain that she must be an impostor, someone trying to dupe me—it was my first thought, of course. So I was careful.'

Keith remained unresponsive but for a chilly smile which showed him skeptical even of her commonsense, she supposed. He considered a moment, fidgeting with a cigarette which he did not light in the end, and she saw his face cloud with a sort of gloomy dissatisfaction. Her surprise increased; not so much because of his incredulity as because of his lack of relish in a sensation—surely a phenomenon. He had not once exclaimed in amazement, or cried out, 'What an extraordinary thing!' She urged arguments upon him.

'But, come, if this girl can never make good her claim, and knows she can't, and knows her evidence will collapse as soon as anyone looks into it, what is she hoping to get out of tricking a few people for a short while?'

A dubious sort of excitement was now reflected in Keith's face and movements. He turned his eyes away, then got up and took his stand before the window, with his back to the light, so that he could look straight down upon her where she faced him and leaned eagerly forward with her question. He continued to speak of the girl as an impostor, though as gently as possible and with a tactful lightness. His manner, in fact, became slightly playful, in that unhumorous way of his. She thought his attention was not wholly in what he was saying.

'What is she hoping to get out of it? I wonder! Well, what if we make a guess? *Your sympathy?* Your pity and sympathy and their practical results? You are a very well-to-do woman—some people would say wealthy.' And he smiled at her kindly. 'And that you choose to live in this comparatively modest style—we all know why that is. You are charitable. You're a kind, simple, charitable creature—everyone can see it at a glance. You look it.' They both laughed, Christine rather painfully and really a little hurt and astonished as she protested, 'Oh, Keith, I don't look simple, surely?' For she knew she was not simple, as we all do. For the rest, the idea of herself as the prey was new and shocked her.

She said, however, with a smile, 'Anyway, I'm not so simple as this poor girl. When I warned her that she wouldn't be able to avoid a good deal of publicity, it seemed as if she hadn't even thought of that and was quite frightened!'

'I will bet she was. Oh, she had thought of it, but had hoped *you* wouldn't. No, then it's plain. I should say she doesn't want any publicity at all. I imagine she has no idea even of trying to claim Lambert's money. Nothing she could produce in the way of evidence would stand up to the legal raking she'd get, and she knows it. No, it's you, undoubtedly—*you* she means to fasten on. I should say she is merely out to collect as much as she can lay hands on before the roof falls in. With *you*, she's the poor waif who cannot claim her rights because she has no proof—because she's too simple—because she could never hope to find her way in the jungle of the law and is afraid even to attempt it. Yes—and I dare say she *is* afraid! . . . And Rosalie? You see, she will not even tackle Rosalie. Good heavens, what reason could the real Vivian have for not going straight to the woman who had brought her up and would be better able to recognise her than anyone else in the world?'

'I do feel that!' Christine admitted.

On that point she was forced to agree with him; the girl must be made to face Rosalie for a start. That—or no sensible person could do otherwise than wash his hands of her.

They went out to lunch. To a stranger, Keith might have appeared in the best of spirits. Fiddling with the table appointments while waiting to be served, he continued playful. 'Who would think you were my mama? You look almost younger than myself,' he said, making one of his peculiar, self-conscious jokes on the subject, as he noted a few eyes turned on their table—one of those jokes which made Mrs Gray wince inwardly. Christine, too, did not care for it, though for a quite other reason. Keith's really attractive manners and moods were all serious ones. But, in a markedly humourless man, these odd capers were less embarrassing than highly disturbing—or so Christine had always felt. They were startling. For they signified, she believed, extreme irritation; so, after laughing a little to please him, she grew nervous and fell silent.

However, a little later, he asked gravely and quietly, in his better manner, 'What do you really think, Christine?'

Her troubled spirit, her impulse to lean on someone, produced a cry from the heart. 'I don't know! I cannot, cannot decide. *I do wish it to be true!*'

'Yes, I can see that,' he said thoughtfully. 'Now, dear, tell me. Have you ever before fancied a likeness to Vivian Lambert in some stranger you passed in the street, for instance? You know what I mean—a sort of momentary little shock. "Whom does this person remind me of? Why, *that child.*" And then, instantly, the unlikeness is apparent. All over in a moment.

Some shadow of a likeness has made the connection. Perhaps it's only a likeness of type. But a mind so predisposed——'

Christine in a low voice confessed unwillingly, 'Yes, I have! Only just at first, though. At a distance I might catch sight of some little girl——Yes, yes! Often!' she said with repressed emotion.

'In short, you intensely wished it?'

She did not answer.

'You wished more than anything on earth to see Vivian Lambert walking towards you, safe and sound. Perhaps you wish it still? Whatever your reason may say to its likelihood, your heart longs for it?'

They returned to the flat in good time, she pale with excitement and walking hurriedly.

'Oh, if only I had had the sense to ask her address!' she exclaimed once, as if in foreboding. Nothing much else was said. Keith was thoughtful.

And the girl did not come, in spite of her promise. Christine would not leave for Hilbery; and Keith, delighted with the excuse, rang up Helena with some vague explanation and himself stayed in town, 'to bring Christine down in the morning'.

TWENTY-SEVEN

Keith would not have repined at any accident which had brought him to London, and he had taken Christine's distressed apologies with the best grace in the world.

He had dismissed the girl for an impostor. 'This fairly proves it. She is not going to face anyone—anyone but you. It was sufficiently odd that she came yesterday evening at all, after you had given her an appointment for today. You should have seen that as suspicious. She was out to avoid a meeting with any business-man of yours. Wasn't going to give you time to take advice which might turn you against her.'

She looked at him as if her mind was so much disturbed that she scarcely took in what he was saying; or took it in a wrong sense. 'Oh, yes, it is quite, quite understandable! The poor girl thought I might set a trap for her. Oh, I hope, I hope my wretched coldness and unkindness on the first occasion hasn't driven her to—give up. Oh, what a wretch I am not to have spoken out more from the heart. To have been more trusting——' Strangely enough, her thoughts kept reverting to the conclusion of the *first* interview, as if she had never said in the end, 'I believe in you.'

Keith could do nothing to comfort her, in spite of conscientious efforts; and so, having added a few last words of kindly admonition, he left the flat with relief.

In the evening, he went to a friend's house in Chelsea, where he found just such a crowded party as he had counted upon. He usually disdained such scrums, but on this occasion was there with a purpose. Having elbowed about restively among the throng for some little while, he caught sight, at a distance, of a large, pale countenance in the centre of which were roughly collected a small, sharp nose, a pair of smaller and sharper eyes, and a thin, long mouth. This unlovely visage, expressive of nothing but sharpness and meanness, filled him with the most joyful emotions. He manoeuvred till he caught the man's eye; then elaborately avoided him.

Sure enough, within a few minutes he was tapped on the shoulder.

'Ah, friend K.!' said a little, sweet, falsetto voice. 'And what of the great work? How goes it? But—hot cakes, hot cakes, you know. If I may venture my poor opinion, there should be no unavoidable delay.'

Keith looked startled; he put on a nervously sensitive face and turned his eyes aside, acting unwillingness touched with annoyance. Indeed, it was hardly acting, for he felt harried. Still, he was pleasantly conscious that the famous critic was examining him with promising interest and attention.

'Well,' he said, taking a clever risk, deliberately giving this acquaintance a cooler reception than was usually accorded him by literary folk, 'there are difficulties. I've come up against certain difficulties I never anticipated. One doesn't sufficiently appreciate the type of obstacle one may come up against in a work of this kind. But now I feel it's strange how little we knew my father—the man himself——' All this he said both dejectedly and with evidences of embarrassment; then broke off and glanced to see what effect it had had.

'But I hear there's a private diary?' the little voice squealed invitingly.

'How on earth did you hear that?' Keith cried, pretending to fall into the trap.

'There *is,* then!'

'However, it could never be published as it stands. I think it quite likely that it will never be published in its entirety,' he said, gravely, firmly, yet with a touch of flurry in his manner.

'"In its entirety"! Dear me! What's this? Why! Is it so—so—so *ample*? Well, I had understood it to be a slight affair which might be included in your preliminary biographical sketch. Would it stand on its own feet, then?'

'It *could*,' said Keith dryly. 'Very much so.'

'Oh, in *that* case, spare the blue pencil, my dear. Come be brave. Posterity will thank you. The relatives are always upset; nothing ever satisfies them. But, in fact, I suppose you and the widow are the only near relatives? What an unparalleled opportunity. Oh, let the grand old man speak for himself! Do let us have it seething in all its native juices——'

Keith pulled himself together with a visible effort, to say with mournful dignity, 'My father and I were very close together—we were very much to each other . . . Certain excisions will have to be made.'

'Yes, yes—understandable. But, oh, do be careful! We all know Thomas's style. As a bird sings! Who could tamper with a bird's song successfully? And if you can remember to give me a tip at the judicious moment, my dear soul—I say *if*——'

Keith applied a few choice words of flattery, which had their effect; and, leaving the party alone and early, he went off in a mood of tense elation.

It was a mood in which he gave scarcely a thought to Christine and her odd experience and the fancies she had built upon it. An impostor was a tiresome complication, to be sure, but he could afford to laugh at this wretched little would-be criminal who had started up out of some squalid underworld to fasten upon an easy prey. He had reason for confidence! *He knew what had happened to Vivian Lambert and that she was not likely to be walking the earth now.*

An astonishing statement—it surprised himself.

Knew? Well, as good as knew.

His knowledge (his all but knowledge), was drawn from the diary; and he believed that to any sane judgment those glaring hints, those phrases of astounding candour, which had spoken so unambiguously to himself, would carry a like conviction.

He was sure—he was almost sure.

To titillate curiosity, he had for weeks past gone about industriously dropping hints designed to give the impression that some scandalous material had come to light, and it now appeared that he had been brilliantly successful in working up a receptive atmosphere. All that remained to be done was to produce the goods. Since the goods were, literally, missing, this would have appeared to some people an insuperable difficulty. But not to Keith. The step between the wish and need to have certain facts established, and their actual establishment, was always unusually close with him, divided only by a hair's-breadth. Had he not always had the knack of making dreams come true?

And so he had gradually seen his way to producing, up to a point, the wares he had already cried.

Up to a point—yes!

But, oh, for a glimpse of those missing pages!

He returned to his hotel room in a truly abnormal mood of contentment with his own company, so sensational were his thoughts—like an artist's, creative. Vague, uncomfortable reminders of the talk with Christine now and again intruded into his excited meditations, but did not seriously disturb them.

With warm self-sympathy, with romantic unction in dwelling upon a trouble marvellously surmounted, he recalled his initial examination of the diary, the first crushing disappointment, the weary and casual fingering and re-turning of the pages—and then his eye and every faculty caught by a brief record of the first visit to Carlotta House; on which Thomas had so oddly commented: 'To the best of my judgment, a place which will be considered *impossible*. Shall I try it?'

Rising interest, careful re-examination of the whole had followed; and it had not been easy to detect pertinent phrases, recognise their relationship and bring them together so as to build up an intelligible story. Usually brief, always cryptic, embedded, as they were, in the stodgy and turgid mass of petty detail which Thomas had reported of his daily life—no, they had not leapt to the eye as they did now, now that he had signalled them out with pencilled lines drawn in the margins. Thus emphasised, they gave the reader a concise, sharp, impressionistic view of a single incident.

Whether it was a correct view, whether a subtle distortion had resulted from words brought into artificial conjunction, he was beyond considering.

Following the first visit, some early negotiations for the property were reported, with amusing evidences of Thomas's weak business-head.

Then the subject changed, but was soon seen merely to have turned a new facet. At this point, Keith had noted in the margin—for his own information?—'Reference to *The Inquisitors*, planned and written at this time'.

'A new experience—a marvellous one. I've been studying my authorities, soaking myself in them, till the atmosphere of tribunal and dungeon has become the only one which does not hinder my breathing. Yet for a long while I had put off the moment of beginning work upon my material—this heap of material which Keith has so ingeniously got together for me. (And was from the first uneasy, disapproving of its trend.) Note that I began these studies with a deep repugnance, and had to force myself on. Courage, Thomas. Cultivate a pretence of detachment, a pose of ironic objectivity, as our clever young people do. "The villainy you teach me I will execute, and it shall go hard but I will better the instructions." I felt something like that ugly excitement and perturbation with which, when very young, one opens some scatological work. Little did I guess the wonderful experience awaiting me . . .'

A lower entry recorded: 'I read slowly the account of the tortures, read and re-read, basking in the sun, sipping my glass of Jersey milk which Keith orders me. What a superb morning!'

Scattered through several pages there followed a number of references to Carlotta House, mostly expressive of business dealings and annoyances generally.

Then, a little later, he had written: 'A long, long, precious week alone with my material. Possession? Suffer us to enter into the swine. Crushed a queen-wasp with relish, slowly, slowly . . .'

But, lest one felt inclined to smile, there came the following entries: 'Remember Keith's words on the value of first-hand experience. Wanted—study of abject fear. Abject helplessness . . .

'The old bus ran well. Arrived about half past one . . .'

And here it was that the disaster had happened, three pages had been ripped out leaving three jagged stubs with not a word upon them.

The first page after the gap commenced with a number of short, disconnected entries, all belonging to the time of the Lambert tragedy—and Keith now saw the double line he himself had drawn down the margin as if it had been drawn in fire.

'I must have been mad.

'Not too late to confess, I suppose. Well, I shall not. Haven't the courage. Besides, I remember nothing clearly. That's the truth. Nothing clearly.

'Oh, that I had been to Granada! My wise boy.'

In the next marked entry, the words themselves were underlined by the attendant pencil:

'I cannot possibly like the place now. But the deed is done.'

The passage following this abounded in an odd way with gushy and redundant exclamation marks, such as are used by naive letter-writers:

'My knees shake still. The police have searched the well-house! They were not looking for the child's body, having no reason to suppose that the murder took place up here——' (The murder? And who had said it was a murder at that date?) '——They were looking for the ornament; and I gather that they would have detained the man if they could have found it and made it out to be his. His bibelots are reported to be of some value. May they find the indescribable something! May they find it! May they find it!

'They have found nothing.'

Some weeks later: 'Finished the play. God knows how. For the spirit failed me. Conducted me into the thick of the battle and there failed me. I came to myself. I went over to the ranks of evil and the Devil mocked me halfway. My wise son. The workmen are still all over the place, and while they are here, I shall have no peace—*I tremble.* Indescribably bad, leaden feeling in the head. Suspect myself of having had more than one slight stroke. On top of which—faithful, faithful, almost wifely letter from K. implying that he will accompany me to the world's end, and is for my sake prepared to put up with Carlotta House . . .'

This was followed by the diary's single and nameless reference to Christine:

'Marriage, perhaps. Marriage is my only hope. It was my original solution of the problem—a practical, commonsense one as conceived, so I think. What is it now? A few weeks ago I saw such a being as, if I were twenty years younger, or only ten——

'Saw this being again. See her as an adequate defence, a surer protection—the adversary being what he is, *a man of conscience*—than the old one. Thomas, Thomas! You lack worldly common-sense, one has heard, but here I think you recognise plainly enough the nature of your argument. Poor little champion, soft-hearted and gentle—and the eyes are still less promising, twilit, dreamy eyes under the straight, golden, delicate brows—weakness, touching weakness lies in them.'

Later, this mysterious sentiment was repeated, this strange preoccupation with 'protection', with a 'champion', cropped up again more than once; a fantasy by means of which, Keith supposed, the wretched degenerate man sought to be saved from himself. The 'adversary'? Did this denote the Devil? And the young girl apparently viewed as a sort of guardian angel?

But this reading seemed far-fetched, and the whole thought was obscure.

Nevertheless, protected as Thomas had been, safeguarded on all sides, by Keith himself, the protection sought could only be moral; which seemed very much to the purpose.

I cannot possibly like the place now. But the deed is done. Could one suppose that Thomas had been so sensitively affected by the thought of a child's death by violence in his garden, a mere figment of popular fancy, never seriously postulated, that it had made the place insupportable to him? And, if so, he was not irretrievably committed to the purchase of the house at that time, as Keith well remembered—he could not have written *of the purchase* 'the deed is done'. What deed, then?

Thomas must have had some good reason for proceeding with the buying of a much too large and entirely unsuitable property against his taste and will. Supposing something had tied him to the place, to some point in the house or garden over which he could retain control only by keeping Carlotta House in his own hands?

In the past, Keith had sometimes even wondered, tense with suspicion and hostility, whether the great man could possibly have found a means of cheating him and leading a double life. Impossible, really. Keith knew his own espionage to have been much too efficient.

But only now was he fully convinced of the futility of such surmises.

The facts were quite otherwise. He had turned up a note of the fearful price paid for a life-time's perilous banking of the central fires of the nature—one terrible, uncontrollable outbreak.

Then Keith's journalistic imagination, which threw out headlines, went to work on the old tale. The child returning to the garden to search for the trinket and someone coming upon her there. Some prowler—some monster—some horrible secret sadist who had all his life passed for an innocent citizen, a peculiarly blameless citizen. Or some good inhibited man who had lived a life of unnatural virtue? A man ripe for excess, for the sudden deed of atrocity, for the sudden, shocking breakdown of a life-time's self-discipline?

Could one really doubt what those missing pages had contained? What but a full description and confession of a crime?

What a tale! What a scoop! (The joyful and artless cry of his trade escaped him.)

But the question of how to reconcile publication of the facts on such lines as these with the behaviour of a devoted son found even Keith at a loss.

TWENTY-EIGHT

It was with a mind which had conveniently disposed of the fact that any hindrance existed here, or any check to his own theories, that he rang up Christine in the morning. Having quite settled that the girl was an impostor, a young crook whose nerve had failed her when it was insisted that she should meet someone capable of unmasking her, he was only prepared to hear that Christine had come to the same conclusion. He found, however, that she was far from taking this view. He was astonished and angry.

He returned to his room in the hotel, flung himself moodily on the bed and began to apply his wits.

Of course he had not assessed the evidence properly at the time. It had seemed scarcely worth while. Now that he did so, he was staggered by its weight, and not so much by its plausibility as by the intelligent precision of the details. There was nothing in the narrative of that disjointed character which betrays the dream origin—none of those missing links in the chain of reasoning, the lack of support, the tell-tale haziness. So here he had to abandon the startling and peculiar and exciting idea which had crossed his mind at the outset, and had recurred as a possibility at intervals during the night; the idea that Christine might have had one of those morbidly vivid dreams which make upon the hapless dreamer an impression of undeniable reality, such as attack the sickening mind. He had suspected long ago that she was one not in good health.

But considering the matter again now, in the critical light of the morning, he felt unpleasantly impressed.

An hour's hard thinking enabled him to account for much of it; and calling on Christine again before leaving for Hilbery, he was able to say, gravely and warningly, 'One has got to face it, dear. I grant you that at first sight much of the evidence appears startling. But the plain truth is that there's nothing—no, absolutely nothing—in all that story she told you that a stranger couldn't have picked up from the Freemantle woman. A stranger meeting her casually in South America, in fact. Simply by listening to her talk. As for a stranger who had been deliberately primed with all those details, what a performance *she* could put up! Now, I wonder if the Freemantle woman is really dead?

'Oh, yes, it's not improbable that the girl actually comes from Peru, or what not. Though, as for the South American adventures——But I'll tell you what has occurred to me about *them* another time . . . Yes, but to have come from Peru—that means nothing. An impostor might very well come from Peru. *Very* well. Just the place to come from. Or Ecuador? Better still . . . Good! So we have Miss Freemantle, possibly still alive somewhere in the South American republics, and this girl coming over at her instigation, primed with the whole story. To lay claim to Lambert's fortune? Perhaps. Or to fasten on *you*, if no better may be and Rosalie proves too hard a proposition? But I seem to feel that she would have someone behind her in this country. What if the Freemantle woman came with her and is lying low somewhere? Lurking. We must remember that she didn't turn up till there was a smell of money—a very suspicious circumstance.

'Well, clearly, my dear, we can't go on at all without some detective work. Official? Or unofficial? If we are really dealing with a nest of crooks, we must take measures accordingly.

'That was a good point you made about her teeth, by the way—a palpable hit. Yes, the child *was* a bit buck-toothed, wasn't she! I remember that point clearly.' And he laughed. 'Did the teeth actually show much, do you remember? Still, you know, they were only her first teeth probably. It would be a good idea, however, to ask her if she ever wore one of those wire contraptions, braces, or whatever the equivalent is in modern dentistry. Try to remember—if ever she turns up again, that is to say . . . What a bad girl she must be! So bad and bold, that, really——But none but a complete innocent would imagine it possible to carry through an imposture on such a scale without quite a deal of backing. And she does not appear to be that. No, she's no simpleton. So either that cannot be her aim and she is just an amateur crook who means to fasten on you alone and be content with small pickings, or else there are others behind her. Do be on your guard with her, won't you. Make no attempt to manage her yourself. Send for me instantly—don't hesitate—forget that I am ever busy! . . . Should you imagine that Miss Freemantle had ever been on the stage?'

But he found Christine immovable in what he considered to be her delusion.

She pointed out that although the girl might have got many of the details from Miss Freemantle, it did not seem as if she could have got all of them. There were facts about Carlotta House as it was twelve years ago, and particulars not only about the exterior, which anyone might be able to note in passing, but about the inside. Facts, too, about people who had been gone so many years from the district as to be forgotten.

But more, much more! There were things which only herself and the real Vivian could have known.

'Known only to you?' Keith murmured, as if arrested by this remark. She did not notice his manner, but, encouraged, cried feelingly, 'Oh, Keith, if only you had seen and heard her for yourself!'

'I begin very much to doubt if I ever shall see her for myself,' he answered in a significant tone which she did not understand, and the upward twist of one corner of his mouth was much in evidence. 'Do you know, I have a queer feeling that our mysterious young claimant is not going to show herself to anyone but *you* . . . Well, in short, I've an idea which I may explain later. Leave it for the present—leave it.' And he waved it aside. 'But, now, dear, consider. Miss Freemantle would probably know the inside of Carlotta House as well as the back of her own hand, and could supply any of these details of twelve years ago which you build so much upon. Consider. Most local people living in the neighbourhood of such a picturesque, derelict old place, break in at one time or another out of pure, idle curiosity.'

Nevertheless, it was fated that he should come back to Hilbery in extreme discontentment with his 'management' of Christine. Excited, carried away by his secret thoughts, he had been a bit premature, and just before leaving her had broached a subject he would have done better to leave to another time. He had turned back to say, with rare impulsiveness, 'Christine, do you remember telling me of that curious glimpse—a sort of psychic experience, you thought at the time, I gathered—that glimpse you had during the lunch-hour in the garden? Seeing something pink through the grass at a distance? The pink of the child's frock, as you first thought?'

'Yes, I do,' she said in a low voice, looking much startled. 'But how was it——? When did I——? Oh, I know. We were stretched out on the lawn after a bout of tennis that first year——'

And she had suddenly raised her head from the grass and begun to pour out her story. Nor had she done it for the sake of comfort. She had spoken of it, as it seemed to her now, without much feeling, with only an excited satisfaction in being able to impress her impressive son-in-law with so strange and interesting an experience. She had told it with a childish sense of importance—almost, as might be said, in a showing-off spirit. The older Christine found such a frame of mind incredible as it was horrible. But she well remembered the temporary state of light-mindedness, or light-heartedness, which she had enjoyed at that time, when perhaps a certain animal satisfaction in her marriage had served to lull her most feeling self, and the whole tragic experience had almost ceased to pain her. Anyway, so it had come about; she had been moved to confide.

She added in troubled wonder, 'I feel it's so odd that I should ever have told you. I never spoke of it to anyone else.'

Keith smiled. 'Well, we're very good friends, dear, aren't we? And were, even in those early days.' (There was no irony in his words; he meant them.) 'But, now, how long was it—could you possibly remember?—before you plucked up courage to go and see?'

After all, now she could think of it as the bad dream it was, consider the terrible query closed for ever. She admitted, 'I suppose, several minutes.'

Then Keith made a blunder. She was at the window, drawing up the blind a little way, only to lower it again, and did not turn round. He could not see her face, certainly; and as he could not imagine it, either, he inquired, 'Several minutes! H'm. Plenty of time, then. Might the child really have been there? Could she have been carried away during the interval?'

There was a silence. She answered at length in a voice cold and trembling with shock, 'Vivian is alive.'

Keith bit his lip, pulled the situation together as well as he could, and rather abruptly took his leave.

He had not been able to persuade her to come down to Hilbery.

She felt cold with distrust.

Something in Keith's manner, even at the beginning, had struck and frightened her, and after he had left her she set herself to grope anxiously for the reason. 'I have a queer feeling that she is not going to show herself to anyone but you.' Blind apprehension stirred in her again. For what could he have meant? She felt that remark, spoken with a significant smile, had had a hidden meaning.

She thought of the many terrible mistakes which had been made by witnesses to identity, many of whom had been so certain, so entirely convinced, that this or that person was, or was not, the one in question; and for a space she concluded, despairing, that she would never be certain enough in her own mind to swear that the girl was Vivian Lambert. Cruel doubts at the heart of it would always remain.

So, painfully she turned to re-examining her experiences, resolved to cast up the points against credulous acceptance rather than for it.

But she was held up at the outset by an odd, an extraneous little memory. For, starting at the beginning, with the meeting on the staircase, she suddenly found herself arrested at that moment when she had turned to the window and looked down into the street with a touch of dizziness. And for the first time she recognised the full singularity of that pair of bizarre figures she had seen strolling on the far pavement. Could such figures really have passed? Or, rather, could they have been quite as she remembered them? With surprise, then with astonishment, she saw in her mind's eye the man's huge hat and striped poncho, the woman's peculiar bowler-like head-gear and wide, swinging skirts which, squat and dumpy as she was, made her look like some sort of toy—a figure weighted at the base, or a top. Many varieties of dark-faced people in barbaric costume were to be seen in that part of London; she supposed she had accepted these two at the time because her mind was so greatly preoccupied. But they were surely South American Indians? And she had never before seen these people in their native dress walking the streets of the West End. Many elaborate African toilets she had seen; but none, she was sure, from that part of the world. She now concluded that imagination must have coloured the memory, in spite of her honest efforts. Indeed, it must be so! The coincidence was too strange.

Still, it was but a detail and did not strictly belong to the encounter at all.

What she had to ask herself was whether she had been quite convinced at the end of that interview on the staircase; and to this she was obliged to answer, no, by no means. Or perhaps her emotions had been satisfied and for the time being had silenced the complaints of her reason. She had parted with the girl with a cold warning, though against her heart; and had come home horribly agitated.

Suddenly she saw, on looking back, that it was the evening visit which had yielded all the clinching evidence. Yes—the whole of it! So she began conscientiously to examine that part of the adventure. 'From the beginning,' she said to herself firmly—and abruptly was faced by the fact that she had no remembrance whatever of letting the girl into the flat, and for some seconds her mind threshed affrightedly, groping for the lost moment. Then she recalled, with flooding relief, that of course she had thrown herself on the bed and had fallen asleep and had waked to find the sallow young girl with the sarcastic eyebrows standing beside her bed in the dim, aqueous light which the blinds let through when the sun had passed off them. Seeing she was awake, the girl had dangled a bunch of keys, saying coolly, 'I thought it was for the benefit of callers, as I couldn't make you hear. You should be more careful, surely, in this honest city—or such is my experience of it.' Then Christine had realised that in her agitation she must have left the keys hanging in the outer lock—an oversight without precedent, for she was nervous and careful, she, who when she stayed with her mother was always on the look-out for such accidents, Mrs Gray being so extremely casual about locks and bolts.

But now another thing struck her, a memory which sent her heart into her mouth. She had not thought of it at the time, but her last consciousness before going off to sleep that evening had been of a glint of metal from the desk, where a thread of sunshine, falling sidelong upon the window at that hour, had slipped through the side of the blind. That gleam had come from the bunch of keys—so she had thought then. *But the keys were then in the lock.* How did she know? Why, simply because they must have been.

Here she ran to the desk—but only to find among the objects strewing it several small metal things which would have glinted in the sunshine. Lying there sleepily, she would easily have taken for granted that the gleam came from the keys.

Then all the evidence of the evening before came flooding back and filled her with fresh courage.

So she was on the whole cheered by this review, and taking herself in hand, thinking of her mother and Helena, she went down to Hilbery on the following day in rather good spirits, although she had heard nothing. The girl would certainly appear in time; any accident might explain her failure—illness, or mere loss of courage and fear of difficulties, or misgivings about the law of a strange country. Besides, it was most likely that she was not a very dependable person.

'She told me a good many little lies, of course I noticed that. She did not remember the ornament, for instance, that was clear, but pretended she did, perhaps thinking it would sound better.' But even if she was cheating a little, here and there, even if some of her evidence had been come by dishonestly—even that did not prove her an impostor, Christine thought in triumph. The girl might have been foolishly driven to supplement her true memories with faked ones. She wished she had remembered to say this to Keith. Yes, still there was hope.

Then she suddenly thought, 'That hair! Why, of course it's tinted!' and laughed at herself for her own lack of common shrewdness.

TWENTY-NINE

Keith came home in excitement and in the fixed determination to run the girl to earth and prove her an impostor. The foolish mystification verged on farce, and yet might be dangerous. It held up his plans, it was a standing threat; he meant to dispatch it quickly. The essential thing was to find the girl speedily and discredit her. Otherwise the story might leak out and inconvenience him, if no worse. The interruption alone was maddening enough. He did not intend to go to the police—he wished no publicity for the matter; and partly for the same reason, and partly because he thought exceptionally well of his own acumen, he would not employ a private detective. He was a practised hunter-up of facts, and not without reason assumed that the little mystery would not detain him long.

A full, sceptical and elaborately witty account of Christine's adventure was brought back to Carlotta House—and somewhat wasted upon the home audience; which grasped the facts with enthusiasm but had no ear for subtleties.

Helena was thrown into delighted amazement. She was at once of the opinion that the girl was an impostor (finding herself rather disappointingly in agreement with her husband), but she prized the adventure for that very reason and hoped for sensation on a big scale.

Mrs Gray, on the other hand, was hardly surprised, now that the thing had happened. She would hear nothing of imposture and seemed unable to entertain the idea. 'Why, what are you saying? *Of course* it's Vivian!' She was astonished that anyone could think otherwise, and treated any who did so to a gentle mockery; for the happy and hopeful tale was always the one her mind most easily credited.

On Keith's advice, it was decided to keep the story between the three of them, and within a quarter of an hour the whole house was agog with it. Keith went into his study and shut himself up to plan his campaign, sending out frequent calls for quiet. But that phrase, 'a nest of crooks', which he had unfortunately indulged in, excited Helena so much that she opened the study door without knocking—a grave misdemeanour.

'I do wonder you left her up there all by herself, Keith! They'll have been down on her as soon as your back was turned.'

He gave it up and came out, infected by the general excitement. Acquaintances dropping in, most inopportunely, were regaled with a few hints and went away with half the story. They were local people and of no influence, but still——Keith shrugged and bitterly blamed Helena afterwards, but in fact had himself talked.

A call to town had set their minds at rest on the score of Christine's danger from accomplices; they learned that none had appeared; and then the next day Christine herself arrived.

She was received with ardour, was questioned exhaustively and met with opinions far less reasoned than her own; and when they had heard her out, enthusiasm mounted higher than ever.

Mrs Gray looked ahead. 'Shall you invite her here, Helena? The poor little thing must be quite friendless.'

'What—have her here?' cried Helena, with her eyes starting. 'Oh, rather, anything you like. Let 'em all come.'

'Yes, we might—so we might,' Keith conceded, laughing, not without malice. But a moment's consideration and perhaps a glance at Christine, caused him to add seriously, 'Well, no, Mother, that would hardly do.'

'Oh, very well, my dear. If it isn't convenient, I'll do it myself. Rosalie may not care to. We must make the poor child welcome.' It seemed as if she expected to see Vivian appear as a small girl in a pink dress, just as she had last been seen.

But at this flight on Mrs Gray's part, and similar ones by the others, Keith took alarm. At this rate, they would all be recognising the young crook if she did turn up, and then a wider public might be similarly inclined, 'No, no, Mother. Wishful thinking won't alter the facts. If this girl appears—*if* I say—we cannot accept her without a shred of real proof. She'll have to make good her claim. We really cannot have a band of crooks fastening upon us.'

In spite of the severity of these words, nobody was much affected by them, least of all Mrs Gray. Helena was again much elated by the phrase 'a band of crooks'. Throughout tea, they talked on the same theme tirelessly. Helena suggested giving a party for the girl, and this happy thought delighted Mrs Gray, who imagined herself saying, 'Now, who do you think this is? Why, it's Vivian Lambert! You remember? Little Vivian Lambert who set us all to turning the place upside-down for her. Well, all the time, she was in South America with that odd, kind woman Miss Freemantle.'

Christine herself, in this uncritical atmosphere, began to yield to something of that same bemusement and intoxication of the judgment which had affected her during the evening visit, the crucial encounter. Almost silent herself, in a mood of buoyancy as sweet as it was new, she listened in absence of mind—though not without an inward gaiety at the extravagances of the debate—while the long, colourful narrative unrolled itself in her memory, falsified a little, brighter, clearer in its more welcome phases, like a dream, a happy dream unconsciously adorned in recollection. In fact, she was tired and at moments almost drowsed in listening. They were talking a good deal of nonsense, of course, and it made her smile; there was no need to go as far as giving parties. Nevertheless, it was true that others had now accepted the possibility of the girl's return and seen nothing incredible about it.

It was Helena, not Keith, who voiced scepticism at last.

'Why, good Lord, you don't really suppose the girl's genuine, do you?' she cried suddenly; and, standing with arms akimbo, over the piled tray, gaped on them all.

'Well, Helena,' Keith said with indulgent humour, 'haven't you yourself been saying you'd make her welcome here? So you were proposing to tolerate a crook in the house, were you?'

'Oh, I don't know—why not? A nice change. A bit of fun. Something funny to think of.' And she plainly meant, 'More fun than if she was the real thing.'

However, this simple expression of scepticism called a halt to fancy. Even Mrs Gray became more sober in her outlook, and no more was said of killing the fatted calf.

The household dispersed and went about its several businesses. Discussion was carried on through open doors, argument continued on stairs or in passages, wherever a pair chanced to meet. Christine, helping Helena in the kitchen, approached the great fireplace where modern cooking appliances were now ranged and studied it with fresh eyes.

'And the old oven, Helena? Do you remember it? I don't think I ever knew there was such a thing.'

'The old oven? What next? Why, there it is, up by the side of the mantelpiece. You can just see the old brick surround under the plaster, can't you.'

'Oh, then I suppose it was bricked up when Thomas took the house. Vivian said it was "deep". She told me she used to think it was a secret passage.'

'Well, I dare say it was a fair size. Fancy, they used to bake bread there. Put in hot coals and then raked out the ashes. What a filthy mess! If Thomas hadn't spoiled it, I suppose I should be doing some period cooking. So "Vivian" remembers the old oven, does she? She's certainly smart——'

But then, drawing her great, red hands out of the washing-up bowl, slowly rubbing them up and down the sides of her apron, Helena turned eyes blank with thought towards the brick surround, and presently added, like one who had discovered a point for herself. 'Why, look here—how does she know about *that*?'

Christine answered triumphantly, smiling, 'Ah, yes—how?'

Helena was much struck; she could not account to herself for the stranger's knowledge of the old oven.

But Keith was no longer amused. At this rate, it would make little difference that the girl was actually an impostor. She would be Vivian Lambert to the crowd, and to all intents and purposes. Rosalie would inevitably be drawn in, and, ignorant and credulous, and without the power to assess evidence properly, as such a woman would certainly be, she might well recognise the long-lost child—even though it was not likely that she would welcome her with open arms. The law itself might be gullible—or at least helpless in such circumstances. The prospect was suddenly threatening.

The very next morning confirmed some of these fears.

Christine, Helena and Mrs Gray, shopping on the Parade, were challenged by Rosalie. They had just dumped the final goods into the back of the car and had settled themselves, Helena at the wheel, when a strident and angry voice bawled into their ears, 'Well, Christine—well, Mrs Gray—what's this I hear?' Rosalie had just burst from the bar-room door of

Hilbery's one 'hotel,' and her face was red and wrathful and her breath smelled of drink. Mrs Gray leaned forward vivaciously from her seat beside Helena and gave her a bland welcome.

'How do we know what you've heard, Rosalie? Who told you?'

'Why, the milkman.'

Mrs Gray was much amused. She began laughing gaily and turning upon the dismayed Helena a teasing eye, which had sprightly reference to Keith in it. This was what came of keeping it a dead secret. And what was there really against broadcasting the wonderful news to the whole world? They offered Mrs Lambert a lift, this seeming to be the easiest thing to do with her.

'Yes, Vivian's alive, Rosalie, she has come back! It was a shame not to tell you at once, my dear, so that you could rejoice with us.' But even Mrs Gray could perceive that Rosalie was not rejoicing.

'So it's true!' And suddenly losing colour and aggressiveness, Rosalie scrambled into the back of the car and collapsed next to Christine amidst a pile of shopping.

'So you're hiding the girl away up there, are you? Waiting till you've fixed things up with the lawyers, etc., to let me have it from both barrels! It's a shame!'

'Vivian? Up at Carlotta House? Oh, no, my dear. How I wish she was! Unfortunately, just at present, we don't even know where she is——'

'Ah, well, now listen!—it won't wash, let me tell you. And if this young baggage, whoever she may be, imagines she's going to walk off with my money as easy as that——'

'But, Rosalie, it's Vivian herself. And about the money she will be, I'm sure, perfectly reasonable——'

'Nice of her!'

So they went on talking confusedly and at cross purposes till they drew up before Rosalie's gate, and here, sitting at rather close quarters, conferring in an atmosphere vaguely spirituous, they at last succeeded in gaining Rosalie's attention with a sober account of the facts.

Mrs Lambert listened open-mouthed, and then was violently indignant, denouncing it as 'a bloody try-on'. She rejected and scoffed at the proofs which they pressed on her—but all this was only a first natural reaction and in a few minutes she grew thoughtful and gazed from face to face in an alarm which verged on tearfulness. And when she was asked, 'Now, Rosalie, what do you think?' she was silent a moment, slumped back in her seat, and then said complainingly, 'Why, now I hardly know whether I'm coming or going . . . I never did like the child, and I've told Christine why—but keep her out of her rightful inheritance I never would want to. It's a blow to me— but it always did seem a bit phoney, me getting all that money. Only, what I say is, to give it up to George's girl would be one thing—though a wrench. But to give it up to a total stranger just because she fancies it—and one who's going to blacken my character, too, you may be sure—that's another pair of shoes. And so,' Rosalie cried, tossing her head with sudden spirit, 'I shall fight it!'

'Of course I told her that she must meet you—and we are all agreed that she must—before anything can be done,' Christine assured her, with the habitual little frown of concentration very pronounced between her brows.

Whereat Rosalie cried out, quite in a tone of alarm, 'Oh, for God's sake, I don't want ever to set eyes on her again!' Then she laughed, dolefully. 'Well, there I go! Talking as if it was really Vivian, which I don't believe, I needn't tell you—not for a minute. In any case, of course I shall have to see this one, whoever she is, if she means business. Pleased to meet her, I'm sure!'

Christine suggested that the meeting should take place either at Carlotta House, or at her own flat in town—anywhere in preference to the house where the child had once lived. 'Then you could ask her details about her old home, things she must remember. That little china cottage, now—the little house which she used to have by her bed with a candle in it, as a treat. No one ever forgets things like that!'

'Why, it's rummy she didn't look me up straight away, when you think of it. If she *is* Vivian——'

They could not deny it.

Rosalie pondered. 'I don't know what to think. I must say, it would be like her. Of course I've always said to myself, "If ever she does turn up, alive or dead, she'll make trouble for me." And here she is, you see. At least——Gosh, yes, I mustn't talk of this one like that, must I? I shall have to be careful. A sharp lawyer'd make something out of that sort of bloomer—if ever it comes to it. Catch me out on that, wouldn't he? What does she call herself?'

'Well—Vivian Lambert.'

'Ah, yes, I suppose so . . . Now, look here. If she can prove it to my satisfaction, I'll just divide the damned money and give her half of it. Settle it out of court. You tell her so from me. Tell her she'll get far more out of it that way than if she goes to law and gets into the hands of those blood-suckers. But, by God, she'll have to prove it. I've got one or two things in mind which she must know, if she is Vivian—things she can't possibly know if she's not . . . I wouldn't, myself, Christine, go too much by looks. Children change so.'

Told of all this later, Keith was ready to tear his hair. 'Very generous of Mrs Lambert, to be sure! She could hardly do anything more foolish. That would be to put a premium on fraud.' But he restrained himself. He judged it was useless. The only thing to do was to get to work without a moment's delay; and this he did.

He had already inserted a notice in the personal columns of more than one of the large daily papers. 'Vivian. Please communicate with C. A.' But nothing came of it. Now he drove Helena to call upon the Chief Constable of the county, with whom she was distantly connected, he being a cousin of her noble father. Keith despaired of her making anything of this mission, however carefully he coached her, and was in ecstasies of impatience at having to employ so inept a tool, where his own charm and diplomacy might have been exerted with such effect. But he fancied himself to be no favourite with his wife's family. Helena came back with a few details which did neither side any good. A mild curiosity had evidently been aroused in Sir Edmund Willows by this sudden interest in the obscure person of Miss Freemantle; but he had not objected to supplying a little information, harmless and of no interest to the police as it was.

Keith retired in moody perplexity.

Far more had been known of Miss Freemantle's affairs and movements at that time than had appeared, as he ought to have suspected. The police had not overlooked her and her timely exodus. She had really gone to South America with a boy, a child of about Vivian Lambert's age. Her English relatives, moreover, had supplied a dossier. She had once brought a child with her when she went to see them and told them it was her own. They had not believed her; they had supposed she had adopted him. She was, they said, a person who enjoyed shocking people, or taking them in; she was, in short, the born hoaxer. Completely untrustworthy, capable of any sort of exhibition, she was a sore trial to decent connections. And clearly these worthy relatives would have been not unwilling to assist her transition to another part of the world, as far away as possible. Perhaps it was they who had done a little wire-pulling for her, while sensibly blind to her motive for wishing to leave the country in something of a hurry. They were a shipowning family, and it was in one of their own vessels that their undesirable relative and her little companion had sailed.

Apparently satisfied that she had nothing to do with the case, the police had not followed the woman any further. She was known to be a rolling stone and might well have rolled from one end of the lower continent to the other in the course of twelve years. Yes, she had also been on the stage at one time. In short, she was an oddity, but not a criminal one. So it was believed. Certainly they could not undertake to trace her—unless there were criminal grounds for inquiry.

Of course Helena, obedient to Keith's instructions, had dropped no hint of the strange revenant on their own doorstep. Yet perhaps Sir Edmund was not unfamiliar with local rumours.

This was discouraging. The facts did not actually favour the girl, but as far as they went they did not quarrel with her story, and certainly they did not eliminate possibility.

For supposing the girl's tale was true? Supposing it was not the boy at Southampton with whom Miss Freemantle had got off in the end, but the girl? A little connivance here and there, a little calculating upon the human disposition to wink at a bold try-on, and a little pulling of strings might have done it, he supposed. Such a woman would obviously have had no deep-laid plans but would have done everything with an impudent simplicity—which in itself might have defeated investigators.

He judged the tale to be almost impossible, and yet not quite so.

But on the immediate and complete unmasking of the pretender hung his whole future. All his hopes depended on it. If he wrote and published Thomas's biography on the lines he had planned, according to the revelation of the diary, what would be the fate of the book, *what would be his own fate*, if a living Vivian Lambert then made her appearance? His position would be horrible. It would not avail him that *he* knew her to be an impostor, if general opinion did not agree with him. The girl must be found and completely discredited.

Other lines of inquiry suggested themselves to him and, during the succeeding weeks and months, he followed them with skill and persistence; but all to no purpose. He had means and sources of information not open to everyone, too. He was passionately impatient for the girl to give a sign, Christine herself could not have been more impatient. But the silence continued. Then, as time went by and there was not a word, not a hint, his spirits rose, if somewhat feverishly. Christine had returned to town. He got to work upon the sketch again and upon the preparation of the diary—a peculiarly exacting task and one which would tax his powers of subtle expression to the uttermost. Blank silence was not what he had hoped for, but it was the next best thing to immediate exposure of the fraud. And it was really extremely odd—interesting. He could not suppose that such a young crook would be working alone—yet a gang would hardly have been scared off so easily. Where had she hidden herself? What had happened? Do what he would, he could come upon no trace of her. And this fact in itself at last impressed him as the most striking of all.

Gradually, an exciting and extremely odd possibility, which had crossed his mind once before, crept back to take possession of him. No sooner had he given the idea harbourage than it obsessed him in the usual way, and he was presently convinced that he had at last found the solution.

A grim one, a tragic one!

THIRTY

The light of a November afternoon closing mistily and showing a carmine, rayless sun through the stripped boughs, entering the hall sparely through one tall window, gave to pale skin a faint, delicate incandescence like a symptom of fever: a light which allied itself with gloom in some strange manner. Christine, standing on the second stair, tentatively put out her hand, touched the rail and at last shook it so that it produced a thin, high sound. She remained pondering. Her face looked a little drawn, with features a shade sharpened, as by illness.

She had been through terrible alternations of hope and despair during the last few months, and had come down from London this afternoon on a crest of hope raised by a new line of search which had been thrust upon her after a long, melancholy space of inaction, and had not yet been proved vain.

She believed herself to have come near to another encounter.

In Oxford Street a few weeks ago she had suddenly felt abnormally tired and, fearful of fainting, had taken a taxi. She had sunk thankfully back into the corner, and then, just as the car started to move, glancing out wearily at the crowd on the pavement, she was presented with a fleeting vision of the missing girl. Standing almost on the kerb—for it seemed there was scarcely two feet between them—the figure was for that very reason seen in a mere flash, a moving glimpse; and with a loud cry, Christine had seized the handle of the door—but the taxi at that moment gathering speed, and a warning and profane exclamation from the driver, had caused her to hesitate fatally. 'Oh,' she had stammered wildly to the man, 'but I've seen someone, I must stop!' The driver, surly, indignant, growling, had drawn up at the next opportunity, and she had tumbled forth, thrust a note into his hand and rushed back to the place. It always seems extraordinary in such cases how far beyond one's mark a vehicle can carry one. Although she had returned as fast as she could press, thrusting along with an unwonted lack of consideration, the crowd did not permit hurry—and then she was not quite sure of the spot.

It was all one; there was no sign of the girl; and distracted, almost out of her senses, she had thrust up and down the street half a dozen times—asked senseless questions of passers-by—had anyone seen a young girl, a short young girl, poorly dressed, standing perhaps at that spot five minutes ago? Most had answered dryly, if at all; one or two had asked questions from curiosity, or perhaps from pity—her sincerity and distress were unmistakable. How was the girl dressed, for instance? In what colour? Strangely enough, she could not say. For was it possible to say pink—bright pink?

Afterwards she could not bear to think of this incident, yet was forced to dwell on it. A certain circumstance increased her horror. It was this. If that air of poverty, of sickliness, had been noticeable before, how much more marked it was now! And her thought was that a young girl friendless in a foreign land, and in all likelihood ill-taught and ignorant, brought to distress by no fault of her own, might easily drift on to the streets in pure desperation. She was ashamed of so readily inclining to this particular dread. But it gnawed at her. From the last glimpse, she had snatched a look of debasement, stamped hard where it had before been shadowed. And the whole range of error and punishment—prison, infirmary, madhouse—which waited on the broken of life, henceforth engaged her fears.

Then the simple, timid, decent woman took to haunting the West End at night, in the artless hope of saving the mysterious one, persecutor or victim, from the classic fate of the lost girl; one who, whether Vivian or not, had appealed to her compassion at least once in vain.

It was no wonder that she had as yet kept all this to herself, for she partly knew her own folly and the fevered tone of her imaginings.

But if the lost would return! Or if the dead would arise to speak one lucid word which would allay for ever killing uncertainty! Once she herself had formed the wild prayer, 'Vivian, if you are dead, rise up and tell me so.'

Lost in these thoughts, she gazed into the dull, red sun with eyes enlarged as by illness and retaining the fearful and dazed expression of the physically preyed upon.

Keith came quietly to his workroom door, which was ajar, and observed her for a few moments through the crack. Feeling him there—for she had hardly heard him—she laid her hand on the rail and again made it utter the thin, faint cry which sounded plaintively in the triste and sombre setting of the twilight. Then she turned round, smiling.

'Such a trifle, Keith! Can you really believe Miss Freemantle would have remembered it—just from the kind of casual look round the house which is all we can suppose she ever had? Now, can you? I know one can't say it's impossible—but it *is nearly* impossible. Anyway—what an imagination she would need to see that a thing like that would be so significant! But an exploring child—yes, *she'd* remember it, to the end of her days. She'd pull and pull at the rail to make the noise again—it would please her.' And she gave him a friendly, coaxing look, wishing so much to charm away this incomprehensible obduracy. For it was a strange, sulky opposition, really antagonistic, and she had had to face it from the beginning, and it had long tormented her. She suddenly resolved to challenge it now.

'Did *you* remember that it creaked, Christine?' he said rather coldly.

'Oh, of course, yes, I knew. Living in the house, as I've done, time and again, how could I not know?'

'Yes, *you* would know.'

Something in his tone struck her more unhappily than ever. She had meant to tell him of the glimpse in Oxford Street; now she felt that it was not the moment. Something else was more urgent. Touching the rail fitfully between her words, she said with great uneasiness, 'You've spoken to me like that more than once—yes, a good many times, I've noticed—saying "But *you* would know"—"*You* would have remembered" this or that. What do you mean? You're not suggesting, I suppose, that she could read my thoughts? That she got things out of my mind? A spectacular case of telepathy!' And she laughed.

Instead of answering or smiling in response, as she had expected, 'What do you really think of the South American part of the story?' he asked gravely. 'Did you really feel that the girl had been in Peru?'

'Of course!'

Keith stood looking on the ground. 'Well, I'm not so sure,' he said in a rather too gentle tone at length. 'Let me tell you what I think of it. In the first place, their itinerary struck me as peculiar.'

'Oh, it was all perfectly clear as she told it. And so vivid!'

'Yes, it was the South American chapter especially which struck me from the first moment as—what shall I say?—*derivative*. It gave me pause—among the many other doubtful points.'

She hesitated. She was conscious of a shade of bewilderment, of confusion; of a breath of vague, baseless fear stealing about her heart. 'Oh,' she murmured, 'what do you mean by that?'

'I mean such details can be got from books—that such information is very easily come by—that it might be taken from a dozen among the hundreds of commonplace travel books which are published every year. It consisted of just such a collection of picturesque details, of colourful incidents—judging by your own account, of course. I have nothing else to judge by! . . . Have you yourself, Christine, ever read any such travel books with that part of South America for its subject? Then you know the kind of thing. Written to popular taste——'

Christine felt an impulse to put her hand to her head, as if she had been asked some very difficult question. 'No,' she said finally. 'No, it all seemed strange to me. And yet I almost felt myself there as she spoke—it was so vivid! You couldn't suppose she hadn't seen it all with her own eyes. You could tell—*it was true.*'

'It seemed to you true because it was familiar? As familiar things seem?'

'How could it be familiar?' she said slowly.

'Well, well—leave it . . . No, but you must have considered that anyone wanting to pass as a Vivian Lambert who had been kidnapped and taken to South America might have got all the local colour out of a book. My dear, of course! Of course she would have mugged it all up—got up the subject to impress you and give realism to her story.'

'Oh, it's simply that you've made up your mind that she's a pretender—made it up from the beginning! You did not want her to be Vivian—I felt you didn't, from the first moment. You've got some reason—for wishing to make her out a criminal. Oh, I feel it!' But her breath failed her. Her gentle nature could not endure contest, or to use hard words to anyone.

He said, after a weighty pause, as if reluctantly, 'A criminal? I may think her something worse than that . . . But—dear Christine!—never mind, never mind what I think. My views may change. Meanwhile, I'll keep it to myself.' He turned away, his eyes still on the ground, while she stared at a grave profile; he moved, he receded, and shut the door of the study as quietly behind him as if he had been shutting it upon a sick-room. This she noted. It distracted her for an instant—a movement so unnatural. However, at last conscious of bewilderment, she found herself asking, '*Something worse?*' And she stared out at the rayless sun. Then she thought suddenly, 'Why did I answer "no" about those books? What a lie!' And she felt shocked and degraded, for she was ordinarily a naively truthful person. She had lied for the reason that children do—because she was afraid. 'But at least it's true that I've not read such a book for many years,' she defended herself.

She returned to considering Keith's manner from the beginning; his reception of her story, and the way he had first reasoned with her, taking great pains to try to convince her that she was deceived. Now she realised that for a long while he had made little attempt to argue; it had seemed as if he no longer tried seriously to combat the evidence she eagerly pressed on him, but merely listened almost with an air of humouring her. Today, for the first time for many weeks, he had reasoned with her again, seriously. Not only seriously—gravely, with a sort of cold displeasure.

Suddenly a painful, incredible suspicion rushed upon her. It was not merely that he did not believe in the girl's claim. *He did not believe herself, Christine.* But this was fantastic; Keith could not suspect her of concocting a lying story, of supplying information to back the girl's tale and help her out! And with what object?

Springing to his door and opening it without ceremony she cried into the room, 'I can't hide it from myself any longer! Can you possibly think I'm making up any of it—any of the evidence?'

Keith had switched on the table-lamp. He was standing with his back towards her and had glanced round at her entrance, flicked her one inscrutable look; then with a ducking movement of shoulders and head, which the light behind his figure accentuated, turned round to the desk again, making a play of interest in something there, rustling papers busily.

'No, I certainly don't think you have consciously made up anything—not consciously,' he said in the quietest tone, as if most carefully avoiding any sort of emphasis. But that inadvertent hiding of the head, as it were, took all her horrified attention for the moment; it was so eloquent of surprised treachery.

She felt, as if he had suddenly put on a hideous appearance, panic-stricken. Little more than that. And she fled instinctively. She found herself back in the hall, which the lamp in the room had plunged into darkness for her eyes, standing again on the stairs, pulling senselessly at the handrail; and here the words 'not consciously' crashed down on her and were like a blow on the head, a stunning blow. Reaching her own room, she did not know how she had come there or what time had passed till the moment when she stood before the dressing-table, saying to herself, 'What does he think? That I am mad!' Then, in the last of the faint, rubious light, she saw her own face in the mirror, pale against the interior darkness, calm, mild, quenched—her own face. A face which gave little satisfaction to herself, in spite of its conventional beauty, for she vaguely felt it to be a face negative and unfinished, faded before ever having blossomed, telling no story, having no story to tell. Still—her own face, unchanged, nothing questionable about it. And she whispered, 'Nonsense, nonsense!' taking heart.

But there came a misgiving about this very certitude, and therefore about herself. She peered closer. The live eyes glittered, the brows arched widely, as she made the effort to search, in that dusky light, her own expression. Such scrutinies always bring a sense of strangeness, a hint of deeper, sinister knowledge in the image. Pensively she turned on the light.

Panic had burned out now, but she was overwhelmed by a sense of weakness and helplessness.

THIRTY-ONE

A little later in the week of her visit, snow fell from the yellow sky which days past had displayed. The fall was not heavy; but frost bound it hard. And the bitterly raw air came as an invader, with the quality of surprise. Yet the glacial crust which the night had produced, the compressed snow on the paths, could be felt to creak as one walked on it—for whether it was felt or heard was in doubt. The frozen crust was shifting upon the warm earth. The sky darkened, however, and snow dry as powder, small and gritty, was whirled off the upper surfaces in the cold gusts, rising in clouds from the boughs and hedges and blowing like smoke against the umber trees of the distance and the dark and low roof of the heavens, which had a scorched tinge, an inappropriately torrid aspect. The icicles started to drip, yet prolonged themselves. In sheltered corners, the snow surfaces of the ground began to soak, to soften, to attain a semi-transparency, the damp spreading along them like water along blotting-paper. Small drops drilled cavernous holes. A warm earth had received the early and sudden snowfall, and two climates seemed to be contending, the upper air icy, the earth still breathing the garnered warmth of the summer.

In spite of these inclement conditions, there was a hammering at the front door in the late afternoon. A caller with a mission of some urgency seemed indicated. Then a strident voice in the hall, amidst exclamations, amidst questions pitched on a note of surprise, announced Rosalie Lambert. That woman! Hearing the formidable commotion from his workroom, Keith flung down his pen, incapacitated. Impossible to go on! What now? Could it be——? Exasperation, consuming curiosity, not unmingled with foreboding, made him fit for nothing.

Much excited, slightly elevated, as was usually the case nowadays, Rosalie had brought strange news. One of her neighbours professed to have seen the girl 'with her own eyes'—yes, seen her walking in the snow at noonday, had come face to face with her and would have known her anywhere. But this woman, although actually living in Hilbery at the date of the tragedy, had made, when questioned, several flagrant mistakes about the child's appearance; and, in short, turned out scarcely to have known the little Vivian Lambert by sight. But superstitious fear had overcome Rosalie's commonsense. Although scoffing at the neighbour's tale as she told it, she was plainly impressed; more, she was upset, even scared. Asked in, she was in no hurry to quit cheerful company; and, seated by the fire, kept peering out at the snowy scene and shivering a little, saying she believed she had caught cold. She continued to describe the neighbour's adventure in a tone of scorn, talking volubly, repeating her facts many times; which nobody minded. Her audience, although sceptical, was an appreciative one. Mrs Jebb, Leslie, Mirry, all the household, gathered to give her hearing.

And Christine, silent in their midst, felt her heart beat fast. Why should not the report be true? Thus did her longing, and her secret panic, make the crude tale seem possible.

The room grew shadowy, the fanning light of the flames began to pulse visibly upon walls and furniture, and with backs turned to the wintry garden they did not realise how much of the suspended daylight was due to the reflection from the snow outside the large bay which came down to floor level. The soft and blanching light under a dark sky had endured from early morning, scarcely changing. Tea had been brought in, Keith called and apprised briefly of Rosalie's story—and in the midst of the slight bustle, the little petulant treble of Mirry was suddenly uplifted.

'Mummy, there's someone out there, a girl. Standing in the snow.'

The clatter of the china abruptly ceased, everyone turned his head and held a rigid pose, staring. And in a silence suddenly grown tense, Keith got up and strolled towards the window, remarking, 'Why, yes, we have a visitor. Who is it?' He went right up to the window and peered outward, with his face close to the pane. They all looked towards the spot on the other side of the lawn to which his attention seemed to be directed. 'Where, Keith?' cried Helena. 'I can't see where you mean.' Keith was suddenly silent.

In that black and white picture, everything was drawn with extreme clarity, shadowless. Yet there were gaps amongst the evergreens, there were sheltered bays and nooks, holes in the bushes, strips of trunk, arbitrary patches of darkness—surfaces from which the snow had already slithered or melted; and the whole scene, with features which appeared so pure and clear-cut, so exceptionally unambiguous, was in fact very confusing at a distance. The air also through which it was seen was many shades darker than one had realised.

If some person had issued from the shrubbery at the edge of the lawn, it looked as if that person had caught sight of their party in the firelit window, seen them all turn and stare, and Keith rise and point, and had taken fright and retreated; retreated so swiftly that not every pair of eyes in the room had had time to see him. Or so some of them thought. The visitor, whoever it was, had had only to take a few paces to pass out of sight behind a great conifer, the lowest branches of which swept the ground. And this she had evidently done.

'Mirry?' Helena said in a hoarse whisper.

'Gone now,' replied Mirry stolidly. 'Ran away—ever so quickly.' The child had returned to bending her head over a small puzzle she had brought in with her, and seemed absorbed in it.

Rosalie had leaned sharply forward at the first alarm with eyes screwed up and a protrusion of the lower lip denoting scepticism in suspension. She now moved and sat back. It was she who broke the shocked pause and broke it with a shocking statement.

'Oh. that wasn't Vivian. Vivian would have been tall. She had those long hands and feet. She would have been tall, like her father.'

'Why, Rosalie, *did you think it was?*' Helena began on a top note of excitement.

But in a voice so breathless and aghast that it caused all eyes to turn on her, 'Are you sure it was not Vivian?' Christine said. '*It was my girl!*'

There was a general gasp of astonishment, of credulity and incredulity mingled; but in fact their attention was at once transferred to Rosalie. And Rosalie's face had already changed; an expression of doubt and alarm had replaced the scornful assurance of the first moment. Still, she repeated, 'I tell you, she'd have been lanky, like her father.—Didn't she sprint, though?' she added, with a hiccup of laughter, which she stifled with her handkerchief.

Mirry looked up and eyed her with contempt.

'Now, what made her do that?' Mrs Gray asked brightly, screwing up her eyes like Rosalie a minute before and stooping forward to peer through the window with elaboration, as if she still hoped to discern a figure walking towards them if only she looked carefully enough. 'She must have seen us. How I wish I'd waved!'

All were then silent again in a sort of unconscious tension, waiting for the figure to appear on the other side of the tree. But they waited in vain. Then Helena declared that she must have gone round the back of the house, down the holly walk. The mouth of this path, which opened off the drive and led to the kitchen garden and the back entrance, was hidden by the tree. So this seemed likely. Tongues were loosened and everyone gave rein to wonder, but in a somewhat hushed fashion.

Keith, who had not uttered another word, suddenly turned from the window with an indistinct, laughing exclamation, strode out of the room and could be heard crossing the hall and opening the front door noisily. The door at once slammed. He appeared to have gone outside. Helena followed, but to plunge down the passage to the kitchen quarters.

The rest of them were now on their feet. Ejaculation and surmise mingled, and a current of uneasy excitement swept from the room to the hall, into which they drifted, one by one. There they stood listening and awaiting the return of the two investigators.

Keith quietly opened the front door again and elaborately rubbed his feet on the mat. He waved them back into the room, drove them before him with playful gestures, smiling, shaking his head mysteriously. 'Well? Anything to be seen?' they asked him. He would not answer. Throwing himself down in an easy-chair, he extended his long legs, thrust his hands into his pockets and lolled his head on the cushion; and from this supine position, in this inert, nerveless pose, he met all their questioning with a provoking, smiling silence. It might have struck anyone there that he was like a man who was considering what to say—a man who had perhaps had something of a shock and was genuinely overcome. At length he laughed in a prolonged, silent manner which seemed artificial. Throughout this, his eyes looked alert. They went often to the window. Finally, he sat up, glanced round, markedly took note of Christine's lingering out in the hall; and with his gaze turned in that direction, he said softly, 'Well, what other proof do we want?'

Louder and ironically, he resumed, 'Come, now. Which of you saw her? Hands up! . . . *I'll* answer for Christine.' Rosalie had made no movement.

Keith threw a smiling, questioning glance round him, but no one responded. 'Leslie?' he said.

'I didn't see anyone,' the girl answered in a low tone, from between her teeth, like one who essays to keep her teeth from chattering; she added, 'Sitting here, rather behind you when you jumped up, I didn't move quickly enough to see anything properly.' Keith gave her a somewhat lingering and intent look; and for a moment more there was no sound in the room but the faint chafing noise he himself was making by rubbing the side of one hand with the forefinger of the other.

'Have you hurt your hand, Mr Antequin?' Mrs Jebb inquired, leaning forward rather officiously.

'Nothing, nothing,' he answered as if in some slight surprise at the question; it seemed that the gesture had been unconscious. He turned from Leslie with impatience. 'But, come, own up!' he cried to the others, in his most spirited manner.

Then Mrs Gray said, laughing a little, 'Do you know, I didn't see anyone at all—while all the rest of you did. Except that at the first moment I saw a shadow, as I thought, at the top of the avenue. But, my dears, that's nothing. You mustn't go by me. My old eyes are not good. It was the little one who saw her first and called out, you know—*not Christine*, Keith. Bless her—children's eyes are so sharp!'

Helena had come silently in and was standing behind Keith's chair, looking down on him.

'Yes, it was Mirry who first saw her,' she affirmed mildly.

'No, Helena,' said Keith in a raised voice, 'she did *not*.' For one instant his face seemed distorted with anger, or with some kindred passion—to such a degree that everyone looked at him in astonishment. He resumed, his tone still pitched to bear down opposition, though he contrived an air of good-humour. 'She did not because she could not. She was mistaken. A blackbird, perhaps. Yes, blackbirds have a habit of flying in the dusk—they fly low and look particularly large in a scene and light like this—and one flying across the snow at the foot of the shrubbery might well give the impression that someone was running beside it.' Then, throwing another of those playful glances towards the door open on the hall (where Christine presumably lingered), and pretending she was out of hearing (a pretence obvious to them all), he observed, with his voice still raised, 'So it has now come to this. That Christine is able to see Vivian Lambert *where there is no one.*'

'What on earth do you mean? No one! Blackbirds! You saw her yourself!' Helena cried, confounded.

'Mercy upon us! Are we *all* taking leave of our senses? Mass hysteria, indeed—or mass insanity! Now, listen—listen carefully. *I was joking.* Yes, I was making a little experiment—just to see how much we *could* see. Of course there was no one there. I saw no one.'

Some hand switched on the light.

Puzzlement, incredulity and even resentment appeared on several of the faces turned on Keith.

'Well, none of us saw her very clearly, I suppose, at that distance,' Helena muttered, clattering the tea-cups. Keith glanced at her sharply. 'Helena, the tea is stewed—you should make some more.' She took no notice. 'Why, look,' she added, 'it's almost dark—no wonder if some of us didn't see much.' But in fact the light having been put on, this was its effect upon eyes turned again on the outdoor scene. Everything outside was sunk in a blue twilight of intensely cold tone in which little could be distinguished beyond the great yellow squares cast by their own window.

'Draw the curtains!' commanded Mirry. Someone did so and attempted to pet the prickly, self-sufficient little girl, thinking she was frightened; but was repulsed. Mirry was not frightened.

'Well, damn it, *I* saw her all right!' the voice of Rosalie cried. She sat up with a jerk and seemed to have hoisted herself abruptly out of a sort of stupefaction into which she had fallen.

'You saw her, Mrs Lambert? And thought it was Vivian! So you did—so you did!' Keith spoke with an air of malicious doubt.

'Oh, I saw her—I'll go as far as that. A rather stocky sort of build. Hasn't grown like I'd have thought she would. What struck me was the rather scowling look—the same that Vivian always had—her eyes rather sunken. But quite dark—gone darker than I should have expected. She'd got her hair plaited and done up in a knocker. A pinkish coat——Funny, that! Same old colour. My word, I'm not keen to meet her, that's all I can say——'

An astounded silence, a frozen silence, was broken by Keith.

'You're amazingly long-sighted, Mrs Lambert, evidently!' he exclaimed with a biting intonation. But a little inadvertent laugh escaped him, almost tremulous. 'Amazingly . . . amazingly . . .' He seemed to play for time. 'You don't mean to tell us that you could see such details as those at such a distance—in such a light? Also—the back of her head, when she was facing us—as I suppose——! Good gracious!'

'Well—what if I am?' Rosalie retorted, looking flustered and sulky, and she relapsed into silence. An apprehensive expression drew down the corners of her mouth. As if she found the room warm, though in fact it was not particularly so, she began to fan herself with her handkerchief.

Keith stood up to hand cakes, and remained standing. 'Of the eight of us, then, only Christine! Or must we add Mrs Lambert? Now, Mrs Lambert——' Suddenly a smiling and mocking expression came into Keith's eyes; and to Rosalie's very face he assumed a slight air of tipsiness, and then, flagrantly over-acting, like a ham actor on a stage, he appeared to be 'seeing things'. And this piece of gross rudeness, this insult to Rosalie, was also an insult to Mrs Gray, and worse, it was singularly cruel—for it could not be overlooked that his mockery was, by implication, a deeper, more injurious thrust at Christine. Mrs Gray quietly stirred her tea and sipped it, her face tranquil, although she glanced at him more than once with mild attention; and Helena, in a panic lest the old woman should see, began hacking off large slices of cake and pressing them upon people who had had enough. But in a minute it was all over.

In a normal, perfectly courteous manner, Keith added, 'Come, Mrs Lambert, I'll put on a coat and go out to where you say she was standing. All you'll be able to see of my face will be that I've got one. Even in daylight that would be so. It isn't dark out there yet by any means, if we turn off the light again.'

'Oh, no thanks, don't bother,' mumbled Rosalie, scrambling clumsily to her feet. 'Well, I'll be going. Such is life.' Refusing the offer of fresh tea Helena pressed upon her with the words, 'Can't face it. Cold's upset my innards, I shouldn't wonder,' and refusing also the offer of a lift home, she went off like one anxious to escape further probing; a retreat which was not without a certain dignity.

Making her reflections to Mrs Gray, who accompanied her into the hall, she continued, 'I wouldn't say so to anyone but you, my dear, but the least drop affects me nowadays in a way I don't like. It didn't used to. I wasn't myself when I saw that back-hair—can't be denied. Couldn't be done. Stands to reason. And I didn't want to stay and be put through it by your gentleman, by Mr Antequin. And have my weaknesses referred to so pointedly, too. Rude, I call it. Very rude. I'm surprised at him. Not such a gent as his father, who once helped me home when I was taken queer in the street and made no reference. I shouldn't wonder if he never went further than this porch—there was no snow on his shoes. Scared—that's what he was, if you ask me. Too scared to go . . . Well, I've got to do a bit of heavy thinking first, before I tie myself down to saying one way or the other. No one's going to persuade me there was no girl there—though I make you a present of the knocker and the eyes. And I'm not going to be bounced into committing myself when I'm not at my best . . . But it's very rummy that the girl really did look to me a bit like Vivian at first sight—I mean, I thought at once, "There she is"—only that I'd expected her to be taller—lanky. You know what I mean. Rather a bean-pole . . . Well, I'll be going. Wouldn't mind getting home before it's dark. Hope I shan't be caught up with by anything on the road—anything I wouldn't wish. Oh, *lor*! . . . Why, it's only Christine, isn't it, wandering out there, all in the snow? What's she looking for? Footsteps?' And Mrs Gray, peering past her shoulder, said in a sad, feeling voice, yes, she had been thinking so.

THIRTY-TWO

'Quite right to deny it. I did quite rightly. A white lie, if ever there was one.'

And having escaped from the centre of the stage at last (for the first time in his life with thankfulness), he dropped down into his chair in the study and leaned back, with hanging arms, feeling more shaken inwardly then he dared to own. On coming in, he had made haste to draw the curtains, the dark, heavy curtains in whose folds the shadows now stood like pillars, having something of a drop-scene effect because of the light placed so low. The reading-lamp, casting its rays down from under a green shade, did not illuminate the room generally, and a wide area of the floor around the desk was thrown into a clear darkness. He was glad of this minimum of light. It was restful.

'Yes,' he continued to think, unconsciously using a rather pompous phraseology, 'I had no choice. To pretend there was no one there was incumbent upon me. For this terrible maggot in her brain must somehow be scotched. One couldn't allow an unfortunate coincidence to strengthen delusion. A figure, seen at that moment, just as the foolish tale was being told—who knew what evil effect it might have on the sick mind?'

As for himself, he had seen the figure from the first, and seen it stand motionless in full view, at the edge of the lawn, against the snow-patched shrubbery.

But he was conscious of a twisting worm of alarm in his entrails. He could not forget or explain the odd fact that all the while it had stood there, openly and in full sight, only three of them, apparently, had looked in the right direction. A presence so very obvious, seen so distinctly!

Straightway, on this admission, an inner voice made itself heard, a stammering voice, unpleasantly near to panic. 'But—but—but——! How could *that* figure ever have been mistaken for the grown Vivian Lambert? It was plainly some child from one of the neighbouring houses, lingering out late in play—it was nothing else. A child drawn on past the gates, fascinated by the spread of untrodden snow. Some little trespasser who took fright on seeing you all in the fire-lit window and finding herself stared at and pointed at. And suddenly vanished. That is,' he amended, as the phrase all at once seemed undesirable, 'beat a hasty retreat.'

Well, the figure of a child, dimly seen, seen momentarily, as the other two had evidently seen it—that would be enough for those already disposed to be grossly deceived.

Then, applying irony to disquieting fact, to laugh it out of court, he rallied himself. 'Come, now! To be so much impressed by Mrs Lambert's brilliant graphic powers!'

It was, of course, desirable to keep an open mind, to assent with intelligent readiness to the exploring of all possibilities. Perhaps it might be argued that a belief in Christine's hallucinated state was in itself hallucination. That the girl, whoever she might be, really existed in the flesh. And perhaps bore some real likeness to the child Vivian? That the figure in the snow was actually 'my girl', as Christine, crying out, had called her; the impostor. That he himself had been deceived as to her stature by a momentary loss of the sense of scale due to the strange atmosphere, to the snowy disguise of familiar ground.

But if he could have believed this, or even suspected it to be possible, he would have admitted it, whatever the cost to himself. Of course! At once! For dear Christine's sake. As it was, it would be as well to face the truth courageously, the sad circumstance of the dear one's illness, so that she might be advised and treated before she was beyond help.

So he repeated, he had done well to deny seeing anyone. Someone there had been, out in the snow—but no impostor, no masquerading girl, for such a creature did not exist, except in Christine's sick mind. He was able to draw forth from the neat pigeon-holes of his brain more than one striking precedent, cases he had heard of where some person on the verge of nervous breakdown had been driven over the edge by just such an unlucky chance event which had seemed to confirm his delusions. He had done well, very well.

Here for a moment or two his thoughts ran on blankly, somewhat out of control. An exhausting hour, an hour of nervous strain, was behind him, and his attention was losing grip and caught at physical trifles in a wave of weariness; and thus he suddenly found himself occupied by a curious sensation in his right hand, which he had allowed to drop over the chair-arm. It could only be described as a warmth, a very gentle and dampish movement of air, as if a slight, tepid, wandering draught now and again encircled the hand rather agreeably. So slight as to be scarcely perceptible at moments; yet no sooner had he dismissed it as fancy than a distinct warmth crept about the hand again. He was a little sleepy, the sensation was not unpleasant, and for some minutes he amused himself by attempting to puzzle out its cause. Then he noticed another thing. This gentle wafting of air was not steady, it came and went; but now he discovered that it came and went with regularity. 'Odd,' he thought, rousing himself. 'Some form of rheumatism, I suppose'; lifted his hand, rubbed it. The sensation ceased.

He had forgotten it the next moment. Indeed, he began to doze.

A physical feeling again aroused him, again in his hand, which he had once more dropped over the chair-arm. This new sensation was gentle and slight, yet perfectly distinct, and was precisely as if some gamesome little animal had caught his hand playfully between its teeth for an instant; so that his first thought was of Mirry's puppy. The thought was natural. But he was startled, for he had shut the door. Calling to the little creature, he jumped up, looked round the desk, searched about under the furniture, in the shadow; then, having had time to note the unlikely stillness, the discreet and crafty inactivity of the little roly-poly corgi, he was brought to realise there was no puppy in the room.

A touch of cramp, perhaps? He had had odd sensations in the hand of late, and hoped he was not about to suffer from some hampering little disorder with a nuisance-value, like fibrositis. The vividness of the momentary delusion he could only judge to have been due to his sleepy state.

He had dozed only a few minutes in reality; yet he felt cold, stiff; and had a dreary and chilly sense of his solitude, which half an hour ago had seemed so desirable.

Leaving the room quietly, he crossed the hall and from outside the drawing-room door heard Mrs Gray saying persuasively to Mirry, 'Tell Granny what you saw, darling.'

'Why, it was a bird—like Daddy said,' Mirry's bored little voice answered clearly. 'I saw afterwards it was nothing but an old bird.'

Keith, with his hand on the handle, paused; Mirry the next moment came out of the room. 'And what are *you* doing?' she asked him with condescension. He eyed vaguely the pallid, consequential little face; then observed it more heedfully. He knew that expression, complacent, conscious. Mirry was feeling clever. Whence did the child derive her unpleasant characteristics? However, so preoccupied was he that he let her go. But it was enough to cause him a second's indecision, as he stood at the door. During this, he witnessed an odd little incident. Past him, out of the room, Leslie shot without seeing him, bearing swiftly down upon the child; and catching up with her in the kitchen passage, from behind, and without a word, boxed her ears violently. In one indoctrinated with a modern child-cult of the purest sentimentality, this primitive act was interesting, was impressive, speaking of bottled-up passion. Keith, a conscientiously modern parent, should have been incensed. He was not; he was pleased. Nevertheless, normally he would have acted as if outraged. But the truth was that in this *distrait* and off-guard moment, he felt quite unable to decide which of the two he disliked more.

Mirry had undoubtedly been clever once too often. The child must have seen the figure clearly enough. He was aware of complexities. But he could not trouble to tackle it now; more serious matters engrossed him and indeed somewhat agitated him.

'Ah, Mother,' he said, going in softly and finding her alone, 'I'd like a little private talk with you——(Oh, nothing, nothing—Mirry has had a little tumble in the passage—but Leslie is there to console her.) A little private talk with you, a few serious words.' And he spoke in tones quite shaken and subdued, modulated by genuine feeling, for he had something dreadful to say to Christine's mother.

THIRTY-THREE

In the hall, having heard Keith say, 'I was joking . . . making a little experiment . . . there was no one there,' Christine threw on an old garden coat, borrowed scarf and gloves and quietly let herself out into the garden, out into the soft, reversed glare from the snow which had prolonged the day so unnaturally. She did not feel the cold. Walking on swiftly under that strange roof of cloud, in which the burning tinge lingered, she went at random wherever space stretched and her feet led her. The park now lay open, shrunken, visibly bounded by walls, searched by an icy wind; the rich pavilions of darkness had long been struck, and the secret nests in the grass, the warm bowers of summer, were open to the sky. All her nooks were exposed, the curtaining tapestry of leaves shaken from the frail screens; she could hardly have told where the arbours were or the sunned banks where she had sat and dreamed the old childish dreams of far, gorgeous lands. Now the eye saw far and wide to the girdling wall; there was no egress and no shelter; nothing but a bounded, frozen world seen in an aghast and chalky light. A silent, dark bird ran over the snow before her. 'I have a queer feeling that she is not going to show herself to anyone but you.' She had a sensation as if her heart turned over, she felt ready to sink down in the cold waste. This dark transparency was the light of nightmare, and the whole garden suddenly seemed to her unutterably mournful and terrible, everything changed menacingly from the norm, and changed for ever.

Her original thought had been to search for footsteps—her secret hope, too wild to be admitted, a meeting in the snow. But her distraction was now too great, she looked in agitation, forgot, walked where the traces might have been. Besides, the snow was thin under the avenue trees, moist and half transparent in many places. And although she might fancy something like a faint trail from the edge of the lawn, other prints more definite were present, probably those made by Rosalie.

'So it has come to this. That Christine is able to see Vivian Lambert *where there is no one.*'

No one, no one? Oh, could it be? That moment of intense suggestion, the dramatic snow-scene, the firelight, Rosalie's tale, the child's sudden cry, her own passionate expectation— had all these combined to call up an abnormally clear mental picture of the girl, which her excited brain had transferred to the outer world?

But Rosalie, she remembered, Rosalie also had seen her.

But her judgment warned her that it was no advantage to be standing alone with Rosalie on the defense side—with a woman a little affected by drink and in a state of superstitious credulity.

Then, glancing back, she saw the door opened, the orange light stream out, and Rosalie and her mother on the threshold; and she instinctively fled to hide her incommunicable terrors in those furthest parts of the garden which no eye could overlook. There, through the thinned trees, she saw the well-house squatting in its hollow field in the white waste, under its fantastic and snow-crowned cap of ivy. Walking to and fro, she had it long in sight. Without being conscious of hurrying, again and again she was obliged to stop, finding herself breathless.

At last she grew calmer. The cold which tightened her brows and made them ache seemed to penetrate her being till at length heart and brain were numb and her passionate fear yielded to lethargy. She did not think clearly.

But with a kind of stupefied resignation she felt that God had marked her out for destruction. Good as she had always tried to be, never having wished ill to anyone, fallen into this very trap through a compassionate impulse, she had somehow, in sheer ignorance, in a moment of inattentive soul-blindness, done something irretrievable in God's eyes. And there was no justice in it, as even she in her humility could see. Or if there was justice, what could a human being care for a justice which no human being could understand?

She had no one to whom she could speak except her mother—and well she knew what her mother's words would be. 'Just trust in God, my darling. You've done nothing wrong. God will never forsake you.' Tender lies. Monstrous lies. For if anything can be predicted of God, it is that He will forsake us, always, always in our worst agony.

'I am cold through,' she felt. She thought of wild creatures whose food was locked in the frozen earth, and forgot herself in pitying them.

Rousing herself at last from her frozen stupor, she returned to the house, and having no energy left to attempt evading contacts and questioning, or even any sensible desire to do so, she came straight into the hall; which was, however, in darkness. But when she had returned her borrowed wraps to their cupboard in the passage, she was suddenly awakened by a thread of light from the door of the drawing-room, the hasp of which had at that moment slipped the lock of its own accord, and caught and fascinated by the enemy voice of Keith still in pressing talk with someone who did not find it necessary to answer. And chance made it seem that he was continuing directly from the very words which had driven her forth, 'Of the eight of us, only Christine saw her. Of the eight of us, Christine alone——'

She went close to the door and listened. She listened as a child might have done, without conscious culpability, because it was essential to her to hear, the matter was desperate, a question of life or death; and the affectations of the civilised were abandoned, as in desperate illness. She listened, and became coolly attentive, sometimes missing a few words but catching the gist of it all perfectly.

'Think what that means. Christine alone! Rosalie, you say? Oh, well, Rosalie! Yes, Rosalie—who all too obviously might have seen anything suggested to her at that moment. Count her out. Christine alone fell into my little trap—failed my little test.'

Thus it was that she came to learn a great deal about herself. She listened, and, while listening, fixed her eyes on the tawny darkness at the top of the window, where dimly appeared the branchy fountains, mere shadows and echoes of the walls and towers, the fortifications studded with blossoms, solid with a thick fell of leaves like the clumsy hands of benign giants, which had guarded her hiding-places and her world of summer. So she learned that she had always been something of a day-dreamer, that she was a person with an especially strong image-making faculty. All these years, she had probably been building up in her subconscious mind a whole protective fantasy around the Lambert case; preparing a reasonable story, thought out intensively, every detail accounted for—and all this strange process, this elaborate self-protective device, had resulted from the emotional shock of finding herself involved in such a tragedy. One could guess how it had weighed on her mind, how she might even have felt herself in some way to blame; and the whole fantasy, the listener should notice, was designed to conjure Vivian back to life and deliver Christine herself from an unbearable thought—the unbearable thought of Vivian murdered.

That was what they had to face. She had made up the whole tale, probably years ago, then shut it away, with all deliberate thought of the tragedy, forgotten it; until a chance word or look, a sound or colour, had suddenly revived need of protection—but by then she did not recognise the origin of the comforting tale, did not recognise it for her own. Dream or hallucination had produced it as an objective experience; an attempt to impose illusion on reality having at last succeeded.

Here someone must have demurred with a look or gesture, for Keith added quickly, soothingly, 'Oh, *unconscious*, yes! Surely I emphasised that? I imagine she has seen someone recently in the street, quite fortuitously, who reminded her so strongly of the Lambert child that it gave her a profound shock, and that touched it off—the fantasy world suddenly merged with reality and she could no longer distinguish the one from the other. Myself, I think the whole thing stems from a mere likeness in a passing stranger, or from some similar incident. It might even be that the talk she told me she had had with Rosalie disposed her to it——'

To the young woman's dismay, it was her mother's voice which answered.

'And he is talking to Mother like that, the coward!' She was so indignant that she was about to throw open the door—but a belated feeling for something in her mother's voice arrested and restrained her.

'Just a hallucination?' said Mrs Gray, speaking up very bravely, considering that she had received news of her daughter's insanity.

Christine, with a woeful glimmer of amusement in the midst of her trouble, reflected that of course Keith could not know that his whole theory would sound perfectly ridiculous to Mrs Gray, and at the same time make her so angry that that long silence in which she had received his solemn exposition had been due, one guessed, to a prayer for heavenly aid before she trusted herself to speak.

'All that sensible, convincing evidence? Made up? Dear me, I had no idea my darling was so clever.'

'Our subconscious selves are often very clever,' Keith said, smiling.

'And I'd never thought of Christine as an unusually imaginative child.'

'Well, no, she would not need to be unusually imaginative. In fact, it's not people of really powerful and original imagination who live in these imaginary worlds—or, rather, who don't keep them in control, or who make the mistake of confounding them with reality. Not the artists, but the weak, uncreative dreamers——'

'Yes, I dare say that is true,' Mrs Gray agreed with a marked and cheerful readiness—noted this time even by Keith, one felt, for he paused. Yes, now surely he must have doubts about his companion's tone. Christine knew (though it was very rare) that gentle, chilling irony which her mother kept only for wicked folly, or what she conceived to be such. In this voice, this light voice of pure judgment, she continued, 'Then we had better be careful what we fancy. For not many of us have "powerful and original imaginations"—so I believe!' And she laughed gaily. 'But, Keith, my dear—now, thinking of what you said to me when you first came in—with the idea of convincing me that there is no Vivian, I suppose——So you have proof—let me be exact—"something like proof" that the child was murdered? Proof taken from Thomas's diary? What *can* it be? Nothing at all damaging to Thomas, that's certain, or you wouldn't dream of publishing it! (He that troubleth his own house shall inherit the wind.) But, Keith—if you will listen to a word of warning from an old woman—it's not, as it seems to me, my poor girl alone who is capable of building fancies on mere suspicions. False suspicions are dangerous things to harbour, I've noticed—all's grist that comes to their mill, and they gather up supporting evidence as a snowball gathers snow. And something else, too, I've noticed. That intelligence, high intelligence, is far from always aiding reason—in fact, that it's apter than stupidity itself to invent ingenious arguments against it. Cherish a "fantasy" of that kind, an evil thought, a folly, of your own creation, and you may raise up a sort of devil to mislead you—God may permit it—not so easily shaken off as conjured up . . . There, quite a little homily! But you see what I mean?'

Christine had drawn back. The familiar, loved voice uttering these dreadful words with characteristic light-heartedness, went home as no other voice could have done, and she was left facing an image of a proved, condemned and punished mental dishonesty.

She retreated quietly to the foot of the stairs, and there paused for an instant to listen again in a kind of cold, absent curiosity. But Keith was silent. Perhaps someone had approached from the little inner room. There were footsteps, the movement of a chair. Something had broken up the talk.

She went up to her room laboriously, conscious of a kind of awkwardness in her body, like a sudden loss of youthful suppleness. A shock, a violent and sickening shock, had been given her. But her brain was cool; she was able to think clearly and to examine with detachment Keith's slick analysis of her state. Its professional jargon was of course absurd, and such prying into one's soul by another must always be an outrage—and yet there was much in it which was hideously acute. It was true, true, for instance, that she had many times tried to imagine Vivian's fate and tried to fit the facts into an imaginary story wherein Vivian survived. (Yet did any story she had ever imagined resemble the one she had heard, or believed herself to have heard, from the girl's own lips? She would have answered, no, none was remotely like it. Ah, but 'unconscious'!)

She saw that all these years she had been weakly trusting in God's mercy, when she should have been trusting in herself; that one cannot place reliance on anyone but oneself, however one may long to. God had done nothing to her, nothing of which she could complain, for He had simply taken no note of her. She had no grievance. Tragic experience had come to her—and why not to her? For the rest, she had brought this fate on herself. Instead of facing the terror, she had hidden her eyes, begging to be told fairytales. She had refused to grow up.

It was certain that the child had been murdered (and had Keith really proof of it? she wondered, trembling), and at the back of her mind she had known from the very beginning that it was certain. She had even selected the scene of the murder— she had chosen the well-house corner. Why had she ever felt that loathing of the well-house? Why had she at that time taken such a scunner at it? She had, of course, heard it called a privy, and that word was already connected with the murder of a child because of the newspaper tale which had just then made a fearful impression on her mind; a word which, affecting her fastidious and half-childish imagination with a deep disgust, had added a last touch of piteous, squalid horror to the fate of the little victim of the story. The well-house, however, was not the privy of the tale. Yet by its kinship it was a place well-disposed to murder. And therefore all her secret, unacknowledged, strangled fears had settled on it.

In short, she had believed in the murder and hidden the belief from herself.

For if it was certain that Vivian had been murdered, then she had been instrumental in the child's death, however innocently. She had seen that even at the time. She had thought, at the time, that if the child's body was found, she would go mad. When it was not found, she had continued to cheat herself with hope, and that was the beginning of the protective screen of falsehood she had put up against reality. That was the beginning of hallucination. And almost certainly she would not *then* have gone mad. Long brooding had not worn her down, as it had now; years of torturing suspicions had not lowered her resistance. Her suffering would have been cruel and deep, but it would have passed, simply because suspense would have been ended and her mind delivered; and she would never have entered the world of imagination so dangerous to the weak.

As it was, she had fled from one make-believe refuge to another, and so she had weakly gone from bad to worse, till she had raised up a spectre to delude her, her own creation, a veritable temptress from hell. Till it had come to the last encounter, when she had seen her far-off and small, in the chalky darkness, and yet in clearest, impossibly clear, detail, with the plaited hair and the deep, frowning eyes, and *no one else had seen her*. 'Of the eight of us,' Keith had said, 'Christine alone.' For if she had been able to transmit that clear figure to the mind of Rosalie Lambert, she had only been able to transmit it to the one of them in whom the faculties were blurred by a drug.

She was terrified to see where her cowardice had led her. But now, weak and demoralised though she was, and of practised dishonesty, she would at last make a stand. She would do it alone, she would not cling and pray. She would give up belief in the living and returned Vivian, everything that appeared like proof she would set down to uncontrolled and desirous fancy; she would face even the prospect of hallucination and, if it happened to her again, force herself to regard it as a temporary sickness of mind which would pass; keep calm and worry no one.

Then she turned on the light, bathed her face and did her hair, and the unnatural strength which had come to her while listening to her heavy sentence returned and upheld her.

Going down quietly to dinner, she spoke collectedly and cheerfully to them all; saying, in the manner of one ready to laugh at herself for an absurd mistake, that on thinking it over she had reached the conclusion that she had been deluded for an instant—excited, as she had been, by Rosalie's tale and deceived by the uncertain light. She agreed that there had been no one in the garden. Then she, who never talked about herself easily, forced herself to discuss her experiences and to admit that she had felt under the weather of late. Perhaps her nerves were a bit wrong. And to let them see how open to reason she was, she made herself speak of the 'evening visit', confessing that she had afterwards felt in perplexity about it, that, on looking back, she had noticed touches in it which seemed dream-like. Indeed, she was sometimes inclined to believe she had dreamed it all, she said, laughing. If she had been ill, she was now on the way to recovery—that was the impression she intended to convey. That she was reasonable now, perfectly reasonable! Thus did she artlessly attempt to forestall loving candour, to avoid being seized and taken in charge for her own good.

But in vain, she saw. Keith listened in silence, sometimes running his hand over his head with a disturbed air. Helena was uneasy, Mrs Gray astonished, at her sudden change.

And after the meal, Keith came quietly upon her at a moment when she was alone, his face drawn with anxiety.

'Christine, let me beg one thing of you—just one thing—for your own sake, dear! Don't try to fight your trouble all by yourself. Ah, just as I feared!—you've made up your mind to do so. Just what I dreaded!—just what I said to Helena!——'

She answered hurriedly, afraid of him, 'I don't want help, Keith. It's nothing. Nothing that I can't manage for myself.' But the tears came into her eyes from pure fright—she was trembling, powerless against that sinister solicitude.

He exclaimed in horror. 'No, no, that won't do. (See how easily upset you are!) Let me at least make inquiries for you——What am I saying? I hardly need to—I can put my hand on the very man who could be your salvation at this moment. One of our very ablest psychiatrists—a brilliant man and most sympathetic. No, no, no—certainly hallucination is no evidence of insanity. Sometimes, of course, it *is* a sign of organic lesion—but, good heavens, we need not consider that! But it is definitely an indication of an abnormal state of mind. An abnormal state of mind should be dealt with at the earliest stage. Don't neglect it, dear! It is *not* nothing.'

Abjectly frightened, she persisted in clinging to the idea of looking for salvation in herself alone.

Then the sense of Keith's hints and suggestions began to take the form of a freezing, monitory whisper in her ear. 'But what if you have not enough judgment left to distinguish the shadow from the real? What if your mind is too far subverted, incapable of interpreting honestly the reports of your senses? If you see Vivian, you will see her, I warn you, as flesh and blood—an imitation of life so exact that you will be unable to do otherwise than believe in her again. Of that, and of nothing else, hallucination consists. The powers of hell are not so easily routed. And your very soul faints within you at the prospect of a repeated visitation, before which you know your brave, new disbelief will collapse.'

She listened, sometimes shaking her head; and came back in a sort of dull surprise to hear Keith's human voice saying almost tearfully. 'You see, you are such an obstinate little person, one must frighten you, I'm afraid, for your own good!'

Yes, Keith was truly distressed. He had entirely convinced himself that he was right in dealing with her like this and was emotionally affected by the painful nature of his duty. In fact, he had quite upset himself and began to feel the premonitory stirrings of a gastric attack.

Still he talked on, while time was given him, and gradually he made his effect; she was worn down. Looking at his yellowing and almost tearful face, she saw with a shock the genuineness of his fears for her; and a terrible mistrust of herself began to exert its paralysing influence.

By the next day she had made up her mind what to do. She would have been unfeignedly glad to fall asleep for ever and to be rid of this haunted life; for she had existed for so many years with the little creature of darkness, bat-like and taloned, clinging to her soul, that the light of the earth had gone out for her. Still, she had journeyed on in a mild, sunless scene without great pain; until this cruel revenant had arisen before her. Called by herself? She feared so now.

But she put the thought of death aside and resolved that for her mother's sake, and her brothers' and Helena's, all her few friends', she would first consult a mental doctor, as Keith advised, terribly as she shrank from such a step. As it was, only her ignorance of these professional healers—for she thought of them as she had been taught to think of doctors as a whole, as benefactors, almost heroes—accounted for this decision.

She would first learn how deeply wrong all her attitude to life had been. She, who was humble, easily overborne, would acquiesce, admit all her weaknesses, make her confession, say (if they asked her—for it was the truth), yes, she had thought of suicide. And then indeed she would be lost. After that, she would 'consent' to anything suggested; enter this or that home, take this or that treatment; and so the pace would grow, till the very sickness which had brought her to this became the live centre, the most vigorous part of her.

THIRTY-FOUR

On a foggy night in December, two people left a party as unassumingly as they had joined it and came down the steps of a large, porticoed house in one of the Kensington squares. The fog was thickening, the street lights burned with a reddish tinge. Distant lamps glowed like spent matches. All light and animation, all of human interest, seemed pressed down into a few yards above the pavements. From the house-fronts, from doorways, from all objects in the open with lights behind them, alternating long, soft, white and dark rays were thrown out on the thick air, so that the whole night seemed crossed and criss-crossed with broad, shadowy random beams. A clubbed tree was crowned with a huge wheel.

The two people proceeded at a saunter along the damp and greasy pavements by the basement railings for some little distance in silence. They appeared so much at ease that they might have been suspected of owning the strange, exclusive disposition of cats to make choice of situations of discomfort. Lingering quite unnecessarily, it was to be supposed, they snuffed up the peppery smell of the fog without repulsion and were evidently in no hurry to shut a door upon it. Something was perhaps congenial to them in the somewhat blackguardly air of the night.

After going a short way, they came to a halt close to a lamp and turned their eyes on each other. Then each softly laughed.

'What an extraordinary thing!' said Mrs Harrel in a tone of high vivacity.

'Well, the story didn't lose in the telling,' answered her son, a dark young man with a Punch-like nose and a bass, nasal voice, singularly unlike his mother. 'K. Antequin's stories never do.'

'But such a different tale—not the slightest resemblance to your own!'

'H'm, yes. That's odd. Of course I *did* supply her with the Carlotta House stuff—or most of it. And I did suggest a South American build-up, as she told me she'd come from there.'

'Well, she was clever enough to improve on your version. For it *is* an improvement, Charlie.'

'Ah! In fact, so woundy clever that I feel a bit flummoxed.'

Mrs Harrel sank into musing. They strolled on beside the railings and porticos, in and out of the rays, the young man, tall and weedy, with his slouching walk, so patently the lounger, the prowler, the creature who lives by its wits; the woman, well and discreetly dressed, with the pleasantest air of amiability, plump, motherly, yet somehow conveying another and deadlier aspect of the same species. Both belonged indefinably to the outskirts. Glancing curiously into every face, every lighted window, she commented pungently on what she saw. Their progress continued leisurely. In passing other couples or parties, these two were always silent and listened.

'So Keith was not taken in,' she said. 'He set her down for an impostor straight away. At least——'

'Very shrewd.'

'Yes, he was careful to put it like that. But, Charlie, those hints! Who could miss them? Not a soul but Christine has ever seen her. He is frankly mystified by Christine's story. And who was it who first dropped the word "hallucination"? Had anyone present had a personal experience? Or did anyone know of any instance at first hand? Till we were all talking about it on those lines. Young Mrs Antequin is suffering from hallucinations— she's not right in the head, poor girl. Not a soul of us who will not have gone off with that impression. Wasn't it cleverly done? Nothing so gross as a direct statement. Did you notice?'

' Yes, I'm very observant.'

'Under what heading did he intend us to put it? Occult? Psychopathic? A case of haunting—obsession? Mental breakdown? Of course, at the time of the marriage, Keith would have liked to wring her neck—it was well known. Have you ever seen young Mrs Antequin, Charlie?'

'Oh, yes—at a distance. A pretty creature. Old Thomas!'

'Oh, he was a good sort. He gave me many a helping hand and asked no questions. One good turn deserves another . . . Yes, she *is* a pretty creature. If there's anything wrong, I'm sorry.' Mrs Harrel added thoughtfully, 'Well, I suppose it must have seemed a bit mystifying—that sudden silence. Sudden silence. Oh, Charlie, what do you feel like? You're to blame, you know.'

The young man laughed without answering.

'Keith has deteriorated a good deal of late. Of course he had a bad time with Thomas towards the end. He looks seedy—look at that!' she said suddenly; and for a minute they both remained staring into the lighted window of a basement where some cat and dog quarrel was in full swing. This spectacle, which would not have struck everyone as comic, amused them both extremely; they hung over it as if they could hardly tear themselves away, and were still laughing as they went on.

They entered presently a long mews which had an atmosphere of smart bohemianism deriving from a small public house at one end with the racy name of The Garden of Eden. At the far end of the passage they came to their own door.

Charlie went into the garage below the dwelling and began tinkering with his car. Mrs Harrel, after removing her party clothes, indulged in an interval of musing of a kind to absorb her, for she loved mysteries and problematical happenings, though she did not like them to remain inexplicable, and she loved worming things out. A disorderly writing-table stood in the window, but after glancing at this in bored indecision, she turned off the light and sat down in the glow of the gas-fire; darkness might favour concentration. Lights from the mews climbed the walls and glided over the ceiling as cars crept down the lane or moved in and out of the garages; wireless blared on both sides, children cried—but all this did not inconvenience Mrs Harrel. She liked a jolly noise, a stir of life. Prolonged silence would have made her uneasy.

But in fact she *was* uneasy. She was intensely superstitious, as only the material-minded can be. The fog pressed closer, a vapour gilded by the lights, with an air of being swept in hastily to conceal something that was going on in the vast, open darkness. The mews quietened to some extent; and once she jumped up at a light, hasty step on the cobbles below, close to their door, and listened for a few moments but did not instantly look out. When she did look, any passing figure had long been engulfed.

Her curiosity had been deeply stirred by the tale she had just been hearing, and perhaps some other emotion besides, one less agreeable, had her in its grip. She remembered visiting Thomas and his story of the lost child, and her feeling that his attitude was odd, that something was not as it should be with the ageing Thomas Antequin. Later, she had concluded that the poor old simpleton had managed to get into trouble somehow. Then Christine, too, flitted through these meditations in a light of sympathy; till she began to feel that, but for laziness, something might be done by her.

'Charlie, bring me a drink,' she called through the half-open door, having heard her son come upstairs into the flat. Her voice was animated. There was a chinking of glasses and in a few moments the young man appeared with two tumblers. He commented on the morbid mentality of people who sat in the dark.

'I do wish that girl of yours hadn't—been so impulsive! I mean, I wish one could produce her. It would be so nice to spoil Keith's game. Anyway—I don't like such happenings—they're dreary.'

'What? Are you still grizzling over that?' Charlie said in a tone of surprise. 'Drink up and forget it.'

'I wonder——Now, it's just struck me—I wonder if there was a line or two somewhere in the papers at the time? She might, you know, have given *that* name. It would be nice to confront Keith with *that*. Have you any idea of the date?'

'No, never knew it. I only picked up the news at her place. I didn't inquire—naturally. That was days afterwards.'

'Well, when you've done that, fetch me some of those papers in the sitting-room cupboard. There's a great stack there—I dare say they go back as far as May. Look out June or May, down to the twenty-first—which was when they met, according to Keith.'

'Ah, why dig it up?' However he brought the papers and they began going over them together, and as they turned out to be not properly in order this took them some time. Charlie fetched more drink. 'Well, you needn't look at the front page, Mother,' he said sardonically. 'Look at the inside columns, towards the foot.'

'Poor little wretch. Don't you feel bad, Charlie?' she asked idly again as they fluttered the sheets.

'No—why?' She was sunk already. 'These Latin girls have only one incentive to decent behaviour—fear of the priest. Once they cut loose——'

'How did you first come across her?'

'Didn't I tell you? I picked her up in The Garden of Eden in the first place. I'd just seen that business in the evening papers—Lambert's hoard, I mean—and of course there was the old tale all worked over again and a photo of the kid, into the bargain. Well, I was sitting there, thinking to myself that the case would make a good film—with the addition of the long-lost girl turning up home again, naturally—when someone leaned over my shoulder, put her finger on the paragraph, and said, "*I* have a right to that money." Turned round and found one of the young merries I'd noticed before hanging about the Garden. "Have you, dear?" I said. She sat down and I gave her a drink. Said she'd come from South America. When my eye lighted properly on her, though, I began thinking, "Why, look at this girl, *she*'d make up all right for the part." For I reckoned there wouldn't have to be much likeness, within reason. There wasn't, of course. Idea amused me. Said I to her, "Look here, you should have a shot at it," or something to that effect. I just meant it as a joke, in the first place. Then, as we talked, it occurred to me, "Well, why not?" At first I just thought I was doing her a good turn—I thought she might collect a bit off the Antequin woman, who's known to be rather mild. Softhearted.

'By degrees I got interested. I thought up a tale. I went to quite a deal of trouble, too, going down there to pick up some useful items . . . By the way, it was funny—I got into the Antequin abode under the wing of an old party who turned out to be Christine's mother. Old dear gave me a jar by being allusive about the Garden of Eden—I thought she was taking a pot at me. All right—nothing in it.

'Well, but, as I was saying, I did tell the young cuss to wait till we were properly primed. I insisted on that. Else I'd wash my hands of it, I said. I warned her to wait till I'd worked it out properly. I couldn't have the thing going off half-cocked—you can see . . . So what I can't understand is how she ever came to meet Christine at all. Girl took a dim view of her chances from the beginning—never really keen on the scheme. Who ever would have expected her to try it on by herself? Very depressed, as I say, when I last saw her, and I was pretty sharp with her. Told me she'd been trailing Christine a bit, just for the sake of sizing her up, which annoyed me. But not a word of speaking to her, mind you. I had a hunch, then, that Christine had made a rather holy impression on her. Discouraging. Depressed, as I say, shrugging, not saying much, and so forth—I did wonder, then, whether she was about to throw in her hand—but I must say, not like *that*! *That* didn't occur to me . . .

'What a sell. It was going so nicely. That tale she'd dished up to Christine was a winner. Makes my little effort look like something out of the Dale saga. Yes, by God, it does,' said Charlie, reminiscently, frowning. 'In fact, it's a bit more than I can swallow, from a girl of her sort. How could she have invented all that, I ask you? Where did she mug it up? Or, if there was anything in it, why didn't she pass it over to me to handle? Well, it beats me . . . Ah, here we are!' he added with satisfaction. He had come upon a few lines of print in the obscure position he had anticipated; and now read these aloud.

'"A South American girl, known as Nina Cazares, about nineteen, of no fixed address, yesterday evening threw herself off Lambeth Bridge and sank before help could reach her. First aid proved useless."'

'Ah, well, there's nothing in that,' sighed Mrs Harrel with waning interest.

'Except the date—except the date, my dear. Twenty-first of May, Keith said? Date of this paper, now I come to use my powers of observation.'

In abrupt silence, with startled, half-comic aspect, they opened their eyes at each other, Charlie rolling his fearfully.

'Tch,' said Mrs Harrel. 'Keith's muddled it.'

The next moment, they both began to laugh according to their flighty custom, both being people to whom most things seemed ultimately funny, even their own losses.

'There, Charlie, clear up all this mess, do.'

Charlie began putting the papers together and she sat without moving, watching him absently. A faintly startled look lingered in her eyes.

'We shall never get to the bottom of it,' she murmured.

'Bottom of what?'

'Well, it would be funny, wouldn't it, if the girl's tale was true—if she really was Vivian Lambert?'

'Sometimes I wondered myself,' the young man answered coolly. 'Of course, she always swore to it. Pooh, no. Why, if she ever was in America, which I doubt, she'd been in England for years, I should say. Long enough to rot.'

'Let me see—let me see——'

'What now?'

'Shall I go and have a talk with Christine? Shall I?'

'Throw me to the wolves if it suits you. Don't hesitate.'

'Oh, I shan't do you any harm. But oughtn't I to go?'

'Toss up for it.' Which she did.

She was not one to fly in the face of superstitious promptings. Possibly nothing less would have overcome her indolence.

Thus it was that Christine had a visit from Mrs Harrel—a reassuring, motherly personality, doing her an act of pure kindness, an old friend of Thomas's. From her she learned that she need never have doubted her senses, that there was a living girl, but (her informant declared) one who was certainly not Vivian Lambert; one who, as Mrs Harrel believed, had now returned to Peru. The pleasant creature's information was a trifle hazy—but it was natural that she should have taken little note of things which had not struck her as important at the time. Supporting dates, anything like precise facts, were lacking; Christine, however, was not of a type, or in a state, to demand them. And so reassuring, so motherly did the young woman find her deliverer, that she ended by telling her everything, all the shadowy fears—of the rose-petal caught in the grass, of the car waiting at the garden door, of the tormenting fancies raised by the talk with Rosalie—thankful to open her heart to one who was not only kind but worldly-wise.

For long hours after her odd ministering angel had left her, Christine lay pondering these disclosures, till they were extended and transformed in sleep; and then, waking some time before seven on the winter morning after she had heard the tale, she was drawn to stumble drowsily to the window of her London flat by a loud, stony clatter echoing from the cliff-like façades, which were all in darkness yet. She looked out into the dark gully. The strip of sky over the roof-tops was piled with flat, black cloud, gashed by a light so keenly silver that the metallic ring of the horse-hooves could be fancied to strike back an echo. Then, indistinctly in the obscurity, she made out the long, approaching cavalcade from the barracks. Two by two, a pair to a rider, the ebony shapes of the horses, seeming a little over life-size, as if the whole procession had some quality of the gigantic, passed before the portico of the hotel over the way, where burned the sole illumination of the scene; and the forms of the powerful, big, black horses, moving at a walking pace in the darkness, suggested the gloomy pageantry of a funeral cortège. They proceeded in a clash of echoes, silent otherwise.

Such an air of phantasmagoria had this glimpse, that she, falling asleep again the next moment, could have believed it part of the inflated symbolism of a dream, a hollow dream, but for the weave of silver scratches which daylight revealed upon the surface of the road.

Yes—dead! Dead long ago. Twice dead! By the morning, she had brought herself to admit it with a new resignation.

THIRTY-FIVE

No sooner was he rid of Christine, and thus of the last fear that his labours might be sabotaged, than Keith went to work upon his biographical sketch; and now for the first time in his life he knew genuine inspiration. Day by day, he was carried along, like one possessed, in a condition of nervous excitement which kept his spirits bounding and raised deep misgivings in the heart of Helena. Passion actuated him and drove his pen with miraculous power. It helped him to produce a work so far above his usual level that it approached brilliance. The passion was hatred. All the secret antipathy to his father, all the bitter jealousy which had accumulated in the young man's mind throughout the years, all the knowledge, never admitted, of their true relations, of Thomas's towering superiority and his own insignificance, and the real hatred springing from the final blow, the cruel mockery of the will, had forced a sort of truth from him at last, an involuntary display of his true feelings. The issue bore likeness to a poisoned flood.

It was a brief work, not quite in the form he had originally planned, for it consisted in large part of extracts from the journal, with commentary passages by himself to make it comprehensible to the general reader; and it was beyond argument that, on this ground, Keith had at last eclipsed his father, his brilliant and spicy interpolations being laid cheek by jowl with the poor jottings which Thomas had indulged in for his own pleasure and comfort. The contrast was cruel. And indeed many felt that it was thoroughly indecent to publish such stuff as these private scribblings which the great writer had obviously never intended any eye but his own to see. Yet it hardly seemed as if Keith was to be condemned; since his little masterpiece was actually impaired, as some thought, by a rather tiresome tone of filial piety.

This important work was published at an advantageous season, and nobody at the first blush could see why Thomas's journal should have been published at all. And one or two unwary people said so. Then there was a hushed pause. Then there was a sensation.

Perhaps it was all Keith had dreamed, and more. Perhaps he triumphed. For not merely the literary part of the press was fluttered and carried its comments, but all the large dailies also took up the story. Thomas Antequin! Thomas Antequin the possible murderer in the thirteen-year-old Lambert case! Thomas Antequin—was it credible?—a public figure, famous and beloved. (So it was said now.) Ah, but then everyone knew he was horribly crazy towards the end. The intriguing revelations made (of course in good faith) by his devoted biographer had left no doubt of it.

But was it really credible that the man's own son, however sunk in adulatory blindness, could publish such a thing in all innocence? One could only suppose, in charity, that, working too near the canvas, he had not seen the pattern as a whole. For the majority, Keith's possible innocence added exquisitely to the sensation. He was known to be devoted to his father, bound up in him, the very soul of loyalty; no one had ever had cause to think otherwise. So a few felt pity. Others knew him too well. All his friends wished to have a look at him, to see what face he put on the matter.

But Keith had gone to earth. He had retired to his 'country place'.

It needed an ingenious ruse to draw him up to London, to be looked at; and such a ruse was finally devised.

Out of the blue, he received a graciously worded invitation to join the Sunday evening gathering of a small and very select coterie which for years had maintained a scathing and destructive public silence about Thomas Antequin and all his works. This group had for its leader the charming hostess, novelist and poet, Mrs Shillingford, and its headquarters at her beautiful little house in Chelsea, Vough Cottage, overlooking the Physic Garden. An invitation coming from such a quarter could only be taken at its face value. It was entirely above suspicion. Biddings to Vough Cottage were usually received with reverence. The house did not open its doors to anything short of high talent; its habitués formed a seriously gifted and superior group, a genuine aristocracy of the intellect. Every member was worthy. A vulgar old campaigner like Mrs Harrel, for all her penetrative powers, could only have hoped for an interior view of Vough Cottage in the capacity of a charlady. And it was no source of surprise to anyone but Keith that he had hitherto never been asked to adorn—though in the character of honourable enemy—a Shillingford gathering. Neither, for that matter, had Thomas; but that, at least, was no mystery. This band of choice aesthetes had its own somewhat perverse standards; not every talent, however authentic, met with its approval, and those which did not were treated with what would have been called, if occurring in cruder circles, an uninhibited intolerance. It was, of course, a damaging intolerance, being both highly articulate and toothed and clawed with irony at its most civilised and most spiteful. And it was from the heart of this small coterie that the fashionable depreciation of Thomas Antequin had received its first impulse.

Naturally Keith was aware of this. Much unkind feeling had always existed between himself and the Shillingford group. However, it is a small mind which cherishes resentment, especially when it appears harmful to its own interests. Keith was flattered. Enough judgment remained to him to value the invitation at something like its true worth and attribute it to common curiosity; yet, at his present strange pass, he felt it might do him good.

Mrs Shillingford's small court was, of course, composed of like-minded people. Yet one or two effective foils were sometimes admitted, by way of seasoning and amusement, people who were not exactly members but protégés; young writers or artists like the brilliant but bearish Robert Gunner, or the forthright, plebeian Hamilton Raven. Mrs Shillingford sometimes took a fancy to budding genius of the rawer kind. It amused her; and also it may be supposed that she felt it contrasted very effectively with her own extreme, spider-thread subtlety. Moreover, she had a cherished and indulged nephew, Roddy, of whom it was said that he had a great artistic future—for what else could have been said of a rather clever boy who was also Mrs Shillingford's nephew?

To this graceless young man the engineering of the unpleasant incident which occurred on the occasion of Keith's visit was afterwards attributed. And of course with some reason. Certainly it was he who contrived to introduce into his aunt's reception of that momentous night one or two members of the younger literary set of such low attainments and general insignificance that their presence in Vough Cottage was even thus hardly accountable.

Such literary riff-raff as Charlie Harrel——Yes, Charlie Harrel, of all people, could tell his mother the whole story as an eyewitness when he strolled into her bedroom next morning to join her at a slovenly, protracted breakfast over the mews.

Charlie was full of triumph. 'How did you do it?' she cried admiringly; and listened with bated breath and many a chuckle to what he had to tell her. He described how a few days previously a little group of young acquaintances had met, everyone agog with the problem of K. Antequin's attitude, and all of the opinion that it was nothing but a shameful, stinking, heartless publicity stunt. A decision was then taken to force the culprit out into the open. They were all indignant on Thomas's account, several of them having cause to remember the old chap with liking, others professing immoderate admiration for his genius (and these were perhaps the vanguard of those who would one day revive Thomas's fame—they were so young). None of them was in a merciful mood.

'Gunner, Eva Wickett and Hamilton Raven, Roddy Shillingford and myself. None of us nice people, you will notice—all truth-lovers, and you know what that means. Yes, it had a bit the air of a bear-baiting, but that didn't worry us.'

'Or a bit of bully-ragging at school.'

'Oh, do you think so?' said Charlie, for once slightly disconcerted. 'Not that one would liken K. Antequin to a bear. A domestic pussy—yes, that's better. Well, say what you like, he deserved it!' cried Charlie with unwonted enthusiasm. 'What? Here's the man holding up before our eyes what look like the plainest proofs of his father's crime, or of poor old Thomas's madness, or whatever it was—as if the monstrous interpretation had never dawned on him. Makes you shudder. Sometimes you quite wonder——'

'Yes, you do.'

'What?'

'Whether it *has* dawned on him—in any real sense.'

'Pooh, near enough. Well, we didn't really get him, of course, but give us time. This is only a start'; and then he went on to describe with relish his and his friends' exploit.

'Yes, everything was under way at the usual stately pace, with five modest young privileged persons in the background, seen but not heard. Then suddenly we five opened fire—we stood up, shouted over the heads of the whole crew and began pelting him with questions, all as crude as you please, not mincing matters. What had he meant by this and that—and we gave chapter and verse, all the worst bits—doing everything we could to corner him and force him to explain himself in the face of the whole crowd—cloud of witnesses, you know, and what witnesses! Each with a tongue in his head, to put it mildly. Scandalised looks among the old habitués—no one intervened, however, no one made any attempt to keep us in order. Yes, that was notable. As for Keith, he was surprised by the attack, that one could tell, nastily surprised, I judged, a bit agitated, but he kept his social face and dodged very cleverly. There was a silence throughout the room, a sort of gradual hush—people drew away, so that there was K. in the midst of us—and I will say he rose to the occasion. I see him yet—the big, bald forehead and the curious smile.

'Well, the ring being formed, as you might say, people then gathered round a little closer, and even elbowed for a front place—no, they were not above that, Mrs Shillingford's hand-picked Intellects. We had a very attentive audience. Breathless silence, and a darting and feasting of eyes—most edifying. And Auntie? Our charming hostess? You may well ask, How was *she* taking it? What was she playing at to allow such a primitive display? You know that ethereal little phiz with the tiny, bright eyes, piercing as gimlets? Shocked, indignant, and the little eyes alight with curiosity and malice. Yes, she was fascinated. She made a few feeble, flustered attempts to regain control, and then left it.

'Keith rode the storm well, I'll say that for him. He wriggled out of it, time and again, always with that nasty, playful air—you know it? Horribly neurotic, really. He slipped round and round, like a cake of soap in a bath, with five pairs of hands grabbing at him. But what a scene, dears! In that refined setting, where intellects revel chastely together every Sunday evening, and one can be as spiteful as one pleases, but never coarsely so. And how the whole crowd enjoyed it. A rather meatier entertainment than usual—they wolfed it down.

'Still, there it was, we weren't making much headway. Eva Wickett at last sang out something to this effect: "But of course you know there's some girl going about laying claim to being Vivian Lambert? How's that? Come, you can't have it both ways, you know. If she's alive, why, you can't have her murdered—and so what's it all about?" Keith threw her a charming, sad smile, an appealing smile. "And I dare say you know very well how such a rumour has arisen, and that it has nothing to do with the true facts, the true story of Vivian Lambert. Those of you who do know, please have the decency to keep it to yourselves." That beat us! Of course we all thought of poor Christine Antequin, and that one ought to spare her and not make a song of her dotty condition—pretty, kind creature. And so there was a pause.

'I thought the game was up. Ham Raven, though, couldn't get hold of the soap and was getting furious. He climbed into the ring. Went right up to Keith and bawled in his face. "But don't you know what they're saying, man? Don't pretend you don't! Everyone has taken your hints to imply that Thomas might very well have committed the murder, and most likely did so. *The Inquisitors*, you say, is a sadistic work, it was written at that time—and it was a sadistic murder of the kind sometimes committed by a virtuous man who breaks down. Come, now, do you mean us to take it that Thomas was the murderer?"

'Had that gone home? 'Pon my word, none of us could tell. At least, it finished us.

'Keith didn't give an inch. Poor old Ham himself ended by being put out of countenance. Keith stared and stared at him, and smiled a little—that curious smile. That slightly deranged smile, I might say. Oh, yes, attractive, rather, but damned odd, can't be denied. He was so obviously moved, shocked, or anyway under strong emotion of some sort—I say, of some sort! Because God knows what, really. I should have thought, simply by looking at him, incredulity. Profoundly shocked, you know, and indignant, incredulous. And righteous, righteous! Astounded at our evil minds. He flicked us all round with a disdainful glance—pretty effective.

'Well, civilisation raised its head again. K. turned with dignity to his hostess, and she at last, as if waking from a trance, took sudden, sharp measures. And I doubt if Roddy will be much in favour in future—Auntie will more and more regret that bit of rough-housing in her chaste halls . . . Not much of a success for us—no, we didn't get him that time. K. left quietly. Oh, but we've not finished with him yet—you'll see——'

Mrs Harrel had listened and kept smiling in lazy amusement; but at last rather as if her thoughts were beginning to work on a theme of her own; and Charlie, noting this, cried shrewdly, 'Any suggestions?'

THIRTY-SIX

Keith left the party, very strung up, in an intensely excited, combative mood, and came out into the street to find a light rain falling. Incapable of bringing his mind to bear on anything but the scene he had just left, the illuminated ring of intelligent, all too intelligent, faces, most of them known to him, and the battery of gloating, appraising, hostile eyes he had so triumphantly confronted, he did not even think to put up his umbrella and commenced to walk, unconsciously glad of the sharp motion, towards the little *pied à terre* he had recently acquired in one of the cul-de-sacs off the Brompton road.

A curious point now was his bitter indignation at the condemnatory tone everyone was taking, at the judgment which had been pronounced upon him, which he had not failed to read that evening written on every face assembled there. (And they were faces which mattered.) In spite of himself, this had profoundly shaken him. His triumph was shot with horror—a horror which gained upon him as he walked and as his brain cooled. Now, for the first time, the beginnings of a proper assessment of his deed made itself felt; that is, he began to see it through others' eyes; a view to which something had so far blinded him. There dawned on him a recognition that he had acted outrageously, impossibly, in the eyes of the world, and had for ever damaged that character, that interesting, likeable personality, which he had spent the greater part of his life in building up. He could scarcely credit the idea that he was perhaps ruined. His head turned at the thought. A shiver of mingled excitement and apprehension of the most desolating kind passed through him; it was not yet remorse, but perhaps a rumour of remorse to come. Also some consciousness of his conduct towards Christine, and of how that must look seen from the outside, seen apart from its true motivation, was at last present. For he did not repent—he did not himself think badly of that cold-blooded ambition of the pettiest kind which had swamped all natural feeling in him, and the treachery which had succeeded—all for an unsavoury celebrity, a trumpery success, transient as the day's news, for the sake of being the hero of a minor sensation. But now he *was* concerned at the judgment of others. To this his deed was reduced in his own estimation—to a solecism of the kind which spells social ruin; one of those deeds, not criminal, not immoral, which yet make an outcast of a man.

The attack had been a shock. Yes, he had borne up against a bad shock that evening. A swift exhaustion threatened to descend on him now, but did not quite do so yet. Like a man fatally hit, he walked on briskly. A slight dizziness troubled him, however—he remembered nervously his father and his father's fate, and felt it was essential to calm himself.

He stopped then; looked about him and discovered himself to have come by a somewhat round-about route and to be standing before the splendid, massive, highly imaginative pile of one of the museums, from the encrusted surface of which a crowd of little shapes and visages peeped or perked against the sky. There it rose before him, a great bestiary in stone; and by its unashamed romanticism, its strongly fanciful character, its emotional intensity, its approximation to all the vigour and colour of Elizabethan poetry, with the same tendency to conceit and rich ornament, reminded him of his own conception of his father's genius, or that aspect of it which had so deeply impressed him at one time; and thus of the most successful part of his life with Thomas.

And, as if nothing had intervened, he was straightway flushed with pride, reflecting, 'It was I who divined him. I created him.'

Here he paused, lost in amazement at the fools who had spoken as if he had done his father any injury, or ever would do so; and then asked, with ironical indignation, what *they* had ever done for Thomas, that they should imagine themselves to have a right to speak. Had *they* created him?

In fact, he did not himself notice this strangest of paradoxes in his own attitude; hating his father while admiring him, jealously cherishing him as his own precious handiwork and possession, whom no one else might decry, while himself calmly savaging him for his own benefit.

He discovered that it was raining sharply, and putting up his umbrella moved off beside the railings, with the stooping gait of an elderly man, sunk in agitated thought.

The house for which he was bound belonged to one of the small, early nineteenth-century terraces of the district, and stood in a narrow, long square, a place of decorative fanlights and miniature iron balconies, where a mingling of ultra-smartness with carefully preserved Regency features alternated with frank decay, and even disrepute. This garden square was all on a small scale and seemed intimate and quiet as he turned into it, after the impression of the vast public buildings by which he had just passed. It seemed small and dark.

The glossy blackness of the rain-swept little cul-de-sac, starred and speared with lesser lights, at once struck him as of a deeper shade than that of the main road. Trees occupying its narrow oblong of garden darkened it upon one hand with a glitter of wet evergreens, from which a whisper sounded of the thin rain on the leaves. Long, frail rays shot from the glassy water-drops which had gathered on the rails, on the glistening iron-work, and seemed to prick the eyes painfully. From the patch of open ground there welled a scent of wet dust, so strong that it was almost rank. All his impressions were intense, sharp, abnormally so. It was as if his senses, after being so flagrantly ignored while his mind was occupied with visionary scenes, had suddenly begun sending through their messages with an angry urgency which positively distorted them. With this went a defect of the sense of proportion, a childish faculty of abrogating it. Walking beside the stream in the gutter, he saw the narrow tress of the black water on a false scale, his mind making of what his vision reported a broad flood of gloomy and dangerous and horribly polluted aspect. As it was magnified so was its defilement. It was like filthy rivers in black cities, which pour over suicides. In short, his imagination had suddenly begun throwing up threatening images in all around him, suddenly ravening out of control. The darkness was bottomless darkness, he saw depths and depths, and himself like a man falling.

Lights hung in brackets of antiquated pattern above front doors, and these and other archaic devices in this small backwater seemed to have a new prominence. He began fancying that the little, flat, old-world faces of the houses breathed a spirit of dark antiquity, something far older than their age. The whole square, seen under the rain, everything painted with the same jetty and wicked glitter, appeared as if drawn in a dark, old wood-cut, like the picture of some place belonging to an age which admitted the terrors of superstition, where still lingered some ancient neurosis, strange and shocking to the modern mind. Thus his thoughts ominously seized on the queer.

Here his solitude was broken. A small figure, that of a young girl, apparently, detached itself from the shadows by the garden railing and, crossing the road, stood in his way.

His nerves quivered. He deflected his course a little, as was necessary, and went past her with averted eyes; and then was conscious that she came behind him, walking lightly, so lightly, indeed, that he could not hear her footsteps for the pattering of the rain on the stretched stuff of his umbrella. But still he was aware of her walking very close on his heels, a little to one side, like a well-trained dog, in a proximity far too close to be accidental.

A respectable man, and not warm-blooded, he was some-what inexperienced in ways of disrepute.

What did she want? Begging? In these days? Bad enough. Surely nothing worse? And he went on, afraid even to glance at her, lest he should encourage her. She followed steadily. Perhaps she was merely frightened in the nocturnal streets and wanted protection on her way home—she was perhaps young enough for that. Then he heard a voice. Behind him there came the words, in a hoarse whisper, 'Sir!' and then, 'Dearie!' He was horrified and incredulous. Why, the figure he had passed with deliberate inattention had been almost a child's, surely? He swung round, and said with frigid severity, 'What are you doing here, child? You shouldn't be out at this time. Go home at once.' But his words ended in agitation. For it was a quite small girl, a child of seven or eight, no more, far smaller than he had at first supposed—and she had imitated that professional murmur of seduction unmistakably, to a shade.

Or so he had fancied. For suddenly he felt he could not have heard aright. And now he looked at her with the keenest scrutiny.

He saw her at close quarters, and saw her very plainly in the light of the lamp which stood a little behind himself. She did not smile, or display any other venal trick. On the contrary, he had, horribly enough, an impression of something sick, sullen, driven by necessity. There was an adult air about her, in spite of her small stature, so that for an instant he wondered desperately whether she might be a dwarf. But clearly she was not that. He saw the rain trickle on the shoulders of her coat, which was already soaked dark, and drip from the scarf she wore over her hair, one drop after another bouncing off. She was intensely pale. The whole effect of her was wretched, unwholesome, and in some obscure manner one almost of deformity. In the light of the lamp the eyes glinted darkly, very close-set. The whole face in that instant struck him as faintly bestial, almost baboon-like in its structure, and he felt there was a natural fierceness about it, very disquieting to a civilised person, like that of a being on the fringes of humanity.

He realised, in some odd fashion a second after the voice had ceased, that she had again spoken; and had said (he thought), 'Leave me alone!' His blood froze. So that was it!

But something else thrust even this from his mind.

A large, prominent mouth—and suddenly his eyes were drawn to that mouth and fixed upon it in fascination. On the underlip, the tips of the teeth rested.

He turned sharply and made for his door.

He was thankful, in a distraught way, to see no light in the house, save for the usual faint one in the fanlight, for he judged that the other tenants were out; while the strains of a wireless behind the drawn curtains of the basement made it likely that the housekeeper and her husband would hear nothing. For now he was deadly afraid, fearing a shriek or outcry on the steps behind him—and then what would become of him, exposed to the accusations of a vicious child? Nothing of the sort, however, happened. He entered and closed the door in the face of this dreadful little hanger-on.

But the house he inhabited consisted of three minute flatlets. The front door was always unlocked on the common staircase, to allow any of the tenants to enter, so that he could not now secure it behind him, though he had quite to struggle against an urge to do so. One dim lamp of the lowest power burned in this entrance passage, and going along it he forgot to put his hand on the switch which lighted the top landing, his own; so bent was he on suppressing a disposition to bolt up the staircase at unnatural speed and gain his own door. The second flight was faintly lighted from below, but at the next turn of the stairs it grew quite dark.

It was here that there was a sound close beside him as if something had lightly brushed the wall—a sensation as if something little and low had run under his elbow, or perhaps someone stooping, running with hands upon the treads. This startled him so violently that, with a loud exclamation of 'Who's there?' he struck out and down with the flat of his hand, trying to grab whatever it was, while missing a step and falling back against the banisters so that they creaked again. The side of his hand just grazed an iron rail set in the wall (as if perhaps some ancient tenant had found the stairs a difficulty), and he even found time to think that he would have got a nasty knock if he had struck out an eighth of an inch wider. Meanwhile, he had felt his hand come down on empty air.

Then a terrible thing happened. Someone screamed— himself! A searing pain had run through his hand, and it took him another instant to realise that something had bitten him, with ferocity, with all the strength of its jaws, right through the side of his palm, under his little finger, so that he had heard the bone crunch.

His own scream continued to ring in his ears with a hideous tone of hysteria.

No further sound reached him. But without so much as stopping to listen, without waiting to gather the movements of this invisible attacker, without thinking of descending and looking over the banisters to see if any one had run down again—in short, in a blind panic—he dashed up the rest of the flight, switched on the light (upon an empty landing), and thought of nothing else but bolting his door against a maniac.

Instinctively, on feeling the blood run, he had whipped out his handkerchief in the dark and swaddled the wound. Now the first thing he noticed was that there was no stain on the thin stuff, which he had expected to see half soaked. He strode into the middle of the room, held his hand to the light and unwound the bandage. For a moment he found he could not see—he was faint.

His sight returned, still somewhat clouded.

Certainly a dreadful injury.

Yet he saw with astonishment that he had been mistaken about the bleeding, though he could have sworn that he had felt the blood run in streams. The skin was unbroken. The peculiar dark red marks, now turning purple, the chain of little oblong dents set in a half circle, showed it plainly enough to be the work of teeth. It was so obviously, so indubitably a human bite, that as he stared down at it, with his head swimming, a strange sense came over him for an instant. Almost too good, too perfect a sample of its genre, so to speak—so precisely what one would expect of the appearance of such an injury! In the midst of it was a tiny graze, hardly a scratch, where he had caught his hand on the rail; on this his attention centred in some odd manner which he could not control and kept noticing. It seemed to stand out too much.

Still the throbbing was fearful, the pain ran up his arm in fiery waves and made him feel ill.

Almost beside himself from shock and pain, he rushed into the little bathroom and held his hand under the tap for a long while—so much distracted that he had no idea what to do with it, nothing but an instinctive feeling that he must bathe a hurt which might be infected. Although the skin was not broken, the feeling persisted that he must wash out poison. For it was surely the bite of a maniac, of a mad dog? Secretly, with dread, with throbbing queries, he recalled the unwholesome look of the young creature in the square. And, shivering as much from a moral distress as with pain, he asked himself how anyone could have run so quickly and quietly up a strange staircase in the dark.

But now he began to agitate himself because the bathroom cupboard was not stocked with any chemist's stuff and there was no antiseptic in the flat. He wrapped the hand in a clean handkerchief and took a little brandy.

The pain did not subside. In an hour's time, in fact, the whole arm was throbbing violently and he was pacing to and fro, incapable of rest. He fancied, besides, that the hand was of a bad colour, and puffy, very inflamed; but this was perhaps the result of long bathing.

It was by now far advanced in the small hours; the square was quiet, he had long ago heard the housekeeper's husband turn out the light in the entrance passage and lock the outer door; and a little while after he heard the tenant below him stirring. This man had come in an hour ago, making little noise, as was his habit.

Then suddenly it occurred to Keith that he had once been told that his neighbour on the floor below had some sort of medical qualifications. He barely knew the man even by sight and had avoided him in the past, suspecting him to be of doubtful reputation, perhaps a doctor who had been struck off the register. Dr Roke's habits were too inoffensive and quiet—they were secretive. But suddenly this rather appealed to Keith than otherwise. He had felt from the first that he should consult a doctor; but a ridiculous little point had prevented him. He did not know how to explain a human bite. He was a vain man, and somewhat prudish. Some low adventure would certainly be attributed to him, something disreputable and undignified. Or even some squalid domestic scene, horribly ludicrous, might be suspected. And his self-esteem, that delicate quality, the flourishing of which was so peculiarly vital to his well-being, trembled on the edge of demoralisation at the bare thought.

But this man of bad character would hold his tongue, would not press indiscreet questions.

After all, he required nothing but a little knowledgeable advice. At the very least, he could borrow some antiseptic, which he lacked.

He was so thoroughly unnerved by the whole adventure, however, that it cost him a great effort to open his door upon the unlighted staircase and make his way down to the next landing to knock up this neighbour of his.

Stooping, with grey hair much in need of a cut, scholarly-looking in some vague, greasy and scruffy manner, wearing a repulsively dirty dressing-gown, the man did not make an agreeable impression. Keith at once noticed a smell of spirits, but nevertheless judged that his neighbour was as good as sober. It was more to the point that he seemed well disposed; for at the explanation, 'I'm sorry to knock you up at such an hour, but I have had a very nasty accident—I believe you're a medical man?' the door was opened to him very readily.

'Certainly . . . do what I can . . . an accident, you say?' Dr Roke's air was obliging, even slightly servile, like that of a man of no reputation eager to make a good showing. The room was extraordinarily full of large, dark furniture, and the greater part of this was cast into deep shadow by a light with a green shade hanging low over the central table. An electric fire created a dry and too fierce heat, and seemed to draw out a smell of ancient upholstery—or was it bed?—and the windows, Keith guessed, were all closed. His malaise increased.

Still, he entered, unwrapped his hand and held it out under the light. For once in his life, he was at loss for words, and made no attempt to give an explanation; while, with alarm and shame, he felt the hysterical tension in his throat. The man bent over the hand as if to examine it closely. He breathed heavily upon it. There was a pause. Then he straightened up and glanced into his visitor's face; and Keith stared back. The doctor was grinning.

He had probably taken out his dentures for the night, for it was now very obvious that he was toothless. And this seemed to Keith an absurd touch, with something deliberate about it, a gratuitous irony. It was like some grotesque symbolical circumstance in a nightmare. And a sense of outrage again tightened his throat.

All he could think was that the worst had happened. The man had at once attached some unsavoury story to such a wound, which was so clearly a human bite. He lied stiffly, he lied badly because he did it deliberately, as he rarely did. 'I came through the mews—it was very dark in that short passage—some cur must have been lurking in the shadow and flew at me . . .'

The fellow suddenly gave a brief giggle, as if in embarrassment.

Keith went on severely, 'I didn't want to turn out in search of a doctor at such an hour. I felt rather ill—faint. The thing is probably not as serious as I suppose—but it pains me—it pains me excessively. I'm a little afraid of septicaemia.'

Laying his head on one side, so that he had still a rather waggish air, in spite of lips now soberly pursed, the doctor again dropped his eyes on to the hand, which Keith kept extended. He did not touch it.

'You can tell me perhaps whether it's necessary to have it dressed, or whether I can safely deal with it myself?'

'Oh—safely, yes! Perfectly safely. Well, you might bathe it, I suppose—and a spot of arnica—it would do no harm.' He was no longer smiling, but still had the embarrassed air, while eyeing Keith furtively. 'Arnica?' said Keith, astonished. 'Trifles sometimes lead to blood-poisoning, to be sure,' the man mumbled. Yet now Keith could scarcely feel that he was being mocked—it was something stranger than that, more inexplicable. The doctor's whole air was curiously jaunty and sheepish, it was the kind of air people put on when unable to see a joke against themselves. It at last struck Keith that he was actually drunk, with the drunkenness of the habitual toper who does not show it.

Nevertheless, he was at such a pass, he felt so desperately nervous, that he positively begged this dubious medico to treat the wound for him; which the man did readily and in what seemed to Keith a reasonably expert manner, first manipulating the hand without causing much pain and then fixing the bandage in a workmanlike fashion. Neither the nameless medicament from a somewhat dusty bottle nor the butt-end of a roll of gauze appealed much to the patient, however, for both appeared to have been lying by for some while without much regard for their hygienic character. All this while, the doctor kept his manner of good-will.

But at the door, on parting with his visitor, 'Why, man, what do you suppose is wrong with your hand?' he suddenly asked, somewhat aggressively, like one tired of a joke.

Keith took him to be asking what specific injury he supposed had been done, and so replied sharply, 'I thought you could tell me that.' Once more, he was faced with the sheepish grin.

The door did not close behind him. He felt that the man was standing there and watching him ascend the stairs with an unnatural interest.

The events of the last few hours had so upset his nerves that on reaching his own rooms he broke down, lamented his whole fortune and wept, while feeling a vague reliance on the thought of God, he being a righteous man.

However, almost at once, as if by magic, the hand began to grow much easier, and saying to himself joyfully that perhaps the old drunkard had known what he was doing, in spite of his offensive and negligent manner, he suffered a complete reaction, his spirits rose feverishly, and he congratulated himself upon having avoided going to a practising doctor, who would surely have demanded a full explanation.

This ugly incident had in fact served to take his thoughts off the attack upon himself at the party. He had been saved from brooding over that, as he would otherwise have done, fretting and raging against it, with smarting vanity. He did not think of it even now. Getting into bed, he at once fell into an exhausted sleep.

THIRTY-SEVEN

'. . . left the car by the door in the garden wall, entered the garden and prowled about in the fierce, jungle-like chiaroscuro. Over-hot, over-tired. Joyful dreams of freedom. My head so full of my *Inquisitors* that I could not look at any living thing without analogous thoughts. As I was meeting Trissingham, the builder, I had no key and so kept to the garden. Too hot, however, and my head felt bad. Had never explored the grounds thoroughly—in particular, had never visited the well-house, and in fact, till today, did not know what use the building had had. Felt curious, and after staring at it from the park side, over the fence between the chestnuts, I went round through the kitchen garden and from there viewed it again. Romantic decay and triste setting. It caught my fancy. Walked along by the elders, nauseated a little by their flat reek, to see the extent of the kitchen garden. Suddenly, out of the corner of my eye, caught sight of some light moving thing in the direction of the well-house, so stopped and looked back at it through the bushes. A third side of the building was now visible to me in narrow perspective and seemed to be entirely covered with ivy, the leaves of which I saw in beaky profile, tapping upon each other when the air stirred. High up, under the eaves, a pale thing waving out of the prick-eared greenery. Mighty curious to know what it was. Entered the small field and circled the house, still at a distance, until I had a full view of that side. Then saw the thing properly. Yes, saw it properly.

'A little head protruding high up out of the wall. As it seemed, clean out of the wall. The hair, a quantity of fair, ragged hair blowing fitfully in the breeze gave an illusion of movement. Turned sideways, laid sideways on the sill of the aperture at a most curious angle—tilted sideways and downwards in an impudent, indescribably waggish posture reminiscent of Punch, the head seemed to be quizzing me—for although the face was turned in my direction, the hair straggling across it concealed its features altogether. Something else about it—of course, its posture, its really impossible carriage——Indescribable! Waited, stupefied, not daring to go nearer—and at last the hair was blown aside.

'She must have shut herself in. But, if so, with what object? The latch may have gone wrong, or the door may have jammed. I did not settle the point, for the whole door was so rotten that, when it would not at once open to my hand, a few kicks caused it to give way on the hinge side and fall inwards. She must have become wild with terror and attempted to climb out through the only aperture she could come at, and this was the little narrow vent under the eaves, which is, however, closed by a few rusty bars. The wall under this aperture having suffered a subsidence has cracked diagonally across its whole width, the lower section projecting on the inside to form a shallow zig-zag sufficiently like a flight of steps to give toe- and finger-hold to a small, active creature. She must have rushed at it, silly with terror, and succeeded in clambering high enough to thrust her head between a pair of bars in the aperture—but of course only to find that her body would not follow. And then a worse, a terrifying discovery must have awaited the little wretch. She could not draw her head in again. This I might have found difficult to credit, but for a previous experience. In just the same way, I once saw an urchin who had rammed his head between the railings over a London area and suddenly found himself a fixture, and that in spite of the advice and assistance of a small crowd. The railings had to be bent before they could release him—an alarming business for the sufferer. I hear his roars yet.

'But this one might have screamed, I suppose, to her heart's content; down in Hilbery, it would merely have been taken for the sound of children playing at a far distance. Hours ago, those screams had ceased. The lark went on singing.

'She must have slipped.

'Succeeded in bending a bar and pulling her down inside.

'Seeing that she was quite dead, and thus violently, I was extremely annoyed. Indeed, I may say that, understanding how all my plans would collapse upon the point of this redundant little corpse, I felt a kind of frustration and rage. Not unreasonably, I think. I believe I kicked it—kicked it savagely. However, there had been a great shock, of course. I became dizzy. I remember my horrible dizziness—and yet, during this, I must have picked her up and carried her out into the open garden, and put her down in the long grass.

'Left her there and walked for a bit, aimlessly, as I seem to remember, trying to collect my wits. It was such a nuisance that the dress was pink. Yes, if the dress had been green, I believe I might have been satisfied to go no further with it. I write as I felt then. Well, never mind—the bright pink worried me. Decidedly I was off my head for the moment. I saw and felt what I was about, but little more. Judgment there was none. Returned, having come to my senses.

'I reasoned thus. I could not, of course, allow this horrible thing to implicate me, as it must do if I permitted it to remain on my own ground. I could not endure such an inquisition as would follow. I foresaw that it would hold up work on the house indefinitely, that even to proceed with the purchase would appear indecent, that so K. would argue and would use it as a lever, that I should be victimised by the press, by the public. And that my work, now at a crucial stage, would suffer unthinkably—in short, I could not face it. Above all, I saw the place, my freedom, slipping out of my grasp, and my head reeled again. Then I had a brilliant idea.

'I examined the corpse carefully and thought that such injuries might well pass for the results of a road accident, and so I determined to remove it and place it in the lane at a little distance.

'After driving a short way, however, I suddenly asked myself, "Why not go further, while one's about it? Why not do the thing thoroughly? Find some spot quite out of my vicinity, at such a distance that no connection with Carlotta House will ever be suspected? Plenty of time, I need not even be late for my appointment with Trissingham. Any river will do."

'Altogether, from then on I acted with great coolness and commonsense.

'*Wrote that yesterday.*

'Impossible to explain my behaviour.

'How it was that I was not caught red-handed——For I took no precautions——Inconceivable!

'Cannot see any means of explaining to anybody my mad act.'

This fragment of narrative, which appeared in the columns of a literary paper shortly after the publication of Keith's book, was there stated to have come from an anonymous correspondent and to have been accompanied by the following explanation.

'The enclosed account is a faithful copy of some writing in my possession, and I think everyone will agree, on comparing the sequences, that the original can only be the three famous missing pages from Thomas Antequin's diary.

'I had better explain briefly how these came into my hands.

'I went to see my friend Thomas Antequin a day or so after the Lambert child was reported missing and found him ill in bed. The situation, his chance involvement in that tragic case has been described in so lively and particular a manner by his recent biographer that I need not enter into it here. On the occasion of this visit, I committed a theft. Antequin was lying down when I went into the room, but had evidently been correcting or making a clearance among his papers; the bed-table was strewn, and beside the bed stood a waste-paper basket, half-full. I suddenly felt I would like to take something—some scrap of his writing—by way of a souvenir. The fact is, I thought him very ill and had a feeling that he wasn't to last much longer. (In this, I was, of course, happily mistaken.) So, stooping down on a pretext, I secretly extracted from the basket the first thing I laid my hand on, which turned out to be a few pages ripped from a notebook—ripped out, torn in halves and thrown away together. Naturally I had taken care not to let him see what I did. In short, I filched them. My first impression was that I had luckily got hold of a discarded part of a manuscript, and I had hopes that it would prove to be some abortive version of a passage in his new work, which might some day be of value as a literary curiosity.

'Does my haul rank as such?

'All things considered, I prefer to remain anonymous.'

But whether these two documents were a hoax or genuine was never to be proved, for the nameless correspondent, challenged to come into the open and produce the original manuscript, remained as anonymous as he had desired and never again broke silence. One could only conclude that it was a hoax; or perhaps had been written by some over-zealous friend of Thomas's, who had chosen this questionable way to defend his memory from a charge of murder.

Others accepted the correspondent's story and thought the fragment genuine in the restricted sense that the words were Thomas's own. It was argued that, with these story-tellers, one could never tell where fact ended and fiction began. Was it, perhaps, they asked, part of a tale made up by Thomas, a mere fancy which his fertile imagination had built up upon the real case, a thing which *might* have happened, a note of an incident which he had once thought to incorporate in some story? This, too, seemed likely.

But there were those, more perceptive and informed, who thought both letter and narrative truthful. They considered that the fragment contained internal evidence of Thomas's authorship, affirming that only a hoaxer of genius, and moreover one with a specialist's knowledge, could have produced a certain peculiar note which it had. For peculiar it was. 'I was extremely annoyed.' 'This redundant little corpse.' 'I hear his roars yet.' What sort of an emotional response was that? Not one word of pity, or even of genuine horror! Actually a touch of humour! These, they thought, were the comments of a person whose values were all wrong; just as were the actions, irresponsible as a child's. Yes, all was askew with that characteristic insensibility, that hopeless loss of a sense of proportion, which were the early symptoms and the fearful signs of Thomas Antequin's insidious illness.

These arguments, however, were too fine-drawn for the majority. It was generally concluded that the whole thing was a hoax; and therefore, although causing a nine days' wonder and producing much correspondence, it was not a matter of lasting interest.

Not a matter of interest even to Keith Antequin. A victim to blood-poisoning, he had by that time achieved reunion with his father. A mere graze on the hand, it was said, a perfectly insignificant wound, had caused his death, he being in such a rundown state after prolonged strain that it had ended thus fatally.

Only Christine profited by the strange sequel.

Of all those who read the story of the missing pages, she was probably the one who had least doubt of its truth. The tale of the well-house was piteous and horrible, yet, as she read it, all her anguish fell away from her; not so much because her guilt was lifted as because now she *knew*. Uncertainty, in the course of time, had become the profoundest cause of her sufferings. She was like a person who, after long years of wandering, loaded with guilt, has at last been arrested and brought to trial, and who hardly cares that she has been miraculously acquitted, only cares that the trial is over.

But as she had never wanted the truth, but only comfort, so she had not now found it.

McNally Editions reissues books that are not widely known but have stood the test of time, that remain as singular and engaging as when they were written. Available in the US wherever books are sold or by subscription from mcnallyeditions.com.